DOSTOEVSKY AND *POOR FOLK*— THE DEBUT OF A GREAT WRITER

"Do you understand what you have written?
You could have written it only with the direct intuition of the artist, but has your mind grasped all the terrible truth you have shown us? . . . This is tragedy. You have pierced to the very heart of the matter, you have shown its whole essence in one stroke. We journalists and critics can only argue, we try to explain in words, but you, the artist, with one line, one stroke, give the essential reality a shape that might be touched with the hand, or fully understood in a flash by the most discerning reader. There lies the mystery of artistic creation, that is truth in art! That is how the artist serves truth! To you as an artist the truth is known and open, it has come to you as a gift; cherish your gift then and remain true to it, and you will be a great writer."

These are the words the great Russian critic, Belinsky, spoke to Dostoevsky on reading his first novel, *Poor Folk*.

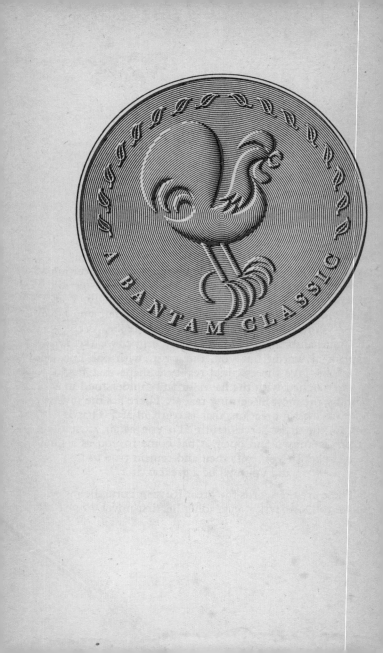

A BANTAM CLASSIC

THREE SHORT NOVELS
by
DOSTOEVSKY

Translated by
ANDREW R. MacANDREW

BANTAM BOOKS

TORONTO / NEW YORK / LONDON

A NATIONAL GENERAL COMPANY

THREE SHORT NOVELS BY DOSTOEVSKY
A Bantam Classic / published March 1966
2nd printing ...... August 1970

Bantam Books are published by Bantam Books, Inc., a National
General company. Its trade-mark, consisting of the words "Bantam
Books" and the portrayal of a bantam, is registered in the United
States Patent Office and in other countries. Marca Registrada.
Bantam Books, Inc., 666 Fifth Avenue, New York, N.Y. 10019.

PRINTED IN THE UNITED STATES OF AMERICA

Contents

THREE SHORT NOVELS
BY
DOSTOEVSKY

INTRODUCTION

Dostoevsky's first novel, *Poor Folk*, caused quite a stir when it was still in manuscript form. The poet, Nekrasov, who at that time was planning to publish the new magazine *Sovremennik* [*The Contemporary*], was so impressed that he rushed it to the ranking Russian literary authority, Belinsky. We are told the great critic read it in one sitting, and that as he was reading it, tears ran down his cheeks.

It was, Belinsky wrote, "the first attempt among us at a social novel." Coming from the social-minded, liberal, pro-Western critic, this was the highest praise. As a result of it, Dostoevsky was lionized in Petersburg's literary salons.

"Well, brother," he wrote to his brother Mikhail on November 16, 1845, "I believe my fame has reached full bloom. I am treated everywhere with amazing consideration and the utmost interest."

Further in the same letter he mentions his next book, *The Double*, on which he was already working. He had the highest hopes for it.

"Golyadkin," he wrote of his protagonist, "is coming along fine. It [*The Double*] will be my masterpiece."

And on February 1st, 1846, he wrote to Mikhail announcing the publication of *The Double*:

"Today, my Golyadkin appears . . . Golyadkin is ten times better than *Poor Folk*. My friends say there has been nothing like it in Russia since [Gogol's] *Dead Souls* and that it is a truly brilliant achievement. . . ."

But this time Belinsky was cool, or at most tepid. Although *The Double*, he maintained, still shows "the most profound and daring insight to grace Russian literature," it also "reveals a signal inability to master and handle economically the overflow of the writer's own creative powers. I should have cut it by one third."

According to Belinsky, *The Double* suffers from yet another major defect—its fantastic setting: "In our day," wrote Belinsky, who, besides being social-minded also championed "realism" in literature, "the fantastic can have a place only in madhouses but not in literature; it is the business of doctors not of poets . . ."

Thus, the ranking authority, who had given Dostoevsky his endorsement for his display of social-mindedness in *Poor Folk,* was withdrawing it now from *The Double* because of the book's undue prolixity and lack of realism, which made it useless from a social viewpoint.

That very same year—1846—Belinsky had also gone sour on Dostoevsky's literary master—Gogol. The publication of Gogol's private correspondence that year had revealed that the author of "The Overcoat" was not at all the champion of the underdog that Belinsky had imagined. Indeed, he turned out to be a reactionary of a rather rabid variety. And this was the writer whose influence showed so clearly in the works of the younger man. In fact, the young Dostoevsky admired Gogol so much that he imitated him while trying to surpass him. Ironically, he was accused of subversion when he was caught red-handed reading an irate letter, in which Belinsky accused Gogol of betrayal, before a group of young "conspirators"—the Petrashevsky group. It was this that landed him in the "House of the Dead"—Siberian exile.

This was a strange quirk of fate, for Dostoevsky was truly and profoundly influenced by Gogol's writings, whereas his friendship with Belinsky was brief and began to fade with the appearance of *The Double.* There was nothing so explicitly "reactionary" in this book, but it certainly seemed to lack the warm sympathy for the "little man" displayed in *Poor Folk.* It was obvious to Belinsky that Dostoevsky was not the "social critic" he was searching for so avidly. And Dostoevsky was equally disappointed. The animosity between the two grew steadily from that moment on.

It is quite evident that Dostoevsky had Gogol in mind when he was writing *Poor Folk*. This comes out explicitly in Makar's indignant letter to Varinka after he has read Gogol's "The Overcoat." Makar, to whom Pushkin's prose was a great joy and a revelation, hates Gogol for invading the privacy of the "little man," for prying indiscreetly into his thoughts, and even inspecting his shabby underwear and patched boots. Gogol's portrayal of Akaky Akakievich was too true, it hurt too much. Makar especially hates the conclusion—the indifference of Akaky's superiors and his miserable death. He could at least have made the "Important Personage" kind to the poor victim, Makar wrote, have had the thief who had stolen the overcoat caught, and given Akaky a promotion.

There is no doubt that this is Makar's view of Gogol and not Dostoevsky's, and that Dostoevsky gives his character a deliberately Gogolian fate. But Dostoevsky's treatment of his hero is strikingly different from Gogol's treatment of his. Gogol never deserts the lofty detachment from which he looks down upon Akaky, struggling like a fly among wasps in a jam pot. But Makar has Dostoevsky's sympathy rather as a fellow fly caught in the same jam pot. Dostoevsky is no detached observer and Makar is treated from within. It was this that made Belinsky state that Dostoevsky was starting where Gogol had left off.

Poor Folk is a tale of two people scrambling desperately to avoid slipping into the pit. However, their efforts to remain above are doomed by poverty, encompassing indifference, and human proneness to take advantage of those whose foothold is precarious. The very virtues—honesty, self-respect, loyalty—which these two poor creatures display are ridiculous and inadmissible in the eyes of the world, because Varinka and Makar are too humble to be able to afford them.

It is small wonder, then, that social reformer Belinsky greeted *Poor Folk* as a great novel of social protest. The stupefying poverty that forces Makar Alexeyevich Devushkin to keep his mind on his patched boots while he feels that his human dignity demands that he rise above such mundane matters; the rapacity of men who feel that Varinka, once she has made a "slip," is fair prey, and Makar's inability to protect her; the shivering beggar child in the street; the coarse and unfeeling fellow lodgers to whom this couple of innocents is merely laughable and who put the lowest interpretations on their ethereal love—all this was meat and drink to

Belinsky, who held that the writer's function was to expose the evils of society. But, in his obstinate search for notes of social protest, Belinsky missed other elements that indicated the seeds of Dostoevsky's conservatism. Thus, it is his fellow clerks who torment poor Makar in the office, while the powers-that-be, represented by "His Excellency," far from being cruel and aloof, display remarkable kindness and understanding. Makar's supreme chief even gives him a hundred rubles to tide him over his troubles. This sounds very much like acceptance of the existing hierarchy.

If *Poor Folk* is an indictment of anything, it is of man's callous indifference to man rather than of any particular social system. But it is equally a eulogy of generosity and devotion as displayed not only by Makar and Varinka, but also by such secondary characters as Teresa and the elder Pokrovsky. And so *Poor Folk* already reflects Dostoevsky's feeling that misery and suffering are man's lot on earth, the only relief from which is to be found in the ability of the individual to love his neighbor. Even then, the young Dostoevsky, while he still considered himself a liberal, did not expect the correction of social ills to bring salvation to mankind.

Although in places *Poor Folk* is somewhat melodramatic, and certain passages are very maudlin indeed, this sentimentality is part of Dostoevsky's characterization of his heroes; it is one of their defenses against the murk and gloom of their existence. Dostoevsky himself faced the world unblinkingly, and pursued its miseries relentlessly to their very end without flinching. This was not always understood and, indeed, Dostoevsky complains in a letter to his brother (February 1st, 1846): ". . . It [the public] will not always perceive that this or that view is expressed by Makar Devushkin and not by me and that he couldn't possibly express himself otherwise."

Makar and Varinka are allowed to delude themselves with sentimental distortions of reality—past and present. Makar writes enthusiastically of the "literary evenings" that are obviously a farce of ignorance and bad taste, and Varinka ascribes a sort of idyllic happiness to her childhood that wasn't really there. But Dostoevsky's own attitude can perhaps best be summed up in the scene of Pokrovsky's death. After a desperate struggle with a tongue over which he has lost control, Pokrovsky manages to indicate to Varinka that he wishes her to open the shutters so that he may have one last look at the world before he dies. She complies. Well, what does he see? The gray Petersburg gloom, clouds and rain. Even in his last moments, a glimpse of the sun is denied to this good and decent man by an inexorable and pitiless fate.

This harsh view of man's fate is driven home even more ruthlessly by the parallel between Makar and Gorshkov. Gorshkov is a few steps deeper in misery than Makar. Makar is wretchedly poor, Gorshkov is destitute. Makar's help to Varinka is only partial, while Gorshkov is responsible for his whole family. Makar's position is lowly, Gorshkov is altogether without position. Makar is threadbare, Gorshkov is ragged; Makar hungry, Gorshkov starving . . . And in each case, just when the situation has improved, Dostoevsky drives them on to final disaster.

Gorshkov, finally exonerated and compensated financially, dies of the shock. This could have been an omen for Makar; however, he doesn't recognize it as such. Soon his own hardships are somewhat alleviated—he receives the hundred rubles from His Excellency, settles his most pressing debts, and also obtains some extra copying work. And it is just when his relations with his landlady and his fellow lodgers have become bearable again that Varinka is snatched away from him and all is lost. Again it is clear that man's salvation is not to be found in this world.

For the character of Varinka, Dostoevsky drew a great deal from his own life. The parallels between her childhood and his are quite striking. Her rapturous descriptions of the countryside where she spent her early years correspond to Dostoevsky's own strong feelings of sudden liberation when he and his family visited their small country estate, escaping from the gloomy atmosphere of the Petersburg hospital where Dostoevsky's father was in charge. These visits may very well have seemed like crumbs of idyllic freedom to the young Fyodor.

Then, Varinka's relations with her parents after the father's loss of his position are in some way similar to Dostoevsky's own family situation. The frail, gentle, consumptive mother and the morose father, always so full of complaints and reproaches, could easily be Dostoevsky's parents. Varinka's father complains that he is spending his last money on her education, while she is lazy and ungrateful. These reproaches sound like the echoes of those heaped upon the young Fyodor when he returned joyously home to a special dinner on Sunday after a lonely week among "strangers" at the boarding school he attended with his brother. And like Varinka, the young Dostoevsky must have understood that these unreasonable complaints were a reflection of his father's unhappy and frustrated mind, that the doctor loved his wife and children in his own peculiar way but was absorbed in his own unhappy situation. That Dostoevsky's father was not really as badly off as he claimed, or as Varinka's father is, does not alter the truth of the psychological portrayal of the man.

Before he wrote *Poor Folk*, Dostoevsky had done a translation of Balzac's *Eugenie Grandet* and written two plays, *Boris Godunov* and *Mary Stuart*, of which the manuscripts have been lost and which were, according to those who read them, slavish imitations of Pushkin and Schiller, respectively. And so, *Poor Folk* can be considered his earliest literary effort, and yet it already contains the hallmarks of the psychological insight so typical of his books. And his next novel, *The Double*, has even more of the ingredients of Dostoevsky's later work.

However, the imitative streak is clear in both books and *The Double* contains more, not fewer "Gogolisms" than its predecessor. Golyadkin's relations with his servant Petrushka are similar to those of Chichikov in *Dead Souls* with his own Petrushka. And the addresses to the reader and the exclamations that the author's pen is too feeble to cope with his task also parallel *Dead Souls*, but while they are in keeping with Gogol's general tone, they echo somewhat artificially in *The Double*. There were so many other elements that hewed close to Gogol that the poet Aksakov was led to brand *The Double* as a flagrant imitation. Possibly, Dostoevsky had imbibed the works of his master so deeply that such "liftings" were almost unconscious. But what is taken from Gogol is not just inserted into the text as a formula of success. Dostoevsky often used his "Gogolisms" very differently from the way their original creator had used them. For instance, the opening paragraph of *The Double*, in which Golyadkin on waking up examines his face in a mirror, is almost identical with the passage in "The Nose" in which Gogol's Kovalev wakes up and looks into a mirror to examine a pimple on his nose. But in his mirror, Kovalev discovers a disaster—that the nose itself is missing—which forms the thread of the entire story. Golyadkin finds that everything is "all right," revealing at once a key feature of his mentality. Throughout the book he keeps pathetically reassuring himself that "everything is all right." Dostoevsky uses the mirror to introduce us to Golyadkin through his mirror image—we see him as he sees himself: a man just like any other. This conveys Golyadkin's almost panicky fear of standing out in a crowd and also prepares us for the introduction of Golyadkin Two—the double. In this saga of a split personality, the other Golyadkin is the mirror image of the first. Time and again Golyadkin One thinks he is looking into a mirror when he catches sight of Golyadkin Two. What is more, the first time he catches sight of him, the description of the double as he strikes Golyadkin's eye is identical with the description of Golyadkin's face as he sees it in the mirror. Thus, Dostoevsky has used Gogol's mirror in a completely original way—this is no mere borrowing.

And again, although *The Double* is a study of deepening madness like Gogol's *Diary of a Madman*, whose protagonist, as it were, records only external events, Dostoevsky, unlike Gogol never releases us from "inside" Golyadkin, even at his most ridiculous moments.

Dostoevsky adheres closely throughout the book to the image of the world as apprehended by a disintegrating mind. We are never sure where reality ends and the hallucinations begin. Has Golyadkin really seen the double? Did he really receive a letter? Did he write one and give it to Petrushka to deliver? Or are these all the figments of his sick imagination? This incertitude provides tension and keeps the reader turning the pages despite the considerable prolixity from which the book suffers, as Belinsky had said quite rightly.

But, obviously this is not a novel of social comment. There is nothing to distract us from Golyadkin's waking nightmare, no external causes are offered to explain it. The picture we are given is not of a man *driven* mad but of the gradual break-up of a personality. Here again, as in *Poor Folk*, the powers-that-be are not cruel and oppressive, but kind and understanding; Golyadkin is treated gently enough. He is not thrown out, but almost delicately removed when he makes his forced intrusions into the social life of his superiors. As to his original exclusion from Olsufy Ivanovich's house—we see it through Golyadkin's eyes as a cruel act of desertion. But we are made to understand what actually happened rather

indirectly in Chapter Ten when Golyadkin's double suddenly says to him: "Come, let's kiss, my pet!" We are told
then that Golyadkin Two's joke seemed to have touched a
responsive chord for it alluded to a circumstance that was
already known to everyone around. Then, a couple of pages
later, Anton Antonovich reproaches Golyadkin for insulting
a young lady, and we realize that it was a suggestion to Klara
Osufievna that she exchange a kiss with him that barred her
father's house to Golyadkin.

Such indirect explanations constitute the story's great
virtue. But, at the same time, it was perhaps the constant view
of the world through a sick mind which accepts all the incon-
gruities and inconsistencies it is faced with, that caused the
most misunderstanding when the book appeared (for instance,
Belinsky's accusation that it departed from "realism" into the
realm of the fantastic). The story is elaborately constructed
and extremely intricate. The demand made on the reader is
considerable, for the explanations of what *really* is going on
are all made indirectly and must be remembered exactly as
they appear, if the parts of the jigsaw puzzle are to fall into
place.

In the very beginning, the psychological aberration by
which Golyadkin strives to make his own situation bearable
is made clear to us when he encounters Andrei Filipovich in
his carriage: "Should I acknowledge him?" he wonders, "or
should I pretend I'm someone else, someone strikingly resembling me?" After which he rushes off to the doctor without
knowing himself what he actually wants of him. He pours a
stream of words over the doctor's head without eliciting
much response or even sympathy, but on leaving the doctor,
he feels "free and relieved" and is even "prepared to claim
that he was the happiest mortal on earth." (A happy state
which doesn't last five minutes.) This seems a rather shrewd
prefiguring of the mechanics of psychoanalysis.

In the conversation with the doctor, Golyadkin has
touched upon all the elements of his situation which seem
threatening to him, and we are given, incidentally, some clear
hints about the real situation. Indeed, we are never going to
be given a clearer picture of it to the end. It is at this point
that we discover that Golyadkin is jealous of Andrei Filipovich's nephew, Vladimir Semyonovich, who has just been
promoted and who is engaged to Klara. These two things
seem to Golyadkin to threaten his position both in the office

and socially. He has already been ostracized from the house of Klara's parents because of his unwelcome advances to her. He feels himself a rejected suitor, although later in the story, when his feverish mind imagines that Klara has offered to run away with him, he will angrily turn his back on her. This is a repeated pattern of his behavior: we also learn during his interview with the doctor that he had promised to marry his German landlady, and then fled in panic when she accepted.

Here again, it isn't the social pressure but his private, internal troubles that are tearing him apart. Golyadkin is afraid of women. He makes approaches to them up to a certain point and then turns and flees in anger when they respond, or when he imagines they have responded, to his overtures. Golyadkin might quite easily be seen as a Makar Devushkin gone mad. Makar too is timid with women, and seems fully satisfied with his immaculately pure relationship with Varinka (his very surname, Devushkin, comes from the Russian *devushka*—a maiden).

There may even be a direct suggestion of a fear of emasculation in Golyadkin, who repeats that he would willingly allow one of his fingers to be cut off in order to have things put straight again (a similar interpretation of castration is often given of Kovalev's loss of his nose in Gogol's story).

There is a further similarity between Makar and Golyadkin. Makar too sits at his desk as if "it had nothing to do" with himself when his name is being called because he has made a mistake in his work. "I pretended I didn't exist," he explains in his letter to Varinka. In Golyadkin this concern with passing unseen is an obsession and when, despite all his efforts, he finds himself exposed on every side to the world's cruel gaze, he feels *naked*. This notion of nakedness is reinforced by his very name (*golyi* meaning naked).

The story is a remarkable anticipation of much later clinical findings. Golyadkin's constant urge to go and see his doctor, as well as his terrible fear of him, is typical of the ambivalent feelings of patient toward doctor. He also often does just the opposite of what he has decided to do, responding thus to subconscious urges. For instance, when he stands hesitating before an apartment door, it is only when he has decided to go away that he rings the bell, thus cutting off his own retreat.

And, finally, there is a complete collapse of the personality, and the double appears on the scene. The build-up before the actual introduction of this sinister character is psychologically revealing. As Golyadkin stands outside Olsufy Ivanovich's back door, his self-hatred reaches its shrillest pitch: he calls himself a fool and a coward and scoffs at his very name and then, when he has decided to rush away home, he enters the apartment instead and breaks in on the party. And it is after he is evicted and is so disgusted with his behavior that he can no longer accept it as his own, that the double appears. And from then on it is the double who commits all the sins that Golyadkin cannot bear to think of himself as committing. And in case we should doubt it, Dostoevsky tells us that as Golyadkin runs along the embankment after leaving the party, "he was trying to run away from himself, to hide somewhere where he would be unable to find himself." And again, when the double appears in the office, Golyadkin feels he is "his shame, his disgrace . . . not the Golyadkin . . . who liked to pass unnoticed . . . whose gait plainly said 'don't bother me since I'm not bothering you . . .'" And although Golyadkin is horrified and disgusted by the things his double does, his one pathetic wish is to "make it up" with him, to live in peace and harmony with him—in fact to be sane again.

Dostoevsky felt that he had hit on a completely new idea, a new conception, with his Golyadkin. And indeed, his story is far subtler than Stevenson's "Dr. Jekyll and Mr. Hyde," written much later, in which the *alter ego* is the exact opposite of everything Dr. Jekyll stands for—a sort of *id* in open warfare with the *ego*. For Golyadkin *is* his double, who mirrors his actual moods and whom he cannot stand precisely because he is himself. And again, in Poe's "William Wilson," which Thomas Mann puzzlingly declared was a better story than *The Double*, a boy is shown at war with his conscience, but here, too, although the mirror symbolism is used at the end, the two fail to overlap and intermingle with each other in the way Golyadkin and his double do. As for the break-up of the personality, Dostoevsky conveys it even more fully than Gogol did in drawing his diary-writing madman.

To achieve such results, Dostoevsky used a very unorthodox approach and met with a great deal of disapproval. *The Double* was published in 1846 shortly after *Poor Folk*, but was received with much less enthusiasm and, as we have seen, Belinsky dismissed it as a departure from "realism," an escape into the realm of the "fantastic" and unfit for the "general public."

The fault, of course, may have been with the closed minds of those who, expecting a civic-minded social novel, did not know what to do with this subtle insight into a disintegrating human mind. Fortunately, however, nothing could deter Dostoevsky from his phychological investigations, although he was yet to face many tougher trials. He went on from there and laid bare to the world many quirks and secret recesses of the human mind, thereby, among other things, establishing for the psychological novel a firm place in the world.

Soon after their three month old daughter died, Dostoevsky's wife, Anna Grigorievna, became pregnant again. This was early in 1869. They were living in Italy at the time, spending the last of the money Dostoevsky had received for his latest novel, *The Idiot*. In fact, it was almost all spent while the debts he had left back in Russia remained unpaid, and he couldn't return there without risking debtors' prison. Yet, in his anxiety for his wife's state after the shock suffered by the loss of their first baby, Dostoevsky decided that she should be confined in Prague where she would at least feel more at home among fellow Slavs. To raise money for the journey, he arranged with the magazine *Zarya* (*Dawn*) for an advance on a novel to be published in installments before appearing in book form.

After some anxious waiting, the money arrived and the Dostoevskys set out. But it so happened that they could find no accommodation in Prague and had to go on to Dresden. By the time they arrived there the advance was almost gone. And so they settled down, waiting for September, when Anna was to give birth to another girl.

It was amidst these vicissitudes—a death, a birth, anxiety for his wife, homesickness, and financial pressures—that Dostoevsky was thinking of his next novel. He hadn't written a word of it yet, but already it was all worked out in his head.

He had written to his friend Strakhov in March, 1869, that he had the story in mind. He explained that he had been toying with an idea for quite a while, indeed, ever since the poet Apollon Grigoriev had praised *Notes from the Underground*, and had advised Dostoevsky to write another book in that vein. To be sure, what Dostoevsky had in mind was in a rather different vein, but still it was centered around what he called "my constant theme."

Writing it turned out to be very difficult in the circumstances under which Dostoevsky was living then, and a few months later (August 28, 1869) he wrote to the poet Maikov:

> I am harassed by worries and endless troubles. Nevertheless I must get down to writing for *Zarya*. After that, I will begin work on that long thing for *Russky vestnik (Russian Herald)*. I am sure I will start off writing feverishly, but I wonder what will come of it. I do have a few ideas for the start but I need Russia.

In fact, Dostoevsky "needed" Russia so badly that further in this same letter he wrote: "I must return to Russia next year even if it means being put in prison for debt."

So he postponed the "long thing" for *Russky vestnik*, which was to become *The Possessed*, and started on the novel for *Zarya*.

The novel in question, *The Eternal Husband*, was completed early in 1870 and was immediately acclaimed as a success.

The literary critic Strakhov wrote to Dostoevsky that it was an "unqualified success," and went on to say:

> This is one of the best thought-out of your novels and, because of its subject, one of the most interesting books you have written. I am speaking now of Trusotsky. Most people will have difficulty understanding this character, but the book is being read and will go on being read.

Indeed, much later, authorities like André Gide proclaimed the novel a "*chef d'oeuvre*," while another Frenchman, Marcel Schwob, went all the way, declaring that *The Eternal Husband* was Dostoevsky's top achievement. This, of course, may sound rather strange when one thinks of such landmarks as *The Idiot*, *The Possessed*, or *The Brothers Karamazov*, but, if the Frenchman's main criterion was perfection of composition, his estimate could certainly be defended.

The novel is a variation on a theme that had obviously been greatly preoccupying Dostoevsky at the time, a theme occurring in his previous book, *The Idiot* (1868), and the book he was already thinking about while writing *The Eternal Husband*—*The Possessed* (1873). But while, in these two gigantic novels, the theme is only one in an intricate symphony of themes, in *The Eternal Husband* it is presented in all its psychological and metaphysical intricacies in a sort of tragic *pas de deux*, punctuated at critical moments by the ringing of bells.

On the surface, the theme is a common and quite simple one: the relations between two men separated or united—depending on the way one looks at it—by a woman. Actually, though, it involves the whole concept of jealousy, love (in the wider sense), and, beyond that, the meaning of life.

The Idiot ends with the Christ-like Myshkin gently stroking, in Christian love and understanding, the face of his predatory rival Rogozhin, who has murdered the woman they both loved.

In *The Possessed*, we again have two men, Shatov and Stavrogin, facing each other, and it is the offended one who finds the strength to love his rival. Here, Shatov, a sort of rough-and-ready saint, lives by an idea he has acquired from Stavrogin. The demoniac Stavrogin is his god, and Shatov longs to kiss the ground he has walked on. The fact that Stavrogin has taken his wife from him, even that he has hurt her, is accepted by Shatov without a murmur, just as he accepts Stavrogin's child with love. He is a species of St. Joseph in Dostoevsky's strange parallel to the Holy Family.

Coming in time between these two huge novels, *The Eternal Husband* is a completely streamlined and concentrated treatment of another such relationship between two men. Trusotsky has discovered that his past idyll was an illusion, and that it was Velchaninov, whom he loved and admired, who had made it so.

Of course, each variation on the theme is a work of art in its own right, since each set of characters consists of fully fleshed, original people, each with his own ailments and idiosyncracies. The three "predatory types," as Velchaninov himself would have called them—Rogozhin, Stavrogin, and Velchaninov, and the three characters offended against—Myshkin, Shatov, and Trusotsky—as well as, incidentally, the three women contended for, are all highly individual characters and, within the framework of the theme, act and feel in a great variety of ways.

Rogozhin, a voluptuous, animal-like creature; Stavrogin, a blasé superman; and Velchaninov, a cynical society man and charmer, are each cast in the role of seducer, and the chief common element in them is their being damned themselves and doomed to hurt the others. The striking feature in the other three men is their natural and rather unconventional propensity to forgive, that is, the strength of their ability to love. Because Shatov and Myshkin are Christian figures in two of Dostoevsky's great religious debates, he has necessarily made them the vessels of Christian love. Both these men are "good" men and Dostoevsky loves them, although, unlike the Idiot, Shatov is "in error." But the third victim, Trusotsky, is a very unlovable figure indeed, and at first glance may seem to be singularly lacking in the Christian virtues of the other two. But if one examines his behavior closely, one finds that he too is dominated by the desire to forgive and to love his rival, whom he greatly admires and whose opinions he repeats, as Shatov does Stavrogin's. But the realization of that love and forgiveness is prevented by his social conditioning, by his very unloveliness, and by his rival's stiff behavior. None of this meek trio, actually, has any place in the society of men, conventional and corrupted as it is.

In *The Eternal Husband*, the very names of the two protagonists indicate their natures: Trusotsky suggesting the Russian *trus*—a coward, and Velchaninov conveying *velichina* —bigness. Their relationship develops in the novel in a ballet-like movement, in which one is trying to pull the past in, while the other is doing all he can to push it away. Trusotsky would really like nothing better than to restore the past. He is longing to obliterate retroactively the terrible betrayal of which he has become aware only after the idyll has been ended anyway by his wife's death.

As for Velchaninov, he would like to blot out the past. Suddenly, as a result of his weakened state, which is caused by worry over financial difficulties (like Dostoevsky's at the time), over his aging and his various symptoms of hidden disease (he is a bit of a hypochondriac, we are told), he is assailed by new moral preoccupations and tormented by a feeling of guilt. He begins to look at life with completely different eyes. His entire *malaise* is symptomatized in a face he does not even recognize at first. Indeed, the mechanism that helps Velchaninov to blot out the past causes him to forget names and faces in general.

When he finally recognizes the face as belonging to the despised husband of his dead mistress, Velchaninov's feelings about Trusotsky are a curious mixture of guilt and scorn. Previously, Velchaninov had despised Trusotsky because he didn't belong to the world by whose code Velchaninov had lived up till then. And he continues to feel scorn for him, although his world seems to be collapsing around him now as his values change. But at the same time Velchaninov feels guilty.

And so, when Trusotsky thrusts himself upon Velchaninov, Velchaninov pushes him away; then, when Trusotsky threatens to leave for good, Velchaninov calls him back, and the whole action is interspersed with paroxysms of insult, retraction, and reconciliation. And when for a while Liza—one more of Dostoevsky's "little girls"—appears, she is all-important to both men. For Trusotsky, she had been the symbol of his idyll with his wife and now has become a token of his ignominy. And yet, although she is the living evidence of Velchaninov's responsibility and guilt, Trusotsky cannot help loving her still. Velchaninov, on his part, welcomes the responsibility with enthusiasm, for it presents him with a possibility of redeeming himself through his love for Liza. So both men love the child. Nevertheless, her very presence is unbearable to Trusotsky and he hands her over to his rival. The child is consumed with shame at being deserted by her father and literally burns out, leaving the two men face to face. It becomes clear then that their only path to salvation lies through each other.

The crisis comes when Trusotsky tries to circumvent Velchaninov and reach salvation by another way. With the child dead, he tries to reconstruct a new idyll for himself, this time a fool-proof one: he plans to marry a fifteen year old girl who, he feels, must be completely innocent and therefore invulnerable to corruption. When, however, he puts this attempt to the test by taking Velchaninov to see her, he finds that she too is susceptible to his rival's charms. His hatred flares up again, although obviously the fault is not Velchaninov's. The simple fact is that Trusotsky's ambition is impossibly idealistic, given his very down-to-earth limitations.

Velchaninov, for his part, is unable to withstand any

longer the moral pressures growing within him, and suffers a physical collapse. Trusotsky has him helpless in his hands, just when his hatred has reached its highest pitch. His efforts to drown out that hatred are frantic and, as he administers hot tea to Velchaninov, he insists that Velchaninov must drink it, for otherwise he might die. This is, of course, a reflection of Trusotsky's secret wish. Finally Velchaninov feels better. At that moment, he knows that "it is all over," he has understood everything—Trusotsky is a better man than he is—and he says so. Thus, in a moment of lucidity reached through pain, he acknowledges the saintly side of that repulsive man. But that is the closest they come to each other, for, half an hour later, Velchaninov has to tear a razor out of Trusotsky's hand to save his own life. And, at the very moment that he gets back on top physically, Velchaninov recovers from his strange mental state.

After that, the old standards reassert themselves and the two men revert to their former selves. The crisis is over and neither is any longer in the supersensitive state of mental perturbation needed, according to Dostoevsky, before salvation can even be sought.

Trusotsky remarries, and becomes once again a henpecked and cuckolded husband, because he belongs to that meek species of men who are born to live as complements to a woman—the species of the "eternal husband." As to Velchaninov, he returns to his free-lancing love life.

And all that is left for either is a scar: a real one across Velchaninov's left hand with which he had caught the deadly razor, and the scar left in Trusotsky's heart by Liza.

Dostoevsky himself had had some personal experience of triangle situations. After his release from the penal settlement, he had to serve another four years in the army in Siberia, and there, in the town of Semipalatinsk, he met a drunken schoolteacher, Isayev, and his wife, Maria. Coming from complete isolation, Dostoevsky fell in love with Maria Isayev; and she, a provincial lady, was duly impressed by the sophisticated intellectual from the capital, especially since she could hardly communicate any longer with her besotted husband. Here, the parallel with *The Eternal Husband* is quite close, with Dostoevsky himself having Velchaninov's role. And later, when Isayev, of whom Dostoevsky had been fond, died, Dostoevsky first reacted with joy at the thought that Maria would now be free, and then was overcome by guilt, just as Velchaninov is tormented by guilt too, although the cause of his guilt is different.

Later, Dostoevsky experienced acute jealousy and rage when the widowed Maria Isayev, whom he hoped to marry, had a passionate affair with a young schoolteacher and seriously contemplated becoming his wife. Then, although suffering torments, Dostoevsky offered help and friendship to the couple and tried to get a better position for the young man. How long this noble self-denial would have lasted remains a matter of conjecture, for the situation reversed itself again and, for better or for worse, Maria ended up by marrying Dostoevsky. Here, of course, Dostoevsky occupied a position somewhat similar to Trusotsky's, wavering between rage and forgiveness. Indeed, he found himself in this position on yet another occasion, when he offered his devoted friendship to his mistress, Paulina Suslova, and the young Spanish student with whom she had deceived him. But here again, the Spanish student vanished from the scene and Dostoevsky remained (a meek slave as opposed to predatory lover) at the feet of the disconsolate lady. Thus, the novel remains firmly rooted in this world, through the creation of characters whose emotions Dostoevsky knew from his own experience.

In general, Dostoevsky's talent for evoking the real world of his time is more readily appreciable in *The Eternal Husband* precisely because this book, unlike his big novels, is deliberately limited in scope, because its composition is so neat and compact in its very complexity. We feel that world through Velchaninov's barren, social meanderings; it weighs on us like a heavy overcast shadowing Trusotsky's provincial bog; it glitters nostalgically around the verandas of the last century's Russian *dachas*. Dostoevsky's picture of the stifling summer in a St. Petersburg deserted by all who could leave comes over in sharper focus when shown to us through the eyes of the dejected Velchaninov in his loneliness and spiritual isolation; while we feel the freshness of the summer garden more acutely, with Nadia and her friends playing their innocent, childish games in it and the callow revolutionary boys hatching their kindergarten conspiracies.

And even when Dostoevsky is concerned with displaying the psychological workings of his characters' minds, he

uses their physical environment to do so. Velchaninov passes
through his temporary psychological state while living in a
temporary apartment full of unfamiliar furniture. And it is
in that apartment that he forgets his razor on the table where
Trusotsky glimpses it, as it were subliminally, to take it later
in the dark.

Indeed, it is strange to think that a man like Stefan Zweig
in his essay on Dostoevsky could repeat such absurd clichés
as that one never remembers what the weather was like in
Dostoevsky's books and that the characters neither eat nor
sleep, when we have just watched Velchaninov get through
one of his dull dinners in the little restaurant on the Nevsky
Prospect and have been nauseated by the sickly sweetness of
Trusotsky's champagne. And as for sleeping—it may be a
disturbed sleep, but one can hardly forget the comedy of
one of the nights Trusotsky spends in Velchaninov's apartment, and the drama of the other. In fact, there is no aspect
of physical life that Dostoevsky neglects, down to the fine
touch of Trusotsky searching for the chamberpot in the middle of the night.

Dostoevsky was indeed one of those writers who felt
he had to live in the land where his novels were set, and
that is why, when abroad, he constantly wrote to his friends
about how much he "needed" Russia. Since he cannot go
back there, he tells Maikov in a letter, he reads three Russian
papers regularly, and talks to Russians in a café whenever
he has a chance. And in a letter to his niece, he writes that
although there is no danger that he will be influenced by his
present environment because, unlike Turgenev, he loathes
the Germans, he does feel "out of touch." Alas, despite his
efforts, he was unable to settle his debts for a long time, and
so both *The Eternal Husband* and *The Possessed* were written in Germany. He need not have worried, though. Apparently, more than he himself realized, he carried his Russia
inside him, and whether he was its prophet or not, he was
its faithful chronicler. On reading his books, one smells it,
tastes it, breathes it. It sticks to one as Dickens' London does,
and one is never really free of it again.

But *The Eternal Husband*, like Dostoevsky's other novels, also reaches deeper and attempts to cope with the problems that constantly preoccupied him. One can say that in
this novel Dostoevsky followed Apollon Grigoriev's sugges-

tion and wrote another book "in the vein of *Notes from the Underground*," vastly different though the two books are.

In *The Eternal Husband*, he comes to grips with some of his "constant" problems from a completely different angle, using a very different character. In this instance he subjects Velchaninov to a complex of mental and physical stresses (starting with financial pressure) that throw him completely off balance and bring him to a physical crisis.

And it is while under stress that Velchaninov suddenly wakes up and becomes aware of the inanity of his past existence, of his guilt, of the permanent responsibility he must bear for his past acts. We are led here into a deeper, "transcendental" psychology, and, like the "Underground Man," Velchaninov suffers from an excess of consciousness, from a too great lucidity. And it is in that state of suffering that he comes closest to his salvation. But, as he almost reaches it, he "recovers" (the recovery subtly crowned by the solution of his financial difficulties), and contentedly resumes the philandering existence he had enjoyed before.

Like so many of Dostoevsky's characters, he has been given only a glimpse of the truth through the murky glass of suffering.

In all three of these short novels, we find the real world impinging upon the individual's world of private ghosts. The intermingling of the two reveals a conception of the human condition which is more painful, but a great deal more subtle, than the ordinary social novel.

ANDREW R. MacANDREW

POOR FOLK

Ah! Those storytellers! They wouldn't think of writing something edifying, pleasant, comforting. They have to dig up all the filth that's buried underfoot. I wish they were barred from writing! Really, it's like nothing on earth: you read, and the next thing you know you're thinking—and all sorts of rubbish comes into your head. Really, I'd bar them from writing; I'd simply bar them from writing altogether and that would be that.

PRINCE V. F. ODEEVSKY

April 8

My Precious Varvara Alexeyevna!

I was happy yesterday, happy beyond measure, unbelievably happy! For once in your life, you obstinate girl, you listened to me. I woke up at around eight o'clock in the evening (as you know, my dear, I like to take a nap for an hour or two after work). I found a candle, prepared my papers, and was sharpening a quill when I looked up by chance and —oh, how my heart leapt! So you understood what I wanted, what my poor old heart wanted! I saw that one little corner of your window curtain was turned back and hooked onto the little pot of balsam, just the way I had suggested. Just then I thought that I caught sight of your little face at the window looking this way from your room, and that you were thinking of me too. And how sad I was, my sweet, because I couldn't see that pretty face of yours clearly! Well, my dear, there was a time when I too could see well. Old age is no blessing, my love! These days, everything's sort of blurred before my eyes. You do a bit of work each evening, write something or other, and the next morning, your eyes are so red and tearful that you feel ashamed in front of people. However, your smile, my angel, your nice, friendly smile, glowed in my imagination, and my heart felt exactly as it did that time when I kissed you, Varinka. Do you remember, angel mine? And do you know, my sweet, that it even seemed you were shaking your finger at me? Were you, you naughty girl? Don't forget to write about all this at length in your letter.

Well, what do you think of our little trick with your curtain? Don't you think it's splendid? Whether at work, going to bed, or waking, I know at once that you're thinking of me over there, that you haven't forgotten me, and that you are well and happy. Lowering the curtain means: "Good-by for now, Makar Alexeyevich, it's time for bed!" And raising it means, "Good morning, Makar Alexeyevich, how did you sleep?" or, "How do you feel? As for me, well, thank God, I'm fine and everything's all right!" So you see, my dearest, what a clever idea it is. We don't even need letters! Smart, isn't it? And mind you, it was my little invention! Now don't you think I'm good at such things, Varvara Alexeyevna?

I must inform you, my dear, that against all expectations, I slept well last night, which was very satisfying, since I usually can't sleep in new places. Everything feels different, you know. I got up this morning feeling keen as a hawk—gay and happy! And what a lovely morning it is, my dear! They have opened the window here; the good sun is shining, the birds are chirping, the air is saturated with spring fragrances, and all Nature is coming to life. Well, and the rest is in keeping—everything is neat and spring-like. I let my imagination run away with me, and I kept thinking of you, Varinka. I compared you to a bird created to delight people and adorn Nature. And just then it occurred to me that we who live in worry and care should envy the carefree, innocent happiness of the birds. Well, the rest was the same sort of thing; that is, I made other far-fetched comparisons. I have a book here, Varinka, which says just the same thing; it's all described there in great detail. What I want to say is that there are all sorts of dreams, my dear. Now, for instance, that it's spring, one's thoughts are so pleasant, sharp, and fanciful, and one has such tender dreams; one sees everything in a rosy light. That's why I've written all this, although I must confess, I took it all out of that book. The author displays the same longing as I. He puts it in verse.

Oh, to be a bird—a bird of prey!

Well, and so on and so forth. There are some other ideas in it too, but they don't matter now.

But tell me, where did you go this morning? I wasn't even ready to leave for the office when you went flitting from your room just like a bird in the spring, and I saw you crossing the courtyard looking so cheerful. It made me cheerful too, just watching you. Ah, Varinka, Varinka, you mustn't be sad. Tears won't help. I speak from experience, my dear—I know. And after all, your life is so peaceful now, and your health has improved a little too. And how's your Fedora? What a good woman she is! Write to me, Varinka, and tell me how the two of you are getting along. Is everything all right? Fedora's a bit of a grumbler, but don't you pay any attention. What does it matter? She's basically a kind person.

I've told you before about our Teresa here. She too is kind and devoted. And I was so worried about our letters, about how we'd manage to get them to each other! And here, by good fortune, God has sent us Teresa. She's kind, meek and quiet. But our landlady is absolutely merciless and wears her out with work as though she were an old rag.

Ah, but what a hole I've come to! What a lodging! As you know, where I lived before was so quiet and peaceful; you could hear a fly buzzing. But here there's noise, shouting, and chaos. You, of course, still don't know the set-up here. Just try to imagine a long corridor completely dark and dirty. To the right is a blank wall, and to the left, a row of doors like in a hotel. People rent these places, each of which consists of just one small room; and in some live two or three people. You can't expect order—it's a real Noah's Ark! Nevertheless, they all seem to be nice, well-mannered, educated people. There's one civil servant (he dabbles in literature) who's a very well-read man. He can talk about Homer and Brambeus, and scores of other writers. He can, in fact, talk about everything—a very intelligent man! Then there are two officers who are always playing cards. And there's a naval man, and an English tutor. Just wait—I'll make you laugh, my dear. I'll give you quite a satirical description of them in my next letter—all the details of what they're really like. Our landlady is a very short, unclean, stumpy old crone who goes about in slippers and dressing gown all day long and keeps nagging at Teresa. I live in the kitchen, or rather, it would be much more accurate to put it this way: I have one room next to the kitchen (and our kitchen, I should say, is a very good one, clean and light). It's a small room, just a modest little corner . . . well, to put it more accurately still, the kitchen is large and has three windows, and is partitioned to form another room. I must say, it's all very spacious and comfortable, and there's a window. So that's my little corner. Now, don't think, my dear, that there's some hidden meaning in what I've just said. Look at that, you'll say, the kitchen! Well, yes, I really am living behind the partition in the kitchen—but it doesn't matter. I'm off by myself here, and I get along all right. Quiet as a mouse I am. I have for myself a bed, a table, a chest of drawers, and two chairs. And I've hung an icon on the wall. I'm sure there are better places to live, much better ones, but convenience is the main thing, and that was my chief concern. So don't think I had any other reason. Your window is across the courtyard from mine, and it's such a narrow little courtyard that I can see you as you go past. That cheers up a miserable fellow like me. Besides, living this way is cheaper. The very worst room, with board, costs thirty-five paper rubles here. That's more than I can afford. And my lodging costs me seven paper rubles, plus five silver rubles for board—that makes twenty-four and a half alto-gether (twenty-four and a half if you count in paper rubles), and before I used to pay thirty, but then I had to deny myself a lot of things.* I couldn't always afford tea, but now I have enough left for both tea and sugar too. And you know, my love, somehow, not being able to have tea seems embarrassing. They're well-off people here, and it wouldn't seem right. And so you drink it because of others, Varinka, for appearances' sake, to keep your standing. For myself, I don't care. I'm not fussy. Well, let's put it this way: Everything costs some money—shoes of some sort, for instance, and something to put on your back. You think there's much left over? No, there goes my whole salary. I'm not complaining, mind you. I'm quite content. For several years now I've had enough. And then there are the bonuses.

Well, good-by now, my little angel. I have bought a little pot of balsam and one of geraniums—very cheap they were. And in case you like mignonette, they have that too. So write and tell me if you do. And mind you, write about everything in detail. But don't you start getting ideas, and

---

* At that time, 1 silver ruble was worth 3½ paper rubles.

don't think ill of me for taking this room. Oh no, it was convenience alone which made me decide. The truth is, my dear, I'm saving money, putting it aside. I've got quite a bit tucked away. I know I'm such a meek-looking fellow that you'd think a fly could knock me over with its wing. But don't go by that. No, my dear, I can look out for myself, and my character is as firm as it should be for a man whose conscience is clear. Good-by now, my little angel! Here, I've covered almost two pages writing to you and I should have left for work long ago. I kiss your fingers, my dear, and remain

> Your most humble servant
> and truest friend,
> MAKAR DEVUSHKIN

P.S. I would ask you just one thing: write to me at length, my angel. I enclose a pound of little candies with this, Varinka, so eat them and be well, and please, for Heaven's sake, don't worry and don't be angry with me. Well, this time, it's really good-by, my dear.

April 8

Dear Makar Alexeyevich,

Do you know what—if this goes on, we'll end up quarreling. I assure you, my kind Makar Alexeyevich, that it makes me feel quite bad to accept your presents. I know what they cost you and how you have to deprive yourself of the most necessary things. I've told you so often that I don't need anything, anything at all, that I cannot repay you for the presents which you have showered upon me up to now. And for what do I need your pots of flowers? Well, the little balsam plant is one thing, but why geraniums? I just have to drop one careless little word, as I did about geraniums, and you go right off and buy one. They surely must have been expensive, weren't they? Oh, the flowers are so pretty! Like little scarlet crosses. Wherever did you find them? I've set them in the most conspicuous place at the window. I've put a bench on the floor beneath, and I'll put more flowers on that—just wait till I become rich! Fedora is delighted; it's paradise in our room now—so clean and bright! Well, and why candy? I guessed right away from your letter that something was the matter with you— heaven, spring, fragrances floating about, and little birds chirping. What's this all about, I thought to myself. There must surely be some verses here. Really, a little poetry is all your letter needs, Makar Alexeyevich! There are tender feelings and rose-tinted dreams—it's all there! And I never even gave that curtain a thought. It just happened to get caught there when I was moving the flowerpots around. So there you are!

Ah, Makar Alexeyevich! Whatever you may say in your letter, however you may calculate your income in order to deceive me and to make me think that you spend absolutely all of it on yourself, you can't hide anything from me. It's quite clear that you deny yourself essentials for my sake. What made you take such a room, for instance? Why, you will be constantly disturbed and bothered; you're cramped and uncomfortable. You like your privacy, and yet what isn't going on right next door to you there? And you could live much better, judging by your salary. Fedora says you used to live much better. Surely you haven't lived all your life in loneliness and privation, without joy, without even a friendly word, occupying a corner in a strange apartment? Oh, my dear Makar Alexeyevich, I feel so sorry for you! At least think of your health! You say you have trouble with your eyes. Well, don't work by candlelight. Why do you have to do that copying? I'm sure your superiors must be well aware of your zeal without that.

Once again, I beg you not to spend so much money on me. I know you're fond of me, but just the same, you're not rich. . . . I also felt very cheerful when I got up this morning. I felt so good. Fedora had been at work for a long time, and she had obtained some work for me too. I was so happy about it. I just went out to buy some silk and then got down to work. I was so happy all morning! But now the black thoughts are upon me again. I feel sad and my heart is heavy.

Ah, what will become of me? What weighs on me is the unknown, the idea that I don't have any future to look to, that I cannot even guess what will happen. And I don't even dare look back. There's so much sorrow there that just remembering it is enough to break my heart in two. I could weep forever when I think of the nasty people who hurt me so!

It's growing dark. I must do some work. I wanted to write to you about a lot of things, but I have no time. There is a deadline for the work, so I must hurry. Of course, these letters are a wonderful thing. They make life much less boring. But why don't you ever visit us? Why not, Makar Alexeyevich? It's not far for you now, and sometimes you must have a spare moment. Please, come. I saw your Teresa. She didn't seem at all well, and I felt sorry for her, so I gave her twenty kopecks. . . . Oh yes! I almost forgot. Write without fail, in the greatest possible detail, all about how you're getting on. What kind of people are living around you, and how you get along with them. I very much want to know. So you be sure to write! Today I'll deliberately turn back the corner of the curtain. You must go to bed earlier. Yesterday I saw your light shining until midnight. Well, good-by. Today I feel unhappy, sad, and bored! Ah well, I suppose it's just not my day! Good-by.

Yours,

VARVARA DOBROSELOVA

April 8

Dear Varvara Alexeyevna,

Well, my sweet, it looks as if it was an unlucky day for unhappy me. Ah, you were making fun of an old man! Well, it's my own fault. I asked for it! I shouldn't have let myself go with all those hearts and flowers and clever hints. An old man like me with nothing but a few tufts of hair on my head! And I'll tell you something else, my dear—sometimes a man can be odd, very odd. And then, good Lord, what he won't talk about! And what comes of it? What are the results? Either nothing or nonsense. I'm not angry, my dear, I'm just terribly annoyed with myself when I think of it all, annoyed with myself for writing you such a stupid, flowery letter. And yet I went off to the office today strutting like a peacock with my heart all aglow. I felt suddenly in a holiday mood. I was in such a happy frame of mind that I began work with great eagerness. But it didn't come to much in the end. Later it disappeared, and everything was just as it had been before—dull and dim. The same old ink spots, the same desks with papers on them, and I too was just the same as before. So what had I been flying around on a Pegasus for? What had caused it all? Was it that the clouds had opened up a bit and the sun had appeared with a corner of azure sky around it? Was that it? And what kind of fragrances can there be with all the things that may turn up in the courtyard under our windows? I must have imagined it all when I was in that dizzy state. Well, it happens sometimes that a man loses his way through his own feelings and just starts spouting a lot of nonsense. That's what comes from stupid and unmotivated enthusiasm. Well, on the way home I dragged myself rather than walked. My head began to ache, and it was really one thing on top of another. (I must have sat in a draft.) I was so pleased to see the spring that, old fool that I am, I went out in my light coat.

As to my feelings, you didn't understand me, my dear. You completely misinterpreted what I said about my feelings. They were inspired by fatherly affection, nothing but the purest fatherly affection, Varvara Alexeyevna. You have been deprived of a father by cruel circumstances, and I only wish I could fill that gap. I say this from the bottom of my heart, with the purest intentions, and as a close friend and relative. For, however you look at it, I am after all a distant relative of yours, even though, as the saying goes, "it's been watered down seven times already." Still, I am a relative just the same and, in fact, your closest relative now and your natural guardian. For, where you had the most right to expect protection and care, you found only betrayal and insult. As for verses, let me tell you, my dear, it wouldn't be fitting for me to start trying my hand at composing poetry in my old age. And anyway, poetry is nonsense! Why, they even whip the brats for writing verse in school these days. That's how much poetry's worth, my sweet.

I don't quite understand, Varvara Alexeyevna, why you write about comfort and quiet and such. I'm neither fussy nor demanding, my dear, and I've never lived better than now, so why should I start being fastidious in my old age? I eat my fill, have clothes on my back and shoes on my feet. So what's it all about? I am not a count, you know. In fact, my father didn't even come from the gentry, and with the family he had, he had an income lower than mine. I've never been spoilt, believe me. I must say, though, my old lodgings were incomparably better, and I was much less cramped in them. But my present room is nice too. It's even more cheerful and, in a way, provides greater variety. That's all very true, and yet I miss the old one. We old, or rather middle-aged, people get attached to things, and they become part of us. Well, that old room of mine was rather small, you know, but then it had real walls. . . . Ah, what's there to talk about? They were like any other walls, and that's not the important part of it. It's just that I become sad when I remember days gone by. It's strange—remembering is sad and yet, at the same time, it is somehow pleasant. And even the unpleasant aspects, things that used to make me angry, now, in my memory, somehow seem free of their unpleasant associations, and I even find them attractive. I lived peacefully, Varinka, with my old landlady, who's dead now. Ah, I feel so sad when I think of the old lady now! She was a good woman, and she didn't charge me much for my room. She used to keep knitting all sorts of rugs and blankets from scraps of material on yard-long needles; she never did anything else. She and I used to share the light, so we worked together at the same table. She had a granddaughter called Masha—I remember her when she was still a child. She must be a big girl now—about thirteen. She was a mischievous little thing, very lively, and made us laugh all the time. So the three of us lived there together. On long winter evenings, we'd sit at the round table, drink our tea, and then get down to our work. And so that Masha shouldn't be bored and start getting into mischief, the old woman would tell fairy tales. And what fairy tales they were! Not only a child, but a sober and intelligent adult would become absorbed in them. Oh yes! I myself included. I'd light my pipe and often become so intent listening to her that I'd forget all about my work. And that child, our mischievous little girl, would grow very thoughtful and lean her little pink cheek on her hand, and her pretty little mouth would fall open, and if the story was at all frightening, she'd press herself closer and closer to the old woman. She was a pleasure to look at, and we wouldn't even notice that the candle needed snuffing or hear if a snowstorm were raging outside or a blizzard blowing. We lived very happily, Varinka. For almost twenty years we lived together.

But, good heavens, how chatty I'm being! Perhaps this subject rather bores you, and besides, it doesn't make me so very happy to remember it all, especially right now when it's twilight. Teresa is fussing noisily about something, my head aches, my back hurts a little too, and in a strange way, it feels as if my thoughts were aching too. Yes, Varinka, I feel rather sad today.

What's this you write about my coming to see you,

my sweet? How could that possibly be? What would people say? Why, I'd have to cross the courtyard and the people here would see me and start asking questions; there would be talk, gossip would start flying, and they'd misinterpret everything. No, my angel, it'd be better if I saw you tomorrow at the vigil service. That would be more prudent, and we wouldn't either of us compromise ourselves. Please don't be too hard on me, my dear, for writing you such a letter. Reading it again, I see it's all rather disconnected. I'm an ignorant old man, Varinka. I didn't have much education when I was young, and if I tried to learn now, I would retain nothing. I know, my dear, that I'm no master at expressing myself, and I don't have to be told or scoffed at to realize that when I am trying to say something a bit more complicated than usual, it just sounds like a lot of nonsense.

I saw you at the window today. You were pulling down your blind. Good-by, good-by, and may God preserve you! Good night, dear Varvara Alexeyevna.

Your disinterested friend,
MAKAR DEVUSHKIN

P.S. I can't write satirical stories about anyone any more, my dear. I am too old, Varvara Alexeyevna, to laugh at people without reason! It's they who'd end up laughing at me instead. As the Russian proverb goes: He who pushes another toward a pit may fall in himself.

April 9

Dear Makar Alexeyevich,

You ought to be ashamed for being so unhappy and ill-humored, my dear, kind friend. Surely you're not offended with me. Heavens, I'm so often careless in what I say, but I never thought you'd take my words as a wicked jibe. Believe me, I would never dare to make fun of your age or your character. It's all because of my thoughtlessness, or rather, because I'm so terribly bored. Ah, the things boredom makes one do! Moreover, I thought you weren't serious yourself in your letter. I felt very miserable when I realized you were annoyed with me. But, my dear, kind friend, you're wrong to suspect me of being insensitive and ungrateful. I do deeply appreciate all that you've done for me by protecting me from wicked people, from their persecution and hatred. I shall always pray for you, and if my prayer is heeded, you will be made happy.

I don't feel at all well today. I have chills and fever in turns. Fedora keeps worrying about me. Now, I don't see why you should find it so embarrassing to come over and see us, Makar Alexeyevich. What business is it of other people's? You are a friend and that's that. Good-by for now. I must stop. I really feel too ill. I only must ask you once more not to be angry with me and to rest assured of my unflagging respect and affection.

With which, I have the honor to remain your most devoted and obedient servant,

VARVARA DOBROSELOVA

April 12

Dear Varvara Alexeyevna,

What is the matter? You give me such a fright each time. In every letter I remind you to be careful, to wrap up warmly, not to go out in bad weather, to take every precaution. But you never listen to me, my angel. Oh, you're just like a small child! I know how delicate you are, brittle as a straw, and you catch cold at the slightest breeze. So you must take special care, look after yourself, avoid taking risks, if only for your friends' sake, so as not to drive them to despair.

You wrote, my dear, that you wished to have a detailed account of my life and of the people and things around me. I'll gladly comply with your wish, my sweet. So let me begin at the beginning. That'll make a tidier account.

First of all, our front stairs aren't too bad, especially the main one; it's clean, light, and wide, all wrought iron and mahogany. But you'd better not even ask about the back stairs. They're dirty, damp, and twisting, many steps are broken, and the walls are so greasy your hand sticks if you touch them. The landings are cluttered with old trunks, broken chairs, and collapsing cupboards; there are rags hanging, and the panes in the windows are broken. By every door there are garbage pails containing every imaginable variety of refuse—dust, egg shells, and even fish guts. The whole place reeks. . . . Well, it is miserable.

I've described the layout of this place before. Well, it's quite practical, as I said, but still, it somehow seems stuffy

—well, not that it really smells but, let me put it this way: There's a sort of slightly rotten, bitter-sweet tang about it. One's first impression is rather unpleasant, but that's nothing. You stop noticing it after a few minutes, because you yourself become sort of permeated by that bad smell; your clothes smell, your hands smell, everything smells, and so you get used to it. But finches die here. The midshipman has bought his fifth now, but they just can't survive in this air. Our kitchen is big, roomy, and light. True, it's a bit smoky in the mornings when they're cooking fish or roasting beef; and then they spill water, and the entire floor is full of puddles. But in the evening, it's truly heaven. There's always somebody's old garments hanging on a line in our kitchen, and since my room is close by, in fact, opens directly onto the kitchen, the smell of the washing does bother me a little. But it's nothing really. You get used to it after a while.

The racket starts here first thing in the morning, Varinka —people getting up, walking around, thumping about. It's all those who have to go to their offices or attend to their business, whatever it may be. So they all have tea. The samovars here belong to the landlady and, as a rule, we find there aren't enough of them. So we take turns boiling our water, and if anyone goes to fill his teapot out of turn, he gets it in the neck. That's what happened to me the first time, and —but what's the point of going into it! Well, that's how I've made everyone's acquaintance here. The midshipman was the first. He's very open—he told me all about his father, mother, and sister (who is married to an assessor in Tula). He also told me about life in Kronstadt. He took me under his wing and invited me to come and have tea with him. I found him in the room here where he and his friends play cards all the time. I was given tea, and they insisted I join their game, although they were playing for money. I am not sure whether or not they were joking with me, but I know that they'd been gambling throughout the night when I came in. There were cards and chalk everywhere, and the room was so full of smoke it made your eyes sting. When they realized I couldn't play, they remarked that I was obviously interested only in high-minded matters; after that no one said another word to me the whole time I was there. I must say, I was rather glad of it. Well, I won't go there again. All they do is gamble, and then gamble some more! Now we have a government employee living here—he has parties, too, but they are more literary, nicer, more quiet, innocent gatherings; and everything there is refined and correct.

Well, Varinka, let me tell you also, in passing, that our landlady is a very nasty woman, a real witch, in fact. You've seen Teresa, haven't you? She looks like a scraggly plucked chicken. Altogether, there are two servants in the house— Teresa and Faldoni, the landlady's valet. (He may have other names, but that's what everyone in the house calls him.) He's a redhead, a Finn or something, one-eyed, snub-nosed, and insolent; he and Teresa are always at each other and sometimes they almost come to blows. Generally, I can't say it's very pleasant living here. At night, it never happens that they all quiet down and go to sleep at the same time. There's always someone playing cards somewhere, and I'd be ashamed to tell you of some of the other things that go on around here. I've grown used to it myself, but I still can't understand how whole families manage to survive in such a Sodom. There's a poor family who lives in an isolated room at the end of the corridor. Nobody has ever heard them make a sound. They live there quietly behind their partitions. The man is a former government employee who was discharged from his position seven years ago and is now without a job. His name's Gorshkov, and he's small, gray-haired, and wears a coat that's so shiny and threadbare it's painful to look at. It's even much worse than mine! He's such a puny, pathetic-looking creature (we meet occasionally in the corridor). His knees wobble, and his hands and head shake—it must be some kind of sickness, I suppose. He's very timid, afraid of everyone, and as he goes by, he always hugs the wall. I'm rather shy myself at times, but he's much worse. He has a wife and three children. The oldest, a boy, is just like his father and just as puny-looking. The wife must have been pretty at one time; you can still see it, despite the miserable rags the poor woman now wears. I've heard they're behind with their rent, and the landlady isn't very kind to them. I've also heard that Gorshkov lost his job through some trouble, and now I'm not sure whether he's being sued, prosecuted, or just investigated. I can say for certain, though, that they're definitely poor. Their room is always so quiet and peaceful that one would never suspect anyone was living there. You don't even hear the children. They never run about or play, and that's a very bad sign. I happened to be passing by their door one evening at a time when the house was unusually quiet. I heard a whimper, then a whisper, and then a whimper again; apparently they were weeping, but so quietly, so pathetically, that it was quite heart-rending. I kept thinking of those wretched people all night and I could not fall asleep.

Well, good-by now, my precious Varinka. I've described everything to you as best I could. I've thought of nothing but you all day long. My heart fails when I think that you don't have a warm cloak, my dear child. And these Petersburg springs, with their wind, drizzle, and sleet—they'll be the death of me, Varinka! God save me from such invigorating air!

Don't be too critical of my letter, my dear Varinka. I know I have no style whatsoever. I just wish I had! I write down whatever comes to my mind, only hoping it will cheer you up a bit. Ah, if only I had some education, it would be a different matter. But what kind of an education do I have? It isn't even worth a handful of coppers.

Your true and loyal friend,
MAKAR DEVUSHKIN

April 25

Dear Makar Alexeyevich,

I met my cousin Sasha today. It was terrible! The poor girl is doomed! I've also heard from someone that Anna Fedorovna is still trying to learn things about me; it seems she'll never stop pursuing me. She says she wishes to *forgive me*, to forget the past, and insists she wants to pay me a visit in person. She says that you're not really a relative of mine at all, that in any case she's much more closely related to me, that you have no right to interfere in our family affairs, and that it is humiliating and highly improper for me to live on your charity and accept your support. She accuses me of forgetting what she's done for me, claims that she saved my mother and me from near starvation, that she fed us for more than two and a half years, spent money on us, and that on top of all this, she forgave us what we owed her. Yet she was so merciless with mother. Ah, if my poor mother knew what they had done to me! Well, God is aware of it all! Anna Fedorovna says that I was too stupid to hold on to my good luck when I had the chance, that she did her best to bring happiness within my reach, and that she was in no way to blame for the rest; and that I was either incapable of protecting my virtue or uninterested in doing so. But, great God, who's to blame here? She says that Mr. Bykov was absolutely right and why should he marry just anyone who . . . but what's the point of going into all that! It's hard to hear such lies, Makar Alexeyevich! I don't know what's come over me now. I keep trembling and crying and sobbing. It's taken me two hours to write you this letter. I thought she'd at least admit that she was at fault before, and now look how she behaves! For heaven's sake, don't be alarmed, my only friend, the only person who wishes me well! Fedora always exaggerates; I'm not really ill. I just caught a little cold yesterday when I went to hear the requiem mass for my mother at Volkovo cemetery. Why didn't you come with me? When I asked you, I wanted you to come so much! Ah, my poor, poor mother, if you rose from your grave, if you knew, if you saw, what they've done to me!

V.D.

May 20

My Dearest Varinka,

I'm sending you a few grapes, my sweet. I understand they're very good for convalescents. And then the doctor recommends them for quenching the thirst, but only for the thirst. The other day you wanted some rolls, and so I'm sending you some now. How is your appetite, my sweet? That's the most important thing. Anyway, thank God that it's all over now and that our troubles are also coming to an end. We'll thank Heaven for that!

Now, as for those books, I haven't been able to find them yet. They say there's one that's quite good and written in a very elevated style; I, myself, haven't read it but it's praised very highly here. I've asked to borrow it, and they've promised to lend it to me. But will you really read it? When it comes to reading, I know how fastidious you can be. It's difficult to suit your taste—I suppose you are mainly interested in poetry, full of sighs and cupids. Well, I'll get poetry for you. I'll get everything for you. There's a notebook full of poems someone has copied.

As for me, I'm fine. Please don't worry about me, my dear. What Fedora told you about me is all a lot of nonsense. Just tell her she's a gossip. Be sure to tell her that! I certainly haven't sold my new frockcoat. There was no need for it, as you can understand yourself. I've been told I'll be getting a bonus of forty silver rubles, so what need was there for me to sell it? Don't you worry, my dear. She just imagines things, that Fedora, and that's all there is to it. We'll be happy yet, my dear girl! You just get better, for goodness' sake, get better, and don't disappoint an old man. Who told you I'd grown thin? It's just more gossip, believe me! I'm as healthy as can be; in fact, I've become so stout that it's even beginning to be embarrassing. I eat my fill and am well content, and everything would be perfect if only you'd get better! Well, good-by now, my angel. I kiss each of your little fingers and remain

Your eternal and unchanging friend,
Makar Devushkin

P.S. Well really, my sweet, what's this you've written to me again? What sort of nonsense is it? How can I possibly come and see you so often, my dear? How, I ask you? I could perhaps have come during darkness—but at this time of year there's hardly any darkness anyway. As it is, my dear little angel, I hardly left you all the time while you were sick, when you were unconscious, you know, and even at that, I don't know myself how I managed to get away with it. And then I stopped coming because people became curious and began asking questions. As it is, there is some gossip circulating. I trust Teresa—she won't talk. But just imagine, my dear, what it'd be like if they all found out about us? What would they think, and what would they say? So you be brave, my dear, and wait till you're well. Then we'll arrange a meeting somewhere or other away from the house.

June 1

My dear Makar Alexeyevich,

I would so much like to do something nice for you, to repay you for all your trouble and effort and for the affection you have shown me. And so, I decided in a moment of boredom to go through my drawer and find my notebook which I'm sending you. I started to write it when my life was still happy. You've often told me how curious you were to know about my former life, about my mother, about Pokrovsky, about the time I spent with Anna Fedorovna and, finally, about my more recent misfortunes. You've asked me so often to let you read this notebook in which, Heaven knows why, I decided to record some of the moments of my life, that I have no doubt you'll be pleased when you get the package. I must say, it saddened me to re-read it. It seems to me that I'm twice as old as I was when I wrote the last lines. It was all written at different times. Good-by now, Makar Alexeyevich. I'm finding life terribly dull, and I'm often bothered by sleeplessness. What a horribly boring convalescence!

V.D.

I

I was only fourteen when my father died. My childhood was the happiest time of my life. It didn't start here, but far away, in the depths of the country. My father was the steward of Prince P.'s huge estate in T. Province. We lived quietly, calmly, and happily in one of the prince's villages. I was a high-spirited child. I used to spend my time running about in the fields, woods, and orchard, and no one bothered about me. My father was absorbed with the affairs of the estate, and my mother was too busy running the house. I wasn't made to study at all, and that pleased me no end. Early in the morning I would run to the pond or into the woods, or go watch the haymaking or reaping. And I didn't mind the scorching sun, or finding that I was far away from the village and not too sure of my whereabouts, or that I was all scratched and my dress was torn. Later they'd scold me for it at home, but I didn't care.

I would have been perfectly happy to spend my entire life in that village. But I had to leave it: I was still a child, only twelve years old, when we came to Petersburg. I remember our sad preparations so clearly! How I cried when I said good-by to everything that was so dear to me. I remember throwing myself on my father's neck, weeping and begging him to be allowed to stay in the country for a little while longer. My father shouted at me. My mother cried. She explained that I had to leave now, that it couldn't be helped. The old Prince P. had died and his heirs had dismissed my father. Father had some money invested with private people in Petersburg, and felt that his presence in the city was now essential. I found all this out later from mother. So we moved here, settled on the Petersburg Side, and remained there until my father died.

It was very hard for me to get used to my new life. We

moved to Petersburg in the fall. The day we left the village it was cloudless, bright, and warm. The work in the fields was coming to an end. Huge stacks of wheat were piled up on the threshing floors, and flocks of birds cried overhead. Everything was so bright and cheerful. But when we got to Petersburg we found rain, sleet, damp, the penetrating autumn chill, and a crowd of new, strange, unfriendly faces, so displeased and sullen. We settled in somehow. I remember how everyone bustled about and fussed, getting into the swing of our new life. Father was never at home, and mother never had a moment's peace. I was almost forgotten. It felt so sad getting up on that first morning after our arrival. Our windows gave on a yellow fence. The street was always muddy. Few people passed by, and those who did were heavily muffled up—everyone seemed to be cold all the time.

And at home I felt terribly sad and bored for days on end. We had hardly any relatives or close friends. Father was on bad terms with Anna Fedorovna. (He was in debt to her for something.) When people came to the house, it was usually on business. As a rule there were arguments, noise, shouting. And after each visit, father was so irritable and gloomy. He would walk back and forth from one corner to the other for hours on end, frowning, and not saying a word to anyone. Mother didn't dare to address him then and kept quiet. I would sit down with a book in some corner, being quiet and good, and not daring to stir.

Three months after we came to Petersburg, I was sent to boarding school. I was very unhappy at first to be surrounded by strangers. They all seemed so cold and unfriendly—the school mistresses were forever scolding, the girls were always ready to sneer, and I was such a wild one! The discipline was strict and exacting. The set hours for everything, the meals taken in common, the boring teachers, all this made me miserable from the start. I couldn't sleep there. Sometimes I'd cry throughout the night, the whole long, cold, tedious night. In the evenings, when we were supposed to do our lessons, I pored over some exercises or some vocabulary, not daring to budge, and all the time I'd be thinking about our little home, about father and mother, about my old nanny and the stories she used to tell— Ah, how homesick you can get! I'd think of even the most trifling little thing at home with pleasure. And I'd keep repeating to myself how nice it would be to be back at home. My family and I would be sitting around a samovar in warmth and familiar surroundings. Ah, how I would hug mother now, so tightly, so lovingly! I'd go on thinking and thinking, until I had to hold back my tears, and then I just couldn't learn my vocabulary. So all night long I'd dream about the teacher, the headmistress, and the other girls; all night long, I'd go over those lessons in my sleep, only to find the next day that I didn't know a thing. So they made me kneel in a corner and gave me only one dish for dinner. I felt wretched and miserable all the time. From the first all the other girls used to laugh at me and tease me. They tried to confuse me when I was reciting my lessons, pinched me when we were walking in line to dinner or tea, and complained to the mistresses about me for no reason at all. But then, what heaven it was when my nanny came for me on Saturday evenings. I'd fling my arms around the dear old thing's neck in an outburst of joy. She used to get my things and wrap me up as we set out, and on the way home she couldn't keep up with me as I chattered away to her, telling her all about everything. And I would arrive home feeling happy and gay and hug everyone as if I hadn't seen them for ten years. There'd be jokes and stories about school, then I'd hug everyone again, giggle, run, and leap about. Then father would ask me seriously about my studies, my teachers, about French lessons and Lomond's Grammar. And everyone seemed so cheerful and happy. It even makes me feel good now, just thinking about those moments. I tried as hard as I could to study well and please my father. I realized that he was spending his last money on me, and for the rest was trying to get by, God knows how. He grew more and more irritable, gloomy, and dejected as his affairs deteriorated further and his debts accumulated. Mother was afraid to cry or say a word for fear of exacerbating him. Her health was poor, and she grew thinner and started coughing ominously. Returning from school, I sometimes found them in a sad state— mother crying softly and father furious. Then the reproaches and recriminations would start. Father would say that I afforded him no happiness, no comfort; that they deprived themselves of everything for my sake and here I still couldn't speak French. In short, mother and I were blamed for all his failures, all his misfortunes, everything. Ah, how he could make my poor mother suffer! It tore my heart just to look at her. Her cheeks were hollow, her eyes sunken, and the red spots of consumption had appeared on her face.

I came in for more trouble than anyone. It always started with some minor thing, but Heaven only knows where it ended up. Often I didn't even know what it was all about. It was a lament about everything—about my French; about my being an absolute idiot; about the headmistress of the school being a negligent and stupid woman who didn't bother about our morals; about father's still not being able to find himself a position; about Lomond's Grammar's being bad, whereas Zapolsky's was much better; about so much money having been wasted on me for nothing; about my being heartless and made of stone. And so I tried my very hardest, preparing my lessons and learning my French vocabulary by heart. It was all my fault and I was blamed for everything! And it certainly wasn't because father didn't love me; he was infinitely devoted to mother and me. It was just the way he had become.

Worries, disappointments, and failures had badly broken my poor father. He grew bilious and mistrustful, and was often on the verge of despair. He started to neglect his health, caught cold, all at once fell very sick, and, after a short illness, died so suddenly, so unexpectedly, that for several days afterward we were unable to recover from the shock. Mother was in such a daze that I feared for her reason. As soon as my father died, creditors started popping up as though from out of the ground. They took everything we had. Our little house on the Petersburg Side, which father had bought six months after we had moved to Petersburg, was sold. I don't know how the debts were settled, but we ourselves were left without a roof over our heads, without food or any resources. Mother was suffering from a wasting disease, we couldn't earn our living, and starvation was staring us in the face. I was only just past fourteen then.

It was at this point that Anna Fedorovna came to see us. She said that she was a landowner and some sort of relative of ours. Mother said it was true—she was related to us, but very distantly. She had never visited us while father was alive. And now, when she came, she said, with tears in her eyes, that she was very concerned about us. She commiserated with us over our bereavement and our disastrous position, remarking though that it was all my father's fault, that he had lived beyond his means, extended himself too far, and placed too much confidence in his own strength. She expressed a wish to become closer friends with us, and suggested that both sides forget the unpleasantnesses of the past. And when mother declared that she had never felt unfriendly toward her, she shed a tear, took mother to the church, and arranged for a requiem to be sung for our "dear one" (that was how she referred to father). After that she was solemnly reconciled with mother.

Having led up to the subject in a very roundabout way, Anna Fedorovna used the starkest colors to depict our poverty, our loneliness, and the hopelessness of our position, and then invited us, as she put it, to "take shelter" at her place. Mother thanked her, but for a long time could not make up her mind. But, as there was nothing else we could do and no other way out, she finally told Anna Fedorovna that we would accept her offer gratefully. I remember so clearly the morning when we moved from the Petersburg Side to Vasilevsky Island. It was a clear, dry, frosty autumn morning. Mother was crying. I was terribly sad too. I was all torn apart inside by some inexplicable anguish. . . . Ah, it was a hard time. . . .

II

Until mother and I got used to our new home, we both felt strange and uneasy living with Anna Fedorovna. Anna Fedorovna lived on Sixth Row in a small house that belonged to her. It had five rooms. Three of these rooms were occupied by Anna Fedorovna and my cousin Sasha, an orphan whom she was bringing up. My mother and I had one of the remaining rooms, and the other, next to ours, was occupied by a lodger, a poor student named Pokrovsky. Anna Fedorovna lived very well, much better than might have been expected, but the source of her income was a mystery. She always seemed to be in a rush, always preoccupied about something; she went out of the house several times a day, but what was the nature of her business I simply couldn't make out. She knew many people and they were of all sorts. Visitors would come to see her at all hours, and God knows who they were or on what business they came, but it never took much more than a minute. As soon as the bell rang, my mother would take me and go off into our room. That always angered Anna Fedorovna. She would say that we were too proud, proud beyond our means, as if we had anything to be proud about. . . . And she would go on like that, sometimes for hours, without stopping. At the time I didn't understand the significance of her reproaches; it is only now that I have found out or, at least, I can guess, why mother was so reluctant to live with Anna Fedorovna. Anna Fedorovna was a spiteful woman and she made us miserable. It is still a mystery to me why she ever invited us to live with her. At first she was quite nice to us, but when she realized how utterly helpless our position was and that we had nowhere else to go, she showed us her true face. Later, however, she became very friendly with me, almost crudely so, even overfriendly. But at first I had to suffer the same treatment as my mother. Every moment of the day she heaped reproaches upon us, or talked of her kindness. She introduced us to outsiders as her poor relatives, a helpless widow and orphan to whom she was giving shelter out of the kindness of her heart. At meals, she watched every morsel that we took; but our not eating caused a furor too, and then she would say we were turning our noses up at her food, that she was doing her best and doubted that we would have had better food at home. And she was continually running down father, saying that he thought he was better than other people, and as a result turned out to be much worse than them, leaving a wife and daughter behind with no place to go; and that if it hadn't been for a kind relative full of Christian charity, they would probably have died of hunger in the street. And she said many more things that were actually more disgusting than painful. And mother was always crying. Her health was deteriorating from day to day. She was visibly wasting away, and yet we worked from morning till night. We got ourselves sewing work on order, a thing Anna Fedorovna strongly disapproved of. Her house wasn't a dressmaker's shop, she kept saying. But we had to have clothes, we had to put money aside for unexpected expenses. We just had to have some money of our own. Besides, we were saving in the hope of eventually moving somewhere. But the work used up the last of mother's strength. She grew weaker with every day. Like a worm, the disease gnawed away at her life and brought her to her grave. I saw it, felt it, and suffered from it. It happened before my very eyes!

Day followed day and each was like the last. Our life was so quiet that we hardly felt we were living in a city.

Gradually, as she came to fully realize the extent of her power over us, Anna Fedorovna began to calm down. Actually, no one ever thought of contradicting her. Our room was separated from her half of the apartment by a corridor, and next to us, as I have already said, lived Pokrovsky. He taught Sasha French and German, history and geography—all the "disciplines," as Anna Fedorovna put it. In exchange he received food and lodging. Sasha was a bright, lively girl, but a bit mischievous. She was thirteen at the time. Anna Fedorovna suggested to mother that I might as well study too since I hadn't finished school. Mother gladly agreed, and for a whole year Pokrovsky taught us both.

Pokrovsky was a very poor young man. His health prevented him from continuing his regular studies, and we only referred to him as a student out of habit. He was so quiet, reserved, and retiring that we never heard him from our room. He was a very strange-looking creature: he walked with a stiff gait, greeted one so awkwardly and spoke so weirdly that at first I couldn't even look at him without laughing. Sasha was forever playing tricks on him, especially during our lessons. But he was a very irritable person, and lost his temper over any small matter. Then he would shout at us, complain, and often walk out on us in a fury before the lesson was over. Most of the day, he sat in his room with his books. He had many, and they were all rare and expensive. He gave lessons somewhere else too, for which he received a little money; as soon as he had any cash at all, he would buy more books.

In time I got to know him better. He was the best, the kindest of men, the most honorable of any I'd met. Mother had a very high opinion of him, and later he became my best friend—that is, after mother, of course.

Big girl though I was, I was in on all of Sasha's pranks at first, and we spent hours devising ways to rib him and make him lose patience. He was terribly funny when he got angry, and it greatly amused us. (I'm quite ashamed to think of it now.) Once we teased him so much that he was on the verge of tears, and I distinctly heard him mutter: "wicked children." And suddenly I felt very embarrassed and sorry for him. I remember I blushed to my ears and, almost in tears myself, begged him not to be upset and offended at our stupid fooling. But he closed his book and went to his room without finishing our lesson. I was torn by remorse all day long. The idea that mere children like us had brought this man to the brink of tears with our cruelty was unbearable. We had expected those tears, wanted to see them; we had succeeded in making him lose control, had forced upon the poor, unfortunate young man the realization of his bitter lot! Annoyance with myself, regret, and remorse kept me awake all night. They say remorse gives relief, but it's just the opposite. I don't know how, but my pride got involved in it too. I didn't want him to consider me a child. I was already fifteen.

From that day on, my imagination was strained by a thousand plans to change Pokrovsky's opinion of me. But, I was shy and timid and being, moreover, in a humble position, I couldn't bring myself to act, and so confined myself to daydreams (and what daydreams they were!). I stopped taking part in Sasha's pranks, and he stopped getting angry with us. But that didn't satisfy my pride.

And now I will say a few words about the strangest, the most unlikely, the most pathetic person I have ever met in my life. I have chosen this particular point in my notes to write about him because up until that time I had practically never paid any attention to him at all—while now everything connected with Pokrovsky suddenly became of interest to me.

Sometimes a little old man came to the house. He wore shabby, grubby old clothes, was short, gray-haired, baggy, and awkward—in a word, altogether odd. He seemed ashamed of something, indeed, ashamed of himself. He seemed to be always shrinking into himself and making faces. His strange ways and tics suggested strongly that he was not really normal. He would come to our house, but then he would stand in the passage outside the glass doors, not daring to come inside. And when one of us passed by him—myself or Sasha or a servant who was nice to him—he would wave and beckon to us, making all sorts of little signs. And only when we nodded and called to him to come in—an agreed upon signal that there were no outsiders in the house and that the way was clear—only then would he quietly open the door and, smiling happily and rubbing his hands delightedly, tiptoe straight to Pokrovsky's room. He was Pokrovsky's father.

Later on, I learned more about the old man's life. He had been in government service once, displayed no ability whatever for his work, and held the very lowest, the least important post. When his first wife (Pokrovsky's mother) died, he decided to marry again. He chose a lower middle-class woman who turned the whole house upside down. That woman wouldn't let anyone live in peace—she had to control everything. Pokrovsky was just ten at the time. His stepmother hated him, but he was lucky. There was a landowner called Bykov who knew Pokrovsky's father, having helped him out at one time. Now he took the boy under his protection and sent him to a boarding school. Bykov took such an interest in the boy because he had known his mother, to whom Anna Fedorovna had been very kind when she was young and for whom she had arranged the marriage with the elder Pokrovsky. Mr. Bykov, Anna Fedorovna's close friend, displayed great generosity and gave the bride a dowry of five thousand rubles. No one knows where that money went. It was Anna Fedorovna who told me all this, for Pokrovsky himself never liked to discuss his family affairs. It seems his mother was very beautiful and it has always seemed strange to me that she should have made such an unsuitable match. She died when she was still young, only four years after she got married.

From the boarding school, the young Pokrovsky went on to high school, and then to the university. And even after that, Mr. Bykov, who often came into Petersburg, continued to concern himself with his protegé. Pokrovsky could not go on with his studies because of his poor health, so Mr. Bykov introduced him to Anna Fedorovna who gave him board and lodging in exchange for tutoring Sasha.

As for old Pokrovsky, his wife's cruelty drove him to liquor and he was almost always drunk. His wife beat him, sent him to sleep in the kitchen, and kept him in such subjection that he finally became accustomed to her blows and ill-treatment and didn't even complain. He wasn't really old then, but his unhealthy life made him look like a doddery old man. The only human feeling he had left was his boundless love for his son. It seems that the young Pokrovsky was very much like his late mother. Possibly it was the memory of his kind first wife that caused the broken old man to love his son so much. Old Pokrovsky couldn't talk of anything else but his son. He visited him regularly twice a week. He didn't dare come more often, for the young Pokrovsky hated these visits. Of all his faults, without doubt the foremost and the gravest was lack of respect for his father. It must be said, though, that at times the old man was just about the most unbearable person on this earth. In the first place, he was terribly inquisitive; secondly, he interrupted his son's studies every minute, asking the silliest questions or making the most trivial remarks, and finally, he would sometimes turn up quite drunk. Little by little the son cured the old man of his foibles, of his inquisitiveness, his eternal chattering, with the result that his father listened to him as if he were an oracle and didn't dare open his mouth without his permission.

The poor old man couldn't sufficiently admire his Petey (that's what he called him). When he came to see him, he almost always looked very worried and anxious, probably because he wasn't sure how he would be received by his son. It usually took him a long time to make up his mind to come in, and if I happened to be around, he would interrogate me for twenty minutes on end about how Petey was, what sort of a mood he was in, and whether he was busy working on something important; what exactly he was doing, whether he was writing or just meditating. When I had sufficiently allayed his fears and encouraged him, he would at last make up his mind and go in. First he'd open the door very, very quietly and cautiously, and just poke in his head. Then, when his son nodded, and he saw that he was not annoyed with him, he would go into the room as noiselessly as possible, take off his wretched overcoat and his broad-brimmed hat which was crumpled and full of holes. He would hang his things on a hook and, tiptoeing very carefully, sit in a chair, and remain there without ever shifting his eyes from his son, taking in his every gesture in the hope of guessing what kind of a mood his Petey was in. And if, by chance, he discerned the slightest sign of irritability, he would immediately get up, explaining that, "Well, you know, Petey, I just dropped in for a minute . . . You see, I had walked a long way and happened to be passing by, so I thought I'd drop in to rest for a moment." And then, humbly and without another word, he would take his wretched coat and battered hat, quietly open the door, and go out, with a forced smile on his face to hide from his son how hurt he was.

But when his son happened to be nice to him, the old man was beside himself with happiness. His joy showed in his face, in his gestures, in his movements. If the son started a conversation, the father would raise himself a little from his chair, answer him quietly, eagerly, almost reverentially, always trying to use the choicest, that is, the most ridiculous, expressions. But he had no gift for words—he always got mixed up and became embarrassed, not knowing where to put his hands, where to put himself; and after that, he would keep whispering under his breath for a long time, as if he wanted to correct what he had said to his son. But when he was satisfied with what he had said, the old man would preen himself, straighten his waistcoat, his tie, his frockcoat, and take on a dignified air. And sometimes he would become so bold as to get up quietly from his seat, cross over to the bookcase, take some book or other and even read something in it there and then, whatever book it happened to be. And he did it all with a feigned casualness, as if he were quite familiar with his son's books, as if there were nothing unusual in his son's forbearance. But once I happened to hear Pokrovsky ask him not to touch his books, and I saw how frightened the poor old man was. He became very embarrassed, and in his haste put the book back upside down. Then, anxious to correct his mistake, he turned it around, putting it with the front side facing outward. He turned very red, smiled sheepishly, and was quite at a loss to know how to make up for his misdeed.

Pokrovsky gradually persuaded his father to give up his bad habits. Whenever the old man had been sober three times consecutively, young Pokrovsky would give him a quarter or a half-ruble or even more as he left. Sometimes he bought him boots, a tie, or a waistcoat. And the old man would be as proud as a peacock in his new clothes. Occasionally he would come and visit us. Now and then, he'd bring Sasha and me gingerbread or apples, and he would always talk to us about his Petey. He asked us to study hard and to be good, and he told us that his Petey was a good son, an exemplary son and, what's more, a learned son. And then he would wink his left eye at us in such a comic way and make such a funny face that, unable to restrain ourselves, we burst out laughing. My mother liked him very much. But the old man couldn't stand Anna Fedorovna, although he was quiet as a mouse and humbler than dirt in her presence.

Soon I stopped taking lessons from Pokrovsky. He still regarded me as a child, a playful little girl like Sasha. This was very painful because I was trying hard to make up for my former behavior. But he didn't notice a thing. This made me more and more miserable. I practically never spoke to him except during class. In fact I couldn't talk to him. I would turn red, feel terribly embarrassed, and then go off into a corner to cry with vexation.

I don't know how it would have ended if not for a strange circumstance. One evening when mother was with Anna Fedorovna, I went very quietly into Pokrovsky's room. I knew he wasn't home. I really have no idea what made me think of going to his room. Until then, I had never so much as glanced in there, although we had lived side by side for more than a year. And now, my heart beat so hard that it seemed to be about to leap out of my breast. I looked around me with a special sort of curiosity. Pokrovsky's room was very scantily furnished and disorderly. Sheets of paper covered with writing lay on the desk and the chairs. Books and sheets of paper! A strange thought occurred to me and gave me an unpleasant feeling of frustration. So it looked as if my friendship and my loving heart wouldn't be enough for him! He was learned while I was stupid, knew nothing, had never read a book.

I looked then with envy at the long shelves almost breaking under the weight of the books, and I felt full of resentment, sadness, and a sort of fury. I decided to read every one of those books, and to do so as quickly as possible. Perhaps I felt that if I learned all the things he knew, I'd be more worthy of his friendship. I rushed to the first shelf and seized the first dusty volume that happened to be at hand. Then, alternately flushing with excitement and turning pale from fear, I carried off the stolen book. I was going to read it by the night light while mother was asleep.

But what was my vexation when I opened it in my room and found that it was only a half-decayed, worm-eaten volume in Latin. So, without wasting time, I went to put it back. Just as I was replacing the book on the shelf, I heard a noise and approaching footsteps in the corridor. I tried frantically to replace the volume, but the books were still so tightly packed that I couldn't wedge in their former companion. I pushed the books as hard as I could and a rusty nail supporting the shelf chose just that particular moment to snap. One end of the shelf slid downward, and the books scattered noisily all over the floor.

Then the door opened, and Pokrovsky came in.

It must be noted that he couldn't stand anyone meddling with his things, and anyone who touched his books did so at his own risk. Now you can imagine my horror when books of all possible sizes and shapes—small, large, fat, and thin—flew from the shelf and went dancing under the table, the chairs, and all over the room.

I thought of running, but it was too late. "This is the end," I thought. "All is lost! I'm behaving like a stupid ten year old girl. I'm a real idiot!"

Pokrovsky was furious.

"That's all I needed!" he shouted. "Aren't you ashamed of yourself? Will you never learn to behave decently?"

He rushed to pick up the books. I bent to help him.

"Leave them!" he shouted. "I'd rather you stayed out of places where you haven't been invited."

But then, somewhat softened by my humility, he spoke to me in his former lecturing tone which he had used not so long ago when I was still attending his lessons with Sasha:

"You know, it is high time you started to behave reasonably. Just look at yourself. You're not a child any more. Why, you're fifteen years old already!"

And, probably wishing to ascertain whether I was or was not still a child, he looked at me, and then turned red to his ears.

I just stood there staring at him in great surprise. He rose from the floor, walked up to me with an embarrassed air and, looking terribly confused, started muttering something. I believe he was apologizing, perhaps for not having realized until then what a big girl I'd become. Finally I understood. I'm not sure what happened to me then. I became even more confused than Pokrovsky, turned even redder than he, covered my face with my hands, and rushed out of the room.

I didn't know where to hide in my shame. The mere fact that he had caught me in his room! For three days I couldn't even look at him. I blushed until tears came to my eyes. The most horrible and ridiculous thoughts whirled about inside my head. Of them all, my craziest idea was to go up to him, tell him the whole truth, and convince him that I had acted with good intentions and was not a stupid little girl. I almost did it too but, thank Heaven, I didn't have the courage. I can just imagine what would've happened if I'd carried out that plan. I'm ashamed when I think of it even now.

A few days after that, mother fell dangerously ill. For two days she was unable to leave her bed, and on the third night she became feverish and delirious. I didn't sleep that night and sat by her bed, bringing her drinks, and giving her medicine at fixed hours. The next night I felt quite exhausted. Sleep kept overcoming me, a green screen kept coming before my eyes, my head spun, and I almost fell asleep with exhaustion. Each time, my mother's weak moans tore me out of it. I started, my head cleared for a second, but soon drowsiness would start to come over me again. It was very painful. I am not sure what (because I can't remember too well) but some horrible dream or vision kept haunting my overwrought mind as I fought off sleep. I woke up terrified. The room was dark. The night light was burning out: the flame kept flaring up, lighting the wall with streaks of light, then almost completely disappearing. Somehow I felt very frightened, horrified. Anguish pressed on my heart. I jumped up from my chair, and was unable to suppress a cry prompted by some painful, agonizing feeling. At that moment, the door opened and Pokrovsky walked in.

I remember only that I found myself in his arms. He sat me down gently in the armchair, brought me a glass of water, and showered me with questions. I don't remember what I answered him.

"You're ill yourself," he said, taking me by the hand. "You're feverish. You're killing yourself. Come, think of your health. Lie down and sleep for a couple of hours. I'll wake you up. Calm yourself. Well, go on, lie down!" he said, giving me no chance to protest. I was too tired. I had no strength left. My eyes were closing by themselves. I stretched myself out in the armchair, thinking I would sleep for half an hour, and didn't wake up until the morning. Pokrovsky only woke me up when it was time to give my mother the medicine.

In the morning, feeling somewhat rested, I installed myself at mother's bedside, determined not to fall asleep this time. But at eleven, Pokrovsky knocked on our door. I opened it.

"It must be boring for you sitting there. Here's a book. Take it. You'll feel less bored."

I took it. I don't remember what book it was, and I don't believe I even so much as looked into it then, although I didn't sleep at all that night. A strange excitement kept me awake. Indeed, I couldn't remain in one place and several times I got up from my armchair and paced the room. An unknown inner gladness pervaded me. I was very happy over Pokrovsky's attentions. I was proud of his concern for me. I spent the whole night thinking. Pokrovsky didn't come to see me again that night, but I knew he wouldn't come and kept thinking of the next evening.

The following evening, after everyone in the house had retired to their rooms, Pokrovsky opened the door and, remaining standing in the doorway, spoke to me. I cannot remember one word of what we said. All I can recall is that I froze with shyness, became entangled in my words, was furious with myself, and wanted the conversation to end as quickly as possible, although I had waited for it all day, thought of it, made up the questions I'd ask him, and the answers I'd give . . .

That evening our friendship began. Throughout my mother's illness, we spent several hours together every night. Gradually I overcame my shyness, although I was still furious with myself after every one of our nocturnal conversations. I noticed delightedly that he was forsaking his unbearable books for me now. Once, the collapse of the bookshelf came lightly into our conversation. I felt very strange. I was somehow *too* open, *too* candid. Carried away by excitement and a strange enthusiasm, I admitted everything—that I wanted to study, that I wanted to know about things, that I didn't like being taken for a little girl, for a child. I repeat—I was in a strange mood. My heart felt all soft and tears filled my eyes. I didn't hold anything back and told him about my affection for him, about how much I wanted to love him, to live in perfect harmony with him, to comfort and console him.

He gave me a strange look, full of surprise and embarrassment and didn't say a thing. I felt suddenly very hurt and sad. I had the impression that he felt like laughing at me. I couldn't restrain myself then and started to cry like a baby, aloud, as if I were in some sort of a fit.

He seized my hands, kissed them, pressed them against his chest. I don't remember what he said, trying to comfort me, but I know that I cried, laughed, and cried again. My face was afire and I couldn't utter one word in my elation.

Through my joy, I noticed, nevertheless, that Pokrovsky still remained somewhat embarrassed and constrained. It looked as though he couldn't get over my excitement, exaltation, and the sudden revelation of my ardent, tender friendship. Well, perhaps it only seemed strange to him at the beginning, because later on he accepted as a matter of fact my feeling for him, my friendly words and the attention I paid him, and replied with the same attention, just as friendly and sincere, very much as an intimate friend or a beloved brother would. It gave me such a nice warm feeling in my heart. I didn't hide anything from him. He knew and saw everything, and with each day became more attached to me.

I really don't remember what we talked about during those painful and at the same time delightful hours we spent together in the flickering light of the little night lamp by the bedside of my poor ailing mother. We spoke about everything that came to our minds, everything that tore itself from our hearts, that clamored to be told. And we were almost happy then. Ah, that was both a sad and a happy time, and I feel sad and happy all at once thinking of it. Memories, whether glad or sad, are always painful. At least, that is how it is with me. But even the painfulness of remembering is sweet. And when I feel oppressed and despondent, my memories are as refreshing to me as the dew of a cool evening to a frail, weak flower wilting from the scorching sun.

Mother was recovering, but I still sat by her bedside throughout the night. Pokrovsky often came and brought me books to read. At first I read them just to keep awake, then more attentively, and finally with eagerness. Suddenly a world I hadn't even suspected opened itself before my eyes. New thoughts, new impressions came in a violent tide. And the more they moved me, the more confused and perplexed I was by the new impressions, and the more I liked them, the sweeter was their impact upon me. They suddenly crowded into my heart, giving it no chance to relax. A strange chaos pervaded me. But that spiritual commotion didn't upset my balance altogether. I was too much of a dreamer and that saved me.

Mother's complete recovery put an end to our nightly meetings and our long talks. We only managed to exchange a few words here and there, often shallow, insignificant words, but I chose to invest those words with special, implied meanings. My life was full, I was happy. It was a sort of quiet, secure happiness. A few weeks passed in this way.

One day, old Pokrovsky came in to see us. He chatted to us for a long time, was in an exceptionally happy mood, laughed, was witty after his fashion, and finally explained why he was in such a state of jubilation: Petey's birthday was exactly one week away, and he'd absolutely have to visit his son on that occasion wearing the new waistcoat and boots that his wife had promised to buy him. In short, the old man felt boundlessly happy and prattled on about whatever came to his mind.

His birthday! The thought of it gave me no rest, day or night. I decided that I must give Pokrovsky something as a token of our friendship. But what? Finally I decided to get him some books. I knew that he would like to have the recent edition of Pushkin's complete works. I decided I'd give it to him. I had about thirty rubles of my own money that I'd earned by needlework. I had put that sum aside to buy myself a new dress. And so I sent our old cook Matryona to learn the price of the full set of Pushkin. Alas! The price of the eleven volumes, including the cost of binding, amounted to at least sixty rubles. Where would I get that sum? I thought and thought, but couldn't decide what to do. I didn't want to take any money from my mother. I'm sure, of course, that she would have helped but, in that event, everyone in the house would have known about our present, and the gift would have been regarded as a token of appreciation for the lessons Pokrovsky had given me for a whole year. I wanted the present to come just from me, and I didn't even want anyone to know about it. As for the trouble he had taken with me, I wanted to remain indebted to him to the end of my life, never trying to repay him except by my friendship. At last, I found a way out of my difficulty.

I knew that at the second-hand book stores in Gostiny Dvor it was sometimes possible, with a bit of bargaining, to buy books at half price. True, they were second-hand books, but some were hardly the worse for wear and looked quite new. So I decided to go to Gostiny Dvor and it so happened that an occasion presented itself the very next day. My mother didn't feel too well, Anna Fedorovna felt lazy, and so it was I who had to run all the errands for the household.

I left, accompanied by Matryona.

I was lucky and found a set of Pushkin in a very pretty binding very quickly. The bargaining began. At first they asked me a price higher than I would have paid in a regular bookstore. But in the end, after considerable trouble and pretending to walk away several times, I succeeded in bringing the price down to ten rubles in silver. Ah, how much I enjoyed that bargaining!

Poor Matryona couldn't understand what had come over me and why I had suddenly decided to buy so many books.

But, oh horror! My entire capital consisted of thirty rubles in paper money and the merchant wouldn't reduce the price any further. So I started begging him. I implored and beseeched and finally he gave in. He knocked off another two and a half rubles, swearing that he was only doing so because I was such a nice young lady and that he wouldn't have done it for anyone else. Since that was as far as he would go, I was still two and a half rubles short and was about to burst into tears of vexation. But then I got some quite unexpected assistance.

Not far away, at another bookstall, I caught sight of old Pokrovsky. Four or five second-hand book dealers were clustered about him. They were harassing him, crowding him, and the old man was almost at his wits' end. Each dealer was offering him his goods, and there were so many things they had to offer and so many things Pokrovsky wanted to buy. The poor old man stood there completely bewildered, not even knowing which of the books to look at. I walked up to him and asked him what he was doing there. He seemed awfully pleased to see me. He was almost as fond of me as of his Petey.

"Well, Varinka," he said, "I'm trying to buy some books for my boy. His birthday is coming soon, you see, and since he likes books so much, I came to buy him books."

The old man always spoke comically and now he was in a state of great bewilderment as well. Whatever he set eyes on cost at least one, two, or three rubles in silver. And so he didn't even inquire how much the bigger volumes cost. He just picked them up, opened them, turned a few leaves, looking at them covetously, then sadly replaced them on the shelves.

"No, no, that's too expensive," he muttered. "But maybe one of these . . ."

And he'd start fingering thin pamphlets, song books, almanacs. They were quite cheap.

"But why are you looking at these?" I asked him. "They are all just a lot of rubbish."

"Oh no," he said, "no, here, just have a look. There are some very, very good books among them."

He drawled the last words in such a sad sing-song that I thought that he was about to cry with vexation because the good books were so expensive, and that a tear was about to roll from his pale cheek onto his red nose. I asked him how much money he had and he said, "Here!" and fished out his fortune wrapped in a grubby piece of newspaper. There was a half-ruble piece, a twenty-kopeck piece and another twenty kopecks in coppers. I took him at once to my merchant.

"Here, these eleven books cost only thirty-two and a half rubles in paper money. I have thirty rubles. If you put in your two and a half rubles, we'll be able to buy those books and give them to Peter as a present from both of us."

The old man was beside himself with delight. He poured out all his coins and the dealer loaded him with our joint present. The old man left with volumes in all his pockets, under his arms, and in his hands. He promised to bring them to me secretly the next day.

On the following day, the old man came to see his son, spent about an hour with him, and then visited us. He sat down next to me, looking very mysterious and very funny. First smiling, then rubbing his hands with a proud and satisfied air, he announced that the books had been smuggled in unnoticed and were now standing in a corner of the kitchen guarded by Matryona. After that our conversation naturally turned to the forthcoming celebration. The old man held forth on how we were to present our gift. But the more he went on about it, the more I felt that there was something on his mind that he didn't dare utter. I was waiting for it and remained silent. The secret joy and pleasure that had been manifested in his strange twitchings and the winking of his left eye vanished. He looked more worried and dejected every minute. Finally he couldn't restrain himself any longer.

"Listen," he said in a low voice, "listen, Varinka, I must tell you . . ." The old man seemed terribly worried and confused. "On Petey's birthday, you'll take ten of those books and give them to him yourself. I mean, as a present from you alone. And then I will take the eleventh and give it to him as my own present. And so, each of us will have something to give him. . . ."

The old man stopped. I looked at him. He was shyly awaiting my verdict in silence.

"But why don't you want us to give him the whole set together?"

"Well, I just feel it'd be better my way. Well, you see, what it amounts to . . ." the old man hesitated and began to stammer. "Well, you know . . ." He got bogged down and

it took him a while to get control of his tongue. "Well, you
see," he said at last, "I indulge myself sometimes . . . Well,
in fact I indulge myself all the time, all the time, and I keep
doing the wrong things . . . You know, it's so cold sometimes
outside, and then there are all sorts of troubles, you know, or
I may feel sad or something, or something bad happens; and
I can't restrain myself, and drink a glass or two too much,
and Petey doesn't like that. You see, Varinka, he takes me
to task and lectures me. So now I'd like to prove to him, by
giving him my present, that I'm beginning to behave, since
I've been able to save enough for a book—and it took me a
long time, because I hardly ever get any money except for
what Petey lets me have now and then. And he knows it. So
he'll see how I use whatever money I get, and he'll understand that I'm doing it for his sake alone."

I became terribly sorry for the old man. It didn't take
me long to make up my mind. The old man was looking at
me anxiously.

"So you know what," I said, "you'll give him the lot of
them."

"What do you mean, the lot of them? You mean all the
books?"

"That's right."

"And tell him they're all from me?"

"Yes."

"From me alone? You mean to make the present just in
my name?"

"Well, of course, in your name."

I thought I had expressed myself very clearly but the
old man couldn't understand what I meant for a long time.

"Certainly," he repeated, thinking very hard, "that'd be
all very nice. . . . But then, what about you, Varinka?"

"There won't be any present from me, that's all."

"What?" the old man shouted, almost in terror. "What
are you saying? You won't give Petey anything? There won't
be a present for him from you?"

He sounded frightened, and I believe that at that moment
he was prepared to pull out of the arrangement so that I
should have something to give to his boy too. He was such
a kind old man and it took me a great deal of effort to convince him that I'd have been delighted to give Peter something, but didn't wish to deprive him of the pleasure.

"If your son is pleased and you are happy," I said, "I'll

be very pleased and, deep down, I will feel as though I too had made him a present."

That reassured him completely. He stayed with us for a couple of hours more, but during that time was unable to keep still; he kept jumping up, fussing around, fooling with Sasha, stealthily kissing me, pinching my hand, making funny faces at Anna Fedorovna. Finally, it was she who turned him out of the house. In fact, the old man had probably never been so exuberantly happy before.

When the awaited day came, he arrived at eleven, directly from church. He wore a carefully darned frockcoat and a waistcoat and boots that were actually new. In each hand he held a bundle of books. It was Sunday, and so we were all sitting in Anna Fedorovna's sitting room, having coffee. I believe the old man began by saying that Pushkin was quite good at turning out verse. Then, spluttering and losing the thread of what he was saying, he suddenly started holding forth on how it was everyone's duty to behave properly, for if one didn't, one was surely indulging oneself, and that bad habits led a man to his downfall and perdition. He even enumerated some tragic examples of overindulgence, and concluded by declaring that he had at last reformed and had been behaving well for some time. He had felt that his son's reproaches were justified even before, he had felt it in his heart then, but now he had finally learned how to abstain. And in proof of that he was presenting his son with these books, bought with savings accumulated over a long time.

Listening to the old man, I couldn't help laughing and crying at the same time. He certainly knew how to lay it on thick when offered an opportunity! The books were carried to Pokrovsky's room and placed on his bookshelf.

Pokrovsky guessed the truth almost right away. The old man was invited to stay for dinner. Everyone was very gay that day. After dinner we played forfeits and cards. Sasha was quite wild and I was hardly less so. Pokrovsky was very attentive to me and kept trying to have a word with me in private, but I evaded him. For me, it was the happiest day in four years.

After that, all I have is sad memories. It is a gloomy story. That's why, perhaps, my pen is moving slower now and refuses to go on writing. And maybe that is also why I have dwelled in such minute detail on the happy days of my poor existence. Those days were so brief, and they were replaced by black misery which will end God knows when.

My unhappiness was ushered in with Pokrovsky's illness and death. He became ill two months after the events I've just described. During those two months he made a great effort to find some secure means of livelihood, for he still didn't have regular work. Until the last minute, like all consumptives, he clung to the hope of continuing to live for a long time. He had been offered a teaching position somewhere but he hated that occupation. And in his state of health he couldn't enter government service. Anyway, he'd have had a long time to wait for his first salary. Now he saw himself as failing in every respect, and he grew peevish and irritable. His health was growing worse, although he didn't notice that. When fall arrived, he still went out every day wearing only a thin topcoat to see whether someone wouldn't give him a job. He had practically to beg, to implore people, and that made him feel very miserable. He would come back with his feet wet, soaked through from the rain. Finally he had to take to his bed, and he never got up again. He died in the mid-autumn, in late October.

I hardly ever left his room during his illness. I looked after him, took care of him. I spent many nights without sleep. He was seldom conscious. In his delirium he said all sorts of things—he spoke about his job, about his books, about me, about his father. And so I learned many things I had never even suspected. During the early days of his illness, everyone kept looking at me in a rather peculiar way. Anna Fedorovna kept shaking her head. But I looked them straight in the eye and no one reproached me any more for my sympathy for Pokrovsky; at any rate, my mother didn't.

From time to time, Pokrovsky recognized me, but very seldom. He was mostly unconscious. There were nights which he spent addressing someone in obscure, unclear words; his hoarse voice resounded in the narrow room as if it were a coffin. It frightened me. On the last night particularly, he seemed to be in a frenzy. He suffered terribly, was in frightful agony; his moans pierced my heart. Everyone in the house was in a strange state of awe. Anna Fedorovna kept praying that God take him quickly. A doctor was called and announced that the patient was certain to die by morning.

Old Pokrovsky spent the whole night out in the corridor, by the door of his son's room. They put some sacking down for him to sleep on. He kept popping into the room, and he was a frightening sight. The blow had been so hard that the old man looked blank and seemed to have no feeling left. His head shook, he trembled, and all the time kept whispering something under his breath, as though debating with himself. I thought he was going out of his mind.

Just before daybreak, the old man, exhausted by his wretchedness, stretched himself out on his sacking and slept like a log. Around seven, his son's end drew near. I woke the father. Pokrovsky, fully conscious, said good-by to us all. It is incredible—I couldn't cry, although my heart was being torn apart.

But the last moments were the worst. He kept asking, begging for something, but he was less and less able to control his tongue, and I couldn't understand what he was trying to say. It was an excruciating feeling. For a whole hour he kept worrying about something, trying to make some sort of a sign with his hands which were growing numb, and then again begging for something in his pitiful, hollow voice. But he just made disconnected sounds that I still couldn't make out. I brought every member of our household to him, gave him a drink. But he just kept sadly shaking his head.

At last I guessed what he wanted. He was asking me to pull back the curtains and open the windows and shutters. He probably wished to have a last glimpse at the world, at the daylight, at the sun. I pulled the curtain aside, but the new day was bleak and sad like the ending life of the dying man. The sun wasn't there. Cottony clouds overcast the gloomy, mournful, drizzling sky. Fine rain rattled against the window panes, washing them with rivulets of cold, dirty water; it was dark and dim. The pale daylight trickled feebly into the room, competing with the flickering of the little lamp burning by the icon. The dying man looked at me very, very sadly and shook his head. One minute later he was dead.

It was Anna Fedorovna who took care of the funeral arrangements. She bought the very cheapest kind of coffin and rented a carter. To cover these expenses, Anna Fedorovna seized all Pokrovsky's books and other belongings. The old man argued with her, protested loudly, got hold of as many books as he could, stuffed them in his pockets and under his hat, and carried them around with him wherever he went, even to church. All those days he seemed to be in a daze, and kept fussing around the coffin with strange solicitude—now straightening the wreath on his dead son's head, now lighting or removing candles. It was obvious that he couldn't fix his thoughts on anything.

Neither my mother nor Anna Fedorovna attended the funeral service. Mother was too ill and Anna Fedorovna, who had been about to go, quarreled with the father of the deceased and decided to stay home. And so only the old man and I attended the church service. During the service, a sort of fear came over me, a kind of sinister foreboding, so that I could hardly wait to leave.

At last the coffin was closed, nailed, loaded onto the cart, and driven off. I accompanied it only to the street corner. The carter set his horse at a trot. The old man ran behind, crying aloud, his crying broken and quivering because he was running. He lost his hat, but didn't stop to pick it up. His head was all wet; the wind was rising, and the sleet lashed his face. The old man didn't seem to feel anything and, weeping aloud, kept dashing from one side of the cart to the other. The tails of his shabby frockcoat flapped in the wind like a pair of wings. Books were sticking out of all his pockets; in his arms he held a huge volume, pressing it desperately to his heart. The people in the street removed their hats and crossed themselves. Some stopped and stared at the poor old man. Books kept falling from his pockets into the mud. People stopped him, pointing out a book he had dropped. He picked it up and rushed on again in pursuit of his son's coffin. At the corner of the street, some beggar woman joined him and followed the coffin in his company. Then the cart turned the corner and vanished from my sight. I went back home and when I got there, I flung myself onto my mother's breast. I pressed myself against her as hard as I could, kissed her, sobbed, held her tight as though trying to retain in my arms the last friend I had left, refusing to yield her to death. But death was already hovering over my poor mother.

June 11

I am so grateful to you, Makar Alexeyevich, for yesterday's excursion to the Islands. It was so lovely there, so cool, and everything was so green! It's been so long since I've seen green leaves and grass. When I was ill, I felt certain that this time I would die. So you can imagine how I feel now!

Please forgive me for having been so sad yesterday. I felt very content, very relaxed, but it so happens that at moments when I am happiest, I somehow always feel sad. As to my crying, that was nothing. I don't know myself why, but I often cry like that. I feel weak and nervous and that is why I react to things in a painful way. The pale, cloudless sky, the sunset, the evening stillness, all that had a painful effect upon me yesterday, although I cannot explain why. I suppose it was just that my heart was asking for tears. But why am I writing you all this? It is all so difficult for the heart to understand, and it is even more difficult to explain. But perhaps you will understand me after all.

It is so sad and so funny! You're really such an extraordinarily nice man, Makar Alexeyevich! The way you looked into my eyes yesterday to read in them what I was feeling, and were so pleased when I looked elated. Whether it was a bush, a garden path, or a strip of water, you stood there, preening yourself and glancing into my eyes, as though you were taking me round your private domain. That goes to show how kindhearted you are, Makar Alexeyevich. And that's why I am so fond of you. Well, good-by. I felt ill again today. I let my feet get wet yesterday and caught cold. Fedora is unwell too, and so we are both invalids just now. Don't forget me, and come to see me as often as possible.

Yours,

V. D.

June 12

My darling Varvara Alexeyevna,

Why, I hoped you'd make a whole poem out of our yesterday's outing, but all you managed to turn out was a one-page letter. Still, though you didn't write much, it is very well and sweetly described. What you say about nature and about various rural landscapes and about your feelings—all that is described really well. But me, I have no talent at all. I can sit down and write ten pages, and still I can't manage to describe anything. I've tried.

You write, my dear, that I am a good, kind man, that I am incapable of harming my fellow creatures, that I appreciate God's blessings as manifested in nature's bounty, and so on, and you go on praising me. All that is true, my sweet, absolutely true. I am really just what you say, I know it myself, but when I read it written by you, I cannot help being deeply moved. After that, all sorts of painful thoughts come to me. And so let me tell you something in my turn, my dear.

I'll begin with when I was seventeen. That was when I entered the government service. I'll have thirty years of service behind me soon. Well, I can say for myself that I've worn out a number of frockcoats, that I have matured, gained experience, seen many people, lived in the world, and once they even thought of recommending me for a decoration. Perhaps you don't believe me, sweet, but really, I'm telling the truth. But then there were wicked people too, my dear. Now let me tell you, Varinka, it's quite possible that I am a stupid and ignorant man, but my heart is just the same as any other man's heart.

Well, I'll tell you now what a wicked man did to me. I'm even ashamed to tell you what he did. And why did he do it? Well, because I'm meek, because I'm quiet, because I'm soft-hearted, that's why! They just took a dislike to me, and that started it all. It began with, "You're this, you're that, Makar Alexeyevich," and then it was "What's the good of asking him anything?" and it came to "No doubt about it—it's certainly all Makar Alexeyevich's fault!" And so everything was blamed on me and they managed to make Makar Alexeyevich a byword all over the department. And that wasn't all—it was not only my name that became a byword and a term of abuse, but they even started on my boots, my frockcoat, my hair, my figure. Everything about me was wrong, everything had to be changed! And, from time immemorial, all that has been repeated every single day. I got used to it because I get used to anything, being meek, being a little man. But what did I do to deserve it? Whom have I ever harmed? As though they'd ever passed over anyone on the promotion list for my sake! Or have I ever tried to discredit a colleague in the eyes of our superiors? Have I ever asked for a bonus? Have I ever gone in for intrigue? Don't think anything of the sort, my dear Varinka! What need would I have of all that? Just think, do I really have the talent required to entertain ambitions and start intrigues? So why must I be accused of all that and suffer for it, may the Lord forgive me for asking. You, for instance, you think I am a decent man, and you are infinitely better than any of them.

Well what, would you say, is the highest civic virtue? So, the other day, in a private conversation, Yestafy Ivanovich said that a citizen's highest civic virtue was his ability to make money. It was meant as a joke (I know it was meant as a joke), but the moral of it was that no one should be a burden to anyone. Well, I'm not a burden to anyone. I earn my own crust of bread. True, it's just plain bread and at times it may even be a bit stale, but still I've had to work for it, I've earned it rightfully, and have nothing to reproach myself with in that respect.

Of course, I realize that I am not performing great deeds in copying documents, but I can't help that. Indeed, I'm proud of doing it because I work by the sweat of my brow. And, after all, what's so disgraceful about being a copying clerk? "Ah, he's just a copying clerk!" Well, is that a dishonest occupation? I have good, legible handwriting. It's a pleasure to look at it and His Excellency is very pleased. I copy the most important documents for him. Of course, I can't express myself in good style. I know that that is just something I haven't got and that is why I haven't made out in the government service, and even now, my dear, that is why I write to you simply, without pretensions, just jotting things down as they come, straight from the heart. I am aware of that, but just think what would happen if everyone started going in for literature? There wouldn't be anyone left to do the copying, would there? That's the question I raise, and I'd like you to answer it, my sweet.

So I realize now that I am needed, indispensable, and that they have no call to drive a man out of his mind with their nonsense. All right, so maybe I am a mouse, if they find I'm like one, but then it turns out that it's quite a useful mouse, that they can ride it, that, thanks to it, some people get promoted and obtain decorations—some mouse, eh?

But enough of this subject, my dear. That's not at all what I wanted to talk to you about. I just got carried away a little. But still, it is quite pleasant from time to time to do oneself justice.

Good-by for now, my dear, my sweet consolation, my kind girl! I'll come to see you soon without fail, my darling. Don't be too bored in the meantime. I'll bring you a book to read. Well, see you soon, Varinka.

Your devoted well-wisher,
MAKAR DEVUSHKIN

June 20

Dear Makar Alexeyevich,

I am writing this in a hurry—I have some work that I must finish in time. There is an opportunity for a good bargain. Fedora tells me that someone she knows has an almost new frockcoat for sale and also some underwear, a waistcoat, and a hat. I understand that the price asked is very reasonable, and I wonder whether you oughtn't to take advantage of the occasion. I believe you're not too hard pressed just now and, anyway, you told me you had some money tucked away. Please, don't stint yourself—you need all those things badly. Just look at the old clothes you go around in! It's really a disgrace how patched they are. You haven't bought yourself any new clothes for a long time. I know it, although you claim you have. Or if you have bought any, you must have sold them again, I don't know on what occasion. So please, listen to me and buy these things. Do it for me—if you love me, buy them.

Now, about that linen you sent me as a present—you're ruining yourself, Makar Alexeyevich. You've spent such a terrible lot of money on me already! Ah, you really like throwing money away! I didn't need it. It was all quite unnecessary. I know, I am convinced, that you love me, and you don't have to keep proving it to me by sending me presents. Especially since it's not easy for me to accept them, knowing what privations they mean for you. Once and for all: no more, understand? Please, please.

You ask me to send you the continuation of my notes. You say you'd like me to complete them. Well, I don't even know how I managed to write what I have already written! I don't think I'd have the strength to speak of the past now. In fact, I'd rather not even think of it, for those recollections frighten me. The most painful thing for me is to speak about my poor mother who left her child to be preyed upon by all those monsters. My heart bleeds at the mere recollection of those days. It is all very fresh in my memory still. I haven't even had time to understand it, let alone to recover from it.

I've told you how Anna Fedorovna feels now. She accuses me of ingratitude and denies any blame for her connivance with Mr. Bykov. She insists that I should go back and live with her, and says that I am living on strangers' charity now, and that I am on a very bad path. I am made to understand that if I go back to her, she herself will see to it that Bykov makes up for what he did and gives me a dowry.

Ah, bother them both! I'm quite happy as I am, with you and my kind Fedora who, in her devotion to me, reminds me of my late nanny. And although you're only a distant relative of mine, nevertheless, your name constitutes a protection for me. As to those people, I want nothing to do with them, and will forget them if I can. What can they want of me now? Fedora says that it's all just idle talk and that they'll leave me alone in the end anyway. I wish to God they would!

V. D.

June 21

My dearest Varinka!

I don't know how to begin. Isn't it strange, my dear, the way we live now, you and I? I say that because I've never known such happy days before. It is as though God had blessed me with a home and a family of my own, my sweet little girl! And what is all this fuss you are making about those four blouses I sent you? Why, Fedora told me you needed them. Let me tell you, it makes me very happy to look after you and get things for you. So please, leave me that pleasure and don't forbid me. I've never been like this before, my dear girl. And I have a very busy social life now. In the first place, my life is twice as full as it used to be, because, to my great joy, you live very close by; and in the second place, I've been invited to tea today by my neighbor Ratazayev, that same government employee I mentioned before who has literary evenings in his room. He has invited some friends, and we will read literature tonight. Well, that's how we are nowadays, my girl! Well, good-by then. I've written all this just like that, for no particular reason, simply to let you know how fine I feel.

I understand from Teresa that you need some colored silk for embroidery. I will get it for you, my darling. I'll get you some without fail. Tomorrow I'll have the pleasure of getting everything you want. And I know where to buy the silk, too. In the meantime, I remain

Your sincere friend,
MAKAR DEVUSHKIN

June 22

Dear Varvara Alexeyevna,

I must inform you that a heartbreaking event has occurred in our apartment. At about five this morning, Gorshkov's little boy died. I'm not quite sure what it was he actually died of. I believe it was scarlet fever or something of the sort—God alone knows. I went to the Gorshkovs. Ah, my dear, they live in such incredible poverty! And what a mess! And no wonder—the whole family lives in one room partitioned only by screens for decency. The little coffin was there already, a very plain little coffin, but rather pretty. I believe they bought it ready made. The boy was about nine, and they say he was quite a promising child. Ah, it broke my heart to see them, Varinka! The mother didn't cry, but the poor thing looked so awfully sad. Well, I suppose that, in a way, they'll be better off with one off their shoulders. Of course, they still have a baby and a little girl not much more than six. There's no joy in seeing a boy suffer and not be able to help him. The father sat there on a broken chair in his greasy old frockcoat, with tears running down his cheeks, not from grief, perhaps, but habit. He's such a strange man! He blushes when anyone addresses him, and gets so embarrassed that he doesn't know what to say. And the little girl, she stood there, leaning against the coffin and looking so sad, the poor thing! Ah, Varinka, I can't stand it when children stand thoughtful and brooding like that. Makes me feel very uneasy, my darling. There's a rag doll on the floor near her, but she won't play with it. She holds a finger to her lips, and just stands and stands without stirring. The landlady gave her candy. The child took it. But she didn't eat it. Isn't it sad, all this, Varinka?

MAKAR DEVUSHKIN

June 25

My very dear Makar Alexeyevich,

I'm sending you back your book. It's a piece of rubbish, not even worth the trouble of picking up! Wherever did you dig up such a treasure? No, seriously, Makar Alexeyevich, do you really like books of this sort? The other day, I was promised something to read, and when I get it, I'll share it with you. And now, good-by, I really have no time to write more.

V. D.

June 26

Dear Varinka,

The trouble is I hadn't read that book myself. It's true, I glanced through it and saw it was nonsense, written just to make people laugh. Well, I said to myself, it seems funny all right, and maybe it will amuse Varinka. And so I sent it to you.

But now Ratazayev has promised to lend me some real literature, so you won't be short of good books any more, my sweet. That Ratazayev knows a lot about literature, and you should see how the fellow writes himself. His pen is nimble, and his style is really great. And he puts so much meaning into every ordinary little word, any word at all, the sort of word I might use sometimes when talking to Teresa or Faldoni—well, he manages to put style into that even! I go to his gatherings. We smoke tobacco there and listen while he reads aloud, sometimes until five in the morning. It's not just literature, it's a real picnic! It's so lovely— just like flowers. You can make a bouquet of words on every page. And he himself is such a nice, friendly man! What am I next to him? Nothing! He is a man with a reputation, while I, I simply don't exist. But that doesn't prevent him from being nice to me. I do some copying for him now and then. But please don't imagine, Varinka, that there's a trick in it somewhere, that he's being nice to me just because I do copying for him. Don't listen to gossip, my dear, to nasty, vulgar gossip. No, I do it of my own free will, and I am delighted to oblige him. Now, if he is nice to me, it is, I suppose, because he likes to please me too. I appreciate his delicate ways, my sweet, and believe me, he is a very, very kind man and an incomparable writer.

Literature is a great thing, Varinka, a very great thing, as I learned from them two days ago. What a profound thing literature is! It strengthens men's hearts, educates their minds, and does all sorts of things, just as it says in that book of theirs. It is very well put, you know. Literature is a picture, that is, in a sense, it is both a picture and a mirror; it is passion, it is expression, it is ever so clever criticism, it is an edifying lesson, and it is also a document. I got all that from them, of course.

Frankly, sweet, I can sit with them, listen to what is said, even smoke a pipe like them, but when they begin to argue about all sorts of lofty matters, I just keep quiet. Yes, dear,

I'm sure that both you and I, we'd have to keep quiet most of the time. I turn out to be a real, poor fool, and I am ashamed of myself sitting there all evening, trying to put in a word on those lofty subjects, but never finding that wretched word! And I'm sorry that I'm not up to them, Varinka, that, as the saying goes, "a man can be fully grown and still have no mind of his own." For what do you think I do with myself in my spare time? Well, I just sleep like a fool. Ah, it'd be better if, instead of wasting my time sleeping, I could do something useful—sit down and write, for instance. It'd be good for me, and perhaps of some use to others. Why, my dear, you can't imagine how much they get for it, God forgive them! And Ratazayev makes pretty good money too. How long does it take him, for instance, to write a signature? On some days he can even turn out five signatures, I'm sure, and I understand he charges up to three hundred rubles for one. He may write a little story, some little yarn, and he wants five hundred for it, and they have to come up with that five hundred, whether they like it or not. And there are occasions when he puts a whole thousand into his pocket. What do you think of that, Varinka? He also has a notebook of poems, rather short poems at that, but you know what he's asking for it? Seven thousand rubles, my dear girl, seven thousand—just think of it! Why, that's the price of a whole property. You can get a whole apartment house for that, you know. He says they've offered him five thousand but he won't accept. I tried to convince him. "Take their five thousand and spit in their eye," I said to him. "It's a good sum, five thousand, after all!" "No," he says, "I'm sure those crooks will give me my seven thousand in the end." He's a real smart fellow, that Ratazayev!

Well, while we're at it, dear, I'll copy a passage from *Italian Passions* for you—that's the name of one of his works. Read it, Varinka, and you'll judge for yourself after that.

. . . Vladimir shuddered. Inside him, his passions gurgled furiously, his blood seethed.

"Countess," he cried, "can you imagine, countess, how terrible this passion, how boundless this madness is? No, my dreams did not deceive me! I am in love! I love exaltedly, furiously, madly! All the blood of your husband is not enough to extinguish the insane, burning, hissing exaltation that has arisen in

my soul! Puny obstacles will prove impotent before
the hellish blaze harrowing my exhausted breast. Oh,
Zinaida, Zinaida!"

"Vladimir!" the countess whispered, beside herself, as she leaned on his shoulder.

"Zinaida!" exclaimed Vladimir Smelsky, seized
with rapture.

A sigh issued from his breast. The flame flared
brightly on the altar of love and scorched the hearts
of the tormented couple.

"Vladimir," the countess whispered rapturously,
her breast heaving, her cheeks turning red, her eyes
blazing.

A new, a terrible union was accomplished!

* * *

Half an hour later the old count walked into his
wife's boudoir.

"What do you say, my sweet, shall I order them
to light up a samovar for our dear guest?" he said,
patting her on the cheek.

Well, what do you think of it, Vărinka? It is a bit out-
spoken, I'll grant you, but isn't it good? And now, let me
give you a little excerpt from his novella *Yermak and Zuleika*.
Imagine, dear, that the Cossack Yermak, the fierce, ruthless
conqueror of Siberia, is in love with Zuleika, the daughter of
Kuchum, the Tsar of Siberia. She is his prisoner. This is an
episode straight from the times of Ivan the Terrible. Here
is a dialogue between Yermak and Zuleika.

"You love me, Zuleika! Oh, say it again!"

"I love you, Yermak," Zuleika whispered.

"May Heaven and earth be praised! I am a happy
man! You have granted every wish I have harbored
in my tormented soul since boyhood. So this is
where you've led me, my guiding star. So this is why
you led me here, beyond the Stony Belt! I will show
my Zuleika to the whole world and men, mad monsters though they are, will not dare to blame me!
Ah, if they could only understand the secret torment
of a tender heart, if they could only recognize that
there is a whole poem contained in my Zuleika's
every tear. Oh, my unearthly one, allow me to dry

that tear with my kisses, let me drink up that heavenly tear, oh you, my unearthly one!"

"Yermak," Zuleika said, "the world is wicked and people are unjust! They will persecute us, they will condemn us, my beloved Yermak! What will happen to the poor maiden raised under her father's tent among her native Siberian snows, in your cold, icy, soulless world? People won't understand me, my dearest beloved!"

"Then my Cossack saber will rise and whistle over their heads!" Yermak cried, a wild flame appearing in his eye.

And now, Varinka, can you imagine what a state Yermak will be in when he finds his Zuleika murdered? Kuchum, the blind old man, takes advantage of a dark night and slips into Yermak's tent while the Cossack is away and cuts his daughter's throat, trying, in that way, to strike a mortal blow at Yermak, who has deprived him of his scepter and his crown.

"The rasp of iron against stone is sweet to my ear!" Yermak shouted in a wild frenzy, whetting his knife of Damascus steel on a magic stone. "I must have their blood! I'll hack them, I'll hack them to little, little pieces!!"

After that, unable to go on living without his Zuleika, Yermak throws himself into the Irtysh. And that is how the story ends.

And what about this now—just a brief excerpt. It is a humorous piece, actually written to provoke laughter.

Have you ever met Ivan Prokofievich Yellowbelly? You know, the fellow who bit Prokofy Ivanovich's leg? Ivan Prokofievich is a hot-tempered man, but also a man of rare virtue. Now, Prokofy Ivanovich is just the very opposite—he loves radishes with honey on toast. Of course, in the days when he was still seeing Pelageya Antonovna . . . You know her, don't you? She's the one who always wears her skirt inside out.

Ah, Varinka, it's so terribly funny! We were literally rolling around with laughter when he read it to us. Ah, what a man, God bless him! But, you see, my sweet, although this piece gets a bit involved and is perhaps too playful at times, it is quite innocent and you won't find any seeds of free-thinking or liberalism in it. I must insist here that Ratazayev is a perfectly well-behaved man, and that is why he is such an excellent writer—not in the least like so many other writers.

But really, one does get ideas sometimes and I wonder what would happen if I sat down and just wrote something? Yes, what would it be like? Just suppose for one minute that a book has been published. You pick it up and it says: *Poems* by Makar Devushkin! So what would you say then, my little angel? How would you feel then and what would you think? For myself, I can tell you one thing for sure, my dear: if that book were published, I'd never dare show myself on the Nevsky Prospect again. For how would it feel if every-one started saying "Here comes that Devushkin, the author and poet! Look, that's Devushkin in person!" What, for in-stance, would I do about my shoes then? Because, as you know perhaps, my shoes have been patched many times and, to tell the truth, the soles tend to break away sometimes, which is a very unseemly sight. So what would happen if everyone realized that Devushkin, the author, had patched shoes? Suppose some duchess or countess noticed that, what would the dear lady say of me? Perhaps, though, she wouldn't notice it, because I don't suppose that countesses are all that interested in shoes, particularly minor officials' shoes (be-cause, as they say, there are shoes and shoes). But I'm sure my own friends would give me away and tell her. I'm sure Ratazayev would be the first to give me away, because he often visits Countess B. He tells me he just drops in on her when he feels like it. He says she's a bright thing, very keen on literature, such a lady, he tells me. Ah, what a rogue that Ratazayev is!

Well, I suppose I've said enough on this subject, for I've been writing all this just to cheer you up a bit, my little angel.

Good-by now, my darling. I have allowed myself to scribble such a long letter because I feel in the happiest frame of mind. We all had dinner together at Ratazayev's today, and they (the bunch of rascals) produced a wonderful bottle of cordial. But I'd rather not go into that.

Only be sure not to imagine things about me, Varinka.

I don't mean it seriously, you know. And you can count on me for the books. I'll send you some without fail. Of course, there's a novel by Paul de Kock circulating here, but you can't have Paul de Kock, that's not for you! They say of him, my sweet, that he is causing righteous indignation among the Petersburg critics now. I am sending you a pound of candy. I bought it especially for you. Eat them, dearie, and think of me every time you put one in your mouth. But don't chew, just suck them, for otherwise you might get a toothache. Tell me, do you like candied fruit? Write whether you do or not. Well good-by, my dear, and God bless you.

I remain

> Your ever faithful friend,
> MAKAR DEVUSHKIN

June 27

Dear Makar Alexeyevich,

Fedora tells me that if I want, some people are very anxious to help me and to get me a very good position as a governess. What do you think? Should I take the job or not? Of course, it would take a load off your shoulders, and the job itself seems to be quite well paid. But then, I am a bit afraid of going to live with a strange family. They are land-owners of some sort, and they may start asking questions about me and get curious, and what will I tell them then? And on top of that, I'm so unsociable. I see very few people, and it always takes me a long time to get used to a new situation. I feel so much better in a place I'm used to, even if I spend half my life grieving about things—it's still better. Besides it means leaving Petersburg and Heaven knows what my duties there will consist of—possibly they just want me as a nanny for very small children. And they seem to be rather strange people too; they've had three governesses in less than two years. So, what do you think, Makar Alexeyevich? Shall I accept or not?

But why don't you ever come in to see me? You hardly ever show your face. And why can't we meet except at Sunday mass? You are just as unsociable as I am! Are you forgetting that we are related in a way? But since you love me, you must know that there are times when I feel very lonely by myself. There are times, especially when it gets dark, when I sit brooding all alone. Fedora goes out somewhere, and I sit and think of the past, both the happy past and the sad. It flashes before my eyes, appearing out of a fog. I see familiar faces (I see them almost as if they were real), and most of all, I see my mother.

And what dreams I have! I feel my health is very poor, that I am terribly weak. This morning, for instance, when I got out of bed, I became giddy. I have such a bad cough too. I feel I'll die soon. Who will accompany my coffin to the cemetery, I wonder? Who'll ever miss me? And now, I may have to die in an unfamiliar corner of a strange house. Ah, life is so sad, Makar Alexeyevich!

Why do you have to feed me candy all the time, my friend? Where do you get the money to buy it? Please, my dear, be careful with your money, please.

Fedora is selling a rug I embroidered. They're offering me fifty paper rubles for it. That's better than I expected. I'll give Fedora three rubles and will make myself a plain, warm dress. And for you, I'll make a waistcoat out of some nice material I'll choose myself.

Fedora got me *The Belkin Stories.* I'm sending you the book in case you want to read it. But please, don't mess it up and don't keep it too long, for it doesn't belong to me. It is by Pushkin.

Two years ago I read these stories with my mother and I felt so sad reading them now. If you have any books at all, send them over to me. That is, just as long as you don't get them from Ratazayev, for he might send something of his own if he's had it published. How can you like his things, Makar Alexeyevich? They sound like such nonsense.

Well, good-by, I have chattered too long as it is! Whenever I feel sad, I am very glad to have an opportunity to chatter about anything. It is like a medicine and makes me feel better right away, especially if I get everything off my chest. Well, farewell, my dear.

Yours,

V. D.

June 28

Dear Varinka,

Stop being so sad! You ought to be ashamed of yourself! How can such thoughts even occur to you? You are not ill, my dear, not in the least ill. In fact, you're blooming.

And what is this about dreams and visions? Shame, my sweet, shame on you. Just forget those dreams once and for all. Yes, just forget them. Why do I sleep well? Why is there nothing wrong with me? Just look at me, my dear—I live quietly, sleep well, and look the picture of health. Come, stop it, dear, don't make me ashamed of you. Be good. I know your little head so well, my pet. As soon as you find something to worry about, you never stop thinking about it. Please, dear, stop it, stop it for my sake.

And what is this about going to work for those people? Never! It's no, no, no! The idea! And it's out of town too. No, my love, I certainly won't let you. I will use every means in my power to stop you from going there. I'd rather sell my old frockcoat, and walk around in the street in my shirt sleeves than see you wanting anything. No, Varinka, believe me, I know you well and it is sheer madness.

And I say it's all Fedora's fault. She's a stupid old woman if she gives you such ideas. Don't listen to her, my dear. You don't know the first thing about that stupid, quarrelsome, absurd woman, who pushed her poor husband into his grave. Or has she angered you in some way or other? No, dear, I won't let you go, whatever you say. Have you thought what would happen to me if you left? What would I do? No, Varinka, just get it out of your little head. What do you lack in your life here with us? We can never have enough of looking at you. We love you, so why can't you just stay quietly with us, just taking in some sewing, reading books— or even without sewing. What's the difference? Just stay here with us. Just imagine yourself what we'd feel if you left us.

Stay here. I'll get you books to read, and one of these days we'll go for another outing. But use your head, my girl, and don't let it get filled with all sorts of nonsense. I'll come and see you very soon, and all I ask of you in exchange is to let me be frank: it's not nice of you, my sweet, not nice at all! Of course, I am an uneducated man and I know I'm uneducated, because I only had a copper's worth of schooling. But that's not what I was trying to say. What I mean is that, whatever you may say, I'll stick by Ratazayev. He does write very, very well. I repeat—very well. I find it quite impossible to agree with what you say about him. He writes colorfully, sharply, with imagery, and he has all sorts of ideas—it is very good! Perhaps you weren't in the right mood when you read it, Varinka. Perhaps you were angry with Fedora, or something unpleasant had happened and you weren't in the right state of mind to feel how good it is. Try reading it when you are in the right frame of mind, when you're pleased and gay, when you're enjoying a pleasant sensation, such as, for instance, when you're sucking a candy. Yes, try then. I won't argue that there may exist writers who are perhaps better than Ratazayev (who could dispute that?); I say they are good, but Ratazayev is good too. They write well, and so does he. He has his own special way of writing, and it's very fortunate that he writes.

Well, good-by, my dear girl, I won't go on with this letter for I must hurry—I have some work to do. So mind, my sweet, take care and God will be with you, as I remain,

Your loyal friend,

MAKAR DEVUSHKIN

P.S. Thank you for the book, my dear; well, I suppose I'll read Pushkin too. And this evening, I will come and see you without fail.

[No date]

Dear Makar Alexeyevich,

No, my dear friend, no. I ought not to go on living among you like this. I've thought it over, and I find that I was wrong to turn down a good job. There, at least, I'd be sure of where my next meal was coming from; I could try hard there and earn the affection of those strangers. I could perhaps even overcome my weakness if I had to. It is, of course, painful and difficult to live among utter strangers, to pretend, to force oneself. But with God's help, I hope to manage. I cannot remain a recluse for the rest of my life. I've had that kind of experience before. I remember, when I was a small girl and went to boarding school. On Sundays, I used to leap around and play at home so much that my mother even scolded me now and again, but what did that matter? I felt so happy, and everything seemed so bright to me. And then evening drew near, and a deadly sadness would start creeping over me, for I had to be back at school by nine, and there everything was strange, alien, and cold, and the teachers were in a particularly nasty mood on Monday mornings. I felt a terrible weight on my heart, and couldn't restrain my tears. So I'd hide myself in a corner and quietly cry there all alone, hiding my tears. They'd accuse me of being lazy, but it wasn't because I didn't want to study at school that I was crying . . .

Well, I got used to it in time and when I left the boarding school, I cried again, that time because I was leaving the other girls. Besides, it isn't fair for me to be a burden upon you both. That thought causes me great torment. I am being frank with you because I'm used to telling you exactly what I feel. Don't I see Fedora getting up before daybreak every morning to launder and working until night? And I'm certain that her old bones clamor for rest. Don't I realize that you grudge yourself every kopeck in order to spend it on me, and that I'm ruining you? You can't go on like this, not with the little you have, my dear friend! You wrote that you'd sell your last clothes to keep me from want. I believe you, my dear, I have faith in your kind heart, but you say all those things now, now that you have come into some unexpected money, that bonus! But what will happen afterward? You know I am ill and can't work as regularly as I'd like. Besides, I can't always find enough work when my health permits. So what is there left for me to do? Shall I become heartbroken from the pain of watching the two of you having such a hard time? How could I be of the least help to you? And why do you need me so? What good have I ever done you? I'm devoted to you with all my heart. I love you very, very much, but, because of a cruel fate, loving is all I am capable of, for there is nothing I can do to repay you for your kindness. So don't try to stop me. Think it over again, and let me know what your final opinion is. In the meantime, I remain

> Your loving,
> V. D.

> July 1

Nonsense, Varinka, sheer nonsense! The things you think up whenever I take my eye off you for one second! You think this isn't right and that's not right, but I can see that it's all so much nonsense. Just tell me, what's wrong with things as they are now? What are you lacking? We love you, you love us. We are satisfied and happy—what more do you want? And how do you imagine you'd feel with strangers? You'd better ask me and I'll tell you what it's like to be with strangers. I know how it feels to eat strangers' bread. I've experienced it, my sweet. A stranger is wicked, so wicked that you'd lose heart; he'd load you down with reproaches, with nagging, with nasty looks. But here with us you're snug and happy, for it is your own nest. Besides, we'd go off our heads if you walked out on us. What would we do without you? What would I, an old man, do, when you were gone? Do you think we don't need you, that you're of no use to us? Just think for a moment, my sweet. How can you say you're of no use? You're of tremendous use. You have such a beneficent effect on me. Just now, for instance, I'm thinking of you, and it cheers me up. And from time to time, I write you a letter, pour out all my feelings in it, and then get an answer from you. I've bought you some clothes and a hat, and if you give me an errand to do for you, I always do it.

No, really, how can you say I don't need you? And anyway, what will I do with myself in my old age if you leave me? What use will I be to anyone? Probably you haven't thought of that, Varinka, and I insist that you give it a thought. I've got so used to you, my dear. And if you leave, what will there be left for me to do? I suppose I'll just throw myself into the Neva and that'll be that. Yes, Varinka, there'll be nothing left for me to do. Ah, my darling, it seems you are anxious for my body to be carted off to Volkovo Cemetery with no one except an old beggar woman to accompany it; you must be in a hurry to have them throw earth on my coffin there and leave me all alone in my grave. It's a sin, my dear, it's a sin on your part.

I am sending back the book you lent me, Varinka, and if you ask me my opinion, I'll tell you that in all my life I've never read anything so good. It makes me wonder, my love, how I could have lived all this time and remained such a fool. What was I doing? What backwoods have I come from? Why, I don't know a thing, my love, not a single thing! I'll tell you straight out, Varinka, I'm an ignorant man and so far I haven't read much. In fact, I've read very little, indeed practically nothing. I've read *The Picture of Man*—a clever book. I've read *The Boy Playing Tunes on Jinglebells*, and I've read *The Cranes of Ibicus*. And that's it. Besides those books, I've never read anything at all. And now I've read "The Stationmaster" in that Pushkin collection of yours and, let me tell you, my dear, it's so strange; one lives without suspecting that he can just stretch out a hand and pick up a book in which his whole life is explained point by point, as if reckoned upon his fingers. And there are things that you yourself couldn't even guess at, which when you get to read them in this book gradually come to you. You remember them, and end up understanding all about them. And finally, I'll tell you why I loved that book of yours so much: there are books which you can read and read and, whatever their worth, you may burst before you understand what they're trying to say, they're written so cleverly. I, for instance, am dull, I'm dull by nature, and so I cannot read very important things, but I read that Pushkin book feeling as if I'd written it myself, as if, speaking figuratively, I'd just taken my own heart, turned it inside out, and showed it to the people for whatever it was worth, describing everything about it in great detail—that's how it feels. And it seems so simple, it looks like there's nothing to it. I get the impression I could've written it myself. And why shouldn't I write in the same way? Why, I feel the same way as that poor Samson Vyrin in that story, and anyway, how many such poor Vyrins we all come across every day! And how cleverly it is all described! I almost shed a tear, my sweet, when I read how that poor fellow took to drink, how he lost his memory and spent days sleeping under his sheepskin coat, drowning his misery in liquor, weeping and wiping his eyes with the dirty skirts of his coat when thinking of the lost lamb, his daughter Dunyasha. Ah, that's something *natural!* Just read it. It sounds *natural* all right! It lives! I've seen it all myself—it exists all around me. Well, no need to go far afield. Take Teresa, for instance, or that poor little clerk—well, perhaps he's just another Vyrin under another name—Gorshkov in this case. Why, it's a thing that happens in life, and it can happen to you and to me and to anyone. And that count who lives on the Nevsky Prospect or on the Embankment—it can happen to him too, although it will look different because they have class and do everything in style. But he'd feel just the same as me if it happened to him.

That is how it is, my sweet, and then you come and tell me you intend to leave us! You really ought to be ashamed of yourself, my love. That could spell the end for both of us. Ah, my darling, get all those wild ideas out of your head and stop torturing me for nothing. How could you, my weak, fragile featherless chickadee, think of feeding yourself, surviving, and protecting yourself from wicked people? Forget it, Varinka! Be good. Pay no attention to gossip and stupid advice. And reread that book of yours, reread it attentively. It will do you a lot of good.

I mentioned "The Stationmaster" to Ratazayev. He told me that it was old-fashioned and that nowadays books with pictures and descriptions are the fashion. I didn't quite get what he was trying to say, but he concluded by saying that Pushkin is good, that he is the glory of holy Russia, and he said many other things about him. Yes, Varinka, it is very good, very, very good, and you ought to read it again attentively. Follow my advice and gladden an old man's heart by listening to me, and God Himself will reward you. I'm sure He will.

Your faithful friend,
MAKAR DEVUSHKIN

[No date]

Dear Makar Alexeyevich,

Fedora brought me fifteen rubles in silver today, and she was so terribly pleased, the poor thing, when I gave her three of them. I am writing this in a hurry. I'm cutting out your waistcoat now—you should see the beautiful material: yellow with flowers on it. I'm sending you a book. It contains several stories by Gogol, some of which I've read. Read the one called "The Overcoat."

You plead with me to come to the theater with you. But won't it be too expensive? Unless you could get seats somewhere in the balcony? I can't even remember when I was last in a theater—it was ages ago. But again, are you sure it won't cost too much? Fedora just shook her head when I mentioned it to her. She says you're living beyond your means now, and when I realize how much you've spent on me alone lately, I think she's right. Watch out, my dear, that may land you in serious trouble. Fedora told me that she'd heard you'd had words with your landlady because you were late with your rent. I'm very worried about you. Well, good-by for now, I am in a hurry. I have a small order—changing the ribbons on a lady's hat.

P.S. If we go to the theater, I'll wear my new hat and my black mantle. Will that be all right?

July 7

My dear Varvara Alexeyevna,

I keep thinking of yesterday. Yes, my dear, anyone, including myself, can be the victim of an aberration. Once, I fell for a little actress. I fell for her head over heels. But that'd be nothing in itself. The strangest thing about it was that I'd hardly seen her. In fact, I'd only been to the theater once, but I did fall for her. At that time I roomed next to five fun-loving young fellows. I couldn't help becoming acquainted with them, although I always tried to keep my distance. Just not to seem too different, however, I agreed with everything they said. It was they who told me things about that actress. Every evening when there was a performance, all five of them went to the theater, to the balcony—although they didn't have a kopeck for the most necessary things—and there they clapped and shouted and kept calling out that actress's name, going literally mad. And after that, they'd let no one sleep all night, talking until the morning about her, each of them referring to her as *his* Glasha, all of them in love with her, each one carrying that same canary in his heart. They got my imagination worked up in the end—I was very young and helpless at the time—and I don't know how it happened, but the next thing I knew, I was in the theater with them, high up in the fourth gallery. I could only see an edge of the curtain from there, but I could hear everything. That little actress really had a pretty voice, a nightingale's voice, clear and sweet. We almost broke our hands clapping, and we hollered so crazily that it got us into trouble. One of us was actually thrown out. Well, when I got home, I felt as if I were drunk. I had one ruble left in my pocket, and the next payday was still ten days off. So what do you think I did, dear? Well, on my way to the office, I spent the remainder of my money on French perfume and some scented soap. And I don't know to this day why I bought it all. Then, instead of going home for dinner, I spent the time walking up and down under her windows. She lived in a house on the Nevsky Prospect, on the fourth floor. I went home, rested for an hour or so, then went back to the Nevsky Prospect, just for the sake of passing under her windows. For a month and a half I went on like that, trailing along behind her, hiring cabs and even private carriages to drive me past her windows. I got quite entangled in debt, but later I got over it and stopped loving her—I got bored with the whole thing. So that's what a little actress can do to a decent man, my dear! But then, I was still a boy at the time, a very young boy in fact.

M. D.

July 8

Dear Varvara Alexeyevna,

I am returning promptly the book you lent me on the sixth of this month, and I would also like to clear up certain matters with you in this letter.

It wasn't nice of you, my dear, to make this explanation necessary. Let me point out to you, my dear girl, that man's fate, whatever it may be, has been ordained by the Almighty. One may be fated to wear a general's epaulettes, while another may be ordained to be a petty government employee; one has been ordained to command, while the other must obey without question, in fear and humility. This is in accordance with men's capacities—some are fit for one thing, others for another—and this is ordained by God.

I have been almost thirty years in the government service now. I have an irreproachable record, am well behaved, have never been involved in any trouble. As a citizen, I recognize that I may have certain faults, but I have my virtues too. I am well considered by my superiors and even His Excellency is quite satisfied with me. He hasn't shown any signs of his satisfaction with me yet; nevertheless I know he is pleased. My handwriting is quite neat and attractive. Not too big or too small. It has a tendency to slant, but it is adequate whichever way you look at it, for in all our department, no one, with the possible exception of Ivan Prokofievich, has such a good hand. And so I have reached an age where my hair has grown gray, and I still have no major sin on my conscience, none that I know of at least. Of course, we are all guilty of little sins, every one of us, my dear, but I can say that I have never been accused of any serious offense or insubordination, of having violated the rules or disturbed the peace. In fact, I almost got a decoration at one point, but why mention that now?

Well, you ought to have known all that, my dear, and so should he, since he has taken it upon himself to write about it. No, my dear Varinka, I never expected anything like this from you! No, certainly not from you.

What does it mean? That nobody can live quietly in his corner—whatever it may be like—live without stirring up mud, as the saying goes, without harming anyone, fearing God? And you only wish that you yourself might be left alone too, that no one should sneak into your hole to find out what sort of life you lead at home, whether you have a new waistcoat or own decent underwear, whether your boots are in a good state and whether they are lined, what you eat and drink, and what sort of things you copy during your free hours. And what's wrong with that, my dear? Why, even I sometimes walk carefully in the street, tiptoeing in places where the pavement is rough, so as not to wear out my soles. And why should anyone write of another person that he's so short of money that at times he goes without tea? As though everyone had to always drink tea! I for one have never looked into a man's mouth to see what sort of food he was chewing. I have never offended anyone that way. No, my dear, I don't see why one should offend people when they are not doing any harm!

Let me give you an example, my dear, and you'll see how it feels. Suppose you work with zeal and devotion and your superiors respect you (that, they do, whatever else they feel); and then, suddenly, someone without any provocation concocts a nasty lampoon like that, right under your very nose. Well, it is quite true that, when you get yourself a new piece of clothing, you get very excited and can't sleep at night. Your heart beats when you put it on—that's true, because I've experienced such joy on seeing my foot in a fine, elegant leather boot—that's accurately described in that story! Nevertheless, I am very surprised that Fedor Fedorovich should have allowed such a book to pass, ignoring it, and not speaking up in his own defense. Of course, he's still very young for a high official, and he loves to raise his voice at people now and then, but why shouldn't he raise it? Why shouldn't he take one of us to task when he feels he has to? Even assuming he bawls out a clerk just to impress his importance upon everyone—well, why shouldn't he? It is a way of impressing us and establishing his standing, because—and let this remain between us, Varinka—the likes of us wouldn't do a thing if they weren't intimidated. All they want is to be on a pay roll somewhere, and then to dodge work as best they can. And, since differences in position do exist and since men in different positions require different ways of being told off, it is natural that the tone differs according to the different rank. That is quite in order. Why, that is the principle upon which all society is built, dear. We all show off in front of one another, and each of us tells off the next man below us. Without that, society would collapse and we wouldn't have any order. And so, I really don't see how Fedor Fedorovich could have ignored this offensive piece!

And what need was there to write a story like that? Who needs it? As though there were any chance a reader might get the idea of offering me an overcoat! No fear of that, Varinka. He'll just read the story and ask for more. And we, we hide ourselves; if we're lacking something we try to conceal it; we're afraid sometimes to show our noses to the world because we fear everything, because they'll laugh at us under every pretext. And now we find that our whole life—as government servants and as private citizens—has been dragged into literature and that everything has been printed, published, read, mocked, and gossiped about! So now we won't be able to go out into the street! They'll be able to tell us just by the way we walk. It'd be all right if he had ended on some redeeming note. After the passage where they shower those bits of paper on his head, for instance, he could have said something about the fellow's being a virtuous man despite everything, a good citizen who didn't merit such treatment at the hands of his colleagues; that he obeyed his superiors (here the author could have given a case in point as an illustration), that he didn't wish any harm to anyone, that he believed in God and that when he died (if the author absolutely wants him to die), he was bemoaned and regretted. But it would have been much better if he hadn't made the poor man die. Instead he could have arranged that the overcoat be found, and Fedor Fedorovich—I mean, the important character in the story—having learned more about the fellow's virtues, could have transferred him to his own office, given him a raise and a promotion. Then we would have seen wickedness punished and virtue triumphant, while the fellow's office colleagues would have been left with nothing to show for themselves. That's how I'd have written it, but as it stands now, what's so great about it? It's just an uninteresting, trivial case from a despicable daily life. I even wonder what made you send me the book, my dear? Why, it's slanderous, Varinka, because it is quite unlikely that such an office clerk could exist. No, Varinka, I have to protest. I will lodge an official complaint.

Your humble servant,
MAKAR DEVUSHKIN

July 27

Dear Makar Alexeyevich,

The latest developments and your last few letters have nonplussed and frightened me, and what Fedora tells me seems to explain it. But why did you have to let yourself go to such lengths of despair and sink as low as you have sunk? Your explanations do not satisfy me the least bit. Now you tell me yourself, was I not right in wanting to take that relatively well paid job as a governess? Besides, this latest thing that happened to me has frightened me. You say that if you have been hiding certain things from me, it is because of your love for me. I realized from the start how much you were doing for me, although you kept insisting at the time that you were only spending the savings you had tucked away in the bank on me. But now, I have found out that you never had any savings. When you found out about my desperate situation, you were moved by it, and you scraped up the money by getting an advance on your salary, and you even sold some of your clothes when I fell ill. So I find myself in a very painful position, and to this day I'm not sure how I should take it all and what I should think. Ah, Makar Alexeyevich, you ought to have contented yourself with that first assistance to which you were guided by your feeling of kinship and by your sympathy for me in my misery. You should never have gone on and squandered your money on things that weren't necessary. You have betrayed our friendship, Makar Alexeyevich, for you haven't been frank with me, and I see now that your last money went on buying me candy, on taking me to the theater, on our outings, and on books—I'm paying a high price for it now in feeling guilty over my lack of responsibility (for I accepted it all without worrying about you). And so everything by which you tried to give me pleasure has now been turned to grief and has left behind it nothing but regret.

Lately, I'd noticed how dejected you were, but, although I myself was expecting something with anxiety, it never

really occurred to me that anything of this sort could happen.
How could you lose courage to such a degree, Makar Alexeyevich? What will all those who know you think and say
about you now? You, whom I myself, as well as everyone
else, have always held in the highest esteem for your kindness,
your modesty, and your good sense. How could you suddenly slip into such a degrading vice, a vice in which, I believe, you never indulged until now? Can you imagine how I
felt when Fedora told me that you were found drunk in the
street and brought home with a police escort? I was dumbfounded, although I was sure something must have happened
since no one had seen you for four days. And have you
thought what your superiors will say when they find out the
true cause of your absence? You say that everyone laughs at
you, that they've all found out about our relations, and that
your neighbors mention my name when they sneer at you and
make nasty remarks. Please, Makar Alexeyevich, pay no attention to that and calm yourself, for Heaven's sake. I am
also worried about that story with the officers. I've only
heard a vague version of it, so please tell me what it's all
about. You say in your letter that you were afraid to tell me
everything because you didn't want to lose my friendship,
that you were desperate, not knowing how to help me when
I was ill, that you sold everything so that I could stay home
instead of being taken to the hospital, that you borrowed
as much as you could borrow, and that every day now you
have words with your landlady about your rent. But in hiding all that from me, you only made things worse. In spite of
your efforts, I have still found out what's been going on.
You didn't want me to realize that I was the cause of your
desperate situation, because you wanted to spare me, but now
you have caused me twice as much grief by your behavior.
All this has surprised me no end, Makar Alexeyevich. Ah, my
dear friend, misery is very contagious. The wretched and
the poor should keep away from each other so as not to become even further contaminated. I've brought miseries upon
you such as you never experienced before in your quiet, se-
cluded life. That grieves me tremendously all the time.

Now, please write to me frankly about everything—
what happened to you and how you came to behave as you
did. Please, reassure me, if that's at all possible. It isn't selfishness that makes me ask you to reassure me, it is my love and
affection for you, which will never be eradicated from my

heart whatever happens. Good-by. I'm waiting impatiently for word from you. You had a very poor idea of me, Makar Alexeyevich.

Your loving,
VARVARA DOBROSELOV

July 28

My precious Varvara Alexeyevna,

Now that it's all over and things are returning to normal little by little, let me tell you something. When you tell me you're worried about what people may think of me, I hasten to tell you, Varvara Alexeyevna, that the most important thing for me is my career. Now, since this is so, in informing you of all my troubles and my disorderly behavior, I wish to make it clear that, thus far, none of my superiors has heard anything and that they won't hear anything in the future, so that I will continue to enjoy their respect. The only thing I'm afraid of is gossip. At home, the landlady can't do more than shout, and now that I've paid her the ten rubles you gave me on account for my rent, she just grumbles. As to my other creditors, they're all right, except that I shouldn't have borrowed any money from them. And in conclusion, let me tell you, my dear, that the main thing for me is your esteem. That I haven't lost it is a great comfort to me now, when I'm going through these temporary troubles. I'm grateful to our Lord that the first blow and the first shock are over, and that you have taken it so well and do not consider me a faithless friend and a selfish man for having kept you near me, for having not had the strength to bear being parted from you, since I love you, my little guardian angel. I've returned to my office, am working assiduously, and performing my duties eminently well. Estafy Ivanovich didn't even say a word when I passed him yesterday. I won't hide from you, my dear, that I am quite harassed by my debts and by the lamentable state of my wardrobe, but, again, it's nothing, and I beseech you to understand that you are in no way whatever responsible for it. Send me another half-ruble, Varinka. That half-ruble will pierce my heart. That's the way it is nowadays, Varinka. It is no longer me, the old fool, who's helping his little angel, it is you, my poor little orphan girl, who's helping me instead! Fedora did very well to get that money. For the time being, there are no real prospects of getting any money. But if any turns up, I'll let you know at once. But what worries me most of all is the gossip. Good-by, my little angel. I kiss your little hand, and I implore you to get better. I'm not writing to you at greater length now because I want to make up for my negligence by even greater zeal than I've displayed before. So I will have to postpone any further account of what happened and my incident with the officers until the evening.

With my profound respect
and all my love,
MAKAR DEVUSHKIN

July 28

My darling Varinka,

Ah, Varinka, Varinka! This time the fault is yours, and it will weigh on your conscience. Your last letter quite bewildered me, and I felt completely at a loss. But after thoroughly searching my heart, I saw that I was unquestionably right. I'm not referring now to my disorderly behavior (ah, the devil take that!) but to the fact that I love you and that it's not at all reasonable for me to love you. You don't know a thing, my dear, but if you knew why it is so, why I must love you, you'd feel very differently. You just say all those sensible things, but I'm sure that deep down you feel quite differently.

Now, my dear, about that incident with the officers. I don't remember too well what happened myself. I must tell you, my little angel, that up till then, I'd been having a very difficult time. Imagine—for a whole month I had been dangling on a slender thread. My situation was quite disastrous. I stayed out of your sight and, at home, my landlady kicked up a terrible fuss whenever she saw me. I wouldn't have cared about that nasty woman's shouting except that, in the first place, it was embarrassing and, in the second, she had somehow found out about our relationship and started screaming things about it all over the house. That made me just freeze with horror and stop my ears. But the trouble is that the others didn't stop their ears; on the contrary, they pricked them up, so that I don't dare to look at them now.

And so, my angel, it was the accumulation of all these troubles that distressed me in the end. And then I heard all sorts of strange things from Fedora: An unworthy adventurer, it seems, called upon you and made you an insulting proposition. He insulted you, insulted you deeply—that I can judge by the way I feel about it myself. It was at this point that I lost my head completely. I rushed out of the house like a madman, wanting to go straight to that unworthy man. I didn't know what I was going to do, but I couldn't bear anyone's offending you. I felt so miserable! And the weather was horrible that day—rain and sleet, a really bleak, foul day! I was on the point of going back . . .

It was then that my downfall came, Varinka. I met Emelyan. He used to be a clerk in our department until he was fired, and I really don't know what he does for a living now—he just hangs around there. And so I went with him . . .

Well then—but I don't suppose you'll enjoy reading about your friend's miseries, the story of his temptations and trials—well then, on the third night, Emelyan egged me on and I went to see him, to see that officer, I mean. I got his address from our janitor. And while we are on this subject, my dear, I'll tell you I've had my eye on that fellow for a long time. I was watching him when he was still living in our building. Now I realize that I didn't act correctly, because I was not in my normal state when they showed me in to him. To tell you the truth, Varinka, I don't even remember what happened, except that there were many officers there, unless I was seeing double—God knows which. I don't know what I said either, only that I said a lot in my indignation. Well, that's when they kicked me out, when they threw me downstairs. They didn't actually throw me downstairs, just pushed me out the door.

Now, you already know, Varinka, how I returned home and that's all there was to it. There's no doubt that I disgraced myself; my self-respect has suffered as a result, but then, no one but you knows about it, and so it's just as though it never happened. Isn't that right? What do you think, Varinka? What I do know for a fact is that last year Aksenty Osipovich assaulted Peter Petrovich in the same way, but, in his case, he did it secretly. He called him into the cloakroom—I saw it all through the keyhole—and there he settled matters in a gentlemanly manner, for no one saw it except me and I didn't count. I mean, I never repeated what I'd seen to anyone. Well, and after that incident, the two went on as though nothing special had happened. Peter Petrovich, you know, is a proud man and so, of course, he wouldn't tell anyone what had taken place, and now they say hello when they meet and even shake hands.

I'm not disputing that I've slipped very low, Varinka. I wouldn't dare contradict you; the worst of it is that I've lost my self-respect, but then, I suppose it was destined to be this way, and who can run from his fate?

So there, now you have a lengthy account of my troubles and miseries, Varinka, and I wish I hadn't read that stuff at such a time. I am not too well just now, my sweet, and I don't feel in too cheerful a mood. And so, I beg you to believe in my devotion, love, and respect, my dear Madam, my gracious Varvara Alexeyevna,

Your humble servant,
MAKAR DEVUSHKIN

July 29

Dear Makar Alexeyevich,

I read your two letters and could only exclaim! Listen, my dear, either you're still hiding things from me, only letting me know some of your troubles or . . . or, really, Makar Alexeyevich, your letters indicate that you haven't quite recovered yet. . . . Please, come to see me this very day. Yes, come over to dinner right away, for I don't know how you live there and how things stand with your landlady. You don't write anything about that, and I suspect that your silence is deliberate. So good-by, my dear, and see to it that you come over today. In general, it'd be much better if you had your dinner here every day. Fedora cooks very well. Good-by.

Yours,
V. D.

August 1

Darling Varvara Alexeyevna,

You're glad, my sweet, that God has sent you a chance to repay kindness with kindness. I believe that, Varinka, and I am sure of the goodness of your heart. I am not saying this as a reproach—but don't say again, as you did once, that I've become an irresponsible spendthrift in my old age. Well, I've been guilty of it, but that can't be helped now. If you insist I acted badly—I did, but it makes me feel so miserable to hear it from you! But don't be angry with me for saying this, because as it is, my heart is all one ache. Poor people are fussy—that's just the way it has been ordained by nature. I felt that even in the past. The poor man is exacting; he takes a special view of the world, he glances suspiciously at everyone he meets and looks worriedly about, pricks up his ears at every word he hears in case they're talking about him. Perhaps they're commenting on his ungainly appearance? Perhaps they wonder how such a man feels? Or what he looks like from this angle or that? And it is a well known fact, Varinka, that a poor man is worse than a doormat, and that he cannot expect respect from anyone, whatever those scribblers may write, and it will always be the same. And why should it always be the same? Because, according to them, the poor man feels just the opposite of what they do and can have nothing sacred, such as secret aspirations and what not. So the other day Emelyan was telling me that they took up a collection for him, and after that they subjected him to a sort of inspection. They thought they were giving him their coins for nothing, but they were actually paying because they were offered a poor man as a spectacle. Even philanthropy is practiced in such a queer way, nowadays, my dear, although they may have always practiced it this way. Either people don't know how to go about it, or they're past masters at it—one or the other. Perhaps you hadn't realized that before, but now you know! I may be ignorant about other matters, but on this subject I'm a real expert. And how is it that a poor man knows all this and thinks of it all? Why? Well simply from experience. Because he knows, for instance, that the gentleman walking into the restaurant at his side may think to himself: "I wonder what this wretched pen-pusher will have for dinner today? I suppose while I'm eating my *sauté papillotte*, he'll be having his plate of gruel without butter . . ." But what business is it of his if I eat my gruel without butter? Yes, Varinka, there exist men who think only of such things. And they go around, those obscene lampoon-writers, and spy on a fellow to see if he is putting his foot flat on a paving stone or walking carefully on tiptoe; or whether such and such a clerk from such and such a department has a hole in his boot and his sock, so that his bare toes stick out and, on top of that, is also out at the elbows. And then they write it down and have it published. Now I ask you, what business is it of theirs if I'm out at the elbows?

And if you'll excuse my putting it crudely, Varinka, I'll tell you that in this respect a poor man feels modesty, like the virgin modesty a young lady like you would feel. And just as you wouldn't undress in front of everyone, if you'll forgive me my bluntness, so a poor man doesn't like anyone to peep into his private hole in order to find out how he lives with his family or something. And so there's no need for you, Varinka, to join my enemies in insulting me and trampling on my honor and my self-respect!

And in the office today, I sat like a lump, like a plucked sparrow, and I almost burned up with shame. I felt so awkward, Varinka! And how can you help feeling awkward when your elbows show through your sleeves and your buttons are dangling on their threads. And it just so happened that, on top of all that, I was in a terrible mess and so I couldn't help feeling quite discouraged.

And what do you think—Stepan Karlovich, who had come to say something to me on business, started speaking and then glanced at me, sort of casually, and said "Ah, Makar Alexeyevich, Makar Alexeyevich! . . ." He didn't explain what he meant, but I understood and blushed so that even my bald patch turned red. It's not really important but still, it makes me think and some rather worrisome things come to my mind. Might they have found out somehow? God forbid, how could they? There's a man, though, whom I rather suspect. Those scoundrels won't stop at anything. They'll sell all your intimate secrets for a copper. Nothing's sacred to them.

Now I know who's behind it all—it's Ratazayev's doing. He knows someone in our department, and he must have told him, in the course of a conversation, everything that happened to me, with some embellishments, I suppose. Or else, he may have told it in his department, and then it spread about and reached my department. As to our apartment, everyone knows about it here and they keep pointing at your window. And when I went over to your place for dinner yesterday, they were all hanging out of the windows, and the landlady made a remark about a devil being after a babe and called you a bad name. But all that is nothing compared with Ratazayev's despicable scheme for getting us into literature and describing us in a subtle satire. He's been telling everyone that, and kind people repeated it to me. I can't think of anything else, my sweet, but I can't decide what to do about it. There's no getting away from it, my angel, we have provoked God's wrath all right!

You wanted to send me some book or other, my darling, so that I should read it and not be so bored, but I say, what's the use of books? A story is just a lie with people in it, and novels are written just for the empty amusement of idle people. Believe me in this, my dear, believe my long experience. And there's nothing to it if they try to outargue you by bringing Shakespeare into it, saying: "You see, there are people such as Shakespeare in literature . . ." Well, my answer to them is that Shakespeare too is just so much nonsense, nothing but nonsense, and just written to jeer at people.

Yours,

MAKAR DEVUSHKIN

August 2

Dear Makar Alexeyevich,

Please don't worry about anything. With God's help, everything will work out right. Fedora has got plenty of work for both of us, and we've started on it feeling very cheerful. Perhaps we shall be able to repair the damage. She suspects that all my recent troubles are somehow connected with Anna Fedorovna, but it doesn't make much difference now. Somehow, I feel especially cheerful today.

As to your borrowing money—Heaven forbid! You'll have no end of trouble when the time comes to pay it back. We'd better all live frugally. Come over more often, and pay no attention to your landlady. As for the rest of your enemies and ill-wishers, I'm sure you're worrying yourself for nothing.

And look out, didn't I tell you last time that your style is extremely uneven! Well, good-by for now and remember, I'm counting on you to come to see me.

Yours,

V. D.

August 3

My little angel, Varvara Alexeyevna,

I'm in a great hurry to let you know, my dearest, that some hope is beginning to stir within me. But just a minute, my girl, how can you write that I'm not to borrow any money? I can't avoid it. I'm in a bad way all right, but just suppose, for instance, something should happen to you? Why, you're such a delicate little thing. And so what I'm trying to tell you is that I must borrow some.

And so I continue my letter. I wish to tell you, Varvara Alexeyevna, that in the office I sit next to Emelyan Ivanovich—not the Emelyan you know. This one is of the same rank as I. The two of us are probably the oldest employees in the whole department. He is a kind, disinterested man, but clumsy as a bear. But he's a good worker, has a good English hand (if I was to tell the whole truth, I'd admit that his writing is quite as good as mine), and is in general a man worthy of respect. We have never been very close, our relations being limited to good mornings, good-bys, and perhaps, if I needed a penknife, I would ask him to lend me his. In brief, just that sort of contact. Well then, today Emelyan Ivanovich says to me: "Why are you so preoccupied today, Makar Alexeyevich?"

I saw that the fellow meant well by me, and I talked openly to him. "This is how it is, Emelyan Ivanovich." That is, of course, I didn't tell him everything. God forbid! I'll never tell, for I don't have the heart to. I just told him a little about being hard up for money and so on.

"Why," he said to me, "you can borrow some from Peter Petrovich. He lends money at interest. I borrowed some from him myself," Emelyan Ivanovich told me, "and he doesn't charge exorbitant interest. His rate is quite decent."

As you can imagine, Varinka, my heart leapt with joy. I thought and thought and I said to myself, who knows, perhaps the Lord will make Peter Petrovich lend me some money too. And in the meantime I began to reckon that I could settle with the landlady, then help you a bit, and tidy myself up some, for it is becoming terribly awkward for me to sit in the office the way I look now, with all the fellows laughing at me. And occasionally His Excellency passes by my desk too and what would happen, God forbid, if he chanced to notice how untidily I'm dressed! For neatness and tidiness are the first things His Excellency demands of us, and although I don't suppose that he himself would say anything, I'm sure I'd die of shame.

And so, I screwed up enough courage, and hiding my shame in my torn pocket, I went to see Peter Petrovich. I was both full of hope and more dead than alive—all at the same time.

And what shall I say, Varinka? It all came to nothing. He seemed to be busy and was having a talk with Fedor Ivanovich. I went up to him and tugged at his arm from the side, as if to say, "Excuse me a minute, Peter Petrovich." He looked at me and I said that I'd like to have thirty rubles or so if it were possible, etc. At first he didn't understand me, but when I explained to him, he laughed. Then he quieted down and I asked him again. "D'you have any collateral?" he asked me, and put his nose back in the file he had been working on, without even glancing at me again. I was somewhat taken aback and told him, "No, Peter Petrovich, but wouldn't it be possible to arrange it somehow nevertheless?" He remained silent, as if he hadn't heard me. I waited for a little while longer; then I decided to try for the last time, and pulled at his sleeve. He didn't say a word, just sharpened his quill and went on writing. So I walked away.

Well, my dear, they may all be very worthy people, but they are so very, very proud and won't have anything to do with the likes of me. They're so much above us, Varinka! And that's why I've written you all this.

Emelyan Ivanovich laughed too when I told him, and just shook his head. He'd given me a hope, our kind and worthy Emelyan Ivanovich, so he promised to recommend me to a man who lives on the Vyborg Side. That fellow also lends money at interest. He's also a government clerk, a fourteenth-class clerk, in fact. Emelyan Ivanovich says that the fellow is sure to lend me some cash, and I'm going to see him tomorrow. What do you say, dear? It'll be awful if I can't get the money! The landlady is just about to drive me out into the street, and she won't let me have my dinners. And my boots are in a dreadful state too, my dear, and I'm short of buttons on my coat and what, in general, don't I need! And what will happen if one of my superiors notices my unseemly appearance? It's awful, Varinka, it's simply awful!

MAKAR DEVUSHKIN

August 4

Dear Makar Alexeyevich,

Please, Makar Alexeyevich, if it is at all possible, do borrow some money and do it as quickly as you can. I would never have asked you to help me under present circumstances but you don't know what a position I find myself in now! It is impossible for us to remain in this apartment. Something awfully unpleasant has happened; you can have no idea how upset and depressed I am. Imagine, my dear friend, a stranger came to see me this morning, a middle-aged, almost an elderly man, wearing several decorations. I was very surprised, wondering what he could want from us. He started to question me on how I lived and what I did and, without waiting for me to reply, announced that he was the uncle of that officer, that he was furious with his nephew for behaving the way he had and for having disgraced us throughout the building. His nephew was just a young hooligan and a scatterbrain and he, the uncle, wanted to take me under his protection. He advised me to be careful with young men, and added that he sympathized with me like a father and that, indeed, he nurtured fatherly feelings for me and was prepared to help me in every way. I kept blushing and didn't know what to think, but I was in no special hurry to thank him. He forcibly took my hand, patted me on the cheek, told me that I was strikingly pretty and that he was delighted with my dimples (God knows what other nonsense he said!) and finally tried to kiss me, saying that it was all right since he was an old man (ah, he's such a repulsive creature!).

At that moment Fedora came in. He became a bit embarrassed and started saying again how much he respected me for my modesty, and that he would be ever so happy if I didn't shun him. Then he took Fedora aside and, under some strange pretext, tried to give her some money. She, of course, wouldn't accept. At last he decided to leave. He repeated once more all his assurances of friendship, said he'd come again and bring me a pair of earrings (I believe he was rather embarrassed himself); advised me to move to another apartment, recommending an excellent one of which he knew, where I wouldn't have to pay rent. He declared he was very fond of me because I was an honest and reasonable young lady, advised me to be wary of loose young men, and finally informed me that he knew Anna Fedorovna, who had asked him to tell me she was going to pay me a visit.

That made the whole thing quite clear. I don't know what came over me. It was the first time in my life I had found myself in that situation; I flew into a rage and told him what I thought of him. Fedora helped me and we almost threw him out of the apartment. We decided that it was all the work of Anna Fedorovna, for otherwise how could he have found out about us?

Now, I am turning to you for help, Makar Alexeyevich. Please, don't abandon me in my present position! Borrow some money, if only a very small sum, for we have nothing with which to move, and remaining here is quite out of the question. Fedora thinks so too. We need at least twenty-five rubles. I'll pay you back; I'll earn them in a few days. Fedora will get me some more work so that an exorbitant interest rate shouldn't stop you. Accept any conditions. I'll pay everything back but please, in the name of God, don't leave us without assistance now.

It costs me a lot to impose upon you when you're going through such a difficult period yourself, but you are my only hope! Good-by, Makar Alexeyevich. Think of me and may God grant you success.

V. D.

August 4

My darling Varvara Alexeyevna,

I feel quite shattered by all these unexpected blows. It is calamities such as these that break my spirit. This scum, those parasites and nasty old men, who are trying to bring you, my angel, to a bed of sickness, are trying to push me to my perdition too. And they'll succeed, the parasites, I swear they will! Why, I'd rather die than fail you now! If I didn't help you now, Varinka, it'd be the death of me, the end of me for good, and if I do help you, then you'll fly off like a bird from her nest when rapacious owls try to peck her to death. And it is this that hurts me, my darling. And you yourself, Varinka, you're so cruel too! How can you be like this? They torment you, make you suffer, and you're sorry to disturb me, and even go so far as to promise to work off the debt which, in view of your weakness, is like promising me you'll kill yourself to help me pay the interest in time. Just think what you're saying, Varinka! Why should you sew, why should you work, why should you worry your poor little head, strain your little eyes, and spoil your health? Ah, Varinka, Varinka! The thing is, my dear, I myself am useless, I know it, but I will do my best to be of some use! I'll overcome all difficulties. I'll find some extra work myself.

I'll do some copying for literary writers. I'll go to see them. Yes, I'll go myself and offer them my services, because they're always on the lookout for good copyists, I know it. But I won't allow you to exhaust yourself. I won't let you go through with that killing plan. I'll borrow the money, my love. I'd rather die than fail to get that sum. And then you tell me, my pet, not to be scared away by the interest rate—I won't be. Nothing will frighten me now. I'll try to borrow forty paper rubles, which isn't a large sum. Don't you think, Varinka, they'll trust me with forty rubles just like that? I mean, do you think I'm capable of inspiring trust and confidence in one who sees me for the first time? Is it possible to get a favorable impression of me from my face? Try to remember, my angel, whether my appearance disposes one toward trust. What do you think? You know, I'm so afraid now, it hurts. Yes, it actually hurts.

Anyway, of those forty rubles, twenty-five will go to you, two silver rubles to my landlady, and the rest for my personal expenses. Of course, I should give the landlady more; in fact she's entitled to more. But just consider, my dear, all my needs, and you'll realize that I couldn't possibly give her more. Therefore, there's no need to talk about it, or to even bring the subject up. For one silver ruble I'll buy myself a pair of boots, for I'm not even sure that I can present myself in the office wearing my old ones again. I am also in great need of a neckpiece; the one I'm wearing will soon be a year old. But since you've promised to make me not only a neckpiece but also a shirtfront out of your old apron, I don't have to worry about that. And so that takes care of boots and the tie. Now, for the buttons, my pet. You must surely appreciate, my pretty little thing, that I can't get along without buttons. Almost half of them have fallen off. The mere thought that His Excellency might notice such untidiness and say . . . Ah, my dear, I won't ever know what he says. I'll be dead from shame before. I'll die then and there, for the thought alone almost kills me.

And so, after all these absolutely indispensable things are taken care of, I'll still have three rubles left. That will be enough for living expenses and also half a pound of tobacco, for it isn't much of a life for me without tobacco. Today is the ninth day since I last had my pipe in my mouth. To tell the truth, I'd have bought some anyway, without telling you about it, but that would have made me feel sort of guilty.

But anyway, you're in trouble, you deprive yourself of bare necessities, while here I am indulging in all sorts of luxuries. And that's why I'm telling you this, because I don't want to feel too guilty. My landlady despises me, no one shows me any respect, and I'm suffering great privations at home. And in the office, where, even before this, my colleagues never treated me too well, things have become really impossible now. I conceal everything. I try to hide my troubles from everybody, and when I come into the office, I sort of steal in sideways, keeping out of their way. Ah, I have only enough strength to admit all these things to you . . .

And what if he refuses to lend me the money? No, Varinka, we'd better not even think of such a possibility, nor torture ourselves beforehand with such thoughts. I'm writing you this just because I want to warn you not to torment yourself with that horrible idea. But, my God, what would become of you then? It is true, though, that you wouldn't be able to move from your present lodgings then and would remain close to me . . . But no, I simply couldn't come back and face you then. I'd rather get lost somewhere.

Here, I have been writing all this time when I ought to have been shaving—it makes me look more presentable, which is always helpful. Well, God help me! I'll say my prayers and go on my way.

M. DEVUSHKIN

August 5

Dear Makar Alexeyevich,

You, at least, shouldn't despair! There's enough trouble without that!

I'm sending you thirty kopecks in silver. I'm afraid I couldn't manage more. Buy yourself whatever you need most urgently. I hope it'll tide you over till tomorrow. This leaves us with almost nothing ourselves, and I don't even know what we'll do tomorrow.

It's a sad state of affairs, Makar Alexeyevich, but still, I don't want you to be too depressed about it—you tried, it didn't work, and so it just can't be helped!

Anyway, Fedora thinks it's not really that terrible, that for the time being we can stay where we are, that even had we moved, it wouldn't have solved our problems, because they would have found us in the end if they wanted to. Nevertheless, it's somehow unpleasant for me to remain here after what has happened. If it weren't so sad, I'd have told you about something in this letter. You've such a strange character, Makar Alexeyevich. You take things much too tragically, and that's bound to make you so unhappy. I always read all your letters very carefully, and I realize from every one of them that you worry about me much more than you ever worry about yourself. Everyone, of course, would agree that you have a very kind heart, but I would say that it is actually too kind. Let me give you some friendly advice, Makar Alexeyevich. I'm very, very grateful to you for everything you've done for me, and I feel very strongly about it. And so you may judge for yourself how I feel when I realize that even now, after all the trouble I've caused you despite myself, you still live by my joys and sorrows! Really, how can one avoid being unhappy if one takes so close to heart the misfortunes that strike someone else? Today, when you came to see me after leaving the office, I was really frightened. You were so pale, looked so frightened, so full of despair, because you were afraid to tell me that it hadn't worked, because you were so reluctant to disappoint me, to frighten me. Then, when you saw me laugh, you seemed so infinitely relieved! Don't be so sad, Makar Alexeyevich. Be sensible, please, I beg you! You'll see that in the end things will take care of themselves and everything will end up all right. Otherwise, if you keep grieving for other people, life will be too painful for you.

Good-by then, my dear friend, and I implore you, don't worry too much about me.

V. D.

August 5

My darling, my Varinka,

All right then, my angel, all right! So you've decided that it's not yet the end of everything because I couldn't raise the money. Good. I'm reassured and feel happier about you. I'm even happy because this way you aren't leaving me behind, poor old man that I am, and are remaining in your apartment. And if I must say everything, my heart brimmed over with joy when I saw from your letter that you thought so well of me and gave credit to my feelings. I don't say this out of pride, but because I can see that you must like me, if you worry about my feelings as you do. But why talk about my feelings? They are what they are. What's the use of telling me, my darling, not to be so downhearted? I know, my angel, I agree with you that it's no good being downhearted but, tell me yourself, my dear, what shall I wear on my feet when I go to the office tomorrow? That's what's worrying me, my sweet, and let me tell you, such worry is also enough to drive a man out of his mind and to spell his end. And the main thing, my dear, is that I am not sorry or suffering for myself—I would think nothing of going out in the bitterest cold without overcoat or boots. I'm sure I'd be able to bear it, because I'm an ordinary, humble man. What worries me, though, is what people will say. What will the wicked tongues of my enemies say when they see me going without my overcoat? Why, I suppose it's for others that one wears an overcoat and even shoes. In the present instance, my dear, I need decent boots to keep up my dignity and my good name, because boots full of holes make you lose both your dignity and your reputation. Believe me—it's true, my dear. Trust the lifelong experience of an old man who knows the world and men, instead of listening to all sorts of scribblers and slanderers.

But I haven't yet told you, my dear, what happened today. I suffered more in this one morning than another man could bear in a whole year. Here's what happened: I left the house very, very early in the morning so as to find the fellow at home and to get to work in time after that. A mixture of rain and sleet was coming down, so I wrapped myself in my overcoat, my pet, and on my way I was thinking to myself, "Oh Lord, forgive me my sins and let my wish be fulfilled." Then, passing by a church, I crossed myself, repented of my sins, and remembered that it wasn't right to try to make bargains with God. And so I withdrew into myself, not looking at anything, or caring about what was going on around me. The streets were deserted, and the people I came across were all busy and in a hurry. And no wonder either, for who'd go out just for a stroll at such an hour in such weather? A gang of workers crossed my path and the rough fellows shoved me a bit as they passed. A terrible timidity came over me. I felt more and more ill at ease and, to tell the truth, I didn't even want to think of that money, but I felt I must go on and take my chances. Just as I reached Vosskresensky Bridge, the sole of my boot came unstuck; from then on I was no longer sure what I was stepping on. Then I met our office messenger, Yermolayev. He stopped, stood stiffly to attention and, as I walked by, followed me with his eyes. "My goodness," I thought, "he's hinting for a tip for a glass of vodka—a fat chance he has." I felt terribly tired, so I stopped to take a breather, and then set off again. I kept looking around for something to take my mind off my preoccupations and to cheer me up a bit, but there was nothing that would hold my thoughts. On top of everything else, I realized that I was all splattered with mud, so badly that I became ashamed of my appearance. At last I saw ahead of me a yellow, wooden house with an upper story in the style of a belvedere. It was just the way Emelyan Ivanovich had described Markov's house (that's the man, you know, who lends money at interest). Nevertheless, I asked the watchman whose house it was, and the uncouth fellow looked as if he didn't even want to talk to me and grunted sort of angrily through his teeth that, yes it was Markov's, whose else's? Ah, those watchmen are such an insensitive lot! But who cares about watchmen?

Well, it all left a very unpleasant impression indeed upon me, because one's impressions always fit one's position and mood. I walked past the house three times and the more often I walked past it the worse I felt. No, I said to myself, he won't let me have the money. I'm sure he won't! Why should he give it to me? He doesn't know me. The proposition I have to offer him is doubtful, and I certainly don't cut an imposing figure. But let fate decide, so I shouldn't later reproach myself later for not having tried; he won't eat me for trying, after all. . . . And so I quietly opened the gate. But there another bother awaited me: there was a mangy cur in the yard, which started barking madly at me. This was one of those small incidents that can throw a man off balance, my dear, intimidate him, take away his determination, and confuse the plan of action he may have carefully prepared beforehand. And so I reached the house more dead than alive, and there yet another misfortune occurred: I couldn't see at first in the darkness and stumbled straight into a woman who was straining milk right by the doorway. The jug of milk spilled; the stupid woman screamed and started berating me, "Where d'you imagine you're going, mister?" and she went on and on, swearing and all. I'm telling you all this, my dear, because such things always happen to me on cer-

tain days—I suppose it's just my fate always to stumble into
someone or to do something I have no business doing. The
noise brought the landlady, an old Finnish hag, and so I
turned hurriedly toward her and asked her whether Markov
lived there. "No," she said and stood for a while examining
me from head to foot, "and what is it you want with him?"
So I explained that Emelyan Ivanovich recommended Markov
to me, and that I must see Markov on business. The old hag
called her daughter, a big, barefoot girl. "Call your father.
He's upstairs with the lodgers." Then to me, "Come in."

I went in. The room was very fine, with pictures on the
walls of important officials and generals. There was a sofa
standing there too, a round table with mignonette and balsam
on it. And all that made me wonder whether it was best to
get out of there while the going was good. And I swear to
you, my sweet, I almost did take to my heels then and there.
I was trying to convince myself that it'd be wiser to come
back the next day—the weather would be better and I'd be
better prepared, because today I'd spilled that milk, and the
generals in the pictures were such an unfriendly lot . . . I
was already moving toward the door when he walked in.

Well, he didn't look too bad really—gray hair, ratty
eyes, a greasy dressing gown tied with a rope round the
waist. He inquired what he could do for me, and I told him
about Emelyan Ivanovich and that I needed forty rubles; but
I didn't finish for I saw by his eyes that I had failed.

"No," he said, "I have no money, anyway, but," he said,
"do you have some collateral or something?"

I started explaining to him that I didn't have any guarantee but that Emelyan Ivanovich had told me . . . well, in
brief, that I needed the money very badly.

He heard me out. "No," he said, "why bring Emelyan
Ivanovich into it—I have no money . . ."

Well, I said to myself, so that's that. I knew it all along!
I'd have rather the earth had opened up under my feet to
swallow me; a chill ran down my spine, my feet went numb,
thousands of ants were crawling all over my back. And I
stood there staring at him, and he stared back at me, as
if to say—Well, what are you waiting for now? Be off with
you! Under any other circumstances, I'd have felt terribly
embarrassed.

"And what exactly do you need the money for?"

That's what he was asking me now, my sweet. So I

opened my mouth just not to stand there as dumb as a post, but before I could utter a word, he said, "No, I have no money. Although," he added, "I'd have been delighted . . ."

Oh, you should have heard me trying to convince him— I needed so little and I'd pay him back, pay him back before the time even, and he could fix any rate of interest he wished and, before God, I'd pay up. I remembered you at that moment, my love, and all the misfortunes besetting you, and I thought of that half-ruble you'd sent me . . .

"Well, I really can't," he said in the end. "What's the use of fixing the rate of interest when you have no guarantee? For, anyway, I have no money. I swear, I have none at all. Otherwise, of course, I'd have been happy to oblige!" and he swore once more that he was telling the truth, the bandit.

Well, after that, I don't even remember how I walked out of there, or how I went down Vyborg Street and reached Vosskresensky Bridge. I was so cold I was shivering, and it was already ten when I got to the office. I wanted to brush some of the mud off my clothes but Snegirev, the porter, wouldn't let me use the brush for fear I'd mess it up, for it is government property. That's how they treat me nowadays, my dear. They look upon me almost as if I were a doormat on which they can wipe their feet.

What gets me, Varinka, is not really the lack of money but all those little troubles life is so full of, all the whispering, all those jeers and jokes. And it is possible that His Excellency may make some remark about me—ah, my dear, the golden days are over for good!

I have reread all your letters today. Made me feel very sad. Farewell, my dear girl, and may God keep you!

M. Devushkin

P.S. I intended to interweave my troubles with jokes when I described them to you, Varinka, but I feel the jokes haven't come off. I was trying, though, to do the right thing by you.

I'll come over and see you tomorrow, my sweet. I'll come without fail.

August 11

Varvara Alexeyevna, my dearest, my darling!

I'm lost! We're both lost, lost irredeemably! My reputation, my self-respect, all is lost! I'm ruined and, together with me, you're ruined too. And it was me, me alone who led you to your perdition. I'm being persecuted, my love. I'm despised by everyone. They laugh when they see me. And my landlady just stood there, shouting at me and berating me, treating me worse than dirt. And in the evening, at Ratazayev's, they read aloud a rough copy of a letter I wrote to you that had fallen out of my pocket. You should've heard, my dear, how it made them laugh! They kept calling us all sorts of things, and then they laughed and laughed, the traitors! I walked in and accused Ratazayev of being a false friend, of betraying me. He answered that it was I who was the traitor, going around and conquering ladies' hearts. "You've been hiding your game from us," he said. "You're really a Lovelace." And so now they call me Lovelace all the time, as though I'd never even had another name before.

Do you understand what this means, my dear? They all know everything there is to know about you now. But that's not all: Faldoni is in it with them too. Today, I wanted to send him to the grocery to get me something, but he wouldn't go, said he was busy. "Why, but you're supposed to go when you're sent," I said to him. "No," he says, "I ain't supposed to, since you aren't paying your rent to my mistress." I couldn't stand that uncouth, illiterate fellow talking to me like that. "You're a fool," I said. "And it's a fool who says so," he came back at me. I thought he was drunk to dare to talk to me like that, and I said to him, "You must be drunk, you stupid bumpkin!" "Why, are you paying for my drinks maybe?" he answered back. "Why, you don't have enough to get drunk on yourself and that's why you go around begging for a few coppers." And he even added: "And that calls itself a gentleman!"

That's the point things have reached, Varinka! I'm ashamed to remain alive! I feel worse than a tramp without a passport, like a real outcast! Ah, what a calamity! I'm lost, I'm simply hopelessly lost.

M. D.

August 13

My dear Makar Alexeyevich,

Troubles keep piling up on you. I no longer know what to do. What will happen to you now? And you cannot hope

for much from me either. I burned my left hand with the
iron this morning; I dropped the iron and bruised and burned
myself, all at the same time. I can't do my work, and what
makes it worse is that Fedora has been ill for the past three
days. I'm very worried. I enclose thirty kopecks in silver.
This is almost all we possess. Ah, God knows how much I
want to come to your rescue in your present difficulties. I
feel like crying in my impotence. Good-by, my dear! I would
feel much better if you came to see us today.

V. D.

August 14

What's the matter with you, Makar Alexeyevich? Aren't
you afraid of God? You'll drive me out of my mind! Aren't
you ashamed of yourself? This will ruin you completely;
just think of your good name! You are an honest, honorable,
and self-respecting man, so think what'd happen if they all
found out about you. Why, you'd simply die of shame! Have
you forgotten your gray hairs then? Have you no fear of
God? Fedora tells me that she won't help you any longer
and even I, I won't let you have any money now. Ah, Makar
Alexeyevich, what are you doing to me? Or do you imagine
that it doesn't hurt me when you behave like that? You have
no idea what I have to go through because of you! I can't
walk downstairs without people staring and pointing at me
and saying horrible things. Yes, they say aloud that I have
become involved with a drunk. You can imagine how it feels
to hear that! When they bring you home, all the lodgers
here point at you scornfully and say, "Here, they're bringing
back that government employee again," and I'm so ashamed
for you that it is quite unbearable. I swear, I'll move away
from here. I'll go and work as a maid or a laundress rather
than stay here.

I asked you to come over here in my letter, but you
didn't come. I suppose you don't care about my tears and
supplications, Makar Alexeyevich! And, may I ask, where
did you get the money? Please, in the name of God, watch
your step or this will be the end of you, and you'll have
asked for it. And what shame, what disgrace! I know your
landlady wouldn't let you into the apartment, and that you
had to spend last night on the landing—I know everything.

If only you knew how it hurt me when I learned about that! Come over to see me—we'll have a nice time. We'll read together and remember the past. Fedora will tell us about her pilgrimages. Please, my dear, don't drive us both to our ruin. Remember, you are the reason why I stay alive, and I will remain by your side. And so, behave like an honorable man, be firm in misfortune, and remember that poverty is no sin. Anyway, why despair, it's all just a temporary hardship, and with God's help things will get better. Just be patient now. I am sending you twenty kopecks. Get yourself some tobacco or whatever you want, but for Heaven's sake don't spend it on drink. And don't fail to come and see us. Perhaps you feel too ashamed to come, but I beg you not to, because it is false shame. If only you could sincerely repent of what you did! Trust in God and He will see to it that things change for the better.

V. D.

August 19

Varvara Alexeyevna, my darling!

I'm so ashamed, my love, I don't know where to put myself. But, after all, what is there so extraordinary about it, my sweet? Why shouldn't a man gladden his heart now and then? If I don't think about my boot soles, my dear, it is because a sole is just nothing and will always be nothing but a common, vulgar, ordinary sole! And boots too are nothing! The wise old men of ancient Greece managed very nicely without them, so why should we bother about such an unworthy item? And so, why must you despise me and say hurtful things about me? Ah, my dear, dear girl, haven't you anything else to write to me about? As to Fedora, tell her she is a headstrong, stubborn, and quarrelsome woman, and a very stupid one to boot! Now, since you mention my gray hairs, let me tell you, you're mistaken there too, my girl, because I am not quite as old as you think. Emelyan sends you his best. You wrote that you were grieving and crying, and so now I'll also write that I'm grieving and crying. In conclusion, I wish you the best of health and happiness. I myself am also in good health and happy, and I remain, my angel, your good friend,

MAKAR DEVUSHKIN

August 21

My dear Varvara Alexeyevna,

I feel I have acted badly toward you, although I don't see what good it does if I feel it, whatever you may say. I felt it even before I went on the binge, but nevertheless, I gave way and did it anyway, knowing all the time what I was doing and feeling guilty. Now, I am neither cruel nor wicked, my darling, and you must understand that to hurt you deliberately, I'd have to be nothing less than a bloodthirsty tiger, when I am much more like a sheep. Also, as you know very well, I have no bloodthirsty leanings whatever. Therefore, my little angel, I'm not altogether to blame, because it was not in my heart and my mind that I sinned. Well, I don't really know what part of me is to blame for it all. It's a very complicated and obscure business, my love!

You sent me thirty kopecks and then twenty more, and my heart began to ache as I looked at that money sacrificed by my little orphan girl. You've burned your hand, and you yourself may go short of food soon, but you write that I should get myself some tobacco. So what am I to do under the circumstances? Or should I start robbing you without any pangs of conscience, my poor little orphan girl? Well, that's when I lost heart, my dear. That is, I felt right away I was no good at all, and that I was hardly better than my boot sole. I felt it unseemly to pretend to myself that I was worth anything at all and started looking upon myself as something shameful, something indecent in a sense. And when I lost my self-respect, when I began to deny any qualities in myself, it was all over with me. It was my downfall, an inevitable downfall that was facing me. Well, that's how fate ordained it and I can't be held responsible for it.

So I went out to get some fresh air at first. And it was just circumstances that brought about what happened next: It was cold and drizzling and then I came across Emelyan . . . You see, Varinka, he had already pawned everything, everything had run through his hands and, when I met him, he hadn't had a thing in his mouth for two whole days. And so he was trying to pawn something that it is quite impossible to pawn, because no one in his right mind would accept a pledge of that sort. And so, Varinka, I dare say he talked me into it, and I yielded rather out of humanitarian motives than because of an irresistible temptation. And that's how I fell into sin, my dear. Ah, you should have heard us weep, Emelyan and me. You should have heard us remembering you! He is a very kind-hearted man, Varinka, a very sensitive man. I am acutely aware of it, my sweet. I feel these things so strongly, and that's one reason why I keep getting into trouble all the time. And I know very well, my dear, how much I am indebted to you. When I got to know you, I came to know myself better too; and, before I met you, my angel, I was so lonely. It was as though I had been sleeping through my life instead of living it. They, my persecutors, used to say that even my figure was indecent and that they were sick of me and so I too became sick of myself; they assured me that I was dumb and I began to believe that I was dumb indeed. But then you came along and shed light over my whole life, kindling a flame in my heart and spirit, and I gained peace of mind, and realized I was no worse than others. There was certainly nothing particularly brilliant about me, but I was a man with a heart and with some ideas even if I didn't have the grand manner and polish. But now, feeling I was a victim of fate and that fate had humiliated me, I renounced all self-respect and, under the weight of my misfortunes, lost heart. And so now you know, my sweet, and I beseech you with tears in my eyes to take no further interest in the matter, because if you persist, you'll break my heart and make things even harder and more painful for me.

I assure you of my deepest respect, my dear, and remain your faithful friend.

MAKAR DEVUSHKIN

September 3

I didn't finish my last letter, Makar Alexeyevich, because it was so painful for me to write. There are moments when I prefer to be alone, alone with my sad thoughts, to keep my grief to myself, without sharing it. Well, such moments occur more and more often. There's something in my recollections that I don't understand, something that absorbs me so completely, so unreservedly, that I remain for hours quite unaware of what's going on around me, completely forgetting the present. And there is no sensation in my present life, whether pleasant or painful or sad, that doesn't bring back to me an identical sensation in my past, mostly in my happy, golden childhood! But I always feel very depressed after such recollections; they weaken me, my dreaminess exhausts me, and impairs my already weak health even further.

But this morning is so bright and clear, a very unusual morning for the fall. It cheered me up and I greeted it with joy. And so it's fall already! Ah, how much I loved the fall when we lived in the country. I was still only a child then, but even so, I felt a great deal. I loved the autumn evenings even more than the mornings though. There was a lake at the bottom of a hill a few yards from our house. That lake—I can see it as though it were before my eyes—was broad, smooth, and clear as crystal. On calm evenings the lake was still, not a leaf stirred on the trees that grew by the water, which was motionless as a mirror. It was fresh, almost cold, the dew glistened on the grass, lights shone in the huts on the shore, the herds were being driven home. It was then that I would slip away from the house to have a look at my lake, and I would gaze and gaze at it and forget about everything. A bonfire lighted by some fishermen at the very edge of the water sheds its light far over the lake. The sky is cold and dark blue, except on the horizon where it dissolves into red, fiery stripes, stripes that get gradually paler and paler; the moon rises; the air is so resonant that one can clearly hear a frightened bird soaring upward, the reeds ringing under the breeze, or a fish splashing. Over the blue water a transparent steam rises. Darkness begins to descend in the distance, and everything is drowning in mist over there, while nearby objects are sharply outlined, as though cut out by a chisel: a boat, the outline of the shore, the islands, some discarded or forgotten barrel floating almost motionless just off the bank, a willow branch covered with yellow leaves entangled among the reeds, a gull taking off, then diving down to the cold water, then soaring up again and dissolving in the mist. . . . I kept looking and listening and I was so marvelously happy! I was still a little girl then, just a child.

I loved the fall so much, particularly the late fall after the harvest had been gathered in, when the year's work was finished, when the peasants began to visit each other in their cottages, when everyone was waiting for the winter. Then, everything becomes bleaker, the sky frowns with clouds, yellow leaves carpet the trails at the edge of the bare forest that now looks bluish and blackish, especially toward evening when the damp fog weighs down on it, and the trees look through the fog like giants, like horrible, frightening ghosts.

At times when I was late, when I had fallen behind the others, I was in a hurry to get home—it was so frightening! I trembled like a leaf, expecting some terrifying creature to peek out of the hollow of a tree. Meanwhile, the wind would tear through the forest, roaring and whistling, howling plaintively, and tearing a cloud of withered leaves from the rickety boughs, whirling them through the air. And the birds would set off in pursuit of them with shrill cries, until they blotted out the whole sky and everything overhead was black. It was all very frightening and then, on top of everything, I'd hear a voice whispering, "Run, child, run, don't be late. It will be terrifying here very soon. You'd better run and not be late," and, with fear gripping my heart, I'd run and run, till I was completely out of breath.

But once I was home, all flustered from running, I'd find everything noisy and cheerful there. They'd give us children some chores to do, such as shelling peas or perhaps shaking out poppy seeds. Damp logs would stick out of the fireplace; mother would smilingly watch us work; old nanny Ulyana would tell us a story of the old days or some scary fairy tale about sorcerers and dead men. We children would press close to each other, smiling. Then, suddenly everyone would fall silent: someone seems to be knocking at the door. But it turns out to be only old Frolovna's spindle, and we burst out laughing. Later, at night, we were so frightened of scary dreams that we tried to stave off sleep. We would wake up at night and lie without daring to stir, trembling under the blanket.

But in the morning, I'd get up fresh as a flower. Outside the window, the whole field and the bare branches are covered with hoar frost; the lake is covered with a thin film of ice and white mist rises from it; birds are calling cheerfully. The sun casts its bright beams upon the lake and the beams shatter the ice as though it were glass. Everything's so bright, light, and gay. The fire is crackling in the fireplace once again, we sit down around the samovar, our big black dog, Polkan, shivering after a night spent outside, peeps in at the window, wagging his friendly tail. A peasant passes under our windows, driving his strong horse to the forest to get firewood. Everyone seems cheerful and content. There's a lot of grain stored in the threshing barns, the huge straw-covered stacks gleam in the sun and are a delight to look at. Everybody feels safe and happy, for God has blessed us all with a bumper harvest. Everyone knows there'll be plenty of bread for the winter. The peasant knows that his family and his children will have enough to eat, and that is why, in the evenings, the resounding songs of the girls never cease, and that is why people have tears of gratitude in their eyes when they say their prayers on God's Sunday. Ah, what a bright and golden time my childhood was!

And here I am crying like a small child, carried away by my reminiscences. I remember everything so vividly. The past stands out so brightly before me, while the present is all dim and foggy. How will it all end? Do you know, I have a feeling, no I am sure that I'll die this fall. I am very ill. I often think that I'll die soon, but I don't want to be buried here. Perhaps I'll have to stay in bed once again, as I did in the spring. But I haven't quite recovered from that time yet. I am not feeling at all well right now. Fedora has gone somewhere for the whole day, and I have been left all alone all this time. For some time now, it has frightened me to be left alone—I am always under the impression that there is some stranger in the room with me, that someone is talking to me, especially when I get lost in my thoughts. Then, when I come out of it, I am frightened. That's why I have written you such a long letter—while I am writing that feeling leaves me. Good-by. I must stop now because I have neither time nor note paper left. Of the money I received for the dresses and for the lady's hat I made, I still have one silver ruble left. I am very glad that you have paid two silver rubles to your landlady—now she may leave you in peace, at least for a time.

You must get your clothes mended somehow. Farewell, I am completely exhausted. I don't understand why I get so weak. The least effort tires me. Now, suppose I do get some work, how will I manage to do it? This is what hurts me most.

V. D.

September 5

My darling Varinka,

I have gone through a lot today. To begin with I suffered from a headache all day. In order to freshen myself up a bit, I took a walk along the Fontanka Embankment. It was a dark, damp evening. It gets dark just after five at this time of the year, you know. It wasn't raining but there was plenty of fog, which is no better than a good rain. Clouds were running across the sky in wide strips. There were masses of people walking up and down the Embankment, and it so happened that they all had such incredibly depressing faces: drunk working men, snub-nosed, booted Finnish women with uncovered heads, tradesmen, carters, cabbies; some of our office clerks out on an errand; street boys; a locksmith's apprentice in striped overalls, thin and weak, his face covered with oily grime, a lock in his hand; a retired, seven foot soldier looking for someone who would buy a penknife or a brass ring from him—you know, that sort of public. Actually, what sort of a public would you expect to be there at such an hour, with the Fontanka being a navigable canal? Indeed, how did so many barges manage to find enough room there! On many of the bridges, women were sitting selling damp gingerbread and rotten apples, and those women merchants were wet and very dirty themselves. Ah, what a sad sight the Fontanka is! Damp granite underfoot and tall soot-stained buildings on either bank; and fog both underfoot and overhead. And this evening was even darker and sadder than most evenings.

By the time I turned into Gorokhovaya Street, it was getting quite dark and the gaslights were being lit. I hadn't had an occasion to walk down Gorokhovaya Street for a long time. It's such a noisy street! What rich shops and stores! Everything glitters and sparkles: beautiful materials, flowers in the window displays behind the glass, beribboned ladies' hats! One would think that these things were decorations, just to make it look beautiful—but no, imagine, there are people who buy them and give them to their wives! It's a rich street indeed! There are many German bakers on Gorokhovaya Street and they are apparently very well-off. There are so many carriages driving by at any given moment, it is really amazing how the pavement can withstand such a battering. Some of the carriages are truly gorgeous, with their windows sparkling like mirrors; inside everything is made of silk and velvet, and the flunkeys wear epaulettes and carry swords. I peeked into all the passing carriages, and in every one of them there were beautifully dressed ladies, all princesses or countesses. It was probably the hour when those people were hurrying off to balls or gatherings. I'd be very curious to see a princess or any distinguished lady at close quarters; it must be very pleasant. I've never had the opportunity; the closest I've ever come was probably tonight, peeping into those carriages.

That reminded me of you, Varinka. Ah, my darling, ah my little sweet! My heart begins to bleed whenever I think of you now. Why must you be so unhappy, Varinka, my dearest angel? You're every bit as good as any of those ladies. You are kind, and beautiful, and so learned! Why, then, must you have such rotten luck? Why does it so often happen that a good person is disinherited, while good fortune keeps thrusting itself upon another? I know, I know, my dear, it's wicked of me to think like that, but, really, in honest truth, why should that raven, Fate, croak good fortune for some people before they're even born while others are destined to start their lives in orphan asylums? And it often happens that luck is with the fools. It is as if fate were saying: "You fool over there, just help yourself from your family money-bags—eat, drink, and be merry! But you so-and-so over there, you must be content to watch and lick your lips. That's all you're entitled to, brother!" I know, my dear, that it is sinful to think like this, but I cannot prevent these wicked thoughts from creeping into my head. And if you had been destined to drive around in a carriage like those ladies, my love, all sorts of bigwigs would be trying to catch your eye, not just poor fellows like me; you'd be dressed in silk and gold, and not a cheap cotton dress. You wouldn't be thin and frail the way you are, you'd have a sweet, plump figure, and a fresh and rosy complexion. As to me, I'd be happy enough just glancing into your brightly lit windows now and then from the street, and perhaps catching sight of just your shadow on the wall; just the thought that you were happy and having a nice time, my sweet bird, would be enough to cheer me up altogether.

But things are so different in reality! Not only have wicked people ruined you, but any worthless, lewd wretch feels free to insult you. Just because he looks so elegant in his frockcoat and because he looks you up and down through his gold lorgnette, the shameless creature imagines that he can get away with anything, and that you must listen indulgently to his indecent speeches! But is it really so, my good friend? And why should it be like that? Well, simply because you are alone and helpless, because you have no strong friend to send the offender packing. And just think—what sort of people would want to go and insult a poor orphan girl just because they feel they can get away with it? They're scum, not people. They're just listed as human beings, but in reality, they don't exist. I'm sure of that. That's the sort of creatures they are. I, for one, my dear, have much more respect for the beggar with the barrel organ I saw on Gorokhovaya Street today than for them. Although he has to drag himself around all day in the hope of getting a few miserable coppers to keep himself alive, he is his own master and he earns his living by his own efforts. Of course, he's a beggar, but he is a respectable beggar; he's cold and tired but still, in his way, he's doing his work. And there are many honest people, my dear, who, although they don't make much money, are paid for their labors, but will bow to no one nor beg for their bread. And me too, just like that organ grinder—that is, not exactly, in fact, not at all like him . . . well, yes, in a respectable way though, I do what he does. I do the best I can. I can't do any better, because my abilities are limited. Well, yes, no one can demand more from me.

I mentioned the organ grinder because it so happened that I felt my poverty twofold today. I stopped to watch the organ grinder. All sorts of thoughts had come creeping into my head and so, to take my mind off them, I stopped for a moment to watch. There were cab drivers standing there, a streetwalker, and also a small girl, a very grubby little girl. The hurdy-gurdy man had stopped under the windows of a house. Then I noticed a little boy of ten or so, a very pretty little boy, but very pale and weak-looking with hardly anything but his shirt on and almost barefoot. He stood there listening open-mouthed to the barrel organ, the way a child does.

He stared at the German's dolls dancing, though his own hands and feet were numb with cold; he was shivering and chewing at the edge of his sleeve. I noticed that he held a sheet of paper in his hands. A man stepped forward and tossed a coin at the barrel organ, and it fell straight into the box in which a toy Frenchman was dancing with toy ladies. At the clink of the coin the boy started and turned his head shyly toward me, apparently thinking that it was I who had tossed the coin. And so he ran up to me. His hands trembled and so did his high-pitched little voice. He handed me the folded sheet of paper and said: "Here's a letter, sir." I unfolded the sheet. Well, it was the usual stuff, you know— the mother of three children dying, the children hungry, please help them and when the mother dies, she will look out for you with gratitude from the other world for having helped her little fledglings. Well, what of it? It was an ordinary thing such as one comes across any day, but what could I give them? I gave him nothing. But I was terribly sorry for that poor little boy all blue with cold; perhaps it was true that he was hungry; in fact, I bet he was. I know something about these things. But what's bad is that those nasty mothers don't spare their children, and send them out into the icy street half-naked with notes like that. Well, maybe she's just a stupid, weak woman without anyone to help her, and so she sits there with her feet tucked under her now. It's quite possible, though, that she's really ill. But why doesn't she see to it that her note falls into the proper hands? Ah, she may be simply a crook who is taking advantage of a weak and hungry child to deceive people more successfully, and doesn't care if it makes him ill. And what sort of things does a little boy learn about life, handing those notes to unknown people? It just coarsens his feelings to go around begging. People are in a hurry. They have no time for him. Their hearts are of stone, and their words are harsh: "Go away! Off with you! Who d'you think you're kidding?" And hearing that from everyone, a child's heart hardens, and he shivers in the cold street all for nothing, like a fledgling fallen from his nest. His hands and feet are frozen, and he gasps for breath. The next thing you know, he'll be coughing, and then he won't have long to wait for the sickness to sneak into his chest like a murderous snake. And by and by, death will be hovering over him as he lies in some dark corner without proper care. And that'll be the end of his life, Varinka. Yes, that's how life is sometimes! Ah, my dear, it's so painful to hear a thin little voice begging "in the name of Christ," and then to walk on without giving anything and just muttering, "God will provide." Well, sometimes it's not all that bad but then, there are different ways of begging "in the name of Christ." Sometimes it's the long, drawling, carrying, professional beggar's whine. It doesn't hurt me so much not to give then, because he's a beggar of old standing, a professional. He's accustomed to it and can take it, you know he can. But sometimes, the phrase sounds unfamiliar, coarse, and frightening. Like today—just when I'd almost accepted the note from that little boy, I heard a man who was standing close to the fence begging; he wasn't addressing everyone but looked at me and said, "Give us a copper, sir, for Christ's sake!" He said it in such a harsh, jerky voice that I shuddered from some uncomfortable feeling, and didn't give him a thing. I didn't have any money anyway. And then, too, rich people don't like poor people to complain aloud about being out of luck—they don't like to be bothered. They don't wish to be imposed upon, for they never pester anyone, never! Yes, poor people are terrible pests, and sometimes their hungry moaning may disturb other people's sleep!

I must confess, my dear, that when I started describing all this I was doing it partly to get it off my chest, but chiefly to demonstrate my good writing style. For, you must admit, my sweet, that my style has rather improved recently. But by now I feel so dejected, because I myself deeply sympathize with myself and the way I feel. Ah, I know very well that self-pity won't do me any good, yet it is the only way I have of being fair to myself. Because, it is true, my dear, that there are other times when, without provocation, one would like to annihilate oneself, when one feels that one is not worth a copper, and when one treats oneself worse than dirt. And I feel like that perhaps because, in a way, I am like that little beggar boy—bewildered, hunted, and downtrodden.

Now, I will explain to you what I mean by illustration. It happens sometimes, my dear, that when, in the mornings, I must hurry to my office I look around me and watch the city waking up, smoking, seething, and rumbling. And the sight makes me feel small, as if someone had given me an edifying poke in my curious nose, and then I drag myself to my office, "quieter than water and lower than grass" as the saying goes. But now have a look at what is taking place inside those big, soot-covered houses, try to understand and then judge whether it makes any sense for me to consider myself so low and to be so mortified. Mind you, Varinka, I say this figuratively, and you mustn't take it in the literal sense. So then, what's going on inside those houses? There, in some dim corner, in a damp hole that he considers his living quarters, some workman is waking up. During his sleep he has, let's say, been dreaming of some boots, which he slit by accident the day before. Now, should a man really dream about such rubbish? But since he's a workman, a bootmaker, he can be excused if he keeps thinking about his trade. His children may be crying and his wife may be hungry. Well, it's not only bootmakers that wake up like that in the mornings, my dear, and it wouldn't even be worth mentioning if it hadn't been for one thing: In the very same house, perhaps a story higher or lower, a rich man in his gilded apartment may also have dreamt of boots. That is, he dreamt of them differently; they may have been boots of a different style, but they were boots all the same, for in this sense, my dear, we're all bootmakers. And even that by itself wouldn't matter, but what is really bad is that there is no one close to that rich man, no one who would whisper in his ear, "You oughtn't to be thinking just of yourself, to be living just for you alone. You aren't a bootmaker, remember, your children are in good health, your wife isn't nagging you for food, just look around and try to find a worthier object for your worries than boots." That's what I was trying to convey to you figuratively, Varinka. Well, it is perhaps too free a way of thinking, my sweet, but the thought does come to me again and again and I can't help it if it bursts out of me in heated words. And so that's why there is no need to estimate myself so lowly, frightened as I was by all the sound and fury. I will conclude by saying that you may fancy I am saying bitter things because I am suffering from a fit of depression, or that I've simply copied it out of some book. That isn't so, my dear, I assure you—I loathe uncalled for bitterness, I am not suffering from depression, and I haven't copied anything out of a book. So there.

I was sad when I got back home. I sat down at my table, put the kettle on, made myself some tea and was about to have a glass or two. Suddenly Gorshkov, that poor lodger in our apartment, comes into my room. I had noticed in the morning that he was hanging around the other lodgers and was also trying to approach me. Let me tell you in passing that the Gorshkovs are incomparably worse off than I, much worse, for he has his wife and children to think of, and I can't even imagine what I'd do if I were in his place. Well then, he comes in and bows to me, and as usual there was a tear hanging on his lashes, for his eyes are always watering. He stood there for a while, shuffling his feet, and unable to say a word, and so I offered him a chair, a broken one it is true, but I had no other. I offered him a glass of tea. He started to demur, demurred for a long time, but in the end accepted. Then he insisted on drinking it without sugar, and started demurring again when I insisted that he must take some sugar. He argued for a long time, wouldn't accept any sugar, and finally put the tiniest lump in his tea, and assured me that it was unbelievably sweet. Ah, to what humility poverty can reduce a man!

"Well, what is it, my friend?" I asked him.

"Ah, kind sir, please, help me out. Help a family in dire distress. There's my wife, my children, nothing to eat . . . You can imagine how a father feels in such circumstances."

I was about to answer him but he interrupted me.

"I," he said, "am afraid of everyone around here, Makar Alexeyevich. Well, not that I'm really afraid of them, but I feel sort of intimidated—they are all such proud, haughty people, you know. And I wouldn't have come to bother you, kind sir, because I'm well aware that you're having your own difficulties, and that you couldn't spare much, but if you could lend me anything, even a very little, do so please. I've dared to come to you," he said, "because I know you have a kind heart and also because you know how it is to be in trouble; in fact, you are in difficulties right now, and so you are certain to feel compassion. And forgive me, please, for presuming, Makar Alexeyevich," he concluded.

I told him then that nothing would give me greater pleasure than to lend him some money, but that I didn't have a kopeck to my name, not a single one.

"Dear Makar Alexeyevich," he said, "I'm not asking for much. Only it's like this . . . my wife . . . my children, you see . . . If only . . ." he turned very red at this point and said: "if only ten kopecks."

Ah, there my own heart sank. Why, I thought, I'm really well off compared with these people! I actually had twenty kopecks altogether, and I was reckoning to spend them tomorrow on my most urgent needs.

"I'm afraid I really can't help you, my dear man," I said to him.

"Please, kind sir, Makar Alexeyevich, just ten kopecks!"

So I got my twenty kopecks out of my drawer, and handed them to him. Some good deed, I thought! Ah, what misery!

We got to talking after that, and I asked him how it had come about he was in such straits, and why he rented a room for five rubles in silver when he was so poor. He explained to me that he had rented the room six months ago and had paid for it in advance, and that it was after that that he had had a streak of bad luck and had been unable to find anything in the way of work. He had hoped that the lawsuit in which he was engaged would in time be settled. It is a very unpleasant case, he told me. You see, Varinka, he is the defendant in that suit, being accused of something or other. He is mixed up in it with a merchant who tried to cheat the government over a contract, was discovered and arrested and now has managed to implicate Gorshkov. But, in fact, Gorshkov was only guilty of negligence, of lack of judgment and zeal in looking after the interests of the government, of which he was an employee. The lawsuit has been going on for years, and snag after snag keeps cropping up.

"I haven't done anything dishonorable," Gorshkov told me. "I am not guilty of any swindle or robbery."

The affair has cast a slur on his name. He has been dismissed from the government service and, although he hasn't been found legally guilty of any crime, to this day he has been unable to recover from the merchant a considerable sum that is due him and which is now the subject of the legal suit. I trust him, but the judges, of course, can't take his word for it. The whole affair is so tied up in knots that it would take a hundred years to disentangle it. As soon as one knot is untied, the merchant manages to tie a new one. I am terribly sorry for Gorshkov, my sweet. I fully sympathize with him. He is without a livelihood, and he cannot get a government post because of his reputation. His savings have been eaten up; the case is very complicated but, in the meantime, they must live; then—the last thing they needed—a new child was born, which meant more expenses; the oldest son fell ill—more expenses; and died—expenses again; the wife is ailing; he himself is suffering from some chronic illness—in a word, he's in trouble up to his ears. But he still says that he expects the lawsuit to be concluded any day now, in his favor of course, and that he has absolutely no doubt about it. Ah, I'm so terribly sorry for him, my dear! I tried to be as nice to him as I could.

Well, so good-by for now, my sweet. May Christ look after you, and you, keep well! Ah, my darling, whenever I think of you, it is like balm to my sick soul and, although I worry for you, even worrying eases my heart.

Your faithful friend,
MAKAR DEVUSHKIN

September 9

My dear Varvara Alexeyevna,

I am quite beside myself as I write this. I am terribly upset by something awful that has happened. My head is spinning. Ah, my dear, what a thing I have to tell you now! This is something we didn't foresee. No, I can't believe I didn't foresee it—I foresaw everything. My heart sensed it all coming! I even dreamt something of the sort a few nights ago.

Here's what's happened . . . I'll tell you about it without paying attention to style, just as it comes to me. This morning I went to the office. I got there, sat down, and began to write. I must tell you here, my dear, that I was writing yesterday too when Timofei Ivanovich walked up to me and told me himself, "This document is needed in a hurry so please, Makar Alexeyevich, copy it very carefully and as quickly as possible—it must be signed today."

I must remind you, my sweet, that yesterday I wasn't myself. I couldn't even bear to look at anything around me. I felt completely weighed down by dejection. There was ice in my heart and darkness in my soul, and I kept thinking of you, my poor little angel. Anyway, I started copying that document. I did it neatly and well, but then—I don't know whether it was the devil himself who confused me, or if it had been predetermined by fate—but I left out a whole line, and God knows what sense it made, or rather it made no sense at all. Well, yesterday, they were too late to take the document to His Excellency to sign, and so they only presented it to him today. Well, today I came to the office at the usual hour as if nothing had happened and installed myself next to Emelyan Ivanovich. I must tell you, my dear, that recently I have become twice as timid and shy as I was before so that now I can't even look anyone straight in the face. I shudder if a chair happens to creak under someone. And so I was sitting there today as quiet as a hedgehog when Yefim Akimovich—the worst tease the world has ever seen— said in a very loud voice, "How come you're sitting there like that, Makar Alexeyevich? What a face—oooh-oooooh!" and he made such a grimace that everyone around fairly rolled with laughter at me, it goes without saying. They went on and on and I sat there blocking my ears, with my eyes half-closed, not daring to stir. I always act like that—I hope they'll leave me alone sooner that way. Suddenly I hear a noise, some dashing about and . . . Maybe I've made a mistake? No, they're calling my name. I'm being summoned—they want Devushkin. My heart pounded, I became terribly frightened, I'm not sure of what, but frightened as I had never been before in my whole life. I sat rooted to my chair as though it didn't concern me, as if I weren't really me. But it came closer and closer and soon I heard by my very ear: "Devushkin! Where is he? Devushkin!"

I raised my eyes and saw Estafy Ivanovich standing there.

"Makar Alexeyevich," he said, "hurry. His Excellency wants to see you! What a mess you made out of that document yesterday!"

That was all he said, but it was enough, don't you think, my dear? I felt cold and numb as I walked over there, more dead than alive. They led me through one room, then through another, then through still another one, and finally I found myself in the private office, facing His Excellency. I cannot tell you exactly what I was thinking then. His Excellency was standing there, and all my superiors were standing around him. I believe I even forgot to bow as I came in. I was so frightened that my lips were trembling. And there was good reason for me to be in such a state. In the first place, I was ashamed of myself—I glanced to the right where there was a mirror, and what I saw in it was enough to drive me out of my mind. In the second place, I've always behaved very quietly, as though I didn't even exist in this world. So that His Excellency would hardly be aware of my existence. He may have vaguely heard that there was someone called Devushkin working in his department, but he had never paid much attention to the matter.

He began angrily: "What's come over you, sir? What were you thinking of? This is an important document and you've spoiled it! How could you?" At this point His Excellency turned to Estafy Ivanovich, and I could only hear the disconnected sounds of certain words: ". . . negligence . . . carelessness . . . cause of unpleasantness . . ."

I opened my mouth, wanting to say I was sorry, but I couldn't; I felt like fleeing but didn't dare budge . . . And then, Varinka, something so dreadful happened that I can hardly hold my pen in my hand for shame . . . One of my buttons that had been hanging on a thread—may the devil take it—suddenly broke off (I must have pulled at it by accident), fell to the floor, bounced, jingled, and then rolled right

between His Excellency's feet . . . And all that in the middle
of a general silence. And so here was my only justification,
my only excuse, the only answer I could offer His Excellency! The consequences were terrifying. It immediately attracted His Excellency's attention to my figure and my dress.
I remembered what I had seen in the mirror and rushed to
pick up my button! What a stupid thing to do! So I bent
down, trying to get hold of the button, but it kept slipping
between my fingers, and I couldn't catch it. In a word, I
didn't impress him with my nimbleness either. Now, I felt
my last strength leaving me and thought that everything was
irretrievably lost, that my reputation was destroyed, and that
I had lost all human dignity. And then, apropos of nothing,
I heard Teresa's and Faldoni's voices ringing in my ears and
echoing inside my skull. Finally, I caught hold of the button
and stood up. Well, after having made a fool of myself like
that, I might at least have stood quietly with my hands at
my sides. But no, I didn't have enough sense even for that!
I began openly fitting the button to the hanging thread as if
hoping to fix it that way and I was even smiling while I
fiddled with it, yes, actually smiling!

His Excellency first turned away, then glanced at me
again. I heard him say to Estafy Ivanovich: "What's this?
Look at the way he's dressed! What the matter with him?"

Ah, I had really distinguished myself! Then I heard
Estafy Ivanovich say:

"No former complaints about him, none whatsoever.
His behavior is exemplary, salary in accordance with his
grade . . ."

"Well, help him out somehow. Let him have an advance
on his pay . . ."

"But he has already taken an advance on his salary, sir.
He must be having some difficulties now, but his behavior
is very good, and there have never been any complaints
against him."

I was dying, my angel, I was burning in the flames of
hell!

"Well," His Excellency said aloud, "that document will
just have to be urgently recopied. Here, Devushkin, come
over here . . . Copy it again, without a mistake this time . . .
Wait a minute . . ."

His Excellency stopped and said something to the others,
who all left. As soon as they were outside, he quickly took

out his wallet, got a hundred-ruble bill out of it and said, "Here, let me help you the best I can. Take it please . . ." and thrust it into my hand.

I shuddered, my angel. My very heart began to tremble. I don't know what came over me. I was about to seize his hand. And he, he went all red, the wonderful man, and—I am not departing one inch from the truth, my dear—and he took my unworthy hand and shook it, shook it as if I were his equal and said, "Go now, I'm glad I can be of use. Try not to make any more mistakes, and now, don't worry, it's all over."

And now, Varinka, here's what I have decided: I'd like you and Fedora—and if I had any children, I'd ask them too —to pray for His Excellency every day for as long as you live, as you wouldn't pray even for your own fathers! And I want to tell you something else still, my dear, and I say this in all seriousness and you listen to me, my sweet: I swear that, however depressed and dejected I was in the worst days of our misery, when I was forced to watch life ill-treating you and myself, realizing my humiliation and how useless and helpless I was—well, despite all that, I swear to you that I treasure not so much that His Excellency gave me that hundred-ruble bill as that he deigned to shake hands with me, a weakling, a drunk, and a man unworthy of trust. By that gesture, he has given me back to myself, has rekindled my spirit, made life more pleasant for me, and I am sure that, however sinful I may be, the Almighty will heed my prayers for His Excellency's happiness and prosperity!

My darling, I'm in a terrible state of agitation now; my heart is beating as if it were about to leap out of my chest, and I feel weak all over.

I am sending you forty-five rubles in bills; I'll give my landlady twenty and keep thirty-five for myself; twenty for putting my clothes in order, and fifteen to live on. But now all the events of the morning have shaken me too much and I must lie down for a bit. I feel at peace, very much at peace, except that something is tugging at my heart and deep within me something is stirring, trembling, quivering.

I'll come over to see you. But now, I feel as if I were drunk with all these impressions . . . God sees everything, Varinka, my irreplaceable little darling!

Your worthy friend,
Makar Devushkin

September 10

My dear Makar Alexeyevich,

I am indescribably delighted at your luck, and greatly admire your chief's kind and noble behavior. At last, you've been given a break, and now you will be able to recover a bit from your hardships. But, in the name of God, don't once again spend the money carelessly. Lead a quiet and frugal life and, from this very day on, start putting a bit aside so as not to be caught without a kopeck if something happens. And please don't worry about us. Fedora and I will manage somehow. Why have you sent us all that money? We don't need it at all. We are content with what we have. It is true though that we will soon need some to move from here, but for that, Fedora reckons to be paid back a certain sum, an old debt that is owed her. Nevertheless I'll keep twenty rubles for extreme emergencies. I'm sending the remainder back to you. Please be careful with this money. Good-by, live quietly, try to be cheerful and to remain in good health. I would have written more but I feel terribly tired. Yesterday I didn't get out of bed the whole day. Please come and see me, Makar Alexeyevich.

V. D.

My dear Varvara Alexeyevna,

I implore you, don't leave me now that I am so perfectly happy and content. My darling, don't listen to Fedora and I'll do whatever you tell me—I'll behave well if only out of respect for His Excellency. I'll be well-behaved and responsible. And you and I will once again write cheerful letters to each other, trust all our secret thoughts to each other, share our joys and our worries, if there should be any worries at all. We shall live in peace and harmony, the two of us. We'll take up literature, my little angel!

Everything has changed for the good in my life. My landlady is much more amenable, Teresa more intelligent, even Faldoni himself has become more prompt. And I've made it up with Ratazayev—in my joy, I went to him. He is really a nice fellow and all those things they say about him are untrue. I have learned since that it was all a despicable slander. It never even occurred to him to describe you and me in a lampoon—he assured me so himself. He read me a new piece of his. As to calling me Lovelace that time, that wasn't in the least meant as an offense or something indecent—he even told me so. It is a word of foreign origin and means literally a *smart fellow*, or to put it in a more literary, cultured way, a young man you must be careful of. So there! It was a quite innocent joke, my angel, as you can see. But in my ignorance, I took offense and so now, I had to apologize. And the weather too is so nice today, Varinka, although an icy drizzle fell this morning as fine as though it were coming through a sieve. Well, never mind. Actually it even made the air a bit fresher. I went out to buy myself some boots, and got a beautiful pair. I took a walk along the Nevsky, and read *The Bee*. Ah, but I'm forgetting to tell you the main thing.

Here's what happened. This morning, I got talking to Emelyan Ivanovich and Aksenty Mikhailovich about His Excellency. Well, yes Varinka, I am not the only one he has treated so kindly. He has helped others, and his kindness is known to the whole world. His praises are sung, and tears of gratitude are shed for him in many places. He brought up an orphan girl in his house, and then he gave her a dowry and married her to a government official working on special assignments in His Excellency's own department. He also got a job in an office for the son of a widow, and has performed many other acts of kindness. Well, I felt then it was my duty to add my little bit, and told them frankly what His Excellency had done for me. I told them all that had happened, without hiding anything. I put my shame in my pocket on that occasion. Indeed, there's no room for pride and dignity in a case like that. Yes, I wanted the whole world to know about His Excellency's noble act.

I spoke enthusiastically, with heat, without blushing. On the contrary, I was proud that I had such things to tell. I told them everything (except about you, my darling—that I sensibly left out), about my landlady, about Faldoni, about Ratazayev and the boots, and even about Markov. I told them everything. Some of them were chuckling, I believe . . . no, in truth, the whole lot of them were chuckling. But I believe they were laughing at the way I looked. I suppose they found it funny in some way. Unless it was my boots . . . Yes, it was my boots, I'm sure. But they didn't have any wicked thoughts. They couldn't possibly have been laughing at what I was saying. I mean, they couldn't have been laughing in connection with His Excellency—that they couldn't possibly do, Varinka, don't you agree?

I still can't get over it, my sweet. All these events have completely befuddled me! Do you have enough firewood? Please don't catch cold, Varinka. It's so easy to catch cold. Ah, my sweet, you depress me so with those sad ideas of yours. I pray to God for you. I pray so hard for you, my darling! Now, do you have woolen stockings, for instance, or warm clothes? Remember, my dear girl, if ever you need anything, in the name of the Creator, ask and do not offend me, an old man! Just come straight to me, and tell me what you need. The hard times are over. And you needn't worry about me—the future is happy and bright!

Ah, we've gone through a sad time, Varinka, but it doesn't matter any more. It's all behind us! Years will pass, and we shall sigh as we think back on these days. I remember when I was young. Why, often I didn't have a copper in my pocket. I was cold and hungry, but I enjoyed life. In the morning, I'd see a pretty face on the Nevsky, and that was enough to keep me happy for the rest of the day. Yes, it was a great and glorious time, Varinka! Especially in Petersburg. Yesterday I was praying with tears in my eyes that God forgive me my recriminations, my liberal ideas, my drinking, and my gambling. I mentioned you ardently in my prayers— you were the only one, my little angel, to give me strength, to console me, to guide me with wise advice. I took your little notes one by one today, and kissed each of them in turn.

Good-by, my dearest. I have heard that there are some clothes on sale somewhere around here. I'll try to find out about it. So good-by then, my little angel, good-by!

Your faithfully devoted,
MAKAR DEVUSHKIN

September 15

Dear Makar Alexeyevich,

I am terribly upset. Listen to what has happened here. I feel there is something sinister in it. Judge for yourself, my dearest friend.

Mr. Bykov is in Petersburg. Fedora met him. He was driving somewhere in a cab. He ordered it to stop, went up to Fedora, and asked her where she lived. At first she wouldn't tell him. Then he scoffed at her, and said that he knew very well who was living with her. (Anna Fedorovna must have told him.) Then Fedora lost patience, and started reproaching him, telling him what she thought of him; that he was a man without a conscience, that he was the cause of all my troubles. He answered that there was no need to go into all that for, anyway, who could be happy without a kopeck in his pocket? Fedora said that I might have earned my living working or might have married someone, or, if that had failed, found a position in a family as a governess, but that as things stood, I had no chance left of finding happiness in life, and that I'd soon die. To that he replied that I was still much too young to die, that my head was full of a lot of nonsense, and that "her virtue is slightly tarnished" (his own words).

Fedora and I thought he didn't know our address, but yesterday, just after I had left to do some shopping in Gostiny Dvor, he suddenly walked into our room. I have the impression that he deliberately arranged it so as not to find me at home. He questioned Fedora at length about our life, kept looking around, examined my work, and at last asked: "Who's the government clerk who comes to visit you?" At that moment, you were crossing the yard. Fedora pointed to you and he snorted. Fedora begged him to leave. She told him that, as it was, there were so many things to upset me that it had made me ill, and that to see him in our room would upset me even further. He said nothing to that, and then declared that he'd just dropped in on us because he had nothing better to do. He then offered Fedora twenty-five rubles. She, it goes without saying, wouldn't take them.

What can it all mean? Why did he come? I cannot understand for the life of me how it is he knows so much about us. I keep making all sorts of wild guesses. Fedora tells me that Aksinia, her sister-in-law, is a friend of Nastasia the laundress who has a nephew working as a hall porter in the office building where a friend of Anna Fedorovna's nephew is employed. But could rumors possibly have reached him that way? But it's quite possible that Fedora is wrong. We don't know what to think. Is it possible that he will come back here? The mere thought horrifies me. When Fedora told me all that, I became so frightened, I almost fainted. What do they want with us? I don't want to have anything to do with them now. They have no business pursuing me here! Ah, I am in such a state of panic that I keep imagining that the door will open at any moment and Bykov will walk in. What will happen to me? What is in store for me, Makar Alexeyevich? Please, come over, my dear friend, come over, for God's sake, Makar Alexeyevich.

[No signature.]

September 18

My dear Varvara Alexeyevna,

Today a very sad and quite unaccountable thing happened in our apartment. Our poor Gorshkov, I must tell you, Varinka, has been completely cleared by the court. The case was concluded quite a while ago, but today he went to hear the final ruling. The case ended very happily for him. He was even exonerated of all blame for negligence of duty. The merchant was ordered to pay him a considerable sum of money, which improved his financial position incomparably and removed all blemish from his honor. So everything turned out for the best, and all his wishes were fulfilled.

But when he returned home at three today, he was a dreadful sight to see—his face was white as a sheet, his lips were trembling as he smiled. He embraced his wife and children. We all went to congratulate him. He seemed immensely touched by our sympathy, bowed to everyone, shook everyone's hand several times. I even had the impression that he was taller and more erect, and that there was no longer that tear from his watering eyes dangling on his eyelashes. The poor man was in a state of tremendous agitation. He couldn't stay in one place for more than two minutes at a time, kept picking up everything within reach, then putting it down again, kept smiling, sat down, stood up, sat down again, muttered something about his honor, his good name, his children—ah, the way he pronounced those words! He even wept. Most of us shed a tear too. Ratazayev, apparently wishing to cheer him up, said:

"What's honor, my friend, when there's nothing to eat; money is the main thing, my friend, and it is for the money you got that you ought to thank God really," and he patted Gorshkov on the shoulder.

I believe Gorshkov was rather offended by those words. Not that he expressed his disapproval directly, but he gave Ratazayev a queer look and removed his hand from his shoulder. He would never have done anything like that before, my sweet! But then, every man reacts to things differently. Take me, for instance, in my joy I'd never have acted so proudly. Why, there are times when I would bow an extra time and accept an extra humiliation just because I'm feeling so happy . . . But I don't come into this, after all.

"Yes," he said, "money is fine too, and I thank God for it."

And after that, all the time we were there, he kept repeating, "Thank God, thank God . . ."

Mrs. Gorshkov ordered a special dinner, and it was the landlady herself who prepared it. She is really a kind woman in her way, our landlady. While they were waiting for the dinner, Gorshkov couldn't stay in one place. He kept rushing into everyone's rooms without being invited, sitting down, smiling, saying something (or sometimes even saying nothing), and then leaving again. At the naval man's, he even took a hand at cards—they needed a fourth. He played three or four cards, got mixed up and gave up, saying, "No, I didn't mean to play, I was just . . ." and left the room.

He met me in the corridor, took both my hands in his, looked into my eyes in such a strange way, shook my hand, and walked off smiling. But his smile, I noticed, was strange and painful, a bit blank. His wife was crying with joy. Their room had a holiday air to it. They ate their dinner very quickly and after the meal he said to his wife:

"I believe I'll lie down for a bit," and he went to bed.

Then he called his daughter to him and, for a long time, stroked the child's hair. Then he turned to his wife and said: "And what about our Peter? Yes, what about our little Petey?" he said. His wife crossed herself and said, "Ah, he's dead . . ."

"Yes, yes, I know. Petey is in God's kingdom now."

Mrs. Gorshkov realized that her husband was not his usual self, that what had happened had given him a great shock, and she said to him, "Why, dear, try to get a bit of sleep."

"Yes, all right. In a minute, I'd like . . ."

He turned to the wall, lay there for a while, then made an effort to turn to her, to tell her something. She didn't hear and asked "What is it, dear?" He didn't answer. She waited for a few moments, then decided he must be asleep and left the room to visit the landlady for an hour or so. When she came back, she found her husband still asleep.

She sat down to do some sewing. She says she worked like that for half an hour maybe and became so dreamy that she doesn't even remember what she was thinking about; she had completely forgotten about her husband. But suddenly she was roused by a feeling of uneasiness, and now the dead silence of the room struck her as uncanny. She looked at the bed, and saw that her husband was still lying in exactly the same position. She walked over to him, pulled the blanket back and there he was lying, cold already. Yes, dear, he was dead, dead all right. What he died of—God alone knows. This death has given me a terrible shock, Varinka, and to this moment I haven't recovered from it. It is hard to believe that a man could just die like that. He was such a poor, unhappy man that Gorshkov! Ah, what a life he had! His wife was in tears and quite panic-stricken. The little girl crept into a corner. It's terrible what's going on in their room! There will be an inquest, I believe, and I'm not sure what else. But what a terrible shame! It's so sad, that one never really knows the day and the hour . . . One dies just like that, for no reason.

MAKAR DEVUSHKIN

September 19

Dear Varvara Alexeyevna,

I hasten to inform you that Ratazayev has found me work with a writer. That writer came to him and brought him a big manuscript so, thank God, there's plenty of work for me now. The only trouble is that it is so illegible that I don't know how to go about it. It has to be done quickly. The manuscript is about something so complicated that it's impossible to understand . . . We agreed that I'll be paid forty kopecks a sheet. I'm telling you all this, my dear, because there will be some extra money around now. Well, in the meantime, good-by, my sweet, I'll start on the work right away.

Your faithful friend,
MAKAR DEVUSHKIN

September 23

My dear, dear Makar Alexeyevich,

I haven't written to you for three days, during which time I've been through many worries and alarms.

The day before yesterday Bykov came to see me. I was alone at home, as Fedora had to go out somewhere. When I opened the door and saw him, I was so frightened that I couldn't budge from the spot. I felt myself turn white. He acted in his usual way, came in with a loud laugh, took a chair, and sat down. It took me a long time to gather my senses, but finally I took my needlework and sat down in a corner. He stopped laughing. I believe that the sight of me shocked him. I have grown very thin recently, my cheeks and my eyes have become sunken, and I was white as a sheet —I imagine that someone who hadn't seen me for a year, would have had a hard time recognizing me. He looked at me intently for a long time, but in the end became gay once more. He said something, I answered him, I don't remember what, and he laughed again. He sat with me for a whole hour, spoke to me at length, asked me all sorts of questions. Then, just as he was leaving, he took my hand and said (these are his actual words):

"Varvara Alexeyevna," he said, "just between us, Anna Fedorovna, your relation and my good acquaintance, is a very despicable person." Here he called her an indecent word and went on: "She has perverted your young cousin Sasha and she has greatly hurt you too. I, too, have acted despicably, in this case, I know, but that's just life I suppose . . ." and he laughed as loud as he could. Then he said he was not very good at coining beautiful phrases, but that what he wanted was to explain certain things that he felt it wouldn't be honorable for him to keep from me and so, he said, he would tell me about it as briefly as possible. Then he asked me to marry him, said he felt it was his duty to restore my honor to me, told me he was rich and that, after we were married, he'd take me with him to his estate which is in the steppes, that he'd trap hares there; he never intended to come back to Petersburg again, because life here disgusted him, and because he had a "worthless nephew" here, as he put it, whom he has decided to disinherit, and that this was the reason that he would like to have legal heirs, for which purpose he was asking for my hand. That was the main motive behind his proposal, he explained. Then he remarked that I lived very poorly and that it was no wonder that I was ill, staying in this miserable tenement, and he warned me that I wouldn't last long if I remained here for even another month. He said that, in general, living conditions in Petersburg were impossible, and finally he asked me whether I needed anything.

I was so amazed by his proposal that I burst into tears. I don't know why. So he mistook my tears for gratitude, and told me that he had always known that I was a kind, sensitive, well-educated girl, but that he hadn't made up his mind to propose to me until he had thoroughly investigated my present behavior. Then he started asking me about you, told me that he had heard that you were a man of principle, that for his part, he didn't wish to remain indebted to you, and did I think five hundred rubles would compensate you for all you had done for me? I replied that what you had done for me could never be repaid in money. He said that was nonsense, that it was all literature and those novels, and that I was still young and went in for poetry; that novels spoil young girls, that books are bad for morals, that he hated books, and that I should first live as long as he had before I talked about people. "It's only then that you'll get to know about them," he added.

Then he said I should give very serious thought to his proposal, for he wouldn't like it at all if I made such an important decision irresponsibly, and he added that it was often impulsiveness and irresponsibility that drove young people to their perdition. But he very much wanted me to say yes, he said, because otherwise he would be forced to marry the widow of a Moscow merchant, "since I've sworn I'll disinherit that useless nephew of mine."

He forced my hand open and pressed five hundred rubles into it. That, he said, was just to buy myself some candy. In the country, he said, I'd become round as a bun, living on the fat of the land. Then he announced that he had thousands of things to do, and had just dropped in to see me between two business visits, and he rushed off.

I thought and thought. I hesitated and wore myself out, but finally I decided—I must accept his offer, my dear Makar Alexeyevich, I will marry him. If there is a human being who can save me from my disgrace, give me back my good name, and pull me out of the life of misery, poverty and hardship, it is he and he alone. What else can I expect? What else can I ask for? Fedora says I shouldn't throw away a lucky chance and, she says, if this isn't a lucky chance, what is? I, at least, cannot think of any other way out for myself, my dear friend. What else can I do? I work so hard that I have completely ruined my health. I won't be able to go on working. So what is there left for me? To become a servant? I'll pine away in despair, and I won't be of any use to anyone. I have a weak constitution and so I am doomed to always be a burden to someone or other. Of course, I know it's not going to be an idyllic existence for me, but I can't help that. What choice do I have?

I haven't asked your advice this time. I wanted to decide it on my own. The decision you have just read is unalterable, and I will immediately inform Bykov of it, because he wants a quick answer. He said his business was pressing, that he had to go back and certainly wouldn't postpone his return for such a trivial matter. God alone knows whether I will be happy; my fate is in His holy and inscrutable power, but whatever it may be, I have made up my mind. They say Bykov is a kind-hearted man. He will respect me, and I will respect him too. What else could be expected from our marriage?

I have told you everything now, Makar Alexeyevich, and I am certain you will understand what a state of anxiety I am in. Don't try to dissuade me from going through with it. Your efforts will be futile. Weigh in your own heart everything that has forced me to act this way. I was terribly distressed at first myself, but I feel calmer now. I don't know what is in store for me. What will be will be—as God wills it . . .

Bykov has just arrived. I leave this letter unfinished. There are many more things I wanted to tell you. Bykov is here already!

[No signature.]

September 23

My dear Varvara Alexeyevna,

I am answering your letter in great haste; I am in a hurry to tell you, my dear, that I am dumbfounded. It all seems sort of, you know . . . Yesterday, we buried Gorshkov. Yes, that's quite right, Varinka, Bykov has acted honorably. Only, you see, my sweet, you accepted it right away like that . . . Of course, everything is according to God's will. That is so and certainly as it should be, and the hand of Providence is in it and fate too, and Fedora too agrees with you and wishes you all the best.

I am sure you will be happy now, my sweet. You will have everything there, my darling, my lovely little girl, my angel . . . The only thing is, Varinka—why must it all be done so quickly? I understand that Mr. Bykov is a busy man. I see, everyone is busy and he is too . . . I caught sight of him as he was leaving your place—a fine figure of a man, a very fine figure. But still that's not the point—what matters is not that he is a fine figure of a man . . . Well, I don't quite feel myself today. And tell me, how will we write to each other now? And what will happen to me when I stay behind alone? I am weighing everything, my angel, everything; ever since I got that letter of yours I've kept weighing in my heart all the reasons you had for doing it. I was already finishing the twentieth sheet of my copying job when the news reached me. But, dear, since you are going on a journey, you must buy yourself all sorts of things—you must get shoes and a dress and what not and, by the way, I know a store on Gorokhovaya Street. You may even remember it. I wrote to you about it in one of my letters.

But no, how can you, Varinka? You can't really think of leaving right away. It's absolutely impossible. Quite out of the question. You have a lot of shopping to do, and then there is the matter of getting a carriage. Besides, the weather is bad. Just look out the window. It's pouring buckets, and the rain is so wet and then . . . and then it's cold. Your very heart will be cold, my little angel. Why, I know you are afraid of that strange man, and yet you are leaving with him. And what will I do here all alone? Sure, Fedora says that great happiness awaits you there . . . but then, as you know, she's a wicked woman and wishes you ill. Are you going to the vigil service? I would have liked to have a look at you. One thing is absolutely true, my sweet—you are well-edu-cated, virtuous, and sensitive, but I still think he'd do better if he married that merchant's widow. What do you say, dear? Let him marry that merchant's widow!

When it starts to get dark, I'll pop over to see you, Varinka, for one hour. At this time of the year it gets dark early, and so I'll be over soon. I must absolutely see you for an hour today, my dear. Now you are waiting for Bykov and as soon as he leaves, like that other time, I'll come over. So please expect me.

MAKAR DEVUSHKIN

September 27

Makar Alexeyevich, my dear friend,

Mr. Bykov says that I must absolutely have three dozen blouses made of Dutch linen. So we must find seamstresses urgently, because we have only very little time left. Mr. Bykov is very irritated and says that all these bits and bobs are a terrible bother. Our wedding will take place five days from now, and we are leaving the day after that. Mr. Bykov is in a hurry, and says he doesn't want to waste a lot of time on all sorts of rubbish. I am exhausted from all this rushing, and can barely stand on my feet. There are so many things to do, and I begin to wish that none of it had happened. Another thing—we must get some more lace, because Mr. Bykov says he doesn't wish his wife to go around looking like a scullery maid, and that I must absolutely "wipe the floors with all the landowners' wives." That's the way he put it. And so, Makar Alexeyevich, please get into contact with Madame Chiffon on Gorokhovaya Street, and ask her to send some seamstresses over here, and then insist that she take the trouble and come here herself too. I am ill today. Our new apartment is very cold, and it is in an awful mess. Mr. Bykov's aunt is so old, she hardly breathes. I am in constant fear that she will die before we leave, but Mr. Bykov says not to worry, that she'll last out. The place is in such havoc and, since Mr. Bykov is not living with us here now, the servants tend to vanish, God knows where. Right now, there is only Fedora to serve us, because Mr. Bykov's valet, who is supposed to look after the place, hasn't shown up for two days. Mr. Bykov comes in every morning. He is very irritated, and yesterday he hit the janitor of the house because there had been some sort of trouble with the police.

There was no one to bring you this letter, so I am mailing it. Ah yes, I almost left out the most important thing—tell Madame Chiffon to be sure to change the lace and to match it with the pattern she showed me yesterday, and ask her to come over to show me the new lace. Tell her also that I have changed my mind about the trimming, that it must be done in crochet. And one other thing yet: The letters of the monogram on the handkerchiefs must be in tambour stitch, and not in satin stitch. Remember—tambour stitch! And something else I almost forgot: For God's sake tell her to raise the leaves on the pelerine and to do the tendrils and thorns in appliqué; and then that the collar must be trimmed with lace or a deep frill. Please, tell her all that, Makar Alexeyevich.

Yours,

V. D.

P.S. I feel very guilty bothering you with all these errands. Two days ago you had to spend the whole morning running around. But it can't be helped! This house is in a mess and I myself don't feel at all well. So please don't be angry with me, Makar Alexeyevich. I feel very miserable. Ah, what will come of it all, my nice, kind friend? I am afraid to peer into the future. I have a strange presentiment, and feel as though I were in a haze all the time.

P.P.S. Please, my dear, don't forget what I have asked you. I am very much afraid you'll get mixed up. Remember—I want tambour and not satin stitch.

V. D.

September 27

Dear Varvara Alexeyevna,

I have carried out your errands very carefully. Madame Chiffon told me that she intended to do them in tambour stitch anyway. She thinks it is more respectable or something, I am not sure, I didn't quite get what she meant. And then, you wrote about a frill, and she said something about that too, but I forget what she told me about the frill. I only remember that she said a lot, the horrid woman. What was it all about though? Ah, I'm sure she'll tell it all to you herself. I, my dear, have completely lost my head. I didn't even go to the office today. Still, I don't see any need for you to despair. I am prepared to go around to all the stores if that can bring you peace of mind. You write that you're afraid to look into the future. Why, you'll find out all about it today at around six. Madame Chiffon will come to see you in person. So don't despair, my sweet, hope, and perhaps everything will turn out for the best—you'll see. Ah, I can't get that miserable frill out of my head! That frill, that frill! I would've liked so much to come over to see you, my angel. I would come if I could. I've even been to the gates of your house a couple of times. But there's Bykov, I mean, Mr. Bykov, and he is always cross and so it's really difficult. . . . Well, what can we do?

Makar Devushkin

September 28

Dear Makar Alexeyevich,

For God's sake, rush over to. the jeweler's right away and tell him that I don't want the pearl and emerald earrings. Mr. Bykov says they would be too expensive, that they would run to too much. He is angry and says that, as it is, the whole thing is costing him a lot, and that we are robbing him. Indeed, he told me yesterday that if he had known it would involve such expense, he would never have got into it in the first place. He says that as soon as we're married we'll leave town, that in the country we'll have no visitors, that I shouldn't hope that there'll be much opportunity for dancing and flirtations there, that the holidays are still a good way off. That's the way he talks. But God is my witness, I never even wanted these things! It was Mr. Bykov who ordered everything himself. I daren't answer him, he is so hot-tempered. What will become of me?

V. D.

September 28

My dear Varvara Alexeyevna,

I . . . that is the jeweler, says it's all right. As for me, I am ill and can't get out of bed. Now, just when there are so many things for me to do, I had to catch this miserable cold! I must tell you that, to top it all, His Excellency was in a very stern mood too, and got very angry with Emelyan Ivanovich, shouted at him, and in the end got quite upset, the poor man. As you see, I keep you posted on what is going on here. I wanted to write more, but I don't wish to impose on you. The thing is, my sweet, I am a common, stupid man, and I write the first thing that comes into my head, while you, over there, you may . . . Well, there's nothing I can do about it!

Yours,

MAKAR DEVUSHKIN

September 29

Varvara Alexeyevna, my dear,

I saw Fedora today, my sweet, and she told me that you're getting married tomorrow, that you're leaving town the day after, and that Mr. Bykov has already ordered the horses for the trip. I have already written to you about His Excellency, my angel. Another thing: I have checked the bills from the store on Gorokhovaya Street. It is all correct, although very expensive. But I can't understand why Mr. Bykov is angry with you. Well, I hope you'll be happy, my sweet! I am very pleased for you and I shall be so glad if you are happy! I would have come to the church, my dear, but I can't with my lumbago. Well, what worries me is our letters—how will we get them to each other now, my dear? Ah yes, you were very kind to Fedora, my sweet. It was very good of you, a very noble deed and, for each noble deed, God will reward you. Good deeds never go unrewarded, and virtue is always crowned by divine justice, sooner or later. Ah, Varinka, there are so many things I would like to write to you. I would like to write to you every hour, every minute of my life, to write and write! I still have your book, Pushkin's stories, you know. Well, don't take it away from me. Give it to me as a present, my dear. I ask this not because I want to read it especially. But, as you know yourself, winter is drawing near. The evenings are getting long, and they'll make me feel sad and lonely, and so I'll read. I will move from my place to your former apartment, and will rent a room there next to Fedora. I'll never part from that honest woman now, my dear, and, besides, she is such a hard worker. Yesterday I went over and had a good look at your deserted room. Your embroidery frame was still there, standing in a corner just as it used to be, with a piece of work on it. I looked at your handiwork. There were also all sorts of little scraps there, and I saw you had begun winding thread on one of my letters. On the small table I found a scrap of paper with the words "Dear Makar Alexeyevich, I hasten . . ." and that's all there was. Someone must have interrupted you at the most interesting point. In the corner behind the screen, I saw your bed . . . Ah, my dearest! ! ! Well, good-by, good-by, and please, please, answer this note quickly.

MAKAR DEVUSHKIN

September 30

My dear, dear friend Makar Alexeyevich,

It's done. The die is cast! I don't know what will happen, but I am resigned to God's will. We are leaving town tomorrow. This is my final good-by, my dearest friend, my own, my benefactor! Don't grieve, live happily, remember me, and may God bless you! I will often think of you, and mention you in my prayers.

So this period of my life is over! There are very few happy memories I have to take with me into my new life, and so the thought of you will be so much the more precious to my heart. You are my only friend, the only one to love me here. I saw everything, you know, I was very well aware that you loved me! Just a smile from me, just one line written were enough to make you happy. Well, you will have to get used to being without me. How will you manage, left all alone? Who will look after you, my dear, kind, unforgettable friend, my only friend? I am leaving you the book, the embroidery frame, and the beginning of the letter. Every time you look at those words, imagine to yourself all that you would have wished me to write to you. And wouldn't I like to write now! Remember your poor Varinka who has loved you so very much. I have left all your letters in Fedora's chest of drawers, in the top drawer. You write that you are ill in bed, but Mr. Bykov won't let me out of the house today. I will write to you, my dear, I promise you, but then, God alone knows what may happen. And so, let's say good-by forever, my dearest, my own friend. Ah, how I would like to hug you just now! Farewell then, my dear, farewell, be happy, look after your health. I will always pray for you. Ah, I feel so sad, there is such a weight on my heart. Mr. Bykov is calling me now.

Your ever loving,
V.

P.S. My heart is brimming over . . . Tears are choking me. I feel torn. Good-by. Ah, my God, it's so sad! Don't forget your poor Varinka.

[No date.]

My dearest, dearest Varinka,

They are taking you away, carrying you off! I would rather they had torn the heart out of my chest! How could you! Here, you are crying, but you're leaving! The letter I received from you was all smudged with tears. So you don't want to leave then. So you are being taken away by force, so you are sorry for me then, so you love me! What will happen

now? With whom will you be now? Your little heart will be
sad, sick, and cold out there; boredom will drain it, and
despair will tear it in half. You'll die there, and they will
bury you in the damp ground, and there won't even be anyone to cry for you. Mr. Bykov will be too busy trapping his
hares. Ah, Varinka, Varinka, why did you have to decide to
go through with such a thing? What have you done? What
have you done to yourself? They'll push you into your
grave over there. They'll be the death of you, my little angel.
Why, you're so delicate, my sweet, you're light as a feather
. . . And where was I all this time? Where were my eyes, old
fool that I am! Couldn't I see that the child was delirious,
that the child's little head was hot and aching . . . Instead of
simply saying no and making an end of it . . . Fool that I am,
it didn't occur to me . . . as though it was all right, as though
it were none of my concern . . . And I even ran to find out
about that frill! . . . No, Varinka, I'll get up tomorrow, for
perhaps by tomorrow I will have recovered and so I will get
up! . . . And then, my dear, I will throw myself under the
wheels; I won't let you be driven away! No really, what's
going on? What right do they have to do it? I'll come with
you; I'll run after your carriage, if you won't take me along.
I will run as hard as I can, as long as there is breath left in
me. Do you have any idea where you are going, my dear?
Perhaps you have no idea. So why don't you ask me then?
There's the steppes there, my dear, nothing but the steppes,
bare like the palm of my hand. The women are insensitive
there, and the men ignorant and drunken peasants. The
leaves have fallen from the trees there, it's raining and cold—
but still you're going there! Mr. Bykov, he has an occupation there—he has those hares, but what about you, my
sweet? So you want to live like a landowner, dear? But just
look at yourself, my cherub. Do you really think you look
like a lady landowner? How can it be possible, Varinka? To
whom will I send my letters now? Yes, just think: whom
will I write to now? Whom will I call my sweet now? Yes,
who will there be to call by that tender name? Where will I
find you now, my angel? I'll die, Varinka. I'm sure I'll die,
for my heart won't stand such a blow! I loved you like God's
world itself, like my own daughter. I loved everything in
you, my sweet, my own. My only reason for living was for
you! I have worked and copied documents and walked
around and written down my observations on paper in the

form of friendly letters—I did all that, my dear, because you were living here, next to me. Perhaps you didn't know it, but it is just as I say! Just listen to me, my sweet, just think— how can you possibly leave us? But you may not go on that journey, my dear. It is absolutely impossible for you to leave! Why, it's raining and, delicate as you are, you are certain to catch cold. Your carriage will get soaked through, it's bound to. And as soon as you drive out past the city barrier, it will break down. Yes, your carriage is bound to break down. Mark my words. They are very bad at making carriages here in Petersburg. I know all the carriage-makers, and I tell you, they are only good for building models of a carriage, a toy, but not for producing something solid. I swear they don't build them solidly. I'll go down on my knees before Mr. Bykov, my sweet. I'll prove it to him. I'll prove everything to him! And you too, my sweet, prove it to him. Make him see reason! Tell him that you're not going with him, that you've decided to stay! Why didn't he marry that merchant's widow in Moscow? She would've suited him much better, I guarantee that! And you, I would have kept you here, near me. And anyway, what is he to you, that Bykov? What could have endeared him to you so suddenly? Was it because he bought you all those frills? Was that the reason? But what are frills? What good are they? It's all nonsense, Varinka! A human life is at stake here, while frills are nothing but rags, after all! Anyway, wait till I get my salary, I'll buy you lots of frills myself, sweetie. There's a little store I know of—well, if only you could wait till I'm paid . . . Ah, dear God! So you feel you must absolutely leave for the steppes with Mr. Bykov, leave and never return! Ah, my sweet! No, write me another letter, telling me about everything. When you get there, write to me again. For otherwise, my heavenly angel, this will be my last letter, and it just cannot be that it is really the very last one! Why should it be, suddenly and for no reason, the very last one! No, no, I'll go on writing and you must write to me too. . . . I am acquiring a style now. . . . Ah, my sweet, what do I care about style! Why, I don't even know what I'm writing now. I have no idea, none at all. I don't reread myself. I don't correct my style. I just write for the sake of writing, just to write to you as much as possible. . . . My Varinka, my dearest, ah, my sweet!

THE DOUBLE

Chapter 1

IT WAS ALMOST eight o'clock in the morning when
Yakov Petrovich Golyadkin, a minor government official,
awoke from a long sleep, yawned, stretched, and at last actually opened his eyes. For a couple of minutes he lay motionless in his bed, as though not quite certain whether he was
awake or still asleep, whether the things around him were
real or the continuation of his chaotic dreams. Soon enough,
however, Golyadkin started to receive the usual everyday
impressions more clearly and distinctly. He recognized the
grimy, greenish walls of his little room, coated with soot and
dust, the mahogany chest of drawers, the imitation mahogany
table and chairs, the sofa covered with reddish oilcloth with
green flowers on it, and finally his clothes which he had taken
off in haste the night before and which now lay on the sofa
in a crumpled pile. Finally the gray autumn day, murky and
dirty, peeped into his room through the pale window with
such a sour expression that Golyadkin could no longer doubt
that he was not in some enchanted land of milk and honey,
but in his apartment on the fourth floor of a rather bulky
apartment house on Six Shop Street, in Petersburg.

Having made this important discovery, Golyadkin shuddered and closed his eyes, apparently regretting his vanished
dream and trying to recapture it for a moment at least. But
a minute later he leaped out of bed, probably having at last
hit on the idea around which up till then his scattered, still
uncontrolled thoughts had been wandering. Once up, he

went straight to a small round mirror that stood on top of his chest of drawers. Although the sleepy, short-sighted face and balding brow that the mirror reflected was so unimpressive that at first sight it couldn't possibly arrest anyone's attention, its owner seemed quite satisfied with what he saw.

"Wouldn't it be something," Golyadkin muttered under his breath, "if there were something wrong with me today, if something weren't right, if, for instance, I found an unfamiliar pimple or some other unpleasant thing? But everything's all right so far, everything's fine."

Golyadkin, very pleased that everything was fine, replaced the mirror. Then, although he was still wearing his night clothes, he scampered over to the window and started looking very intently for something in the yard which the window of his apartment faced. Apparently he found what he was seeking, for his face lighted up with a self-satisfied grin.

Then he peeped behind the partition into the cubicle of his servant, Petrushka. Finding that Petrushka wasn't there, he tiptoed to the table, unlocked a drawer, fumbled in its farthest corner, fished out a greenish, worn-out wallet from under a pile of yellowed papers and all sorts of junk, carefully opened it, and looked inside a secret pocket. Apparently the wad of green, gray, blue, red and multicolored bills was a gladdening sight to Mr. Golyadkin's eyes for, smiling brightly, he placed the open wallet on the table in front of him and rubbed his hands as a sign of the greatest delight. Then he pulled out the comforting wad of bills and, for the hundredth time since the day before yesterday, recounted the money, daintily holding up each bill between his forefinger and thumb.

"Seven hundred and fifty rubles in bills," he announced to himself in a half-whisper. "A respectable sum, a very nice sum," he went on in a weak voice which quivered slightly with pleasure. "Anyone would be delighted to have such a sum; I have yet to meet a man for whom such a sum would be trivial. That much money could take a man very far. . . . But where on earth is Petrushka?" Mr. Golyadkin suddenly thought.

Still wearing his night clothes, he peeped behind the partition once more. Petrushka still wasn't there, but the samovar was huffing and puffing angrily on the floor, beside itself with fury and threatening to run away as it lisped something heatedly at Golyadkin in its complicated language, probably something like: "Please take me, can't you, man. I'm boiling and quite ready."

"Where can that damned Petrushka be hiding?" Golyadkin thought. "The lazy animal is enough to drive a man mad."

In righteous ire he stepped out into the entry, which consisted of a short passage at the end of which was the door leading onto the landing. He opened the entrance door a crack and caught sight of his servant surrounded by a considerable crowd of flunkeys and other rabble. Petrushka was holding forth on some topic while the others were listening.

Golyadkin must have disapproved of the topic of conversation or of the very fact that it was taking place at all. Looking displeased, even upset, he ordered Petrushka to come in at once. Then he went back to his room, thinking: "That brute would sell anyone for half a kopeck, especially his master, and I bet he's already sold me. I'm sure he has, and maybe for less than a kopeck. . . ."

"Well, what's going on?" Mr. Golyadkin asked.

"They've delivered the livery, sir."

"Put it on and then come here."

Petrushka put on his livery and, smiling stupidly, came into his master's room. His outfit was rather striking. He now wore a green, considerably worn livery, with frayed gold braid, that had apparently been made for a man a yard taller than he. In his hand he held a hat also trimmed with gold braid and with green feathers in it; at his side dangled a flunkey's sword in a leather sheath. To complete the picture, Petrushka, an informal dresser by inclination, was barefoot, as he usually was at home.

Golyadkin examined Petrushka from all sides and seemed satisfied. Obviously the livery had been rented for some special, solemn occasion. During this inspection, Petrushka looked at his master with an air of strange expectation, watching his every movement, which embarrassed Mr. Golyadkin extremely.

"Well, and what about the carriage?"

"The carriage is here too, sir."

"For the whole day?"

"Yes, sir, and it'll be twenty-five rubles."

"And the shoes? Have they brought them?"

"They have."

"Ah, you damn fool! Can't you say, 'They have, sir!' Bring them in here!"

Golyadkin found that the shoes fitted well and expressed his satisfaction. Then he ordered Petrushka to bring him warm water to wash and shave, and to serve him his tea. He was very thorough about his washing and shaving, took a few swallows of tea, and attacked the final phase of his toilet. He slipped into an almost new pair of trousers, put on a shirtfront with brass buttons, donned a waistcoat adorned with rather bright and attractive flowers, tied a multicolored silk cravat round his neck, and finally put on his formal dress coat, which was also quite new and very carefully brushed. As he dressed, Golyadkin glanced lovingly at his shoes several times, kept lifting first one foot then the other, admiring the style of his footwear, all the time whispering something under his breath, and now and then winking understandingly at his own thoughts.

Actually he was very absent-minded that morning for he went on like that, hardly noticing the grins and smirks Petrushka was directing at him as he helped him to dress.

At last, when he felt he was dressed and ready, Golyadkin put his wallet in his pocket and threw an approving glance at Petrushka who, in the meantime, had put on his boots and was thus also quite ready. And since there was nothing more to delay them, Golyadkin fussily and hurriedly trotted downstairs, his heart throbbing slightly.

A pale-blue hired carriage decorated with some sort of coat of arms rolled up to the doorstep with a thunderous rattle. Petrushka, exchanging winks with the driver and some loiterers, assisted his master into the carriage and, only just managing not to burst out into idiotic laughter, shouted to the driver, in an unnatural voice, "Let's go," and jumped onto the step. Then the whole turnout, rattling, rumbling, ringing, and clattering, rolled toward the Nevsky Prospect.

As soon as the blue carriage drove out of the courtyard gate, Golyadkin nervously rubbed his hands together and went into a soundless chuckle, like some gay blade who had just pulled off an amusing trick and was now delighted by it. But the fit of glee vanished almost at once, and a strangely preoccupied expression appeared on Golyadkin's face. Disregarding the damp and unpleasant weather, he lowered both windows of the carriage and proceeded to scrutinize the people on either side of the street, immediately assuming a dignified air when he became aware that someone was looking at him. As the carriage turned from Liteinaya Street into Nevsky Prospect, Golyadkin suddenly shuddered at an extremely unpleasant sensation, as if someone had stepped on a sore corn, and he huddled hastily into the darkest corner of the carriage, looking quite frightened.

The trouble was that he had caught sight of two young clerks who worked in the same government department as he. They, it seemed to Golyadkin, were also rather bewildered at seeing their associate like that; one of them even pointed his finger at him. Then Golyadkin thought he heard the other clerk call out his name quite loudly, which, of course, was very unseemly in the street. So Mr. Golyadkin ducked out of sight and didn't respond.

"The stupid young fools," Golyadkin thought, "what's so strange about a man riding in a carriage? A man needs a carriage and so he hires one. What nonsense is this? They're nothing but nasty brats and what they need is a good thrashing. All they think of is playing games while drawing their salaries . . . I could tell them what I think of them, but why bother . . ."

Suddenly his thought snapped off and he gaped, terrified. A familiar pair of spry Kazan horses hitched to a flashy carriage was passing him on the right.

The occupant of the vehicle, chancing to notice Mr. Golyadkin who had imprudently stuck his face out of the carriage window, was apparently equally surprised at the encounter. And so, leaning out as far as he could, he was now trying to look into the darkest corner of the carriage, to which our hero had withdrawn. The gentleman's name was Andrei Filipovich, section head of the government department in which Golyadkin was employed as assistant to the chief clerk.

Golyadkin, realizing that Andrei Filipovich had recognized him, that he was now staring at him round-eyed, and that there was no place to hide, blushed to the roots of his hair.

"Should I bow or shouldn't I? Should I acknowledge him? Admit that it is me? Or should I pretend I'm someone else, someone strikingly resembling me, and look completely indifferent?" Golyadkin asked himself in indescribable anguish. "Yes, that's it: I'm not me and that's all there is to it," he thought, his eyes fixed on Andrei Filipovich as he took off his hat to him.

"I, I, I . . . no, nothing, sir," he stammered in a whisper. "The fact is, it's not me . . . Yes, that's all there is to it. . . ."

Soon, however, the carriage passed and the magnetism of the chief's eyes ceased to affect him. But Golyadkin continued to blush and smile.

"I'm a fool," he muttered to himself, "not to have hailed him. I should have taken a bolder line. It would've been more dignified . . . I ought to have simply said, as it were, 'Well, sir, it just happens that I too have been invited to dinner. . . .' That was all I had to tell him."

Then, remembering how he had failed to do so, our hero flushed as hot as fire, knitted his brows, and directed a challenging and threatening glance at the opposite corner of the carriage, a glance intended to reduce all his enemies to ashes. Then, prompted by a strange inspiration, he pulled the cord attached to the driver's elbow and ordered him to turn around and drive back to Liteinaya Street. The reason for this was that Golyadkin suddenly felt he had to impart something most interesting to his doctor, Christian Ivanovich, at once, something which, he thought, would make him feel better. And although he hadn't known the doctor for long—in fact had seen him only once, a week or so before, to consult him about something or other—nevertheless, as they say, a doctor is a bit like a priest, and it would be stupid to hide things from him, for it was part of his duty to know his patients really well.

Golyadkin ordered the driver to stop at a five-story house on Liteinaya Street and, as he stepped down, he thought: "Is it right, though? Is it the proper thing to do? Is it appropriate?" But as he was going upstairs, breathing hard and trying to calm his heart that had a bad habit of pounding when he was going up an unfamiliar staircase, he decided: "Why, after all, the matter concerns only me and there is nothing wrong in my . . . It would actually be very stupid for me to hide things. Well, I will pretend that I just dropped in on him as I was driving by. . . . He'll realize that and see that it's all quite proper."

Reasoning thus, Mr. Golyadkin reached the second floor and stopped before the door of apartment number five, on which there was an attractive plate with the inscription:

CHRISTIAN IVANOVICH RUTENSPITZ
DOCTOR OF MEDICINE AND SURGERY

Our hero stopped and assumed a dignified, casual, rather friendly air before pulling the bell cord. Before he actually pulled it, he asked himself a rather appropriate question: Wouldn't it be better if he came back the next day, since anyway there was nothing urgent about his visit? But, hearing steps on the stairs at that moment, he immediately decided that, since he was already there, he might as well go through with it, and, looking most determined, he pulled the bell cord.

Chapter 2

CHRISTIAN IVANOVICH RUTENSPITZ, M.D. and surgeon, was a vigorous although quite elderly man, endowed with thick gray eyebrows and whiskers, an expressive and sparkling gaze which by itself could cure all ailments, and an important decoration in his lapel. That morning, he was sitting in a comfortable armchair in his office, drinking coffee brought to him by his wife, puffing from time to time at a cigar and writing out prescriptions for his patients. After he had prescribed some medicine for a little old man complaining of hemorrhoids and had seen the aged patient out of the side door, Christian Ivanovich sat back in the armchair, waiting for the next patient. And in walked Mr. Golyadkin.

Apparently Christian Ivanovich hadn't expected to see Golyadkin, nor did he seem in the least delighted at the sight of him, for his face expressed embarrassment at first and even had a certain air of displeasure. For his part, Mr. Golyadkin almost always stumbled most unfortunately and felt quite lost when he had to approach someone about his private affairs, and so now, having failed to prepare the opening words, which were like stepping stones for him in such cases, he became completely confused; he muttered something that might perhaps have been an apology and, not knowing what to do next, took a chair and sat down.

But realizing immediately that he had sat down without having been invited to do so, he stood up again, hoping thus to retrieve his faux pas. Then, vaguely realizing that he had made two faux pas one after the other, he immediately decided to commit a third and, smiling brightly, muttered some explanation, then turned beet red, lost the thread of what he was saying, became expressively silent, sat down, and this time didn't get up again. But, to be on the safe side, he looked straight ahead with that withering gaze which had the imaginary power of reducing all Mr. Golyadkin's enemies to dust and ashes. In addition, this gaze expressed Mr. Golyadkin's independence, informing the world that there was nothing wrong with him, that he was just like the next man, and that, in any event, he didn't meddle in other people's affairs.

The doctor coughed, grunted, apparently approving and accepting it all, and fixed on Golyadkin the questioning eye of an inspector.

"I must bother you for a second time, doctor," Golyadkin said with a smile, "and, for the second time I must beg your indulgence. . . ." Obviously, he was having difficulty finding the right words.

"Hm . . . yes!" the doctor said, spouting a jet of smoke from his mouth and putting his cigar down on the table. "But you absolutely must stick to the prescribed treatment. Why, I've explained to you that a change will do you good. You need distraction, you see. Well, I mean something like visiting friends and also remember that the bottle is no enemy either. You understand, keep up with good company, hmm?"

Still smiling, Mr. Golyadkin hurriedly remarked that it seemed to him he was just like everyone else, that he had his own place, that he distracted himself just like the next man, that, of course, he could go to the theater if he felt like it, because he could afford it just as well as anyone, that during the day he was in his office and in the evening in his apartment, and that he was really fine. He even managed to put in, apropos of nothing, that as far as he could see he was no worse than others, that after all he lived in his own apartment and, finally, that he had a valet, Petrushka. At this point, he began to cough and stopped short.

"Hm, that wasn't really what I meant," the doctor said. "I didn't ask you that at all. What I was trying to find out from you was whether, in general, you like gay company, whether you spend your time pleasantly . . . Well, whether you arrange your life according to a sad pattern or a gay one?"

"You see, doctor . . ."

"Hm! . . . I was trying to say," Christian Ivanovich said, "that you must radically change your way of life and, in a sense, your character must *break*." Christian Ivanovich stressed the last word heavily and paused for a moment with a very meaningful expression on his face. "You must not shun a gay life; you must attend theaters, go to your club and, whatever you do, display no hostility toward the bottle. And sitting at home is harmful for you. . . . Whatever else you do, sitting at home is out for you."

"The thing is, doctor," Golyadkin said, casting a significant glance at Christian Ivanovich and apparently searching for the right words to express his thought, "I like quiet, and there's no one in my apartment except myself and Petrushka . . . I mean my servant, doctor. I mean by that, Christian Ivanovich, that I follow my own path, my own personal road. I am an independent man, doctor, and as far as I can see, I do not depend on anyone. And then, doctor, I do go out for a walk now and then like everyone else."

"What? Ah, I see! But, these days there's nothing so specially pleasant about going out for a walk, since the weather is so bad."

"That's right, doctor. Well, you see, doctor, although I am a quiet man, as I've already had the honor of telling you, nevertheless, my path is a separate one, doctor. The path of life is wide . . . I mean by that . . . What I am trying to say, doctor . . . Well, you must forgive me, sir, I'm not a very eloquent talker."

"Hm . . . We were saying . . ."

"I was about to ask you to excuse me for not being an eloquent speaker," Golyadkin said in a half-offended tone, stumbling and nearly losing the thread of what he was saying. "In this respect I am not like others," he added with a strange smile. "Indeed, I am unable to speak for a long time and I haven't learned to make my words sound beautiful. But, when it comes to deeds, doctor, I do act. Please believe me, doctor, I do act!"

"Hm . . . What do you mean when you say you act?" the doctor inquired.

A brief silence followed. Christian Ivanovich gave Golyadkin a strange, distrustful look and he, in turn, cast an incredulous, sidelong glance at the doctor.

"I, doctor," Golyadkin resumed in his former tone, slightly taken aback and irritated by the doctor's stubbornness, "I happen to like quiet rather than worldly hustle and bustle. In high society, a man must be good at polishing parquet with his shoes." At this point, Golyadkin slightly scraped his foot on the floor. "That's what they demand of you. And on top of that, they demand that you be a wit. But I, doctor, have never learned their tricks, never mastered all those clever ways. I've had no time. I am a simple, unpretentious fellow, doctor, and there's nothing conspicuously brilliant about me. I must concede, doctor, that, in that sense, I lay down my arms."

Golyadkin said all that with an expression which conveyed that he was not in the least bit sad at "laying down his arms," and that he was not sorry at "not having learned their tricks." Indeed, just the opposite. Christian Ivanovich listened to him with an extremely unpleasant grin, as if expecting something to happen. When Golyadkin had ended his tirade, a long and heavy silence followed.

"I believe you've strayed from the subject slightly," the doctor said at last, "and I confess I didn't quite follow you."

"Well, I'm no orator. I'm not very good at expressing myself eloquently, doctor, as I've already had the honor of telling you," Golyadkin said with sharp determination now.

"Hm . . ."

"Doctor," Golyadkin began quietly but in a weighty, rather solemn tone, pausing after every sentence, "doctor, when I stepped in here, I started by apologizing. Now, I repeat, and ask you once more to bear with me for a bit. I have nothing to conceal from you, doctor. I am an insignificant man, as you well know, but, luckily, I do not mind being insignificant. In fact, I am proud not to be someone important, but just a little man. I am also proud that I do not go in for intrigue. I do not do things behind people's backs, but openly, and although I could have harmed many if I had chosen to do so—and I know very well whom I could harm and how—I do not wish to dirty myself by doing so, and in this sense, doctor, I wash my hands." Here Golyadkin, who had been speaking with meek passion, lapsed into a brief and dramatic pause.

"So I go my way, doctor," he went on, "straight ahead, scorning devious paths which I leave to others. I do not despise those who are, perhaps, worse than you and us—I mean them and us—I didn't mean to involve you, doctor. I dislike insinuations, I have nothing but contempt for duplicity and do not go in for gossip and slander. I only put on a mask when I go to a masquerade, and don't wear one every day when I meet people. The only thing I wish to ask you, doctor, is how would you avenge yourself on your worst enemy—on a man whom you considered such?" And Golyadkin looked challengingly at Christian Ivanovich.

Although he had spoken with the utmost clarity and assurance, weighing the effect he was producing, there was an uneasiness, indeed, an immense uneasiness in his eyes as he looked at the doctor. He had become all eyes now and was watching Christian Ivanovich timidly, anxiously, and impatiently.

But to Golyadkin's great surprise, the doctor just mumbled something under his breath, pulled his chair closer to the table and, very dryly, although courteously, said something to the effect that he didn't have any time to spare, that, somehow, he didn't quite understand; that, although he would have been happy to do anything he could for Mr. Golyadkin, he had to decline to get involved in things that were none of his concern. Then he tore a piece of paper from his prescription pad, picked up a pen, and informed Golyadkin that he was about to prescribe what he needed.

"No, doctor, no need for that, no need for that at all!" Golyadkin got up and seized the doctor's right hand. "No, doctor, I'm sure there's no need for it."

But while Golyadkin was saying this, a peculiar change came over him. His gray eyes flashed in a strange way, his lips trembled, all the muscles of his face were set in motion, all his features began to twitch. Then the whole of Golyadkin began to shake. Having followed his impulse and stopped the doctor's hand as it was preparing to write, Golyadkin now stood motionless, as if not trusting himself and waiting for an inspiration to act further.

Then a very unusual scene occurred.

Christian Ivanovich was slightly puzzled and seemed to have grown into his chair. He was staring at Golyadkin, who was staring back at him. At last Christian Ivanovich scrambled to his feet, taking a gentle hold of the lapel of Golyadkin's coat. For several seconds they stood there without taking their eyes off each other. Then this caused another very peculiar thing to happen to Golyadkin: his lips twisted, his chin started to jerk up and down, and he quite unexpectedly burst into tears. Sobbing, shaking his head, pounding his chest with his right hand while his left caught the lapel of the doctor's coat, he tried to speak, to explain something, but was unable to utter a word. In the meantime, the doctor recovered from his surprise.

"Come, calm yourself, sit down," the doctor said, trying to install Golyadkin in the armchair.

"I have enemies, doctor, vicious enemies, who have sworn to ruin me," Golyadkin mumbled in a terrified whisper.

"Oh, come now, what enemies can you have? No need for you to be thinking of enemies, no need at all. Just sit down, please, sit down," the doctor said, determinedly pushing Golyadkin into the armchair.

Finally Golyadkin sat down, his eyes still glued on the doctor, who was now pacing from one corner of the room to the other, looking highly displeased. A long silence followed.

"I'm very grateful to you, doctor, very grateful indeed. I greatly appreciate what you've done for me. As long as I live, I'll never forget your kindness, doctor." And Golyadkin stood up, looking very hurt.

"Stop it, stop it. I'm asking you to stop it," Christian Ivanovich said, rather sternly, once again sitting Golyadkin back in the armchair. "Well, tell me. What is the matter with you? Tell me what is bothering you. And who are these enemies you mentioned? What's going on? Tell me now."

"No, doctor, we'd better leave that for now. We'll get to it at some more appropriate time, when everything comes out into the open and when the masks fall from certain faces. But for now, after what has happened between us, you must agree yourself, doctor . . . Well, allow me to wish you a good day, sir." This time Golyadkin stood up with real determination and picked up his hat.

"Well . . . hm, suit yourself . . ." the doctor said and after a long pause added: "I, for my part, am doing my best . . . and I wish you the very best too."

"I understand, doctor, I understand you perfectly now . . . In any case, please forgive me for having disturbed you, sir."

"Hm, that's not really what I meant. But suit yourself. As to the medicines, just go on with the same doses as before. . . ."

"I will go on taking your medicines and I'll keep buying

them at the same chemist's. Nowadays it's certainly a great business to be a chemist, isn't it?"

"What? In what sense do you mean?"

"In the most usual sense, doctor. I mean that that's the way the world spins these days."

"Hm . . ."

"And every young fellow—and not only a chemist's assistant—looks down on a respectable man."

"Hm, and how do you account for that?"

"I have in mind a well-known person, doctor, a man we both know, Vladimir Semyonovich, for instance. . . ."

"Ah!"

"Yes, sir, and I also know people who do not feel bound to always follow public opinion and aren't afraid of the truth now and then."

"Ah, and how is that?"

"Just like that. But then, this has nothing to do with what we have been talking about. I simply meant that there are people who occasionally know how to butter you up."

"To do what?"

"To butter you up, doctor. It's just an expression. It means there are people who know how to congratulate some-one at the right time."

"Congratulate?"

"Yes, congratulate, just as one of my very close acquaint-ances did a few days ago!"

"One of your close acquaintances? . . . Ah! How is that?" the doctor asked, looking intently at Golyadkin.

"Yes, a very close acquaintance of mine congratulated another acquaintance of mine—and, what's more, a friend, a dear friend as they say—on having been promoted to the rank of collegiate assessor. It was as if it just came out by accident: 'I'm delighted,' it said, 'to offer you, Vladimir Semyonovich, my warmest congratulations, my most *sincere* congratulations, on your promotion. And I am so much the more delighted in that, as all the world knows, old women who tell fortunes have died out now.'"

And Golyadkin, screwing up his face, looked slyly at Christian Ivanovich.

"Hm, so that was the way he put it."

"He did, and as he said it, he gave Andrei Filipovich, our dear Vladimir Semyonovich's uncle, one of those looks. But what is it to me that he has been promoted? What do

I get out of it? But he wants to marry, even though his mother's milk, if you'll pardon the expression, isn't even dry on his lips. That's exactly what I said, too. I said to him, 'Vladimir Semyonovich, I've said what I had to say and so, with your permission, I'll take my leave.'"

"Hm . . ."

"Yes, doctor, that's what I said. 'I'll take my leave.' But then, while I was at it, I decided to kill two birds with one stone. After giving it to that young fellow with that remark about fortune-telling grannies, I turned to Klara Olsufievna (this happened the day before yesterday at Olsufy Ivanovich's), as she'd just finished singing a very moving romance, and I said to her, 'You certainly can sing those touching songs, but people don't listen to your singing with pure hearts,' and by that I was hinting clearly to her that they weren't really looking at her, but past her. . . ."

"Well, and what did the young man do then?"

"He just had to swallow it, as the saying goes, doctor."

"Hm."

"Yes, doctor, and then I said to the old man himself, 'Olsufy Ivanovich,' I said, 'I know how much indebted to you I am for all the kindnesses you have bestowed upon me since I was hardly more than a boy, but open your eyes, Olsufy Ivanovich,' I said. 'I am being frank and aboveboard.'"

"Ah, so, I see."

"Yes, doctor, that's how it is."

"So, what did he say?"

"Well, what can I tell you, doctor? He just mumbled something about knowing me for a long time and that His Excellency was a gracious person and so on and so forth. . . . Well, looks as if he's got a bit shaky in his old age."

"So that's how it is."

"Yes, doctor, and that's the way we'll all end up. Poor old fellow! He has one foot in the grave already, but as soon as it comes to a bit of gossip, there he is with his ears pricked up, listening. He's in on everything."

"Gossip, did you say?"

"Yes, doctor, they've been spreading a certain rumor around, and our Bear's got involved in it too, and his lovely nephew. They're in league with the old cronies and, of course, they cooked up the whole business. And what do you think they've thought up? Nothing less than murder."

"Murder?"

"Yes, doctor, murder. The moral assassination of a human being. They have spread ... I'm still talking about my friend, of course."

The doctor nodded.

"They've spread a rumor about him. ... I feel positively embarrassed to talk about it, doctor."

"Hm."

"They've spread a rumor that he gave a written promise to marry, that, on the other hand, he was already engaged ... Now take a guess, doctor, whom is he to marry?"

"Well, whom?"

"A German woman of shaky reputation who runs an eating house where he takes his meals. They claim that instead of paying the bill for his meals, he is offering her his hand."

"Is that what they say?"

"Would you believe it, doctor? Marry that nasty, vulgar, repulsive, shameless German woman, Karolina Ivanovna, if you know ..."

"I admit that, for my part ..."

"I understand what you mean, doctor, and I feel that way myself."

"Tell me, please, where do you live now?"

"Where do I live now, doctor?"

"Yes ... I wanted ... I believe you used to live ..."

"Right, doctor, I used to ... I used to ... just as you said. I don't deny it." Golyadkin accompanied his words with a little chuckle and saw that Christian Ivanovich was somewhat disconcerted by his reply.

"No, you didn't get me right; for my part, I wanted ..."

"I also wanted, on my side," Golyadkin said with a laugh. "But I feel I have detained you long enough, doctor, and I hope you will allow me to wish you good day now."

"Hm."

"Yes, doctor, I understand you now, I understand you perfectly," Golyadkin said, showing off slightly before Christian Ivanovich. "And so allow me to wish you a pleasant day."

And, clicking his heels, he walked out, leaving the doctor extremely perplexed.

As he went downstairs, Golyadkin smiled and rubbed his hands. On the doorstep he took a breath of fresh air, feeling free and relieved. He was even prepared to claim that he was the happiest mortal on earth. He was about to start walking toward his office without thinking, when suddenly his carriage pulled up to the curb with a rumble. The sight of it reminded him of everything. Petrushka opened the door. A peculiar uneasiness gripped Golyadkin. For one second, he looked embarrassed. Something had stung him. He had already raised his foot to the carriage step when he turned round and glanced at Christian Ivanovich's window. And sure enough, the doctor was standing there, stroking his sidewhiskers with his right hand and looking at Golyadkin with considerable curiosity.

"He's stupid, that doctor," Golyadkin thought, taking refuge inside the carriage, "extremely stupid. He may be good at curing his patients but that doesn't prevent him from being as stupid as an old log."

When Mr. Golyadkin was comfortably installed, Petrushka shouted, "Go!" and the carriage rolled toward Nevsky Prospect.

Chapter 3

THE WHOLE MORNING was spent rushing madly around. When they reached the Nevsky Prospect, Golyadkin ordered the driver to stop at the Gostiny Dvor arcade. Leaping out of the carriage, he darted under the arcade, followed by Petrushka. There, he went straight into a store that handled gold and silver items. One could tell by just looking at Mr. Golyadkin that he was a terribly busy man, indeed that he had his hands full. After some energetic bargaining, he agreed with the merchant on a complete dinner and tea service for fifteen hundred rubles and then talked the man into letting him have a cigar case of ingenious design and a complete silver shaving set for the same price. He also inquired about the prices of several other pleasant and useful items and ended up by promising to come without fail the next day, or perhaps even to send someone over that very day to pick up the selected articles. He even took down the exact address of the shop, and listening attentively to the merchant's pleas for a small deposit, promised that he would have it, when the time came.

Then, hurriedly leaving the perplexed shopkeeper, he set out along the line of stores followed by a whole flock of hangers-on. He kept turning toward Petrushka to consult him, all the time busily searching for some other store. On his way, he stopped in at a money-changer's and changed all his big bills for ones of smaller denominations, and although he came out of this transaction a bit poorer, his wallet was now considerably fatter and that obviously pleased him no end.

He stopped at last in a store where they sold ladies' dress materials. Again, after picking out goods for an impressive sum, Golyadkin promised the merchant to come to collect his purchases later, again wrote down the address of the store, and, when again asked for a little deposit, gave the same answer—that the deposit, too, would be taken care of at the right time.

After that he visited several more shops, in every one of which he inquired the price of various items and bargained with the shopkeeper, sometimes at great length, walking out two or three times, then coming back to bargain some more. In brief, he displayed tremendous activity.

From Gostiny Dvor, Golyadkin went to a famous furniture store and chose furniture for a six room apartment, admired a lady's dressing table in the latest style, promised the merchant that he would have the furniture picked up, and promised a deposit too. After that he stopped somewhere else and did some pricing and bargaining there. There seemed to be no end to all the things he had to take care of. Finally, Golyadkin himself appeared to grow quite sick and tired of it all. Indeed, God knows why, he even felt some pangs of conscience.

He would have hated, for instance, to meet Andrei Filipovich or even the doctor now.

At last the town clock struck three and Golyadkin climbed back into the carriage. All he had to show for his morning's shopping was a pair of gloves and a bottle of perfume worth one and a half rubles. Deciding that it was still too early for what he had to do, he stopped his carriage near a famous restaurant on the Nevsky Prospect, which he only knew by hearsay, and walked in to have a bite and relax for a while, until the time came.

He ate lightly, just to keep himself from starving, like a man who has a big formal dinner party ahead of him, drank one glass of vodka, sat down in an armchair, and, after taking a quick, shy look around, settled down behind a thin nationalist daily. He read a couple of lines, got up, glanced into a mirror, straightened his cravat, smoothed his hair, walked over to the window, and checked whether his carriage was still there. Then he resumed his seat and again picked up the newspaper. He was visibly agitated. He glanced at the clock and saw it was only a quarter past three. He had still a long time to wait. Deciding that it was awkward to just sit there like that, he ordered himself a cup of chocolate, although he didn't really want it at all right then. He drank it, saw that the time had gone ahead a bit, and was going to pay at the desk when suddenly someone slapped him on the shoulder.

He turned around and saw the two clerks from his department whom he had met that morning on Liteinaya Street, two fellows still young in years and junior in position. Golyadkin was neither on friendly nor on openly hostile terms with them. They had kept up decent relations but had never reached a stage of familiarity, nor could they possibly have. Meeting them now was very unpleasant to Golyadkin. He screwed up his face slightly and for a moment felt rather at a loss what to do.

"Mr. Golyadkin! Yakov Petrovich Golyadkin!" the two young registering clerks chirped excitedly. "What's the great oc . . .?"

"Oh, it's you, gentlemen," Golyadkin interrupted hurriedly, a bit embarrassed and irritated by the clerks' surprise at seeing him there and by their familiarity, but playing the part of a good fellow which was forced upon him. "So I see you have deserted the office and your duties, gentlemen, ha-ha-ha!"

Then to emphasize what an easy-going person he was, without, however, lowering his prestige as a superior dealing with young clerks from whom he felt he had to keep a proper distance, Golyadkin decided to pat one of the young men on the back. But this attempt at familiarity didn't succeed and his gesture looked anything but brief and dignified.

"And what about the Bear, fellows, is he still sitting in the office?"

"Who's that, Mr. Golyadkin?"

"Why, the Bear, of course—as if you didn't know whom they call that!" Mr. Golyadkin laughed and turned toward the cashier to pick up his change. "I was, of course, talking about Andrei Filipovich, gentlemen," he said, in a quite serious tone now, having finished with the cashier. The two young clerks exchanged an understanding glance.

"He's still sitting there and, in fact, asked where you were, Mr. Golyadkin," one of them said.

"So he's still sitting in the office, is he? Well, let him sit there to his heart's content. And you say he asked for me, did he?"

"He did, Mr. Golyadkin, he did. But what's come over you, sir? You're so elegant and perfumed and pomaded and all. What's happened?"

"You don't say, gentlemen, you don't say."

And Golyadkin looked away with a forced smile. Seeing him smile, the two clerks burst out laughing, which offended Golyadkin and made him pout a little.

"Let me tell you something as a friend, gentlemen," he said, in a tone that implied he had decided to condescend and reveal something to the clerks. "Although you know me, you actually know only one side of me. No one is really to blame for that, in fact I must take a part of the blame upon myself."

He pressed his lips tightly together, looking very meaningfully at the two clerks, who again exchanged furtive glances.

"So far, gentlemen, you don't know me at all and this is not the proper time and place for me to explain to you. I'll tell you only a few things in passing. There are people, gentlemen, who dislike devious ways and who only put on masks at masquerades. There are people who do not hold that a man is destined to polish the parquet with the soles of his shoes. There are people who do not feel they are happy and leading a full life just because, for instance, they wear a nicely cut pair of trousers. Finally, there are people who do not enjoy leaping around pointlessly and uselessly, currying favor and flattering and, above all, sticking their noses into places where they haven't been invited. And now, gentlemen, having said what I had to say, I must be off."

Golyadkin stopped talking, since what he had said ought to have been sufficient explanation for the clerks. However, the two young men suddenly started literally rolling around with laughter. Golyadkin flushed.

"You may laugh, gentlemen, laugh now, but we'll live and see," he said with an air of offended dignity, picking up his hat and beginning to move toward the outside door. But then he stopped again and added: "And let me tell you something else. We're alone here, without witnesses. Here is my rule: If I fail, I don't lose courage and if I succeed, I persevere, but without ever trying to undermine anyone. I don't go in for intrigues and I'm proud of it. I would make a very poor diplomat, I know. They say that the bird flies toward the hunter. There's some truth in that. But it isn't certain yet who's the hunter here and who's the bird."

Golyadkin lapsed into an eloquent silence, and with a most dignified expression, that is, with his eyebrows raised and his lips pressed together as tightly as was possible, he bowed to the men and walked out, leaving them in a state of utter bewilderment.

"Where do you wish to go?" Petrushka asked in a rather gruff tone, for he had grown rather tired, waiting in the cold. "Where do you wish to go now, sir?" he repeated, weathering the terrifying, annihilating glare that his master had already used on him twice that day and which he felt he had to employ for a third time now, as he went down the steps from the restaurant.

"To the Izmailovsky Bridge."

"The Izmailovsky Bridge, driver. Let's go!"

"They won't sit down to dinner until after four, perhaps even five," Golyadkin was thinking. "Isn't it a bit early still? But I suppose it won't matter if I get there a bit on the early side. After all, it's a family affair and I don't really have to be all that formal, since we are among the right kind of people, all of us. The bear, too, said it wouldn't be a formal affair, and so I can also . . ."

But while Golyadkin was thinking along these lines, he was becoming more and more worried. Obviously he was preparing for something that was bound to cause him a lot of bother to say the least. He kept whispering under his breath, gesticulating with his right hand, and ceaselessly peeking out of the carriage window. No one who had seen Mr. Golyadkin at that moment would ever have guessed that he was simply going to a family dinner, an informal affair, *sans-façon*, among the right people.

At last, near the Izmailovsky Bridge, Golyadkin pointed out a house, and the carriage, rattling noisily, rolled through the gate into the courtyard.

Catching sight of a female figure in the window, Golyadkin threw her a kiss. Actually he didn't know very well himself what he was doing because he was half alive and half dead at that moment. He was very pale as he stepped out of the carriage and looked completely lost. He walked into the house, removed his hat, unthinkingly straightened his cravat, and started upstairs, feeling that his knees were quivering slightly.

"Is Olsufy Ivanovich in?" he asked the servant who opened the apartment door.

"Yes, sir . . . That is, no sir. The master isn't at home."

"How's that, friend? Why, I've come for dinner. You surely must know who I am, don't you?"

"Certainly I know, sir, and I've been ordered not to let you in."

"You . . . you must be mistaken, friend. It's me, and I've been invited to dinner," Golyadkin said, removing his overcoat and leaving no doubt about his intention of going inside.

"Please, sir, you can't come in. I was told not to let you. That's how it is!"

Golyadkin turned white. At that moment the door leading to the rest of the apartment opened and Gerasimovich, Olsufy Ivanovich's old valet, appeared in it.

"The gentleman wishes to come in, Gerasimovich, and I am trying to tell him . . ."

"You're a fool, Alexeyevich, go back inside and send Semenych here. You can't come in, sir," Gerasimovich then said politely but firmly to Golyadkin. "They present you with their apologies for being unable to receive you."

"Is that what they said: they couldn't receive me?" Golyadkin asked hesitantly. "But, excuse me, Gerasimovich, why can't they receive me?"

"They just can't. When I announced you, they said, go and apologize and tell him that we can't receive him."

"But why, why?"

"Please, sir, please . . ."

"But it's quite inadmissible! Go and tell them I'm here. . . . How can they? I've come to dinner. . . ."

"Please, sir, don't make it difficult!"

"Well, after all, if they told you to apologize . . . But still, Gerasimovich, what's going on?"

"Please, sir," Gerasimovich said, very determinedly brushing Golyadkin aside with his hand to make way for two gentlemen who had entered the hall at that moment.

It was Andrei Filipovich and his nephew Vladimir Semyonovich, and they both looked at Golyadkin in great surprise. Andrei Filipovich was on the point of saying something but Golyadkin had quickly decided that it would be best to leave and was already starting to go down the stairs. He was very red in the face, kept his eyes on the ground, and wore a miserable smile.

"I'll come in later, Gerasimovich. I'll sort things out, I hope this misunderstanding will be cleared up soon," he said when he was already on the stairs.

"Mr. Golyadkin! Mr. Golyadkin!" he heard the voice of Andrei Filipovich who had followed him out.

"What can I do for you, Andrei Filipovich?" Golyadkin asked in a quite determined voice.

"What's the matter with you, Yakov Petrovich? What's happening?"

"Nothing, sir, I am here all on my own, and it is a private matter."

"What did you say?"

"I said that this is a private matter and, as far as I can see, has nothing to do with my official duties and my official superiors."

"What do you mean, my good sir? What's this about your official superiors? What's come over you?"

"Nothing, sir, nothing at all. An ill-bred young lady, that's all. . . ."

"What? What did you say?" Andrei Filipovich was completely bewildered. Golyadkin, who until then had been standing on a lower step of the staircase as he spoke to Andrei Filipovich and had been glaring at him as though about to leap at him, now realized that his chief was a bit off balance and took a step toward him. Andrei Filipovich stepped back. Golyadkin went up one step and then another. Andrei Filipovich glanced apprehensively behind him. Then Golyadkin ran quickly upstairs and Andrei Filipovich was even quicker to dart into the door of the apartment and close it behind him.

Golyadkin remained all alone. The world spun before his eyes. He was utterly nonplused now and stood in a sort of stupor, as though trying to make out something that had just happened to him that didn't make sense. "Ah . . . ah . . ." he mumbled, smiling with the effort. In the meantime, voices and steps came from the foot of the stairs, probably more guests who'd come to have dinner with Olsufy Ivanovich. Golyadkin, having partly recovered, raised his raccoon collar to hide as much of his face as possible and went down the steps, stumbling and slipping. He felt numb and weak. He was in such a state of confusion that, when he reached the bottom of the steps, instead of waiting for his carriage to drive up to the door, he started to walk toward it across the muddy yard. When he reached it, Golyadkin thought how nice it would be if he could sink into the ground or hide in a mousehole, carriage and all. He had the impression that all the people inside the house were watching him from the windows, and he felt that he would die then and there if he just turned around.

"Why are you laughing, you fool?" he snapped at Petrushka, who was helping him into the carriage.

"I'm not laughing, sir. What is there for me to laugh about? Where are we off to now, sir?"

"Home, tell him to go home."

"Home!" Petrushka shouted, jumping on to the footboard.

"He caws like a crow," Golyadkin thought.

When the carriage had already driven a good distance past Izmailovsky Bridge, Golyadkin suddenly pulled violently at the cord tied to his driver's arm and ordered him to go back forthwith. The driver turned the horses around and a few minutes later they drove into Olsufy Ivanovich's courtyard once more.

"No, you idiot, not back here, not back here!" Golyadkin shouted, and the driver, as though expecting that order, drove around the yard and out into the street again.

Instead of driving home, Golyadkin stopped the carriage near a rather unprepossessing tavern just past Semenovsky Bridge. He stepped down and paid the driver, thus getting rid of his carriage. He ordered Petrushka to go back home and wait for him there. He himself entered the tavern, took a room there, and ordered that his dinner be brought up to him. He was feeling quite low, and there was complete havoc inside his head. He paced the room for a long time. At last he sat down to the table, rested his forehead on his hands, and tried hard to solve certain aspects of his present situation.

Chapter 4

I̲T̲ ̲W̲A̲S̲ ̲T̲H̲E̲ ̲B̲I̲R̲T̲H̲D̲A̲Y̲ of Klara Olsufievna, the daughter of State Councilor, Olsufy Ivanovich Berendeyev, who at one time had been Golyadkin's benefactor. The day was marked by a brilliant and sumptuous dinner such as had not been seen for a long time in the houses of the officials living around Ismailovsky Bridge. It was more like some Belshazzarian feast than a dinner. There was something Babylonian about the luxury and ritual of it. It included such items as Veuve-Clicquot champagne, oysters and fruit from the Eliseyev and Milyutin stores, and all sorts of fatted calves. And the whole hierarchy of officials was present. This gorgeous dinner was followed by a brilliant ball, a small, private, family ball, but in the very best taste, very civilized and full of decorum. Of course, such balls are given, but only very rarely. They are really more like family celebrations than balls and can only take place in houses like that of State Councilor Berendeyev. What's more, it is very doubtful that all state councilors are capable of organizing such balls. Ah, if only I had been a poet—of course, I mean a poet such as Homer or Pushkin, for it would be hopeless to attempt it with less talent—I would have depicted that whole glorious and sumptuous night for you, oh readers, with a broad brush and bright colors! But I would have started my poem with the dinner. I would have particularly emphasized the striking and memorable moment when the first goblet was raised to the health of the queen of the occasion. I would first have described the guests for you, plunged, at the beginning, into a reverent and expectant silence, that was more like the eloquence of Demosthenes than an ordinary silence. Then I would have presented Andrei Filipovich, the ranking guest, a man quite entitled to his seniority, adorned by white hair and the decorations that should go with white hair. It was he who raised the goblet of sparkling wine especially imported from a remote kingdom to be drunk at such moments, that is more like heavenly nectar than just another wine. I would then have depicted the parents of the queen of the ball and the other guests, who raised their goblets as Andrei Filipovich did and whose eyes, so full of expectation, were fixed on his. Then I would have told you how the so often mentioned Andrei Filipovich, having dropped a tear in his goblet, congratulated the queen, wished her happiness, proposed a toast, and drank to her health.

But here, I must admit, I would have failed to convey the triumphant impact of the moment when Klara Olsufievna, the queen of the ball herself, blushing like a rose of spring with bliss and modesty and overcome by emotion, collapsed into the arms of her loving mother, whereupon that loving mother burst into tears, which made the State Councilor himself sob, that venerable old gentleman, Olsufy Ivanovich, who had lost the use of his leg during his long and distinguished service and who had now been rewarded for his zeal with a neat little amount of capital, a house, an estate including several villages, and a beautiful daughter. Indeed, the old man cried like a baby, managing, however, to exclaim between his sobs something to the effect that His Excellency was a most gracious man.

Nor could I possibly have conveyed to you the rapture felt by all those present when Andrei Filipovich had spoken. For instance, a young registering clerk (who at that moment looked more like a state councilor than a registering clerk) also burst into tears as he listened to Andrei Filipovich.

For his part, Andrei Filipovich didn't at all look like a collegiate councilor and the head of a government section at that moment—but like someone quite different . . . I couldn't tell you like whom exactly, but certainly not like a collegiate councilor. He was greater . . . Ah, well . . . Oh, why don't I possess the secret of a noble, mighty, solemn style that would enable me to convey those beautiful and edifying moments of human life which seem to exist as proof that virtue triumphs over subversive views, free-thinking, vice, and envy!

So I will say nothing about it, but in my silence—that is more pertinent than any oratory—I shall point to the happy young man entering on his twenty-sixth spring, to Vladimir Semyonovich, Andrei Filipovich's nephew; he in his turn rose to propose a toast and on him were now fixed the tearful eyes of the queen's parents, the proud eye of Andrei Filipovich, the shy glance of the queen of the ball herself, the enraptured gazes of the guests, and even the properly envious eyes of the brilliant young man's young colleagues. So, although I will say nothing, I cannot fail to note that everything about this young man—who, in a favorable sense, was really more like an old man—everything, from his ruddy cheeks to his assessor's rank, seemed to say at this triumphant moment, see how far correct behavior can take a man!

I shall not describe how Anton Antonovich Setochkin, head clerk of the departmental section, a colleague of Andrei Filipovich's and once of Olsufy Ivanovich and, at the same time, an old friend of the household and godfather to Klara Olsufievna, a completely white little old man—how, when it was his turn to propose a toast, he suddenly crowed like a cock and recited some gay verses; how with that breach of etiquette, if we can call it that, he made everyone laugh till they cried and how Klara Olsufievna herself, to reward him for his gaiety and amiability, kissed him when her parents told her to do so.

I will only say that the guests, who after such a dinner were bound to be filled with close, brotherly feelings for one another, at last rose from the table and that the old and middle-aged, after spending some time in friendly talk, including even the exchange of some confidences—it goes without saying only friendly and amiable confidences—passed quietly into another room and, without wasting any more time, broke up into two groups, and then, full of a feeling of their own dignity, sat down to green baize tables. The ladies installed themselves in the drawing room, suddenly became immensely amiable, and proceeded to discuss various topics. And finally, the venerable master of the house, who had lost the use of his leg while serving his country with loyalty and zeal and had been rewarded for it as we mentioned earlier, suddenly picked up his crutches and started

walking among his guests, supported by his daughter and
Vladimir Semyonovich; he, too, had suddenly become incredibly amiable and he decided to improvise, then and there, a
modest little ball, regardless of the expense. Then, with that
objective in view, the agile young man, who during the dinner had looked more like a state councilor than a young man,
was sent to get a band, which he did, bringing back with
him a group consisting of no less than eleven musicians. And
so, at exactly eight-thirty, the opening bars of a French
quadrille resounded, followed later by a variety of other
dances. . . .

There is no need for me to say that my pen is too weak,
too sluggish, too dull to present a proper picture of the ball
improvised by the gray-haired host on an impulse of extraordinary warmth. Anyway, how could I, the modest narrator
of the, it must be said, rather curious adventures of Mr.
Golyadkin—how could I convey that seemly blend of beauty,
elegance, decency, gaiety, respectable amiability and amiable
respectability, playfulness and joy, the games and the jokes
of the officials' ladies who were more like fairies than ladies
(in the favorable sense) with their lily-white and rose-pink
shoulders and faces, with their ethereal figures, their playfully
agile, homeopathic (to use exalted language) feet? How,
finally, could I describe the brilliant knights of officialdom,
the gay young men and the solid, sedate, happy gentlemen,
all of them decorously foggy, smoking their pipes between
dances in a small, isolated green room, all of them, from first
to last, bearing good names and holding good positions, gentlemen deeply penetrated by esthetic feeling as well as by a
feeling of self-respect, gentlemen who mostly addressed the
ladies in French and, if by chance they used Russian, kept
to expressions in the best tone, to compliments and profound
statements—except in the smoking room where they indulged
in some phrases which denoted friendly familiarity, such as,
"I'm telling you, Peter, you old so-and-so, you sure gave
your all in that polka," or, "Well, Vaska, my boy, looks as
if you've got her just where you wanted her!"

All this, as I have told you, dear readers, is too much
for my pen to convey and so I remain silent. Let us rather
go back to Mr. Golyadkin, the only true hero of our truthful narrative.

The thing is, he was at that moment, to say the least,
in a very strange position. He was also there. I mean not at

the ball, but almost there. He was perfectly all right but, although he was minding his own business, it would be impossible to say that at the moment he was on an absolutely straight path. Where he actually was—it is even strange to say it—was in the back entrance hall of Olsufy Ivanovich's apartment. Well, that was all right. He was standing there, huddled in a spot that was perhaps not the warmest but certainly the darkest, between old screens and a huge cupboard, among all sorts of junk and rubbish. He was hiding until the time came to act and, while he was waiting, he watched the further development of events as an outside spectator.

So now he was just watching, gentlemen. And why, gentlemen, he too, if he had so chosen, could have walked in. So, why not walk in then? All he had to do was to go ahead and he'd get in, he'd get in very easily. And now, having stood in the cold corner among the junk and litter, he kept encouraging himself by repeating under his breath a saying of the French statesman Villèle: "Everything comes to those who can wait."*

Golyadkin had found that phrase in a book that had nothing to do with the present situation, but now he remembered it and found it very useful. It seemed to apply so well to his position and, then, what wouldn't come into the head of a man who had been standing for almost three hours in a dark, cold corner, waiting for a happy ending? And having quoted the former French minister Villèle, Golyadkin somehow also remembered the former Turkish vizier Martsimaris and then the beautiful Margravine Louise, whose story he had once read in another book. Then he remembered that the Jesuits made it their rule to approve of any means as long as they helped them to reach their goal. But having drawn some encouragement from that historical point, Golyadkin proceeded to ask himself, "Well, what of it?" and "Who were those Jesuits?" Well, they were a bunch of fools and he could outdo the lot of them. Well, as soon as the servants left the pantry empty (the pantry door gave onto the back entrance where Golyadkin was hiding), he, ignoring all Jesuits, would walk straight through the pantry into the tea room, then into the room where they were now playing cards, and then straight into the drawing room where they were now dancing a polka.

---

* Actually a quotation from Rabelais' *Gargantua.*

Yes, he'd get through, he'd get through, slip through without fail and that'd be that, and no one would notice him; and once there, he'd know what to do next.

Well, gentlemen, this is the position in which we find the hero of our very truthful story, although it is very hard to explain the state he was in at that moment. The thing is, he had succeeded in getting as far as the service stairs and then up to the back entrance of the apartment because there was nothing much to it really and anyone could have got that far. But he obviously didn't dare to go any farther, that is to say, there was nothing particular he was afraid of, but he simply didn't wish to force his way in, and felt it was better for him to slip in quietly. And so, gentlemen, he was now biding his time on the quiet, and had been biding it for exactly two hours and thirty minutes. Well, why shouldn't he wait?

"What has Villèle to do with me?" Golyadkin thought. "Why should I care about Villèle? What about just going in there, without any further ado? Ah, you damned dummy!" he said, pinching his frozen cheek with his numbed fingers. "Ah, you poor fool, you miserable idiot, you golliwog, Golyadkin!" But this gentle reproach addressed to his own person was just a general remark made in passing.

Then he decided to go ahead. It seemed to be the right moment. The pantry was at last empty of people—the moment had come. Golyadkin could see that through the window. In a couple of strides he reached the door and started to push it open.

"To go or not to go? Well, shall I go in or not? I'll go. Why not? To the bold all roads are open!"

But having given himself this pep talk, our hero hurriedly retired behind the old screens again.

"No," he thought. "What if someone walks in? And that's right—there, someone's just come in. Why did I waste all that time while there was no one in the pantry? I could have just walked in. Now, how can I get in there with my nature? What despicable tendencies I have! I really didn't have the guts. To lack guts—we can always be counted on for that. We can also always be counted on to mess things up. You don't have to worry about that. And so I have to stand here like a dummy without getting a thing out of it. At home I could have had a cup of tea at least. I certainly would enjoy a cup right now. If I get back late, Petrushka will grumble. Shouldn't I really be on my way back home? Ah, to hell with everything, I'm going home, and that's that."

And having thus settled his present dilemma, Golyadkin moved forward as if propelled by a spring. In two strides he reached the pantry, threw off his overcoat, took off his hat, hurriedly pushed them into a corner, straightened his clothes, smoothed his hair and . . . and proceeded into the tea room; from there he darted into another room, slipping almost unnoticed between the card players, who were engrossed in their games, and then . . . then, Golyadkin forgot what was going on around him and, like a bolt from the blue, burst into the ball room.

It just so happened that they weren't dancing at that moment. Ladies were strolling all over the room in colorful clusters. Gentlemen stood in circles or roamed around inviting the ladies for the next dance. But Golyadkin saw nothing of that. He saw only Klara, with Andrei Filipovich near her, then Vladimir Semyonovich and two or three other young men, quite promising and bright, who had, as far as one could judge from looking at them, already realized some of the things expected of them. . . . He also saw a few other people. Or, no, he did not really see anyone else or look at anything else—he was simply propelled forward by that same spring which had pushed him uninvited into the ball. And so he moved on and on and on again, butted into a councilor, stepped on the man's feet while he was at it, also stepped on the dress of a venerable little old lady, tearing it slightly, shoved a servant carrying a tray, shoved someone else, all without noticing or, to be more accurate, noticing but disregarding it, just not looking—for what was the good of looking at this point?—moving ahead and ahead until he found himself in front of Klara Olsufievna herself.

No doubt he would have chosen, without blinking an eye and with the greatest of pleasure, to sink into the ground, but what was done was done and couldn't possibly be undone. So what was there for him to do? "If I fail, I don't lose courage; if I succeed, I persevere . . . Golyadkin certainly doesn't go in for intrigue, and polishing the parquet with the soles of his shoes isn't for him. . . ."

And so, indeed, it proved. Moreover, the Jesuits had a hand in it too . . . But what did Golyadkin care about them now! All the people who had been walking, talking, laughing, and shouting suddenly became silent and gradually surrounded Golyadkin. But he didn't seem to hear or see anything; he couldn't look. Nothing in the world could have made him look. He lowered his eyes and just stood there, having vaguely given himself his word of honor to shoot himself somehow that night. Having made himself that promise, Golyadkin said to himself inwardly, "Here goes" and then, to his own infinite astonishment, started to speak.

He began with congratulations and the appropriate wishes. The congratulating part went off fine but when it came to the wishes, our hero, who had felt beforehand that if he got stuck the whole thing would be a mess, did get stuck. And so when he did get stuck and bogged down, he turned red, lost control of himself, and raised his eyes; and having raised his eyes, he looked around. And he was petrified. They were all standing around him, all silent, all waiting. Then, a bit farther away from him, they were whispering; a bit closer, they laughed. Golyadkin cast a doggish, submissive glance at Andrei Filipovich, who responded by a look that, if it failed to kill our hero then and there, made sure that a second such look would finish him off. And the silence continued.

"This concerns my private life and home, Andrei Filipovich," Golyadkin said in a hardly audible voice. "It has no connection with my work as a government employee. . . ."

"You ought to be ashamed of yourself, sir!" Andrei Filipovich said in a half whisper, looking outraged. And having said that, he took Klara's hand and turned his back on Golyadkin.

"There's nothing for me to be ashamed of," Golyadkin said, also in a half-whisper, looking around miserably, as if trying to find, among the bewildered people thronging around him, a way out that would enable him to save his social position.

"Well, what of it, gentlemen? This could happen to anyone," Golyadkin whispered, moving back a little and trying to get out of the human ring.

They let him pass, and he squeezed through two rows of surprised and curious guests. He was propelled by his fate. It was his fate, he felt, that was pulling him away. Of course, he would have given a lot to be in his former hiding place by the back entrance now. But since that was impossible, he tried to escape into some other corner, hoping to stand there quietly and humbly without bothering anyone, without attracting their attention to himself, but at the same time gaining the indulgence of the guests and of the host. Golyadkin also felt that the floor was swaying under his feet and that he was about to fall.

He managed to reach a corner though, and stood there like an indifferent observer, resting his hands on the backs of two chairs, of which he thus took possession, and trying to look cheerfully at Olsufy Ivanovich's guests who had gathered around him. The nearest of these guests was a tall, handsome army officer next to whom Golyadkin felt like a bug.

"These two chairs, lieutenant, are reserved for Klara Olsufievna and Princess Chevchekhanov who is now dancing. I am holding these chairs for them," Golyadkin said breathlessly, looking beseechingly at the lieutenant.

The lieutenant said nothing, then turned away with an annihilating smile.

Having failed with the lieutenant, Golyadkin tried his luck with an important councilor with an impressive star around his neck, but that gentleman replied with such a cold gaze that Golyadkin felt as though a bucket of icy water had been poured over his head. He grew quiet.

He decided that the best thing for him to do was to say nothing, for that would show that there was nothing special the matter with him, that he was just like all the others and that, as far as he could see, his position was very acceptable. And so he riveted his eyes on his cuffs. When at last he raised them, they rested on a very respectable-looking gentleman.

"That gentleman is wearing a wig," Golyadkin decided, "and so if that wig were pulled off, he'd have a head just as bare as the palm of my hand."

Having made that important discovery, Golyadkin remembered the Arab emirs who, under the green turbans they wear to show their family ties with the prophet Mohammed, have equally bare, hairless heads that would be exposed if the turbans were removed. Then, probably through a peculiar association of ideas, Golyadkin passed from the Arabs to the Turks and from the Turks to Turkish slippers, which made him think that Andrei Filipovich's shoes looked more like slippers than shoes.

It was clear that Golyadkin had partly adapted himself to the situation.

"If that big overhanging chandelier," Golyadkin thought, "suddenly fell in the middle of the company, I'd rush to save Klara and, having saved her, I'd say to her, 'Please don't worry, ma'am, it's nothing, and I am your savior.' And then . . ." At this juncture, Golyadkin turned his head, searching for Klara Olsulfievna, and caught sight of Gerasimovich who, with a very solemn expression on his face, was working his way straight toward him. Golyadkin shuddered and frowned, experiencing an unaccountably unpleasant sensation. Unthinkingly he looked around, feeling that it would be nice to slip away from trouble somehow, to pretend that none of what was happening had any connection with him whatsoever. However, before our hero had time to decide upon further action, Gerasimovich was standing in front of him.

"See that candle up there, Gerasimovich," Golyadkin said with a little grin, "in the chandelier, I mean. Well, it's about to fall. So you'd better see that someone puts it straight."

"The candle? No, sir, that candle is straight. But there's someone asking for you, sir."

"Who is asking for me, Gerasimovich?"

"I can't tell you exactly who, sir, a servant in the employ of some people. He came and asked for you. 'Is Mr. Yakov Petrovich Golyadkin here?' he said. 'Please inform him that he is needed urgently. . . .' So you see, sir . . ."

"No, Gerasimovich, there's no one asking for me. You must be mistaken, I'm sure."

"That's unlikely, sir."

"No, Gerasimovich, there's nothing unlikely about your making a mistake, nothing unlikely at all. There's no one asking for me. Indeed, there's no one who could be asking for me, Gerasimovich."

Golyadkin took a deep breath and looked around him. Sure enough, that was it! All the people in the drawing room had their eyes and ears riveted on him in a sort of solemn expectation. The men were crowding closer around him, listening. Behind them, the ladies were exchanging alarmed whispers. The master of the house was not too far away either, and although he didn't let on that he was taking a direct hand in the further fate of Mr. Golyadkin—the opera-tion being carried out with delicacy—the hero of our story realized nevertheless that the moment of decision had arrived. He saw that the time had come for him to strike and put his enemies to shame. He was inspired and greatly agitated as he addressed Gerasimovich in solemn and quivering tones:

"No, friend, no one is asking for me. You were mistaken. And I will say more: you were also mistaken earlier today, when you told me . . . I mean when you tried to assure me that . . ." Golyadkin raised his voice, "that Olsufy Ivanovich, my benefactor for so many years, a man who, in a sense, has taken my father's place, had closed the door of his house to me on the occasion of a solemn family celebration that is a joy to his parental heart." Looking a little smug but profoundly moved, Golyadkin gazed at the faces around him, with tears trembling on his eyelashes. "I repeat, my friend," Golyadkin concluded, "you have made a mistake, a cruel, unforgivable mistake."

It was a solemn moment. Golyadkin felt that it had had the right effect. He stood with lowered eyes, expecting Olsufy Ivanovich to rush over to him and throw his arms around him. There was an obvious stir among the guests. Even the terrifying Gerasimovich stammered as he tried to say again, "unnn-nn-likely . . ."

But suddenly the merciless band struck up a polka. All was lost. It dispersed the effect like a blast of wind. Golyadkin shuddered, Gerasimovich reeled back, the whole room seemed to be set in motion like an agitated sea; Vladimir Semyonovich was already flying across the parquet with Klara, and the handsome lieutenant with Princess Chevchekhanov. The spectators, enthusiastic and curious, watched the polka—a fascinating, fashionable dance that had caught everyone's imagination. For the moment, everyone forgot about Mr. Golyadkin.

Then there was a new stir among the guests, everyone became excited and agitated. The music stopped . . . a strange thing happened. Klara Olsufievna, gasping for breath after the polka, her cheeks afire, her breast heaving, let herself fall into an armchair. All hearts flew out toward the charmer, everyone rushed toward her to tell her how charming she was and how they appreciated the pleasure she was affording them. And then, lo and behold, Golyadkin too was standing next to her. He was pale and looked very depressed. Like her, he seemed completely out of breath, completely exhausted, and hardly able to move. There was a strange grin on his face and his hand was extended imploringly toward her. Taken by surprise, Klara didn't have the presence of mind to pull back her hand. Unthinkingly responding to Golyadkin's invitation, she stood up. Golyadkin swayed, lurched forward, once, twice, then lifted a foot, then clicked a heel, then stamped his foot, then stumbled . . . He too wished to dance with Klara.

She screamed. Those around them rushed to free her from Golyadkin and he found himself separated by at least ten paces from her by the onrush of the crowd. A tight ring formed around him too. Two old ladies, whom he had almost knocked over while being pushed back himself, squealed and shrieked. The havoc was indescribable; the whole place was in an uproar; people were asking questions, shouting, commenting. The band was silent. Golyadkin was turning inside the human ring and mumbling, with a blank half-smile, something to the effect that, "Why not after all?" Inasmuch as he viewed the polka as a new and interesting dance, made to please the ladies, he didn't see why he shouldn't . . . , but since it was this way, why, he was willing to agree. But it didn't look as if anyone was going to bother to ask for our hero's agreement just then. He felt a hand clutch at his arm, then another hand pressed hard against his back, and he found himself being guided somewhere with very firm solicitude. Soon he realized that he was moving straight toward the door. Instinctively, he tried to laugh it all off. Finally, he felt them putting his coat on him and pulling his hat down over his eyes, and then he realized that he was on the stairs, in the darkness and the cold. He stumbled and felt he was falling into an abyss. He was about to scream but, at that moment, he found himself out in the yard. The impact of the fresh air made him stop and, just then, he heard the band strike up another dance. Suddenly, Golyadkin remembered everything and had the impression that the strength that had abandoned him was now flowing back. He had been standing as though riveted to the ground, but now he tore forward and began to run, to run madly, straight ahead, anywhere, toward the fresh air, toward freedom, just ahead.

Chapter 5

Aʟʟ ᴛʜᴇ ᴘᴇᴛᴇʀsʙᴜʀɢ clock towers were striking twelve when Golyadkin, beside himself, ran out onto the Fontanka Embankment by the Izmailovsky Bridge, fleeing from his enemies, persecution, the kicks aimed at him, the screams of the old crones, the moans and groans of the ladies, the annihilating glare of Andrei Filipovich. Golyadkin had been killed—actually killed in the full sense of the word, and if he had still preserved the ability to run, it was through some sort of miracle, a miracle in which he himself refused to believe. It was a horrible November night—wet, foggy, rainy, snowy, fraught with head colds, flu, inflammations, all sorts of fevers—in brief, with all the boons of a Petersburg November. The wind howled in the deserted streets, raising the Fontanka's black water above the mooring rings and recklessly swinging the meager streetlights on the embankment so that they responded to its howlings with a shrill, strident creak, producing that concert which is so well known to every resident of Petersburg. It was raining and snowing at the same time. Displaced by the wind, the rain spurted almost horizontally, as though shot from a fireman's hose, and stung poor Golyadkin's face like a thousand pins. In the silence of the night, broken only by the distant rumbling of carriages, the howling of the wind, and the creaking of the streetlights, one could hear the mournful splash and gurgle of water streaming from every roof, every doorstep, every drainpipe, and every cornice onto the granite sidewalks.

There was not a soul in sight, either nearby or at a distance, and it seemed quite impossible that anyone would venture out in such weather. And so, all by himself, Golyadkin trotted along the Fontanka Embankment, trotted in his usual short, quick steps, trying to reach as quickly as possible his fourth floor apartment on Six Shop Street.

Although the snow, the rain, the fog, and all the nameless horrors that make up a November storm in Petersburg pounced upon Golyadkin when he was already broken by misfortune, showing him no mercy, giving him no respite, drenching him to the bone, sticking his eyelids together, blowing through him from every angle, making him lose his way and the last thread of reasoning capacity—although all these trials were hurled at him as if by a prearranged agreement with his enemies to give him a day, an evening, and a night to remember, yet Golyadkin remained almost unaware of this last manifestation of fate's hostility toward him, being much too shaken by what had happened to him a few minutes earlier in the house of State Councilor Berendeyev.

Had some stranger, some uninvolved outsider, caught sight of Golyadkin's gloomy, trotting figure, he would at once have grasped the bottomless horror the man had just faced and would have certainly said that he was trying to run away from himself, to hide somewhere from himself. Yes, that was certainly it! We can even go further and say that Golyadkin was not merely longing to escape himself, but was anxious to annihilate himself, to reduce himself to dust. He didn't see anything around him, understood nothing, and seemed quite unaware of the wretched weather, of being so long exposed to rain, snow, wind, and every discomfort. One rubber, which had slipped from his right shoe, remained stuck in the muddy snow of the Fontanka Embankment, for Golyadkin never even missed it. He was so absorbed in his thoughts that he stopped several times and, disregarding the howling wind and rain, stood still as a post in the middle of the sidewalk, visualizing his recent degradation, dying, vanishing during those seconds, then, suddenly tearing off like a madman and running straight ahead without looking back, fleeing something even more terrifying that was pursuing him. . . . He was really in a desperate situation.

At last, at the end of his tether, Golyadkin stopped, leaned against the railing of the embankment and, looking like a man suffering from a sudden nose bleed, stared into the Fontanka's black waters. It's hard to say how long he remained standing there, but it can be said that by then he had reached such depths of despair, was so torn, tortured, and tormented, that the remnants of his already shaken spirit collapsed and he forgot everything, including the Izmailovsky Bridge, Six Shop Street, and even where he was. . . . But then, what did it matter? Why should he care? He had done what he had to do; his decision had been made, confirmed and approved, so what was there for him to worry about?

Suddenly . . . suddenly a shock passed through his whole body, and he instinctively leaped a couple of steps back from the railing. He looked around with unaccountable apprehension. But there was no one in sight. Nothing special had happened, and yet . . . and yet he was under the impression that just a second before someone had been standing near him, leaning, like him, against the railing and, incredible as it might seem, had said something to him. He had said it very quickly, quite abruptly and not very clearly, but it was something that closely concerned him.

"I guess I must have imagined it," Golyadkin said, looking all around him, "but what am I doing, standing here? Ah, that . . ." He shook his head, looking dejectedly and apprehensively into the murky dampness, trying hard to pierce the dusky space with his nearsighted eyes. But Golyadkin could make out nothing suspicious, all was in order, only it was snowing rather harder now—the flakes were larger and there were more of them—so that one couldn't see much more than twenty paces away; the streetlights were creaking a bit more shrilly, and the wind was a little whinier and sounded like a beggar imploring a passer-by to give him a kopeck to buy himself some food.

"Ah, what's the matter with me after all!" Golyadkin said, starting on his way again, but still looking cautiously around him. Then a new feeling pervaded him. It was rather like fear and anguish, but it was different from either. A feverish shudder ran through him. It was an unbearably unpleasant moment.

"Well, never mind," he said, to cheer himself up, "perhaps it was completely unimportant, and no one's honor has suffered from it. Perhaps it just had to happen," he went on without quite understanding what he was saying, "perhaps in time it will turn out that everything that has happened is for the best and there will be nothing for me to complain about and everything that has been done will be vindicated."

As he said this, feeling a little relieved by his own words, Golyadkin shook off the snow that had formed a thick layer on his hat, collar, overcoat, cravat, shoes, and everything, but did not succeed in shaking off the strange feeling of anxiety that had filled him.

A cannon boomed somewhere in the distance.

"What terrible weather!" our hero thought. "I'm afraid there may be a flood. Looks as if the water has risen very high."

No sooner had Golyadkin said this than he saw someone walking toward him, probably just another belated passer-by like himself. It seemed a quite ordinary, natural occurrence, but somehow Golyadkin was troubled, even frightened. It wasn't really that he was afraid of some evil stranger but, "Who knows," the thought flashed through his head, "perhaps he doesn't just happen to be walking here, perhaps he's out to cross my path deliberately, to provoke me."

It's possible that Golyadkin didn't actually formulate this supposition to himself in so many words, but he did feel something of the sort at that second and the feeling was a very unpleasant one indeed. But he didn't have much time either to think or feel, for the stranger was already within a couple of paces of him.

As usual Golyadkin hurriedly assumed his special air which made it clear that he, Golyadkin, minded his own business, that he didn't wish to interfere with anyone, that the road was quite wide enough for everyone, and that he, Golyadkin, had no wish to look for trouble from anyone.

But suddenly he stopped as though struck by lightning. Then he quickly turned back and stared at the man who had just passed him. He had turned as if something had pushed him from behind, like a weathercock turned by the wind. The stranger was rapidly sinking into the snowy darkness. He too was walking fast and, like Golyadkin, was all bundled up, and he, also, trotted in short, bouncy steps along the Fontanka Embankment.

"What does this mean?" Golyadkin whispered, smiling with incredulity. An icy shiver ran down his spine and his whole body shuddered.

By now the passer-by was out of sight; even the sound

of his steps could no longer be heard. But Golyadkin still stood and stared at the spot where he had vanished.

When he snapped out of it at last, he thought with vexation: "What's the matter with me, after all? Am I really going out of my mind or what?"

He turned and resumed his way, walking faster and faster, and trying not to think of anything at all now. And to succeed in this, he even closed his eyes. Suddenly through the howling of the wind he once again heard someone's footsteps. He shivered and opened his eyes. A man was coming in his direction. He was about twenty steps away now. The man was trotting, apparently in a great hurry, and the distance between them was rapidly decreasing. Soon Golyadkin could even discern the features of the other man. He discerned them, and let out a shout of surprise and terror. He felt his legs giving under him. It was the passer-by who had passed him ten minutes earlier, and who now once again had somehow reappeared in front of him. But it was not just this ordinary circumstance that made Golyadkin stop and cry out. He turned toward the stranger, tried to say something to him, called out, asking him to wait. The stranger obliged, stopped ten paces away, as it happened under a street lamp, so that his entire figure was lighted, and turning toward Golyadkin, waited with an air of worried impatience.

"Forgive me, I may have made a mistake," our hero said in a trembling voice.

The stranger said nothing, turned away in annoyance, and walked on in a great hurry, as though he were trying to make up the few seconds he had been forced to waste on Golyadkin. As to Golyadkin, he began to shake, his knees buckled under him, and he had to sit down on the edge of the curb. And he had a very good reason for being so overwhelmed. He was under the impression that he had seen the man before. Well, that would be nothing still. But he recognized the man, recognized him for sure. He had seen him, seen him very recently in fact. But when was it? Yesterday perhaps? But then, that Golyadkin had often seen him before was not what mattered. Besides, there was nothing so special about him; he wouldn't have attracted anyone's attention at first glance. He was apparently a respectable man, looking like all respectable men, and he probably had some quite considerable merits—in brief, he was a man like any other. Golyadkin didn't feel any hatred, hostility, or even the slightest dislike for him; in fact, if anything he felt just the contrary, and yet (and this was just the point) he wouldn't have wanted to meet him for anything in the world, especially under circumstances such as those in which he had met him just now. Golyadkin knew very well who the man was, he even knew his first and last names, but then again, he wouldn't have wanted to pronounce that name, to have acknowledged that the man had such and such a first and last name.

I couldn't tell you how long Golyadkin remained there in a quandary, how long he sat on the edge of the sidewalk, but I can say that when he had recovered a little from his shock, he jumped up and started running without looking back, running as hard as he could, out of breath, stumbling, twice almost falling, which caused his other shoe to become orphaned of its rubber.

When at last Golyadkin slowed down a bit to catch his breath, he glanced around him and realized that in running along the Fontanka Embankment, he had already passed Anichkov Bridge, and after that had covered a good stretch along the Nevsky Prospect and was now standing near the corner of Liteinaya Street. Golyadkin turned into that street.

At that moment his position was like that of a man in front of whom the earth is splitting open, the ground swaying under his feet, the abyss drawing closer and closer—he is already slipping, about to fall into the bottomless gap, but he hasn't the courage either to leap back or to turn his eyes away. The abyss fascinates him and, in the end, he jumps into it himself, thus speeding the moment of his death. Golyadkin felt, knew, indeed was absolutely certain that something untoward would happen to him on his way home, something unpleasant, like meeting that man once again. But strangely enough, he was looking forward to that meeting in a sense, considered it inevitable, and only wished that everything would come to an end quickly, that the situation would be settled, no matter how, but quickly. And, in the meantime, he ran ahead as if pushed by some outside force, for all his being felt weak and numb; he couldn't even think straight, although all sorts of thoughts caught on to him the way scraps catch on a bramble bush.

A mangy little stray dog, soaking wet and shivering, had attached itself to Golyadkin and was now trotting by his side, its ears drooping, its tail between its legs, from time to time casting shy, questioning glances at him. Some far-away, long-forgotten thought—a memory of something that had happened very long ago—descended on him and kept hammering at his brain, pestering him, refusing to leave him in peace.

"Ah, that nasty mutt," Golyadkin whispered without understanding himself.

It was at the corner of Italian Street that he saw the stranger. But this time the man was not coming toward him, but was running in the same direction as Golyadkin, preceding him by a few steps. And thus they entered Six Shop Street. Golyadkin's breath caught in his throat when he saw the stranger stop in front of Golyadkin's own house. The bell rang and immediately afterward the iron bolt grated. The gate opened, the man bent forward, and in a flash vanished inside. Golyadkin followed on his heels and also darted through the gate. Ignoring the grumbling janitor, he rushed into the inner yard, and at once his eyes fell on his mysterious companion whom he had lost sight of for a few seconds. The stranger had just entered the door giving onto the staircase that led to Golyadkin's apartment. Golyadkin followed him. The stairs were dark, damp, and dirty. All sorts of junk belonging to the tenants was piled up on the landings, so that an outsider coming to visit might spend half an hour picking his way through it in order not to break a leg, all the while cursing his acquaintances for having chosen such a place to live in. But Golyadkin's companion seemed to be quite familiar with the place. He had no difficulty whatever in making his way through all the obstacles. Golyadkin had almost caught up with the stranger and a couple of times was so close behind him that the skirts of the man's overcoat brushed against his nose. His heart contracted. The mysterious stranger stopped in front of Golyadkin's apartment, knocked on the door and, as if he hadn't gone to bed at all, Petrushka opened the door right away—a thing that would have surprised Golyadkin at any other time—and holding the candle in his hand, followed the stranger inside.

The hero of our story tore into his place quite beside himself. Without bothering to take off his overcoat, he went through the narrow little corridor, then stopped at the door of his room as though struck by lightning. All his forebodings had come about. Everything he had feared and foreseen was now becoming reality. It cut his breath. His head spun. The stranger, also still wearing his hat and overcoat, was sitting on Golyadkin's bed, looking at him with a little smile and, his eyes slightly screwed up, greeting him with a friendly nod.

Golyadkin wanted to scream, but couldn't, to protest, but he didn't have the strength. His hair stood on end, and he had to sit down, unable to remain on his feet in his terror. And he had good reason to be terrified too. Now Golyadkin had really recognized his companion of the night. It was none other than himself, another Mr. Golyadkin, but exactly the same as him—in other words what is called a double, a double in every respect. . . .

Chapter 6

On the following morning at eight o'clock, Golyadkin woke up in his bed. Right away, all the peculiar things that had happened on the previous day and the wild, incredible night with its unbelievable adventures came back to him in all their horrifying detail. Such diabolical viciousness on the part of his enemies, especially this last manifestation of it, froze Golyadkin's heart. But at the same time it all seemed so strange, incomprehensible, and inane, and it was hard to believe it had really happened. He would almost have been inclined to dismiss it all as a nightmarish vision, a temporary aberration, or a paralysis of reasoning power, had he not known from bitter experience how far an enemy's hatred can lead him when he tries to avenge himself for a slight to his honor and pride. Besides, the stiffness of his limbs, his fuzzy head, his aching back, and his wicked sniffles attested to the reality of his lengthy nocturnal escapade, and thus confirmed everything that had happened to him during that nighttime adventure. Anyway, Golyadkin had known all along that they were concocting something, that they had someone else on hand. But what was it? After giving it considerable thought, Golyadkin decided to keep quiet, for the time being, not to protest. "They may have decided to scare me," he thought, "but when they see that I don't protest, that I accept it with resignation, they'll give it up themselves. They'll be the first to call it off."

Golyadkin was thinking along these lines, stretching his

sore limbs in his bed, and waiting for Petrushka to appear, as the fellow did everyday. He waited for fifteen minutes, listening to Petrushka fussing unhurriedly over the samovar behind the partition, but somehow not daring to call him. We may even declare that Mr. Golyadkin was rather afraid of confronting Petrushka.

"God only knows what that ne'er-do-well thinks now. He doesn't say so, but he sees plenty," Golyadkin thought.

At last the door creaked and Petrushka appeared carrying a tray. Golyadkin glanced at him out of the corner of his eye, wondering whether the fellow wouldn't mention a certain occurrence he had witnessed the night before. But Petrushka said nothing. In fact, he seemed more taciturn, gloomy, and sulky than ever, was obviously displeased about something, and never once looked at his master, who felt slightly vexed at this. Having put the breakfast on the table, Petrushka went off behind his partition without opening his mouth.

"He knows, he knows everything, the good-for-nothing," Golyadkin grumbled, sipping his tea. But although Petrushka kept coming into the room for various reasons, Golyadkin couldn't bring himself to ask him about what he wanted to know.

Golyadkin was in a state of great anxiety. He was afraid to go to the office. He had a strong foreboding that something had gone wrong there. "If I went there," he thought, "I just might run into something bad. Wouldn't it be wiser to be patient, to wait? Let them do as they please over there, but me, I think I'd rather wait this day out, recuperate a bit, regain my strength, think it over a bit more and then, biding my time, come down on them like a bolt from the blue without blinking an eye myself."

Thinking along these lines, Golyadkin smoked pipe after pipe without noticing how fast the time was passing. When he looked at the clock, he found it was already nine-thirty.

"It's too late to go to the office anyway," he decided, "and on top of that, I feel sick. Of course I'm sick, no doubt about it, and I'd like to see anyone who'd dare say I'm not sick. What do I care? Let them come and check. Let them send their doctor over. My back aches, I'm coughing and sneezing; and really, I can't possibly go out in this weather. I might fall ill and die. The mortality rate is really quite high nowadays. . . ."

Using this line of reasoning, Golyadkin succeeded in calming his scruples, and consoled himself in advance for the telling off he'd get from Andrei Filipovich for his failure in duty. In general, Golyadkin was in the habit of justifying himself in his own eyes by using all sorts of irrefutable arguments to the effect that he couldn't have done other than what he had decided to do, and thus setting his conscience at rest. And so, having soothed his conscience, he took a pipe, filled it, and started to puff away at it. But just as he had his pipe going nicely, he suddenly jumped up from his sofa, put the pipe down, washed, shaved, smoothed his hair, and, donning his frockcoat and all the rest, took some papers and rushed off to the office.

Once in the department, Golyadkin walked timidly to his office and, trembling with anxiety, sat down, expecting something unpleasant to happen—an expectation which, although vague and unformulated, was nonetheless extremely unpleasant. He sat down timidly at his desk which was next to that of the head clerk, Anton Antonovich Setochkin. Then, without looking around, without letting anything distract him from his concentration, Golyadkin plunged into the papers that lay before him. He had resolved to avoid as far as possible anything that might provoke them or compromise him, such as indiscreet questions or jokes, all unseemly allusions to last night's party; he decided even to abstain from the routine amiabilities with his colleagues, such as inquiries about their health and the like. But he realized very well that he couldn't keep this up for very long. The worry that there was something he didn't know and that might concern him always upset him more than the thing itself. And that is why, despite his resolution not to bother with what was going on around him, and to avoid everything he could, Golyadkin now and then kept stealing glances right and left, trying to make out his colleagues' expressions, trying to figure out whether anything new had happened that concerned him and that was being concealed from him. He assumed that what had happened yesterday must necessarily be connected with what was going on around him now. Finally, in his anguish, he started wishing that things would come to a head quickly, whatever the outcome, even if it were bound to end in disaster. . . . But here, fate took Golyadkin at his word. Before he had even finished formulating his wish, all his doubts were dissipated in the strangest and most unexpected way.

The door to the next office screeched very gently and discreetly, indicating that the person about to walk in was in a very menial position. Then a figure who was very familiar to Golyadkin came in and walked shyly up to the desk where our hero was sitting. Golyadkin didn't raise his head, but having caught sight of the newcomer out of the corner of his eye, he already knew all about him, down to the tiniest detail. He was burning with shame and trying to bury his poor head in the official papers as an ostrich hides its head in the burning sand to escape hunters. The new arrival bowed to Andrei Filipovich, and then the chief's voice spoke in the tone in which kindly superiors address new subordinates in their departments.

"Sit here," Andrei Filipovich said to the new man, pointing to Anton Antonovich's desk, "right here, next to Mr. Golyadkin. We'll find some job for you soon enough."

Andrei Filipovich concluded by gesturing in an authoritative and dignified manner to the new man, after which he plunged into the intricacies of the papers piled before him.

Golyadkin finally looked up, and if he didn't faint, it was only because he had had a foreboding that something like this would happen long before and, deep down inside him, had guessed who the new man was. Golyadkin's first reaction was to look quickly around to make sure that no whispering had started yet, that no one's face was twisted by some joke being made about him and, finally, that none of the clerks had fallen off his chair in fright. But to his great surprise, he found no sign of any such reactions. His colleagues' behavior amazed Golyadkin. It didn't make any sense to him and he felt quite frightened by the unusual quiet. The fact was there for everyone to see, and it certainly was a strange, monstrous business, certainly enough to stir a person out of his indifference. Of course, all these thoughts only flashed through Golyadkin's mind as he sat there simmering on a low flame. And he had good reason to simmer too. The man who sat opposite Golyadkin was his shame, his disgrace, his horror, his nightmare of the night before. In one word, it was Golyadkin himself. It was not the Golyadkin who was now sitting in his chair with his mouth wide open and a pen in his frozen hand, not the Golyadkin who was the assistant to the head clerk in his office and who liked to pass unnoticed, burying himself in the crowd, not the Golyadkin whose very gait plainly said "don't bother me and I won't bother you" or "don't bother me since I'm not bothering you." No, this man was another Mr. Golyadkin, quite different, but one who, at the same time, resembled the first Mr. Golyadkin exactly—the same height, the same build, the same clothes, the same bald patch—in brief, with nothing neglected to make the resemblance perfect so that if they had been stood up next to each other, no one would have been able to tell which was the real Golyadkin, which was the old and which the new, which the original and which the copy.

Our hero was now in the position of a man on whom some practical joker has surreptitiously directed a captured sun ray through a convex lens.

"What is it? Am I dreaming or is it real?" Golyadkin was thinking. "Is this reality or the continuation of last night? But how can it be? Who authorized the hiring of this new employee? I must be dreaming, having delusions . . ."

He tried pinching himself, even vaguely considered pinching someone else. . . . No, it wasn't a dream and that was all there was to it. Golyadkin felt he was dripping with sweat, that something unprecedented and unheard of was happening to him and that, to top his misfortune, what was happening to him was a shameful, indecent thing, and he felt acutely the terrible disadvantage of being the first to go through such a ridiculous experience. He even began to doubt whether he really existed and, although he had been prepared for it and had actually wished to have his doubts settled one way or the other, yet what had actually happened was certainly no better than the anxiety of expectation. He was oppressed and tormented by anguish. There were moments during which he completely lost his memory and the ability to think coherently. When he snapped out of such moments, he found himself mechanically moving his pen across the paper. Distrusting himself, he tried to check everything he had written before, but he couldn't understand what he was reading. At last, the other Golyadkin, who up until then had been sitting very quietly, got up and, for some reason, went out through the door leading to another section of the department. Golyadkin looked around the room. All was quiet, the only sound being the scratching of pens against paper and some whispering around Andrei Filipovich's desk from the opposite side of the room. Golyadkin glanced at Anton Antonovich and, in all probability because our hero's face reflected the state he was in and was in harmony with his feelings, the kindly head clerk put down his pen and inquired with great concern after Mr. Golyadkin's health.

"Thank God, Anton Antonovich, I'm perfectly fine," Golyadkin stammered. "I'm quite all right now, Anton Antonovich," he added hesitantly, still rather distrustful of the head clerk.

"Well, it just looked to me as if you didn't feel too well. It wouldn't be too surprising, anyway, there are so many colds around. Do you know that . . ."

"Yes, Anton Antonovich, I do know that there are a lot of colds around. That's not what I had in mind, Anton Antonovich," Golyadkin said, looking intently at the old man. "I don't even know how to tell you. I mean, I'm not sure how to start, Anton Antonovich. . . ."

"What is it? I must admit I don't follow you too well. . . . You know, you'd better explain in what way you find it difficult to tell me. . . ." Anton Antonovich said, also finding it rather difficult to express himself when he saw tears in Golyadkin's eyes.

"I mean, Anton Antonovich . . . you see, there's a new clerk here."

"Well? I still don't understand you."

"I mean to say that there is a new man working here."

"Well, yes, a namesake of yours. So, what of it?"

"What did you say?" Golyadkin cried out.

"I said he's a namesake of yours; his name is Golyadkin too. Is he your brother perhaps?"

"No, Anton Antonovich, I . . ."

"Hm, I was sure he was a close relative of yours somehow. There seems to be a sort of family resemblance, you know."

Golyadkin was quite flabbergasted. For a few moments he was speechless. What a way to treat such an unprecedented abomination, such a freak coincidence that ought to have struck even the most unobservant man! How could Anton Antonovich talk about a family resemblance when Golyadkin saw a mirror image of himself?

"If you'll take my advice, Yakov Petrovich," Anton Antonovich said, "you'll go and consult a doctor. I don't think you look too well. Your eyes especially . . . There's a peculiar expression in them, you know."

"No, no, I assure you, I feel perfectly all right, Anton

Antonovich. I simply wanted to ask you something about that clerk."

"Well, what is it?"

"Didn't you notice anything special about him? Something that struck you particularly?"

"Such as what?"

"Such as his striking resemblance—his resemblance to me, for instance, Anton Antonovich. Well, you mentioned in passing our family resemblance. You mentioned it quite casually, Anton Antonovich. But, you know, there are twins who look exactly alike, like two drops of water, so that they can't be told apart. Well, that's what I was thinking of."

"Well, yes," Anton Antonovich said, after a moment's thought, as if he had just become aware of the fact. "Yes, you have a point there—a really rather striking resemblance, and you are right when you say it is hard to tell you two apart," he went on, opening his eyes wider and wider. "And do you know what, Yakov Petrovich, it is really an incredible resemblance, a fantastic one, as they say. I mean, he is exactly like you. I wanted to ask you about him, Yakov Petrovich, but, I admit, I hadn't realized the full extent of the resemblance at first. It's a real marvel, I'm telling you, a real marvel! Tell me now, Yakov Petrovich, you're not a native of this part of the country, are you?"

"No, I'm not."

"Neither is he, you know. Perhaps the two of you hail from the same parts then. May I ask you, where did your mother live mostly?"

"You say, Anton Antonovich, that he doesn't come from around here?"

"That's right, he doesn't. Indeed, it's all very strange," continued Anton Antonovich, for whom a chat was always a treat. "There's something here that might arouse one's curiosity, although we pass by and brush against so many curious things without noticing them. But I wouldn't worry too much about it, if I were you. Things like this do happen. You know, the same thing happened to a maternal aunt of mine; she saw her double just before she died. . . ."

"No, I—please forgive me for interrupting you, Anton Antonovich—what I was trying to find out is on what basis that clerk is here."

"Well, he has been appointed to replace the late Semyon Ivanovich. There was a vacant position and so he got the job.

Ah, poor Semyon Ivanovich, I understand he has left three tenny-weeny children behind him. His widow came to beseech His Excellency. But I've heard she really has a little capital tucked away . . ."

"No, Anton Antonovich, I still want to find out about that other thing."

"What do you mean? Ah, yes, but why should it bother you so much? I'm telling you, don't be embarrassed. It's to some extent only a temporary thing and, anyway, it's none of your doing. It's God's will and it'd be a sin to complain against it. You can see His wisdom in it. And as far as I can see, Yakov Petrovich, none of all this is your fault at all. There are plenty of strange things in the world; Mother Nature is generous and you won't be held responsible for it. Now, for instance, take those—ah, what do you call them?—ah yes, Siamese twins, with their backs joined together. Well, they manage to live like that, eat and sleep together and, I understand, make a lot of money."

"Just a minute, Anton Antonovich. . . ."

"I understand, I understand! But really, what of it? Believe me, there's nothing to get upset about. What's the matter then? Well, he's just another government employee and looks like a competent fellow. He claims his name is Golyadkin, that he doesn't come from this part of the country, that he has been employed as a government clerk before. He had a personal interview with His Excellency."

"And what did His Excellency say?"

"Why, nothing special. I understand he gave satisfactory answers to the questions asked, gave his reasons for applying —being without means, he'd apparently decided to take a post and insisted he was very anxious to work 'under your orders, Your Excellency,' and well, he said all the right sort of things and put it well enough. Seems like a clever fellow. And, of course, he came with a recommendation. He wouldn't have been hired without one, of course."

"And who gave it to him? I mean who had a hand in that disgraceful business?"

"I understand he had a very good recommendation. His Excellency had a good laugh about it with Andrei Filipovich."

"Had a laugh with Andrei Filipovich?"

"Yes, although actually Andrei Filipovich just smiled and

said that as long as the fellow did his duty, he had nothing against taking him on."

"Well, and then? You reassure me a little, Anton Antonovich, please go on."

"Again, I don't quite understand you . . . Well, nothing very complicated. It's a very simple matter and as I said, there's nothing for you to get upset about, nothing that could reflect upon your . . ."

"What I wanted to ask you, Anton Antonovich, is whether His Excellency didn't say anything else, anything concerning me, for instance?"

"Oh, to be sure! Well, yes . . . No, nothing. You needn't worry about it. Of course, it is quite striking when one first realizes it . . . Now, take me for instance. I hardly noticed anything at first. In fact, I can't understand now how I could've failed to notice it before you called my attention to it. But you can rest assured that His Excellency said nothing about it, not a word," said the kindly Anton Antonovich, getting up from his chair.

"And so, Anton Antonovich, I am . . ."

"You'll have to excuse me now. As it is, I've been chatting here about all these trivial matters, quite forgetting that I have to finish some important business. I must go and inquire about it now."

"Anton Antonovich!" Andrei Filipovich politely called the head clerk. "His Excellency has been asking for you."

"Just one second, Andrei Filipovich, I'm coming," Anton Antonovich cried out and, picking up a file of documents, he rushed off, first over to Andrei Filipovich's desk and from there into His Excellency's office.

"So what's going on around here?" Golyadkin thought. "So that's the game they're trying to play! I see, that's the way the wind's blowing now then. . . . Well, it's not too bad. Indeed, it looks as if things had taken a most favorable turn," he muttered to himself, rubbing his hands with glee and no longer feeling his chair under him in his joy. "So my affair turns out to be a quite ordinary matter and everything will turn out all right. Yes, no one's whispering anything, and each one of these crooks is just sitting there and minding his own business. That's just great! I've always liked a kind man and am always prepared to respect him . . . Although, I must say, when one thinks of it, I'm somewhat afraid to trust that Anton Antonovich. His hair is too white and he's getting a bit shaky in his old age. But the most important and the most glorious thing is that His Excellency didn't say a thing and thus must have ignored the matter. That's wonderful and I can only approve of it. Only, why does Andrei Filipovich have to interfere with his snicker? What business is it of his, anyway? The old creep! Why does he always have to get in my way? Why must he always run across people's paths like some black cat? Just to spite people, I guess. . . ."

Golyadkin looked around again, and was again cheered by hope, although a vague apprehension still remained. Now it even occurred to him that he might perhaps try to approach the other clerks himself, to get talking to them as they left the office, or to approach them in the course of his work, and tell them, or just hint to them, something to the effect that: You see, here's how it is, such a striking resemblance, such an incredible occurrence, such a trick of fate—that is, to take the whole thing as a joke, while gauging the extent of the real danger. "Because under the still waters of ponds, wicked water sprites may live," our hero concluded.

Actually, Golyadkin didn't toy long with the idea of approaching the clerks; soon enough he changed his mind. He realized that this would be going too far. "That's just my nature," he said, slapping himself lightly on the head. "As soon as you're pleased about something, you go completely wild. Ah, you're much too open-hearted, Golyadkin. You'd better wait and see!"

Nevertheless, he was filled with new hope and felt like a man raised from the dead. "Never mind," he thought, "I feel as though five hundred pounds had been lifted from my chest. But the solution was quite simple—just like in that fable of Krylov's. The way to open the box was simply to lift the lid, the simplest way, and, as in the fable, there was no need for all those complications. Ah, what a good fable and what a smart fellow that Krylov was, what a great fable writer! And as to that clerk, good luck to him. Let him work in this office and, as long as he doesn't interfere with others and doesn't try to harm anyone, he'll have my complete approval!"

Meantime, the hours were flying by and the next thing Golyadkin knew, the clock was striking four. The office closed. Andrei Filipovich took his hat and, as usual, all the others followed his example. Golyadkin deliberately took his time and left the office last, after all the others had already gone, each his separate way. In the street he felt as if he were in paradise; he decided to take a longer way home that would take him to the Nevsky Prospect. "This is the life for you," he said to himself. "What an unexpected turn of events. And the weather is turning nice, clear and cold, and it's freezing and soon we'll be riding in sleighs. Cold suits the Russian for the Russian gets on wonderfully in cold and snow, and I love the Russian people so, and I love the first snow on the ground, which is the right time to go shooting hares, hunters say. Ah, it's really great. Well, never mind."

This is how Golyadkin expressed his joy at being alive, although something was still nagging him, something that perhaps wasn't exactly anguish but that was strong enough to make his heart pump so hard that he didn't know how to relieve the pressure.

"It's really wiser to wait for the morning before rejoicing. But what's it all about? All right, let's try to work it out. Well, let's think it out, my young friend. In the first place, here's a man exactly like you, exactly the same. Well, what of it? Should I weep because he is like me? What is it to me? I don't care. I just go walking on my way, whistling. All right, let him work in the office. Well, it may be freakish and all, and then there are those Siamese twins . . . But what have Siamese twins got to do with it? All right, they're twins, but then some great people have also had a freakish air about them. It is a well known historical fact, for instance, that the great General Suvorov liked to crow like a cock. . . . Well, but then he did that for political considerations and the great military leaders. But what have the military leaders to do with it? As for me, I just mind my own business. I don't wish to get involved with anyone and, in my innocence, I despise my enemies. I don't go in for intrigue and I'm proud of it. I'm clean, straightforward, neat, pleasant and forgiving."

Suddenly Golyadkin's train of thought snapped. He began to shiver and even closed his eyes for a second in the hope that the cause of his terror was only an illusion. Then he opened his eyes and cast an apprehensive sidelong glance to the right. No, it was no illusion!

Walking next to Golyadkin in quick little steps was his new colleague. The man was smiling, looking into Golyadkin's face, and apparently waiting for an opportunity to get into conversation with him. But somehow the conversation wouldn't get started. They walked along next to each other like that for fifty yards or so, with Golyadkin trying to hide as much of his face as possible under his coat collar and hat, aware all the time, to his greater mortification, that his companion's coat and hat looked as though they had just been pulled off Golyadkin's back and head.

"My dear sir," our hero brought out at last, almost in a whisper and without looking at the other, "I don't believe we're going the same way. . . . I'm even quite sure we're not," he added after a brief pause. "And lastly, I'm quite certain I've made myself clear," he concluded quite firmly.

"I would have liked," Golyadkin's companion said finally, "I would have liked . . . I'm sure you'll be generous enough to forgive me . . . I don't know whom else I could have approached here . . . my position—I hope you will forgive my boldness—I even had the impression that you had displayed some sympathy for me this morning. For my part, I immediately felt attracted toward you . . ."

At this point, Golyadkin silently wished that his companion might be swallowed up by the earth.

"If I dared to hope, Yakov Petrovich, that you'd have the indulgence to hear me out . . ."

"We . . . here . . . No, let's go to my place instead," Golyadkin decided. "We'll cross the Nevsky Prospect here. It'll be more convenient for us to go that way, then we'll take that narrow sidestreet. . . . Yes, we'd better do that."

"Very good, let's go by the sidestreet," said Golyadkin's companion in a shy tone, thus indicating that he was in no position to choose whether they were to go by sidestreets or not. As for Golyadkin, he was utterly at a loss and did not realize what was going on. Indeed, he hadn't yet had time to recover from his surprise.

Chapter 7

H<small>E RECOVERED A BIT</small> as they were walking upstairs.
"Ah, what a blockhead," he said, reproaching himself in his
thoughts. "Where do I think I'm taking him? Why do I have
to put my own head in a noose? What will Petrushka say
when he sees us together? What will that good-for-nothing
imagine now, suspicious lout that he is?"

But it was too late to change his mind. Golyadkin
knocked at the door. It opened and Petrushka started to help
the visitor out of his overcoat. Golyadkin glanced at Petrushka, trying to guess what was going on in the fellow's
head. To his great amazement, he saw that his servant manifested no surprise at all. Indeed, it looked as if he had been
expecting some such thing to happen. Of course, even now,
he had a wolf-like look and kept his head averted, as though
preparing to devour someone.

"Could it be that someone has bewitched them all today?" Golyadkin thought. "Some devil must've put his spell
on them. I'm sure there's something peculiar about everyone.
Ah, hell!"

Such were Golyadkin's thoughts and reflections as he led
his visitor into his room and invited the man to sit down.
The guest seemed to be in a state of extreme agitation. He
shyly watched his host's every move, tried to look into his
eyes and, thus, apparently, to guess what Golyadkin was
thinking. There was something humble, downtrodden, and
frightened about all his gestures and, if we may make the

comparison, he was like a man who, not having anything to put on, dresses in clothes belonging to someone else and finds that the sleeves keep pulling back and uncovering his arms and that the waist is almost up around his neck, so that he has to keep pulling down the ridiculously skimpy waistcoat, at one moment trying to conceal his ridiculous figure and at the next, trying to catch people's glances to see whether they are laughing at him or are ashamed of him—and the man blushes and loses countenance, and his self-esteem suffers.

Golyadkin put his hat on the window sill too close to the edge, and the hat fell to the floor. The visitor hurried over and picked it up, brushed off the dust, and replaced it on the window sill. He put his own hat on the floor by the chair, on the edge of which he modestly seated himself.

This little incident indicated to Golyadkin that the man had great need of him. And so he stopped worrying about how to open the conversation, very properly leaving that to his guest. But for his part, the guest, either out of shyness or because he believed that it would be more polite to wait for his host to speak first, also remained silent. In the meantime, Petrushka appeared in the doorway and stared into the corner of the room farthest from where his master and the guest were seated.

"Must I get two dinners?" he asked hoarsely in an off-hand tone.

"I don't know . . . What about you? . . . Yes, all right, get two dinners then."

Petrushka left. Golyadkin glanced at his guest. The guest blushed to the roots of his hair. Golyadkin was a kind man and so concocted a whole theory then and there: "Poor fellow," Golyadkin thought, "and it's his very first day on the new job. I'm sure he's suffered a great deal in his time. Probably the quite decent clothes on his back are his entire possessions, and he hasn't even enough money to buy himself dinner. Just look at him, how downtrodden he seems! Well, never mind, I suppose it's better this way . . ."

"Forgive me for . . ." Golyadkin began, "but if I may ask, what shall I call you?"

"I'm . . . I'm Yakov Petrovich Golyadkin," the visitor said almost in a whisper, as though he were terribly ashamed of also being called Yakov Petrovich Golyadkin and were begging his host to forgive him.

"Yakov Petrovich!" our hero repeated, unable to conceal his shock.

"Well, yes, that's right. I'm your namesake, sir," replied Golyadkin's humble guest, daring to smile and to speak in a light tone. But he at once drew back and again looked grave and embarrassed, realizing that his host was in no joking mood.

"I would like to ask you what made you decide to do me the honor . . . ?"

"Knowing of your kindness and generosity," the guest said quickly, although in a timid voice, rising slightly from his seat, "I dared to turn to you and seek your acquaintance and your protection . . ."

Apparently the guest found it hard to choose the right words; he was trying to sound neither too flattering nor too self-deprecating, as that would have humiliated him too much, but at the same time, he didn't want to lay a brash claim to equality. In general, it may be said that Golyadkin's visitor was behaving like a well bred beggar in his patched frockcoat, a gentleman's passport in his pocket, a beggar who hadn't yet mastered the art of stretching his hand out, palm up.

"I am still at a loss," Golyadkin said, glancing at himself, at the walls of his room, then at his visitor. "In what capacity can I . . . I mean how can I be of any service to you?"

"I, Yakov Petrovich, I felt drawn to you at once, and please forgive me, I built my hopes—I dared to hope . . . I'm poor, Yakov Petrovich, and I feel completely lost here, being new to the place. And when they told me that, besides your innate kindness, you had the same name as me . . ." (Golyadkin screwed up his nose in distaste at this point) "and that you hailed from the same part of the country as I do, I made up my mind to turn to you and explain the painful position in which I find myself."

"All right, all right, I really don't know what to say just now," Golyadkin said in an embarrassed tone. "Let's have our dinner first and we'll talk about it later."

The guest bowed and soon the dinner was brought in. Petrushka set the table and both host and guest proceeded to appease their appetites. The meal didn't last very long; both men were in a hurry, the host because he was ill at ease over the poor quality of the dinner—he would have liked to offer his guest some nice food and also to show him that he didn't live too badly. For his part, the visitor seemed terribly embarrassed: having helped himself to one slice of bread, he didn't dare to stretch out his hand to take another; he wouldn't accept the jucier morsels, assuring his host that he wasn't really hungry, although the dinner was sumptuous, and that he greatly appreciated the invitation and would be grateful as long as he lived. When they had finished eating, Golyadkin lighted a pipe and offered one to his guest. They sat down facing one another and the visitor began to tell his story.

It took the visitor three or four hours to tell his story. It consisted, however, of the most trivial incidents and was unrolled against what we may describe as a rather sordid background. It had to do with service in some provincial court, with prosecutors and judges, with intrigues and corruption, with a certain court clerk and an inspector. An unexpected change of governors had made the second Mr. Golyadkin an innocent victim and brought hardship upon his elderly Aunt Pelageya Semyonovna. Losing his position through the intrigues of his foes, he set out on foot for Petersburg, where for a long time he was unable to find a position and suffered great misery once he had spent all his money. He almost had to spend his nights in the street, ate stale bread, washing it down with his tears, slept on the bare floor . . . At last, some kind person interceded for him, gave him a generous recommendation, and got him a job.

Golyadkin's visitor kept wiping his tears with a blue check handkerchief that looked very much like oilcloth for a table. He ended by admitting that he had, for the time being, no means of subsistence, no money to rent a room or even to buy himself some clothes; that he couldn't afford a pair of decent shoes and that the frockcoat had only been hired somewhere for a short time.

Golyadkin was genuinely moved. And, although the visitor's story was rather trivial, each word of it fell like heavenly manna on his heart. Golyadkin had discarded his misgivings; he allowed his heart to reign freely and, in the end, decided that he had been a fool. It had all come about very naturally. Of course, there was still that rather awkward circumstance—but there was nothing that disastrous about it: How could a man's honor be tarnished and his career ruined by something that was not of his making, when Nature herself had taken a hand in it? And then, his guest was asking him for protection, his guest was weeping, complaining about the cruelty of fate, his guest seemed to be such a helpless, harmless, artless person, so weak and pitiful, and he was probably quite oppressed by his strange resemblance to his host. The guest behaved in a seemly manner, appeared anxious to please his host, and had the look of a man who feels guilty before another man. When, for instance, the conversation touched upon some controversial point, the guest hurriedly agreed with the host; and if, by chance, the visitor happened to express an opinion which Golyadkin, as it turned out, didn't share, he quickly retracted what he had said and announced that he actually felt, thought, and understood it exactly the way his host did. In short, the visitor did his utmost to please Golyadkin and Golyadkin was finally compelled to conclude that his guest was a very amiable companion indeed.

It was close to nine o'clock when tea was brought in. Golyadkin was in a very cheerful mood. He had completely relaxed and was now letting himself go. He talked with great animation. When in high spirits, Golyadkin was fond of telling amusing stories, and so now he held forth to his visitor about the beauties and pleasures of Petersburg; about the theaters and clubs; about Bruylov's painting of the "The Last Days of Pompei"; about the two Englishmen who had come all the way to Petersburg just to take a look at the iron railings of the Summer Gerden, and having taken a look had immediately gone back; about the office; about Olsufy Ivanovich and Andrei Filipovich; about Russia progressing daily toward a state of perfection and how the arts and humanities were flourishing; about an anecdote he had read recently in the Northern Bee about a boa constrictor of extraordinary size found in India; about the literary critic who wrote under the pseudonym of Baron Brambeus, and so on. In short, Golyadkin was pleased because, in the first place, he felt quite safe; in the second place, he was not only not afraid of his enemies now, he was prepared to challenge them all to merciless combat; and in the third place, he now had someone he could patronize while accomplishing a good deed.

However, he admitted to himself that there was still a tiny worm gnawing at his heart—oh, just a tiny one—that prevented him from being perfectly happy. The thought of last night's party at Olsufy Ivanovich's still hurt him, and he would have given a great deal to undo many of the things that had taken place there.

"But what does it matter, after all?" Golyadkin decided at last, firmly resolving to behave well in the future and never again to be guilty of such a lapse.

And, since Golyadkin was now quite excited and felt almost perfectly happy, he decided to taste the joys of life. Petrushka brought in some rum and they prepared a punch. Host and guest emptied a couple of glasses apiece. The guest became even more amiable than before, and kept demonstrating his frankness and his easy-going nature. He contributed greatly to Golyadkin's enjoyment and seemed, indeed, to derive enjoyment from watching Golyadkin's pleasure, obviously regarding him as his only true benefactor. At one point, he took a sheet of paper and a pen, asked Golyadkin to turn away while he wrote something, and when he had finished, showed his host what he had written. It turned out to be a quatrain written with a great deal of feeling, in good style, and in beautiful handwriting. Apparently it had been composed by the amiable guest himself:

> If you ever should forget me,
> I for one will not forget,
> For in life all things may happen,
> So remember—we have met.

With tears running down his cheeks, Golyadkin embraced his guest and, quite overcome by emotion, told him some of his most intimate secrets and private affairs, in which Andrei Filipovich and Klara Olsufievna figured quite prominently.

"Well, I'm sure we'll get along fine, Yakov Petrovich," our hero assured his guest. "We'll live together like fish in water, like brothers. And then we'll scheme too, my friend, we'll plot together, just to spite the lot of them. But don't you ever trust any of them, Yakov Petrovich, because I know you well and understand your nature perfectly. You are a man who'll go and tell anyone everything he has in his heart. You're so artless, so straightforward! No, brother, you'd better keep to yourself with those people."

The guest fully agreed. He thanked Golyadkin again and again, and in the end also shed some tears.

"You know what, Yasha," Golyadkin said in a voice

weak with emotion, calling his guest by the diminutive of his first name, "why not come and stay with me for a time? I'm sure we'll get along fine. Well, what do you say? And another thing, don't let that strange coincidence bother you, Yasha, for what's the good of protesting—that's just nature for you. Besides, let me tell you something. Mother Nature is generous, believe me. I tell you that from the bottom of my loving heart, Yasha, like a brother to a brother. And remember, we're going to scheme. We'll undermine them all and show them what's what!"

When each had emptied his third and then his fourth glass of punch, Golyadkin became aware of two sensations: The first was that he was an extremely happy man and the second that he could no longer stand on his feet. It goes without saying that the guest was invited to stay for the night. They improvised an emergency bed out of two rows of chairs. The guest explained to Golyadkin that, under a friend's roof, even the bare floor would feel soft to his body; that he was sure he would sleep anywhere with gratitude and humility; that now he felt as if he were in paradise; that he had gone through so much misery and hardship in his life, and who could tell what the future had in store? Perhaps he'd have to go through all those things again.

Golyadkin protested against such a pessimistic view and declared that one must put one's faith in God. To that the guest readily agreed and said, of course, there was no one like God. This made Golyadkin remark that, in a sense, the Turks were right to call out the name of God even in their sleep; as a matter of fact, he didn't go along with certain scholars in some of their slanders about the Turkish prophet Mohammed whom he, Golyadkin, considered a great statesman. From there, Golyadkin passed on to a very interesting description of an Algerian barbershop which he had found in the supplement of a magazine.

Host and guest laughed at the simple-mindedness of the Turks, although they felt obliged to pay tribute to the Turks' fanaticism, exacerbated by the use of opium.

The guest began to undress and Golyadkin went behind the partition, partly out of kindness, not to embarrass the other if he didn't happen to have a decent shirt, and partly to see how Petrushka was taking it all, to try and cheer the fellow up, so that everyone should be happy and pleasant.

For it must be noted that Golyadkin still felt a bit uneasy in Petrushka's presence.

"You can turn in now, Petrushka," Golyadkin said, stepping meekly into his servant's cubicle. "Go to bed now and wake me up tomorrow at eight. Do you understand, Petrushka?"

Golyadkin said this in an unusually nice and friendly tone. But Petrushka didn't answer. At that moment he was puttering around his bed and didn't even look at his master, as he should have, if only out of politeness.

"Did you hear what I said, Petrushka?" Golyadkin said. "You go to bed now and wake me up tomorrow at eight. Do you understand?"

"Sure I do. There's nothing special about it," Petrushka muttered indistinctly.

"That's fine, Petrushka. I only said it so you shouldn't worry, so you'd feel happy. Everyone is happy and comfortable and I wanted you to feel happy and comfortable too. And now, good night and sleep well, Petrushka. We all have to work to earn our living, you know, and I don't want you to think . . ." Golyadkin interrupted himself, wondering whether he wasn't going a bit far. "I'm almost overdoing things," he thought, and left Petrushka's cubicle rather displeased with himself. Besides, he was a little offended by Petrushka's rudeness and unresponsiveness. "I was trying to be nice to the brute. He should be pleased and honored, but he doesn't appreciate it in the least," Golyadkin thought. "Well, I suppose that's just the way that sort of person is!"

Golyadkin returned to his room, swaying slightly and, seeing that his guest had settled himself in for the night, sat down for a moment on the edge of his bed.

"You might just as well admit, Yasha," he began in a whisper, shaking his head, "that you're a rascal and that you're guilty toward me. For, let me tell you, my dear namesake, you're something of a . . . well, you know . . ." Golyadkin went on playfully, feeling very free and easy with his guest now.

Finally, Golyadkin said goodnight and went to bed. At once, the visitor began to snore. Making himself comfortable, Golyadkin chuckled and whispered to himself: "Why, you're drunk tonight, you rascal you, Yakov Petrovich Golyadkin, with that cockeyed name of yours! And what is there for you to be so pleased about? Well, tomorrow you'll weep, you miserable cry-baby, you. Ah, what is one supposed to do with a fellow like you?"

Suddenly a strange feeling—a mixture of regret and misgiving—descended upon Golyadkin.

"I've let myself go too far," he thought, "and now my head is buzzing and I'm drunk. I couldn't control myself and blurted out at least three bagsful of nonsense. And to think I had intended to be on my guard. Sure, I know that forgiving and forgetting is the first virtue, but still . . ."

And Golyadkin got out of his bed, took the candle and went to have another look at his guest. He stood over the bed of the sleeping man and thought: "What a most unpleasant sight! It's a sort of practical joke, a real practical joke being played on me! Yes, that's what it is!"

Finally he really got into his bed. His head was buzzing, ringing, creaking. He began to doze off. He was on the point of remembering something, of thinking about something very interesting, solving some very important, intricate business, but he couldn't stay with it. Sleep overwhelmed his perturbed head, and he slept as non-drinking people usually do when they have downed five glasses of punch during a reunion with a friend.

Chapter 8

On the following day, Golyadkin woke up at eight as usual. At once everything that had happened the evening before came back to him and made him screw up his nose. "Ah, I really did let myself go like a fool last night," he muttered to himself, sitting up and glancing toward his friend's bed.

But what was his amazement when he saw neither his companion nor the emergency contraption on which he had slept.

"What's happened?" Golyadkin almost cried aloud. "What can this mean? What's this new mystery now?"

While Golyadkin was gaping at the empty spot, Petrushka walked in, carrying his tea on a tray.

"Where is he?" our hero asked in a hardly audible voice, pointing to the place where the guest's bed had stood the night before.

At first Petrushka didn't even answer, didn't even look at his master. Instead, he turned his eyes to the corner of the room to his right, so that Golyadkin also looked at that corner. But then, after a silence, Petrushka himself volunteered the following information: "The master isn't at home," he said rudely, in a hoarse voice.

"What are you talking about, you fool?" Golyadkin said, breathing very hard and staring at his servant. "I'm your master and I'm here."

Petrushka didn't answer but gave Golyadkin a look that

made him blush to the roots of his hair. The look was so insulting and so full of indignation that it felt just like a torrent of abuse. Golyadkin felt like giving up when Petrushka informed him that the *other one* had left an hour and a half before and had said he wouldn't wait. What Petrushka said was very likely true; it was obvious he wasn't just inventing it, that his insulting looks and his use of the words the *other one* were due to the depressing circumstances we have already mentioned. Still, Golyadkin felt that there was something more behind it all and that fate had yet another unpleasant surprise in store for him.

"All right, we'll see," he thought. "We'll watch it, we'll understand in good time what it's all about. . . . Ah, good Lord!" he whimpered in conclusion, in a quite different tone. "Why on earth did I have to invite him here? What was it that drove me to do it? Why, I'm deliberately sticking my head into the noose those bandits are preparing for me. Ah, what a stupid blockhead! Couldn't I resist one minute before letting out all those lies—like some street urchin or some pen-pushing clerk of no rank, like a wet rag, like a stupid old woman, a damned gossip! Ah, damnation, that poem the animal wrote and all the protestations of affection he made! Now what will be the best thing to do if he comes back? Should I just point to the door? I'm sure there are many ways and means of handling such a situation: 'Well, you must understand that, having to live on my small salary . . .' Or I could just scare him off by asking him to contribute one-half of the expenses for the room and board, and demanding that he pay in advance. No, to hell with that! It'd make me sound cheap. Unless I could perhaps get Petrushka to rub him the wrong way, to be rude to him or something, just to make him leave? I could try to set 'em against each other. . . . Ah, damn it, that'd be too dangerous and, from a certain point of view, it wouldn't be right. Ah, what's the use! And what if he doesn't come back here? Well, that'd be bad too, for I did much too much talking last night. It's a really bad business I've got myself into. Ah, what a stupid, stupid fool I am! Seems I'll never learn how to conduct myself properly. Now, suppose he does come back and tells me he's decided not to accept my offer to move in? I hope to God he does just that! I'd give anything to see him do that!"

Golyadkin thought all this as he was drinking his morning tea, continually watching the clock on the wall of his room.

"Quarter to nine, almost time for me to go. What will happen now? I'd like to know what's behind all this: What's the object, the aim of all these tricks? I'd give a lot to find out what all those people are after and what their first move will be."

Golyadkin couldn't endure it any longer. He abandoned his unsmoked pipe, dressed, and ran all the way to the office, hoping that his presence might forestall the danger threatening him. As to the existence of such a danger, he had no doubt about it.

"Well, now we'll appraise the situation," Golyadkin said to himself, removing his overcoat and overshoes in the entrance hall. "We'll get to the bottom of it."

Having decided that, our hero straightened his clothes, satisfied himself that he had a dignified and official air, and was about to pass into the room adjoining the entrance hall when, in the very doorway, he butted into his companion of the night before. It looked as though Golyadkin Two hadn't noticed Golyadkin One, although they almost touched noses. Golyadkin Two seemed very busy, obviously in a great hurry to get somewhere. He was quite out of breath and wore such an official and important expression that one could read all over his face: "I have been charged with a special errand."

"So there you are, Yakov Petrovich," our hero said, grabbing his previous night's guest by the arm.

"Later, later, excuse me. You'll tell me everything later," Golyadkin Two shouted, trying to free his arm and dash on.

"No, wait. It seems to me, Yakov Petrovich, that you wanted . . . you wanted . . ."

"Wanted what? Would you please be quick and tell me what you have in mind?"

The guest of the previous night stopped reluctantly and put his ear right up to Golyadkin's nose.

"I must tell you, Yakov Petrovich, I'm rather surprised at your ways. I never expected anything of this sort from you."

"There's a proper form for everything. You must present your petition to His Excellency's secretary, after which you'll have to go through the proper channels to the head of the office. Do you have your petition here with you?"

"Really, Yakov Petrovich! I don't understand you at all. Do you really not recognize me? No, you must be joking— you're such a gay, fun-loving person."

"Ah, so it's you!" Golyadkin Two said, as though he had just recognized Golyadkin One. "Well, how did you sleep?"

Golyadkin Two smiled. It was a rather stiff, official smile, not at all the smile that might be expected from a man who had a debt of gratitude. And having smiled thus, he declared that he was delighted that Golyadkin One slept well. Then he leaned to the left, shuffled his feet for a while, glanced to the right, then to the left, lowered his eyes, took aim at a side door, whispered quickly, slurring his words, that he was on an urgent errand, darted through the door, and vanished.

"That's really something!" our hero whispered, feeling a bit numb for a moment. "That's really, really something!" And Golyadkin felt as if thousands of ants were running up and down all over his body. "But then, after all," he said to himself as he went to his desk, "wasn't I aware all along that he was here on a special mission. Yes, that's exactly what I said yesterday. There can be no doubt about it, he is here on a special errand for someone."

"Have you finished the document you were working on yesterday?" Anton Antonovich asked as soon as Golyadkin had installed himself at his desk. "Do you have it here, please?"

"Yes, it's here," said Golyadkin, looking helplessly at the head clerk.

"Good. I asked you because Andrei Filipovich has inquired about it twice. His Excellency may send for it at any moment."

"I've finished with it, Anton Antonovich."

"Well, very good then."

"It seems to me, Anton Antonovich, that I've always done my work properly and I've always scrupulously discharged the duties entrusted to me by my superiors."

"Well, yes. But why do you say that now?"

"For no special reason, Anton Antonovich, I was simply trying to say that . . . that sometimes ill-wishers and envious people spare no one in their search for their abominable daily bread . . ."

"I'm afraid I don't quite understand you. What person are you alluding to?"

"All I was trying to say, Anton Antonovich, is that I believe in following a straight path, I scorn devious ways. I don't go in for intrigue, and I am proud of my conduct, even if I say so myself."

"Yes, sir, that is all very true, and I fully agree with your views on the subject. But now allow me to tell you in my turn, Yakov Petrovich, that offending people is not really permissible in good society, that I can stand being slighted when I am not present because who is not abused behind his back? But, whatever you say, I won't allow anyone to be insolent to my face. No sir, my hair has turned gray in the government service, and I certainly am not going to stand for impertinence."

"No, no, Anton Antonovich, I don't think you understood me right. Believe me, I would consider it only as an honor . . ."

"Well, and you'd better forgive us too, because we've been trained in the old school, and it's too late for us to learn your new ways. So far, though, our understanding of things has proved adequate to the service of our country and, as you are well aware, I'm sure, I have a medal for twenty-five years of service without a blemish. . . ."

"I agree, Anton Antonovich, I fully agree, but that is not what I was talking about. I was speaking of a mask, Anton Antonovich."

"Of a mask?"

"I'm afraid you may once again misinterpret what I say, Anton Antonovich, the meaning of my remarks, that is . . . It's only a theory I have . . . Well, I feel that people who wear masks aren't very rare nowadays, and that it is becoming increasingly hard to recognize a man under his mask."

"I don't think it is all that hard. In fact, there's often nothing easier, and there's no need to go far to find him."

"No, Anton Antonovich, I don't agree. Speaking of myself, I, for instance, I only put on a mask when I have to, for a carnival, for gay parties, in the direct sense, but I do not wear a mask every day, when I deal with people. I mean it not in a literal but in a more subtle, figurative sense now. And that's what I wanted to tell you, Anton Antonovich."

"Well, anyway, we'd better leave it for the time being. I'm rather busy," Anton Antonovich said, picking up some papers to go and make a report to His Excellency. "As to the business that you're so worried about, I'm sure it will all come clear soon enough and you'll be able to judge for yourself whom to suspect and whom to accuse. In the meantime I'd greatly appreciate it if you'd dispense with any further private comments and explanations that interfere with our work."

"No, no, Anton Antonovich," Golyadkin said, turning a little pale and addressing the retreating figure of the head clerk, "I had no such idea."

Alone, after Anton Antonovich had gone, Golyadkin thought: "What's going on now? What new winds are blowing here and what's this new snag?"

And at the very moment when our crushed and bewildered hero was trying to solve this new enigma, a sound of bustling about came from the next room, the door opened, and Andrei Filipovich, who had just returned from His Excellency's office, appeared breathless in the doorway and called Mr. Golyadkin. Knowing what it was about and anxious not to keep Andrei Filipovich waiting, Golyadkin leaped up from his chair and, fussing madly, started gathering up the file in question and preparing to follow the file and Andrei Filipovich into His Excellency's room. Suddenly, slipping almost under the elbow of Andrei Filipovich, who was standing in the doorway, Golyadkin Two darted into the room. In a great hurry, huffing and puffing with a very solemn and official expression on his face, he rolled right up to Golyadkin One, who was completely taken aback by this forceful assault.

"Those papers, Yakov Petrovich, let's have those papers! His Excellency wants to know whether they're ready," Golyadkin Two chirped stridently. "Hurry, Andrei Filipovich is waiting for you. . . ."

"I don't need you to tell me he's waiting," Golyadkin One said in a quick whisper.

"No, you don't understand me, Yakov Petrovich, I'm speaking as a friend. I'm moved by heartfelt sympathy for you . . ."

"I'd greatly appreciate it if you'd spare me your friendship and sympathy. And now, I hope you'll excuse me. . . ."

"Wait, Yakov Petrovich, you'd better put those sheets into a folder and put a marker at page three. . . ."

"Please, let me take care of it myself, after all."

"But there's an ink blot here, Yakov Petrovich. Hadn't you noticed that ink blot?"

Andrei Filipovich called Golyadkin for the second time.

"I'm coming, Andrei Filipovich, I'm coming right away. I must just . . . Listen, don't you understand plain language?"

"I think the best thing would be to scrape it off with a penknife, Yakov Petrovich, and if you'll take my advice, you'll let me do it. I shouldn't try to scrape it off yourself if I were you."

Andrei Filipovich called Golyadkin for the third time.

"But what are you talking about? Where did you see an ink blot?"

"It's a huge blot. There it is! I saw it just a second ago. Let me take it off for you. I'll do it with a penknife . . . I'm doing this for your sake, Yakov Petrovich, in all sincerity. And here we go and that's the end of it."

And catching Golyadkin completely unaware, Golyadkin Two snatched the file out of his hands. But, instead of trying to scrape off an ink blot with a penknife as he had been going to do for friendship's sake, he thrust the folder under his arm and in two bounds was standing next to Andrei Filipovich, who hadn't noticed the maneuver. And the two of them hurried into the Director's office while Golyadkin One remained as though riveted to his seat with his penknife still in his hand, seemingly preparing to scrape something off with it.

Our hero hadn't yet fully grasped the new situation. He hadn't quite recovered. He felt the blow but hoped that somehow nothing would be changed. Finally, he managed to tear himself from his seat and, in indescribable anguish, rushed into the Director's office, praying as he went that everything would turn out all right, that nothing horrible would come of it.

In the room which adjoined the Director's office, he butted into Andrei Filipovich and his namesake who were already on their way back from the Director's. Andrei Filipovich seemed to be in a very cheerful mood and Golyadkin Two, smiling sweetly and walking respectfully one step behind Andrei Filipovich, was enthusiastically whispering something in his ear, at which Andrei Filipovich kept nodding approvingly.

Now our hero grasped the situation. As a matter of fact, his work (as he found out later), besides being completed in good time, had almost surpassed His Excellency's expectations. His Excellency was extremely pleased. It seemed that His Excellency had even said thank you to Mr. Golyadkin Two, a very warm thank you indeed, and promised him that his zeal would be remembered when the time came . . . .

Obviously, the first thing Golyadkin felt impelled to do was to protest as strongly as he could. Almost beside himself, pale as death, he rushed toward Andrei Filipovich. But hearing that Golyadkin wanted to talk to him about a private grievance, Andrei Filipovich refused to listen to him, declaring that he didn't have a single minute to spare for private talks.

The dryness of his tone and the curtness of his refusal struck Golyadkin. "Perhaps," he thought, "I'd better try another channel. I'd better go and see Anton Antonovich."

But unfortunately Anton Antonovich wasn't at his desk; he was engaged elsewhere.

"I'm sure his asking me to spare him private talks and explanations is most significant," our hero reflected. "So this is what he had in mind, the old snarer! Well, in that case I suppose I'd better dare to go all the way. I'll go and implore His Excellency himself to listen to me."

Still pale and still feeling thoroughly upset, not knowing what to do next, Golyadkin sat down in his chair. "It would be so wonderful if it all turned out to be just nothing," Golyadkin repeated to himself. "It's so sinister it's quite unbelievable. In the first place, it's too absurd, and in the second it's quite impossible. Most likely someone must've dreamt it all up. Or perhaps it just seemed that way but didn't actually happen—perhaps it was I myself who was in His Excellency's room . . . yes, and after that, somehow, I mistook myself for someone else . . . Oh, it's really a quite impossible business."

Just as Golyadkin had decided that it was all quite impossible, Golyadkin Two, carrying papers in both hands and under his arms, burst into the room. He whispered some urgent message to Andrei Filipovich, exchanged a few hurried remarks with someone else, paid a compliment to another man, cracked a joke with yet another, and, apparently having no more time to spare, hurried toward the door, stopping as he was about to leave the room to have a few words with some young officials who were just coming in. Golyadkin One took advantage of this delay and rushed over to Golyadkin Two, who noticed the maneuver and looked worriedly about him, trying to find somewhere where he could take shelter. But before he had time to move, our hero took a firm hold of the sleeve of his visitor of the previous night. Those around them stepped back and waited with curiosity to see what would happen. Then Golyadkin One realized that public opinion was not on his side, and he saw clearly that there was a plot on foot against him. But that made it even more necessary to stand up for himself. It was a decisive moment.

"Well?" Golyadkin Two said curtly, glaring arrogantly at Golyadkin One.

Golyadkin One could hardly breathe.

"I am at a loss," he began, "how to account for your behavior toward me, sir."

"Well? Go on, please," Golyadkin Two said, looking around and winking at the witnesses as if intimating that the farce was about to begin.

"Your impudence and the shameless way you've treated me have unmasked your true character even better than . . . than my words could do. But if I were you, I wouldn't rely so much on your acting ability; it's not really that great. . . ."

"Now, you tell me, Yakov Petrovich, how did you sleep last night?" Golyadkin Two said, looking straight into Golyadkin One's eyes.

"You forget yourself completely, sir," Golyadkin One said, hardly feeling the floor under his feet. "I hope you'll change your tone. . . ."

"Oh, my dear, sweet man," Golyadkin Two replied, making a quite unseemly grimace. Then, all of a sudden, on the pretense of making a friendly gesture, the new Mr. Golyadkin seized his senior's rather pudgy right cheek between two fingers.

Our hero flared up. Apparently realizing that Golyadkin One, who was shaking with fury, speechless with indignation, and red as a boiled lobster had now been driven to the limit of his endurance and would probably even risk a frontal attack, Golyadkin Two decided to forestall him in this too. He patted him a couple of times on the cheek, tickled him a little under the chin, played for a few more seconds with his victim, who was quite paralyzed with rage, and then, to the great delight of the young clerks, gave Golyadkin One a hearty poke in his rotund belly, and, with a venomous smile loaded with threatening hints, said: "You don't say, brother? You don't mean it seriously? Remember, we're in this together, Yakov Petrovich, and we'll outmaneuver the lot of them!"

And before our hero had time to recover from his attack, Golyadkin Two (after exchanging an understanding smile with the audience) assumed a frightfully busy air, lowered his eyes, shrank, contracted, muttered something about being on "an urgent errand," kicked the air with his stumpy leg, and darted into the next room. Our hero, still unable to believe his own eyes, could not gather his wits together.

When he finally came to his senses, he saw in a flash that he was lost, in a sense annihilated, that his reputation had been stained and damaged, that he had been treacherously mocked and bespattered in the presence of other people by a man whom only yesterday he had considered his most reliable friend, that he had indeed failed utterly and hopelessly. And having seen all this in a flash, Golyadkin One rushed out in pursuit of his foe, refusing to think, at that moment, of those who had witnessed his ignominy.

"They're all plotting against me," he muttered to himself. "They're all in it together, setting each other on me." But after having taken ten steps or so in pursuit, Golyadkin One realized that his efforts to catch up with his enemy were futile and he returned to his starting point. "You won't get away," he mused. "You'll get what's coming to you in good time; the world will pay for the tears of lambs!"

With ferocious composure and fierce determination, Golyadkin One reached his chair and sat down. "You won't get away," he said again. It was no longer a matter of passive defense but of full-scale attack, and if anyone had watched Golyadkin at that moment when, flushed and hardly able to control his excitement, he thrust his pen into the inkpot, and had seen the fury with which he started scratching something on a sheet of paper, that person would have understood that the business would not end just like that, and that Golyadkin was not going to take it meekly, like a woman. In the depths of Golyadkin's soul, a resolution had taken shape, and he swore in his heart of hearts to carry it out.

Although to tell the truth, he wasn't quite sure yet what he was going to do. Indeed, he didn't have any idea at all. But never mind. "No one can get away with imposture and shamelessness in our times, my dear sir. Imposture and shamelessness land people in a noose, my good man! There was only one man—Grishka Otrepiev—who managed to deceive people by passing himself off as the Tsar, and even he didn't last long."

But despite this last circumstance, Golyadkin decided to continue waiting until the masks fell off and certain faces were exposed to the light. Since that couldn't happen during office hours, Golyadkin wished the time would pass quickly and decided not to undertake anything until they had. After closing time, he'd do what he had in mind. And after he had done that, he had a whole plan of action ready to shatter the horn of pride and scornfully crush the snake groveling in the dust. In any case, Mr. Golyadkin couldn't allow them to make a doormat out of him. He couldn't allow it, especially as things stood now. Perhaps if the latest indignity had not been inflicted upon him, he might still have decided not to protest violently, to let it go at that, to resign himself. He would've just argued a bit for form's sake, to show them he was right, and then would have made a little concession. Later, perhaps, he would have conceded a bit further still, and then finally conceded completely, especially if his opponents had recognized that he was actually in the right. And later, later he might have forgiven, and who could tell, it is even possible that a warm friendship would have been reborn, a friendship even warmer and more encompassing than it had been yesterday, a friendship such as could have completely overshadowed the unpleasantness of the rather unseemly similarity of their two faces, so that the two clerks would have both been very happy and would have gone on living together until they were a hundred years old, and so on. To tell the truth, Golyadkin ended up by regretting that he had attempted to stand up for himself, since it had done nothing but land him in trouble.

"If he should say he's sorry," Golyadkin thought, "just say that he meant it as a joke, I'd forgive him. I'd even forgive him all the rest too, if he would only admit publicly. But I'm no doormat, and I won't allow anyone to wipe his boots on me—no one, and certainly not a depraved person like him. No sir, I'm no doormat and you'd better remember it!"

In brief, our hero had made up his mind. "You have only yourself to blame, my dear sir!" Golyadkin thought and decided to protest, to protest with all his strength to the very last. Yes, that's the sort of man he was. He couldn't allow anyone to insult him, and especially not to take him for granted, as if he were a doormat, and certainly he was not one to let a depraved man get away with it.

Actually, we won't assert that, if someone had really set out to accomplish it, if he had really tried hard to make a doormat of Mr. Golyadkin, that he couldn't have done so. He'd probably have managed it, and he might not have met with resistance or any great danger (there were moments when Mr. Golyadkin felt this himself), and the result would have been a doormat, a dirty, sordid doormat; but not just an ordinary one. It would have been a doormat with aspirations, with emotions, with feelings, and although those aspirations, emotions, and feelings would be ignored, somewhere at the bottom of the grimy bristles of the doormat, there would remain the hidden feelings—unseen, but feelings nevertheless.

The hours crept by with unbearable slowness. At last it struck four. Soon afterward, everyone got up and, following their chief's example, they all went home. Golyadkin joined the throng, keeping his eyes on the man he wanted. He saw his friend rush up to the hall porters who were handing out the officials' overcoats and, in his usual despicable way, start buzzing around the attendants while waiting for his coat. This was the moment of decision. Golyadkin managed to elbow his way through the crowd and, not wishing to be outdone, also started demanding his overcoat. Nevertheless, it was Golyadkin's friend and namesake who got his coat first, for obviously here too he had managed to intrigue, to whisper the right things into the right ears.

Golyadkin Two put on his coat and glanced sarcastically at Golyadkin One. He was acting with the overt and quite unabashed impudence that was his personal mark. He shuffled about a bit, looked around, apparently to observe the impression he had made upon the other employees, made a friendly remark to one, exchanged a few whispers with another, bowed respectfully to a third, smiled at a fourth, shook hands with a fifth, and darted downstairs.

Golyadkin One tore after him and, to his indescribable joy, caught up with him on the bottom step and seized him by his coat collar. It looked as if Golyadkin Two were taken rather by surprise, for he glanced around with a quite disconcerted air.

"How am I to take this?" he whispered at last in a weak voice.

Fury made Golyadkin One speechless for a second. "If you're an honorable man, sir, I hope you'll remember our friendly relations of yesterday," our hero said at last.

"Well yes . . . Why? You slept well, I hope, didn't you?"

"I did sleep well . . . But allow me to tell you, sir, you're playing a very shady game. . . ."

"Who says that? My enemies must have said it!" the man who claimed his name was Golyadkin answered sharply and, as he said it, he suddenly wriggled himself free of the real Mr. Golyadkin's feeble grip. Once free, he rushed out of the building, looked around, saw a cab, hailed it, jumped into it and, in one second, had vanished from Golyadkin One's sight.

Golyadkin, dejected and feeling abandoned by everyone, looked helplessly around, but couldn't see another free cab. He tried to pursue him on foot, but his legs gave way under him. He leaned against a lamppost and remained standing there for several minutes with his mouth wide open, feeling shrunken and annihilated. All seemed lost for Mr. Golyadkin.

Chapter 9

Iᴛ ʟᴏᴏᴋᴇᴅ ᴀѕ though nature itself was up in arms against Mr. Golyadkin. But he was still on his feet and wouldn't concede defeat. He felt he hadn't lost yet and was prepared to fight on. He rubbed his hands with such feeling and energy that just by looking at him it became quite clear that he was not going to yield. Yet the danger was obvious and imminent, and Golyadkin knew it. The only question was how to cope with that danger. For a second he even wondered whether he shouldn't simply drop the matter at the point it had reached: "Well, shouldn't I just leave it all the way it is, just disregard it? What of it? Nothing. I'll stay out of it, as if it weren't me," Golyadkin thought. "I'll let it all pass me by. It's not me, and that's all there is to it. And he too, perhaps he'll stay out of it, perhaps he'll drop the whole thing. He'll buzz around for a while, and then he'll give it up and drop it all. That's how it'll be! I'll overwhelm them all with sheer meekness. Anyway, how can it all endanger me. Where's the danger? I would like to see the person who could point out what possible danger it could present? It's nothing at all, just a trivial affair that's not worth mentioning . . ."

At this juncture Golyadkin's thought snapped. The words died on his lips. He even reproached himself for thinking that way. He accused himself of cowardice. That, however, didn't advance him any further. He felt that he had to decide something right away, and he would have given anything to the person willing to tell him what he should decide. But how could he guess? But, anyway, there was no time for guessing and, so as not to waste time, he hailed a cab and drove home.

"Well, how do you feel now? Are you satisfied with the way things stand today, Yakov Petrovich Golyadkin? What's your next move, you miserable, scheming little wretch? You've brought all this misery down on yourself and now you're weeping and whimpering."

Golyadkin kept baiting himself as the cab jolted over the cobblestones. At that moment, he enjoyed baiting himself, rubbing in his humiliation. It even gave him a strange, voluptuous feeling.

"Now imagine a magician coming to me and saying . . . Or even better, suppose they made me an official offer, something like: 'If you let us have a finger from your right hand, Golyadkin, we'll call it quits; there will be no other Golyadkin any more and everything will be fine, except that you'll be one finger short.' Well, I'd give them that finger without blinking an eye. . . . Ah, the hell with the whole damned business!" Golyadkin exclaimed in a sudden wave of despair. "Why did this have to happen to me? Why just this thing and not something else? Everything was going so well. Everyone was so happy and pleased, and then this had to happen! But what's the good of talking? It's deeds, not words, that are needed."

And so Golyadkin arrived home almost resolved upon some action and, without wasting one second, seized his pipe and started puffing away furiously, sending jets of smoke right and left, as he darted back and forth across his room.

When Petrushka came in to set the table, Golyadkin suddenly laid down his pipe, grabbed his overcoat, told his servant that he wouldn't be home for dinner, and rushed out. Petrushka tore down the stairs after him and handed his master the hat he had forgotten. Golyadkin took his hat and thought he ought to say a word or two to explain his forgetfulness, in case the fellow started getting ideas. But since Petrushka didn't even look at him and went back upstairs without waiting, Golyadkin donned his hat and went on downstairs, repeating under his breath that possibly everything was for the best, that things would somehow turn out right, although he felt a cold chill right down to his heels. In the street, he took a cab and drove over to Andrei Filipovich's.

When he already had the bell pull in his hand, he began suddenly to wonder: "Wouldn't it be better to see him tomorrow? Anyway, what do I have to tell him that's so special? In fact, I have nothing very special at all. The whole business is just a miserable, sordid little affair, hardly worth bothering about . . ." And Golyadkin suddenly pulled the cord. The bell rang. Someone could be heard walking inside the apartment. Golyadkin cursed himself for his impetuosity and audacity. The recent unpleasant incidents and his brushes with Andrei Filipovich, about which he had almost forgotten, suddenly came back to him very vividly. It was too late to retreat, though. The door opened.

By a stroke of luck he was told that Andrei Filipovich hadn't returned from the office and wasn't expected home for dinner.

"I know where he dines—he dines near the Izmailovsky Bridge," Golyadkin thought, suddenly feeling very pleased. When the servant asked whether there was any message he wished to leave and who he should tell his master had called, Golyadkin said that it wasn't urgent, that he'd come over later. "Thank you, my friend," he said, and ran downstairs feeling positively cheerful.

In the street, he decided to dismiss the cab and settled with the driver who asked for a tip because of the long wait and because he hadn't spared the horse but had driven there at full speed at his fare's insistence. So Golyadkin gave him five kopecks quite willingly and started out on foot.

"Of course, I can't leave things as they are," Golyadkin thought, "but when you come to think of it, does it really matter all that much? Well, let's see—is it really worth kicking up so much fuss about? Is there enough in it for me to suffer over, to tear myself apart, to worry the way I do? In the first place, the damage is done and can't be undone. Let's put it this way: A man presents himself, he has a good recommendation, he's supposed to be an excellent clerk and well behaved; he just happens to be in a difficult financial situation, being a victim of circumstances—vicissitudes of some sort—but, after all, poverty is no sin. So, none of that had anything to do with me. No, really, what is this nonsense? Just because nature has willed it that a man should look like the exact copy of another man, is that a reason to refuse him a job in the department? Since it is the fault of blind fate, why should the poor man be thrown out like an old doormat and not allowed to work? What kind of justice would that be? He is a poor, lost, scared man, and it is impossible not to feel compassion for him. A good thing our chiefs didn't feel as I did! Ah, what a stupid fool I am. I carry enough stupidity around in me to fill three heads. No, no, I'm terribly glad and I'm grateful to our superiors for having given a job to the poor man when he'd seen so many hardships in his life! And now let's just imagine we're twins, that we were just born this way and that's all there is to it. Well, so what? So nothing! It will be very easy to accustom all the other employees to that fact . . . And, of course, if an outsider happened to chance by, he certainly wouldn't find anything prejudicial or shocking about it. In fact, there's something touching about it: God had the idea of creating two altogether identical twins and their superiors in government service decided to give each twin a niche. Although, of course," Golyadkin went on, taking a deep breath, "it would have been even better if there were no such touching business, if there were no twins at all. . . . Ah, devil take them! What need was there for the whole story? Ah, good Lord! It's a real witch's brew or something! And, I must say, that fellow's so tricky, so vicious by nature, he's such a shifty, scheming fellow, such a boot-licker, such a toady. That Golyadkin! I expect he'll do something so unspeakable it'll disgrace my name. And so I'll have to spend my whole time keeping an eye on him, trying to keep him satisfied. Ah, what a nuisance! But, actually, why should I bother? All right, I grant you he's a nasty crook. So, let him be a crook, and I'll be an honest man, and people will say that Golyadkin is a crook, don't bother with him, but don't confuse him with the other Golyadkin, who is a decent, honest, virtuous man, a friendly, reliable public servant who ought to be promoted to a more responsible position. That's fine, but what if they . . . What if our superiors get mixed up? Why, you can expect anything from that man. Ah, dear God, he won't hesitate to step all over a man, as if he were a doormat! Ah, God, what a horrible business it all is!"

Moaning and arguing with himself thus, Golyadkin was running straight ahead, with no idea where he was going. He recovered his senses on the Nevsky Prospect, and then only because he butted into someone so hard that sparks flew. Golyadkin muttered an apology without raising his head, and it was only after he had heard the passer-by let out some rather unflattering remark about him and had already gone on a few steps, that he stopped and looked around to see where he was. He was near that same restaurant into which he had gone to have a snack before going to Olsufy Ivanovich's select dinner party; the thought made our hero feel pangs and rumblings in his stomach, and he remembered that he hadn't eaten yet. So, since there was no dinner party forthcoming, he went into the restaurant and tore hurriedly upstairs to order something to eat. And although everything was rather expensive in that establishment, Mr. Golyadkin decided that that wouldn't stop him this time and, anyway, he had no time for such trifling considerations just then.

In the brightly lighted room, customers were crowding around the counter on which were displayed all those items that decent people delight in eating and drinking. The barman was hardly able to keep up with pouring drinks, handing out snacks, and taking in money. Golyadkin, after waiting his turn, modestly stretched out his hand to pick up a meat pie. Then he went quietly to a corner, turned his back to the company, ate the pie with great appetite, replaced the plate on the counter and, knowing the price of the pie, took a ten kopeck coin from his pocket, placed it on the counter and, catching the barman's eye, pointed to the coin, sort of signifying to him, "Here, this is for the meat pie."

"That'll be one ruble ten kopecks," the barman said through clenched teeth.

Golyadkin was very surprised at that statement.

"Were you addressing me? But I . . . I believe I helped myself to just one meat pie."

"You helped yourself to eleven pies," the barman said with assurance.

"It . . . it seems to me . . . I believe you're making a mistake. . . . Really, I believe I took just one pie."

"I counted them. You took eleven. You've eaten them and now you must pay. We don't give anything away for nothing here."

Golyadkin was flabbergasted. "What is it, after all?" he thought. "Am I the victim of an evil spell or something?"

The barman was waiting. A circle formed around Golyadkin who was already putting his hand into his pocket to fish out a silver ruble and so avoid a row.

"Well, if he says eleven, let it be eleven," he thought, turning crimson. "Suppose even that I ate eleven pies—what of it? All right, a person is hungry and eats eleven pies, so more power to him, there's nothing to laugh about. . . ."

Suddenly something made him feel uncomfortable. He turned his eyes and at once understood the sort of spell he had been made a victim of. The whole mystery was solved. . . .

Behind the barman's back, in the doorway leading to the next room, which until then our hero had mistaken for a mirror, there stood a man. The man was Mr. Golyadkin himself. But it was not Mr. Golyadkin the hero of our narrative. It was the other Golyadkin, the new Mr. Golyadkin. And this new Golyadkin seemed to be in an excellent mood: He was smiling broadly and nodding in a friendly way to Golyadkin, winking understandingly at him; he took a few mincing steps without moving from the spot, but looking prepared to take off at the first alarm and if need be to leave the building by the back stairs, so that all attempts at pursuit would be quite futile. In his hand he was still holding a piece of meat pie and, as Golyadkin looked at him, he put it in his mouth and smacked his lips with delight.

"He's taking advantage of our . . ." Golyadkin thought, his face burning with shame. "He doesn't seem to mind making a public show of it. But how is it that no one seems to even notice him?"

Golyadkin threw his silver ruble on the counter, as though it had burned his fingers and, ignoring the barman's arrogant smirk, so full of triumph and awareness of his power, he elbowed his way out of the room without looking back.

"I have to thank that crook for not disgracing me completely!" Golyadkin One thought. "I have to be grateful to him and consider myself lucky that everything was settled peacefully. Of course, the barman was rude, but he was within his rights in asking for one ruble ten kopecks. 'We don't give things away for nothing!' Well, I suppose the lout could have been a bit more polite."

All this went through Golyadkin's mind as he walked downstairs, but as he reached the last step he stopped dead and turned red, his eyes filling with tears from an overflow of mortification. But after he had stood there like a post for half a minute, he rushed out of the building and ran all the way to Six Shop Street without even feeling tired. At home, he didn't bother to take off his office clothes, although he usually liked to be at ease, and he didn't light his pipe, but sat down directly on his sofa, drew the inkpot toward him, took a pen and a sheet of notepaper and, his hand trembling with excitement, proceeded to write the following letter:

Dear Yakov Petrovich:

I should never have taken up my pen if I had not been pushed to it by you and by circumstances. Believe me, it is dire necessity that induces me to enter upon this explanation. And therefore, I beg you above all not to consider this as a deliberate attempt to insult you, my dear sir, but rather as the inevitable consequence of the circumstances that link us.

"Sounds all right—it's dignified, polite, and at the same time quite forceful and firm. . . . I don't think there's anything in it he could take offense at. Anyway, I'm fully within my rights," Golyadkin decided after rereading what he had written.

Your strange and sudden appearance on that stormy night, my dear sir, just after I had been so rudely and vulgarly treated by my enemies (whom I shall not mention out of scorn for them), was the source of all the misunderstanding existing between us at the present time. Your obstinate persistence in breaking in on my existence and violating my privacy goes against the civilized code of behavior and the most elementary politeness. I do not think, dear sir, that I need remind you here of the occasion when you misappropriated the file on which I had worked, in order to gain the favor—the unearned favor—of our superiors. Nor is there any need for me to mention your deliberately insulting refusal to discuss your actions with me. Finally, I won't go into your last strange performance in the restaurant. I would be the last man to protest against the pointless—from my viewpoint—expenditure of one ruble; but I cannot abstain from voicing my indignation at your action, which was a slur upon my good name, and which was perpetrated, moreover, in the presence of several witnesses, who, although unknown to me, were certainly persons of good breeding.

"Aren't I going a bit far?" Golyadkin wondered. "Aren't I saying too much? Isn't it a bit too offensive? For instance that hint about good breeding? Ah, never mind, I must show him that I can be firm. Anyway, I can soften the effect a little by buttering him up a bit toward the end. Let's see . . ."

> I wouldn't have bothered you with this letter, my dear sir, if it had not been for my firm conviction that the nobility of your feelings and the straightforwardness and forthrightness of your nature would show you the means of putting right all these failings and repairing the damage.
>
> I have full confidence that you will not misinterpret my letter or see in it anything disobliging, and at the same time, that you will not refuse me a written explanation, which you could send to me by my man.
>
> In expectation of your reply, I remain,
>
> > Your obedient servant,
> >
> > YAKOV GOLYADKIN

"Well, that's done and it seems quite all right. If it has reached the stage of writing, he is the one to blame for it. He has pushed me to the extreme and I feel obliged to demand a written document from him. Yes, and I have a good right to it too. . . ."

Golyadkin reread the letter once more, folded it, sealed it, and called Petrushka. Petrushka appeared, as usual, sleepyeyed and in a foul mood.

"Here, my friend, you'll take this letter, understand?" Petrushka remained silent.

"You'll take it to my office. There, you'll find the clerk on duty; today it's Mr. Vakhrameyev. Do you follow me?"

"Yes."

"Don't say just 'Yes,' say 'Yes, sir, I do.' Well, so you'll ask for Mr. Vakhrameyev and you'll tell him that your master sends him his regards and wonders whether he would oblige him by please looking in the employees' address book and finding the domicile of the clerk Yakov Petrovich Golyadkin. Do you understand?"

Petrushka remained silent and Golyadkin had the impression he was grinning.

"And so you'll ask for the address, Petrushka, and find

out for me where that new clerk called Golyadkin lives, all right?"

"Yes, sir."

"And once you've been told his address, you'll take him this letter. Is that clear?"

"It's clear."

"Now if that gentleman, that Mr. Golyadkin, to whom you are to deliver this letter, happens to be at home . . . Well, what are you laughing about, you fool?"

"Me? What's there for me to laugh about? I wasn't laughing. The likes of me never laugh. . . ."

"Well then, if that gentleman begins asking you something like, what did your master . . . Well, what was it your master . . . Well, if he tries to find out all sorts of things about me, you mustn't answer him. Just tell him that your master requests that he give you a written reply to this letter. Is that clear?"

"It's clear."

"All right, off you go."

Golyadkin thought: "It's a real bother having anything to do with that idiot. Why does he have to keep laughing all the time? Well, I've really got myself into deep trouble this time . . . although, after all, everything may turn out well in the end. Now, I bet the lout will vanish somewhere for a couple of hours. It's quite impossible to send him anywhere without his getting lost. Ah, what misery has descended upon me!"

Wallowing thus in his misery, our hero decided to delay any further active moves for a couple of hours, while awaiting Petrushka's return. So for an hour he paced his room, puffing at his pipe. Then he discarded his pipe and sat down with a book. A little later, he stretched himself out on the sofa. But soon enough, he lit his pipe again and went back to pacing the room. He tried to think of something, but there was absolutely nothing for him to think about. Finally, the agony of inactivity reached the last degree and Golyadkin decided to act.

"It will be at least another hour before Petrushka comes back. So I could leave the key with the doorman while I do a little investigating on my own," Golyadkin said to himself.

Without wasting time, since he was in a hurry to conduct his investigation, Golyadkin took his hat, walked out of his apartment, locked it, and downstairs gave the key and ten kopecks to the doorman, having become extraordinarily free with money. Then he set out toward the Izmailovsky Bridge. It took him half an hour to get there; when he had reached his objective, he walked directly into the yard of the familiar house, and looked up at the windows of Olsufy Ivanovich's apartment. All the windows were dark, except for three which were covered with red curtains.

"Looks like Olsufy Ivanovich has no guests today; they must've all stayed home," Golyadkin concluded.

Then, after standing in front of the windows for a few minutes, our hero felt he had to make up his mind and do something, but apparently it just wasn't written in the books that any resolution of his should be carried out, for he suddenly shrugged and walked out of the yard into the street.

"No, this wasn't where I was supposed to go. What am I supposed to do here? Well, I suppose I'd better, you know . . . I'd better do a bit of investigating."

And to follow up on that resolution, Golyadkin set out for his office. It was a good way off, the sidewalk was very muddy, and wet snow was coming down in big flakes. But nothing seemed difficult to our hero at that moment. True, he was getting quite wet and rather bespattered with mud. "But what does that matter, as long as the objective is attained!" he thought, when he was already quite close to his objective, and the heavy bulk of the government office building loomed black and foreboding before him.

"Hey, halt, what do I imagine I'm going to do in there?" the thought occurred to him. "Suppose they tell me where he lives? What will I gain, since by now Petrushka must be back and waiting for me with his reply? I'm just wasting precious time, that's all. But never mind, I can still make up for it. Still, shouldn't I go in and see Vakhrameyev? No, what'd be the point of that? I can see him some other time. So it seems I didn't really have to go out at all. Ah, I'm so restless by nature! Whether it's necessary or not, I'm always rushing headlong . . . Hm, what time is it? I bet it must be nine. What if Petrushka came back and didn't find me at home? It was plain stupid of me to dash out like that. Ah, what a nuisance!"

Having admitted sincerely that he had made a blunder, our hero rushed back to Six Shop Street. He arrived home quite exhausted. Downstairs, the doorman informed him that Petrushka hadn't returned yet.

"I thought something like this would happen," our hero thought. "And to think it's nine already. I bet he's getting drunk somewhere. Ah God, what a day, what a day!"

Plunged in these bitter thoughts and recriminations, Golyadkin unlocked his apartment door, lighted a candle, undressed, lit a pipe and, dead tired and hungry, lay on the sofa waiting for Petrushka to return. The candle was burning dimly and the fluttering flame was reflected on the wall. . . . Golyadkin mused and mused, looked and looked, and finally fell into a deep sleep.

It was already quite late when he woke up. The candle was just about to go out. It was sputtering and smoking. Golyadkin leaped up and shook himself, and everything came back to him. Behind the partition Petrushka was snoring thickly. Golyadkin rushed over to the window. All was dark. He opened the window. Everything was quiet. The city seemed to have become deserted. He thought it must be about two in the morning. And sure enough—just then, the clock behind the partition struck two. Golyadkin rushed behind the partition.

It took him some time and effort to wake up Petrushka and pull him into a sitting position. And just as he achieved it, the candle went out altogether. It took Golyadkin about ten minutes to find another candle and to light it. In the meantime, Petrushka went back to sleep.

"You lout, you good-for-nothing lout!" Golyadkin said, shaking him. "Are you going to get up, yes or no?"

After half an hour of desperate effort, Golyadkin finally succeeded in bringing his servant back to consciousness, and dragging him out from behind the partition. It was only then that our hero realized what a drunken state Petrushka was in and how precariously he kept his feet.

"You lazy good-for-nothing!" Mr. Golyadkin began to shout. "You'd have thought nothing of cutting my head off my body, you murderer, you! Good lord, I wonder what he did with the letter! Why on earth did I have to write it at all, I just ask myself! I let myself go again, fool that I am! Ah, all that stuff about honor and self-respect! Here's some self-respect for you, you stupid coward . . . But you, what did you do with that letter, you murderer? Whom did you give it to?"

"I never gave that letter to no one; I never had no letter . . . So there!"

Golyadkin wrung his hands in despair.

"Listen, Petrushka, just listen to me, just listen . . ."

"I'm listening . . ."

"Where have you been? Come on, answer me!"

"Where was I? I guess I went to see some nice people, that's where I went."

"Ah, good God, tell me where you went first. Did you go to my office? Listen Petrushka, perhaps you're drunk?"

"Me drunk! May I never budge from this spot, may I . . ."

"Listen, I don't really mind whether you're drunk or not. I was just wondering. In fact, I'm rather glad you're drunk. Well, never mind, Petrushka, perhaps you just forgot, but you'll remember everything now. Well, try to remember then—did you see Mr. Vakhrameyev, the clerk on duty at the office, you know?"

"I didn't go there and there wasn't any clerk there, and may I never budge from this spot if I ever . . ."

"No, Petrushka, you still don't get me. I'm not reproaching you for anything. It's so cold and damp outside that no one could possibly blame a man for having a few drinks. There's absolutely nothing wrong with that. Let me tell you something—I myself have been drinking today. . . . Now, tell me, did you see that clerk Vakhrameyev?"

"As I say, may I never budge from this spot. I did go, and if I didn't may I . . ."

"That's good, Petrushka. I'm very glad you went there. I'm not angry at all. . . . There, there," our hero said, patting his servant on the back and smiling in a desperate effort to mollify him. "I can see you've had something to drink, you rascal—I bet you had a good ten kopecks' worth of drinks. Am I right? Ah, you crook! Well, never mind, I won't hold it against you. Do you understand? I won't hold it against you."

"No, I'm not a crook and have never been one. . . . I just went to see some nice people, just like I told you. . . ."

"Ah, try to understand that I'm not reproaching you for anything, and I didn't mean it seriously when I said you were a crook. I even meant it in a flattering sense. You know, like telling a man he's a real bandit, when you mean he'll get anything he sets his mind on and won't let anyone stop him. That was the way I meant it, Petrushka. So now tell me in all frankness, did you go to the office, did you see Vakhra-meyev, and did he give you that address?"

"Yes, he gave me the address too and everything and he's a good clerk that Mr. Vakhrameyev and he says to me, 'Your master's a good man,' he says, 'a very good man. And you can tell your master,' he says, 'that I like him and re-spect him a great deal, and since you're working for him, Petrushka,' he says to me, 'you must be a good fellow too, and so Petrushka,' he says . . ."

"Ah, good Lord, and what about the address, you Judas, you?" Golyadkin almost hissed this last epithet.

"And the address, and the address, he gave me that too."

"So he gave it to you? So where does he live, that Golyadkin fellow?"

"'And that Golyadkin,' he says to me, 'he lives on Six Shop Street, that Golyadkin. You'll find him on the fourth floor,' he says to me, 'on the right. That's where he lives, that Golyadkin,' he says to me, just like that."

"Ah, you good-for-nothing cheat!" Golyadkin shouted, beside himself. "You murderer, you! Why, that's my own address you're giving me and it's about me myself you're talking!"

"Suit yourself. I've nothing to do with it. Just suit your-self. . . ."

"And what about the letter?"

"What letter? There was no letter. I never saw a letter."

"What did you do with it, you lout?"

"I gave it to him and he says, 'Give my regards to your master, he's a good man, your master is, and I want you to give him my regards . . . '"

"But who said that? Was it Golyadkin said that?"

Petrushka didn't answer, and suddenly smiled broadly, looking straight into his master's face.

"Listen, you cutthroat!" Golyadkin hissed breathlessly, his whole body shaking. "Can't you see what you're doing to me! Tell me, you Judas, why did you have to kill me and cut my head off my shoulders, you monster!"

"Say whatever you want, it's got nothing to do with me," Petrushka said in a determined tone, retreating behind the partition.

"Come here, come here at once, you bandit!"

"I'm not coming. I won't come no more ever. I don't care. There are good, nice people I know and I'll go to them . . . They're decent people, they live honestly, they don't need lies and there are never two of them at a time. . . ."

Golyadkin's hands and feet turned to ice and he was unable to breathe.

"Sure," Petrushka went on, "there's never two of them because they never offend God or plain honest people. . . ."

"Ah, you nasty, drunken oaf! Go to sleep now, you freak. You'll pay for this tomorrow," Golyadkin added in a voice hardly audible.

Petrushka could be heard muttering something for a while, after which his bed creaked, he yawned protractedly, stretched, and fell into what is usually referred to as the sleep of the innocent. Petrushka's behavior, his strange hints which were nevertheless rather vague and so shouldn't be taken seriously, especially as they had been made by a drunken man, and, in general, the whole unpleasant turn the affair had taken had shaken Golyadkin to his foundations.

"Why on earth did I have to take him to task in the middle of the night?" Golyadkin said to himself, trembling and feeling painfully uncomfortable. "What the hell did I want to get into an argument with that drunk for, anyway? How could I expect any sense out of him? He can't say a word without lying. But what was he hinting at, the bandit cutthroat? And, God almighty, why did I have to write all those letters? What was I trying to do? To kill myself? To dig my own grave? I seem to be unable to keep quiet. I had to open my big mouth once again! And what am I making all this fuss about? I'm going to pieces anyhow. I'm becoming nothing but an old doormat, but that doesn't prevent me from going around holding forth about my self-respect and talking about saving my honor! Ah, I'm nothing but a suicide, that's all I am!"

Golyadkin sat on the sofa, so frightened that he didn't dare to move. Suddenly his attention was attracted by something. Fearing that the object that had caught his eye might prove to be a delusion, a figment of his imagination, he reached out for it with his hand, tense with hope and curiosity. . . . No, it was no optical illusion, it was a letter all right, a letter addressed to him. He picked it up from the table. His heart was pounding wildly. So it was true. That lout had brought it, put it on the table, and then forgotten

all about it. That's what must've happened. . . . The letter
was from Vakhrameyev, a young colleague and an erstwhile
friend of Golyadkin's. "I really had a sort of presentiment
about it all," Golyadkin thought, "and I also have a presentiment about what's in this letter."

The letter read as follows:

Dear Yakov Petrovich:
    Your servant is drunk and it is quite impossible
to get any sense out of him and, for this reason, I
prefer to reply by letter. In the first place, let me assure you that the service you ask of me, namely, to
transmit your letter to the person in question, will be
carried out promptly and without fail. The person in
question, who has taken the place of a friend of mine
whose name I shall not mention (not wishing to cast
aspersions upon the reputation of an innocent man)
now lives with me in Karolina Ivanovna's apartment
in the room that used to be occupied by a transient
infantry officer from Tambov when you yourself
used to live here. Anyway, you can always find
the person in question in the company of honest,
straightforward people, something that cannot be
said of everybody.
    I also wish to notify you hereby that I intend to
break off our formerly amicable relations, feeling
that it is impossible for us to remain on a friendly
footing any longer. In view of this, I would appreciate it very much if upon receipt of this letter you
would let me have back the two rubles you owe me
for the razors of foreign make that, if you remember, I sold you seven months ago on credit, this transaction taking place while we were both domiciled at
Karolina Ivanovna's, a lady for whom I have the
highest esteem. I have taken the above decision because, according to reports coming from intelligent
people, you have recently lost all sense of propriety
and self-respect and have become a threat to the
innocent and uncontaminated, for some people do
not bother with the truth, their words are fraudulent
and their dignified airs are put on.
    Let me tell you also that it is easy to find many
people who would be only too anxious to stand up

for Karolina Ivanovna, a lady who has always been of irreproachable conduct, who, in the second place, is an honest woman and, what's more, a maiden, despite the fact that she's no longer so young, though she comes from a good foreign family. I have been asked to mention this in this letter in passing, but I am also speaking in my own name. In any case, you will find out about it soon enough, if you haven't found out already, although you've made yourself notorious from one end of the city to the other, according to reports I've heard from people who are intelligent, and must therefore have intelligent information.

To conclude this letter, let me inform you, my dear sir, that a person you know and whose name I won't mention for reasons of honor, is greatly respected by right-thinking people. Moreover, he is of a gay and pleasant disposition. He is equally successful with his superiors at the office and with any person of common sense, is true to his word and a reliable friend, and does not say disparaging things to their faces about the persons with whom he is friendly.

In any case, I remain,

Your obedient servant,

N. VAKHRAMEYEV

P.S. You had better get rid of your servant who is a drunkard and must give you a great deal of trouble and take in his stead Éstafy, who used to work for us and is now without a job. As to your present servant, he is not only a drunk but also a thief, for last week he sold a pound of lump sugar to Karolina Ivanovna at a reduced price, which, in my opinion, he could not have done if he hadn't maliciously stolen it from you, accumulating that quantity little by little. I write this to you as a well-wisher, despite the fact that certain people know only too well how to deceive and insult their fellow men, preferably honest, good-natured men; and what is more, they revile them behind their backs and misrepresent them out of sheer envy and because they themselves have no qualities to match theirs.

V.

Having read Vakhrameyev's letter, our hero sat on his sofa for a long time without stirring. Some light seemed to be breaking through the thick fog of mystery surrounding him. He was beginning to understand. He tried to get up from the sofa, to pace his room for a bit, in order to pull himself together, gather his scattered thoughts, and concentrate them on his situation. But when he actually tried to stand up, he immediately fell back onto the sofa, feeling completely weak and helpless.

"Actually I had a feeling something like this would happen. But what's this he writes and what is the true meaning of his words? The meaning, of course, I know. Still where will it all lead? Why couldn't he say simply, this is what I want and this is what I demand? I could have complied then. But now the whole business is taking a very unpleasant turn. Ah, I wish it were tomorrow already, and I could get to work! But I know what to do now. I'll tell him that I am open to reasonable suggestions, but that I will never sell my honor . . . As to that one, I can't see how that malicious person could have become involved in it. Why should he be involved precisely in this? Ah, I wish it were tomorrow already! All sorts of nasty rumors may be going around about me, for they keep plotting all the time, and would do anything out of sheer spite. The main thing is not to waste time, to write that letter, let him know a few things, and tell him that I would agree to this, that, and the other. And I'll send the letter first thing tomorrow morning, while I myself rush off to the office, to get there before those dear friends of mine . . . Ah, they'll spread all sorts of stuff about me. I can count on that!"

Golyadkin drew the notepaper to him, took a pen, and wrote the following reply to Vakhrameyev's letter:

Dear Nestor Ignatievich:
   I read your falsely well-wishing letter with pained surprise. I find it insulting, for I clearly realize that when you speak of certain unworthy persons you mean me. It is with genuine sorrow that I see how successfully and how rapidly the calumny has spread, and how deeply it has taken root to the detriment of my good name, my honor, and my welfare. What hurts me even more and offends me deeply is that even honorable and high-minded people, and

notably, people with straightforward and open characters have deserted the cause of honorable men and attached themselves, through the best qualities of their hearts, to pernicious rottenness, which unfortunately has spread so wildly and so dangerously in our immoral times. In conclusion, let me tell you that the two silver rubles, that you mention in your letter as owed to you by me, will be returned to you in their entirety since I consider it a sacred obligation.

As to your references to a certain person of the female sex, let me assure you, my dear sir, that I never clearly understood certain hints made by her concerning her intentions, hopes, or future plans. And so, please allow me, dear sir, to preserve my lofty way of thinking and my honorable name undefiled. Whatever it may be, I am prepared to accept an explanation, a face-to-face explanation rather than one in writing, for I feel it would be more likely to be successful and, moreover, I am prepared to make various peaceful concessions on condition, of course, that the concessions are mutual. With this in view, I would be obliged to you, sir, if you would tell the lady in question of my readiness to discuss things with her, and at the same time, name the place and day of the meeting.

I felt very bitter when I read your hints, my dear sir, implying that I had betrayed our erstwhile friendship, and that I had said unflattering things about you. I must ascribe this misunderstanding to the vicious libel, envy, and ill-wishes of those whom I can justifiably call my worst enemies. But those people probably do not know that innocence is strong by its very innocence, that the shameless impudence and shocking familiarity of certain people will sooner or later earn itself the brand of disgrace, and that those people will one day perish of their own wickedness and corruption.

In conclusion I would ask you, dear sir, to tell those people that their strange claim and their vile and fantastic pretensions to squeeze others out of the position those others occupy will earn them contempt, pity, and the madhouse. Moreover, such claims are forbidden by law, and in my opinion justly so, because every man should be content with his lot. Everything has its limits, and if this is a joke, it is an indecent one. I would even go so far as to say that it is a quite immoral one, since I dare assure you, dear sir, that my own views concerning *one's own place* are of the highest moral caliber.

In any case, I have the honor to remain,

Your obedient servant,

YAKOV GOLYADKIN

Chapter 10

IN GENERAL, it may be said that the previous day's events had shocked Golyadkin to his very foundations. Our hero slept very poorly, indeed he never remained completely asleep for more than five minutes at a time. It was as though some practical joker had scattered bristles in his bed. He spent all night half-asleep, half-awake, turning from side to side, moaning, groaning, one minute dozing off, the next waking up again, the whole time suffering from a strange feeling of anguish, vague recollections, hideous visions—in short, everything unpleasant that it is possible to think of. Now, Andrei Filipovich's figure appears before him in a strange, mysterious half-light, a dry, unfriendly figure with a hard gaze and a stiffly polite expression of disapproval. . . . And as soon as Golyadkin tries to go over to Andrei Filipovich to somehow justify himself as best he can and prove to him that he, Golyadkin, is not at all as his enemies have tried to represent him, that he is, in fact, like this, and that on top of his innate qualities, he displays such and such advantages— that notorious individual immediately appears on the scene and, using some shocking, sickening device, brings all Golyadkin's intentions to nought, and there, before Golyadkin's very eyes, the man thoroughly blackens his reputation, tramples his self-respect in the mud, and then is immediately given Golyadkin's place in the department and in society.

Then Golyadkin's head smarts from a blow he has received recently and humbly accepted during the performance

of his duties, a blow against which he finds it very difficult
to protest. . . . And while Golyadkin racks his brains, trying
to understand why he should find it so difficult to protest that
blow, the thought gradually takes on another shape, the shape
of some large or small despicable action which he has either
witnessed, heard of, or in which he was involved himself,
and often involved not at all out of any nasty motive, nor
even on a nasty impulse, but just like that—sometimes out of
delicacy, sometimes out of utter helplessness and, at last, because . . . Ah, Mr. Golyadkin knows perfectly well *what*
caused it! Then Golyadkin turns red in his sleep, and to
make up for his shame, he mutters that he could show his
strength of character; that he could, if he wished, prove his
strength of character, his considerable strength of character.
. . . But then he concludes with, "What's strength of character anyway? And what has strength of character got to do
with the present situation?"

But what enrages Golyadkin more than anything is that
a certain person never fails to show up at such a moment
and, disregarding the fact that the matter has already been
settled, also starts muttering, with an unseemly little grin,
"What's strength of character anyway? And what's strength
of character got to do with the present situation?"

Then Golyadkin fancies he is in a select company
reputed for its wit and distinguished manners. But even in
this company, Golyadkin stands out because of his wit and
gallantry, and everyone grows fond of him, including some
of his enemies who are also present, and that is very pleasant
indeed for Golyadkin. Everyone agrees that he is the most
brilliant person in the company, and at one point Golyadkin
overhears the host telling some of his guests how highly he
thinks of him, Mr. Golyadkin. . . . And then, all of a sudden,
that evil individual, notorious for his bestial impulses, appears and, just by his very appearance, completely eclipses
Golyadkin's triumph. Golyadkin Two tramples Golyadkin
One into the dirt and proves irrefutably that Golyadkin One,
the genuine Golyadkin, is really not the genuine one at all,
but a fake; that the only true Mr. Golyadkin is he, Golyadkin Two; that Golyadkin One is not at all what he appears to
be, but just a so-and-so who has no right to mingle with respectable people or to be received in decent society. And all
this happens so quickly that Golyadkin One doesn't have a
chance to open his mouth. Everyone has already gone over,

body and soul, to that wicked sham, and scornfully rejects the true and innocent Golyadkin. There is no one left whose opinion the hideous Golyadkin Two hasn't twisted his way; and there is no one in that company, not even the most insignificant, whom that false and useless Golyadkin won't stoop to flatter, upon whom he won't fawn, before whom he won't burn sweet incense that will make the person sneeze till his eyes fill with tears as a mark of tremendous delight and appreciation. And the most striking thing about it is that it is all done in one second; the speed with which the shady Golyadkin moves is really remarkable! No sooner has he finished charming one when, before you know it, there he is, already working on the next. He'll pour some honey over that other person, pluck a benevolent smile, then he'll give a kick of his short, fat, although rather wooden-looking leg and be off wooing the third, and, lo and behold, he's already made a great friend of him; and before you have time to open your mouth in your amazement, he's busy with a fourth, is indeed already on the same terms with him too. It's really frightening—witchcraft, that's the only way to describe it.

And everyone seems pleased to see him and praises him and declares that his courtesy and sense of humor are infinitely superior to the courtesy and sense of humor of the real Mr. Golyadkin, and they mock the genuine Mr. Golyadkin, and reject and push him away and start kicking the genuine Mr. Golyadkin!

Full of horror and anguish, the genuine, broken-hearted Mr. Golyadkin rushes out into the street and tries to hail a cab to drive over to His Excellency's or at least to Andrei Filipovich's but—oh horror—no cab driver will take him. They say, "Sorry sir, we cannot take two gentlemen exactly like each other; a decent man must live honorably and never comes in twos."

In great shame, the perfectly honorable Golyadkin looks around and realizes that the cabbies and Petrushka, who is in league with them, have a good point, because the depraved Golyadkin is standing not very far away and, with typical depravity, is obviously contemplating committing some very shocking act quite unfitting for a well-bred person, although the loathsome Golyadkin Two likes to brag about his refinement at every opportunity. Beside himself with shame and despair, the defeated although perfectly righteous Golyadkin rushes headlong away, not caring where he is going; but every time his foot hits the granite of the pavement, there springs up from under the ground an identical Golyadkin, but depraved of heart. And as soon as they appear all these exactly identical Golyadkins begin waddling along one after the other, like a file of geese, following the poor, worthy Golyadkin One whose breath comes short in horror when he realizes that there is no possible escape for him from the chain of exactly identical Golyadkins. In the end, the whole city becomes flooded with identical Golyadkins, so that the police authorities, in the face of such a breach of the peace, are forced to collar all these duplicates and lock them up.

Numb and horrified, our hero would wake up and then, realizing that the reality was hardly any rosier, he would grow even more numb and horrified. It was torture. At times he felt as though someone were gnawing at his heart.

In the end, Golyadkin couldn't stand it any longer. "This shall not be!" he yelled determinedly, sitting up in his bed, and that yell brought him fully awake.

The day must have started long before. The room was rather unusually light. Sunshine filtered through the frosty window panes and scattered generously all over the room. Golyadkin was rather surprised for he was under the impression that the sun only shone into his room at around noon. He could not remember that heavenly body ever having deviated from its course. And while he was still wondering about that phenomenon, he heard the hissing that always preceded the striking of his wall clock. "Now!" Golyadkin thought, in suspense, preparing to listen. . . . But, to his immense amazement, the clock took a deep breath and struck only once.

"What's going on?" our hero cried, leaping out of bed and, dressed just as he was, rushing behind the partition. It was actually one o'clock. Golyadkin glanced at Petrushka's bed, but the cubicle didn't even smell of his servant. The bed was empty and made. He couldn't see Petrushka's boots anywhere—a sure sign that the fellow wasn't at home. Golyadkin rushed toward the door and found it locked. "But where can he be?" Golyadkin whispered in terrible agitation, feeling that his limbs were beginning to tremble. Suddenly an idea flashed through his head. Golyadkin rushed to his desk, searched all through it, and in the drawers. That was it! That letter he had written yesterday to Vakhrameyev was not there. Neither was Petrushka in his cubicle behind the partition. The clock said it was one, and in his letter of the day before Vakhrameyev had made some points, points which, although they were made quite obscurely and vaguely, became quite clear now. So Petrushka had been bribed. Yes, yes, no doubt about it!

"So this is how the main plot is shaping up," Golyadkin cried, slapping himself on the forehead and opening his eyes wider and wider. "So it is in the nest of that niggardly German woman that the headquarters of evil is located! So she was just trying to divert my attention for tactical reasons, indicating the Izmailovsky Bridge. She was trying to put me off balance, the horrible witch. That was how she undermined me! Yes, there's no doubt about it, if we look at it from this side, no doubt about it at all! And that also accounts for the appearance of that scoundrel. It all fits in perfectly! They were holding him in reserve for a long time, keeping him for an emergency. So that's the way the whole business turns out! Ah, the way it's all come out into the clear! Ah, it's still not lost. There's still time to cope with it."

But suddenly Golyadkin remembered that it was past one o'clock, and a moan escaped from his breast: "No, no, they're lying. They couldn't possibly have had the time," he muttered. "We'll see yet . . ." And dressing hurriedly, he seized notepaper and a pen and delivered himself of the following missive:

Dear Yakov Petrovich:

It is either you or me—it cannot be both of us! I must therefore inform you that your strange, ridiculous and, at the same time, inadmissible desire to look like a twin of mine and to pass yourself off as such can only lead to your utter undoing and disgrace. Consequently, in your own interest, I suggest that you step aside and make room for people of true good will. If you do not comply with this, I am prepared to take extreme measures. I lay down my pen and wait. Nevertheless, I remain ready to oblige you in any way, including the way involving pistols.

YAKOV GOLYADKIN

After he had written this note, our hero rubbed his hands together fiercely. Then, having donned his hat and coat, he unlocked his door with a spare key and went to his office.

He reached the office building, but didn't dare walk in—it was really too late, half-past two by Golyadkin's watch. Suddenly an apparently insignificant circumstance decided Golyadkin's last doubts: A breathless, flushed little man appeared from behind the office building, looked around furtively, and then darted into the building like a rat. It was Ostafiev, the copying clerk who, Golyadkin knew, could be a very useful man, ready to do anything for a ten kopeck piece. Now, surmising that after his visit to a certain establishment Ostafiev would be particularly interested in ten kopeck pieces, our hero decided not to stint him any, and also darted into the building, and then followed Ostafiev into the lobby. He took the man aside into a quiet corner behind a huge iron stove and started questioning him.

"Well, my friend, how are things up there? Know what I mean?"

"Yes sir, very good sir . . ."

"All right, my friend, all right, I'll show you my appreciation. So tell me, how is it?"

"What do you wish to know, sir?" Ostafiev asked, supporting his jaw with his hand because his mouth had fallen slightly open against his will.

"You see, my friend . . . I don't wish you to imagine anything . . . Well, is Andrei Filipovich here?"

"Yes sir, he is."

"And the other officials are here too?"

"Yes sir, they're all here as usual."

"And His Excellency?"

"His Excellency is here too, sir."

At this point the copying clerk had to again support his mouth which kept opening. He gave Golyadkin a strange and curious look, or at least that was how it seemed to Golyadkin.

"And nothing special has happened?"

"No sir, nothing at all."

"Wasn't there anything about me, anything . . . I mean anything concerning . . . I'm just asking by the way, you understand?"

"No sir, so far I haven't heard a thing . . ."

The man again had to prevent his mouth from falling open and gave Golyadkin another queer look. The thing is, our hero was now trying to read Ostafiev's face to see whether there wasn't some secret hidden behind it. And, in fact, it seemed there might very well be a secret, for Ostafiev was becoming noticeably more reticent and abrupt, and was not listening to Golyadkin's questions with the interest he had displayed at first. "Well," Golyadkin thought, "it's his right not to be interested. What am I to him? Anyway, he may have been bribed by my opponents already, since he slipped off on that urgent little errand of his. Well, I suppose I'd better . . ." And Golyadkin decided that the time for the ten kopeck piece had arrived.

"Here, this is for you, my friend."

"I deeply appreciate it, sir."

"I'll give you more."

"Thank you, sir."

"I'll give you another one now and, when we're through, I'll give you that much again, understand?"

The fellow said nothing. He just stood to attention, staring at Golyadkin.

"All right, tell me now: have you heard them say anything about me?"

"Seems to me that so far, sir . . . well, nothing yet, sir, I believe," Ostafiev answered with deliberation, trying to assume an air of mystery like Golyadkin, slightly knitting his brows, looking down at the ground, trying to fall into the appropriate tone, in brief, trying to earn what Golyadkin had promised him, because he considered what he already had in his hand as his by right.

"And nothing is known?"

"Up till now, nothing, sir."

"But listen . . . tell me—isn't there anything in the wind even?"

"Well, to be sure, sir, it'll perhaps become known later on."

"Sounds bad," our hero thought, looking at the copying clerk.

"Here's some more for you, friend."

"I appreciate it very much indeed, sir."

"Was Vakhrameyev here yesterday?"

"Yes sir, he was."

"And wasn't there anyone else here? Try to remember, my friend."

The fellow ransacked his memory for a moment, but couldn't come up with anything appropriate.

"No, sir, there was no one else."

"Hm," Golyadkin said, and a silence followed. "Listen, friend, here, take this. And tell me everything without dissimulation."

"Very good, sir," Ostafiev said, turning smooth as silk again now, which was exactly how Golyadkin wanted him.

"I want you to tell me now, my friend—what footing is he on here now?"

"Well, sir, quite all right, sir," Ostafiev said, staring wide-eyed at Golyadkin.

"What exactly do you mean by 'all right'?"

"Well, just exactly that, sir . . ." And Ostafiev twitched his eyebrows meaningfully. He was completely at sea, though, and didn't know what else to say.

Golyadkin thought: "It sounds quite bad" and went on to ask: "And, tell me, aren't they up to something new, Vakhrameyev and he?"

"It's still the same thing, sir, nothing new."

"You'd better think hard."

"Well, sir, I heard they were up to something new."

"And what is it?"

Ostafiev had once more to hold his lower jaw up with his hand.

"Aren't there any letters for me from there?"

"Well, sir, today the janitor Mikheyev went to Vakhrameyev's lodgings, at that German woman's, you know, sir, and so I'll go and ask him if you wish me to."

"Please do that, my friend, do it in the name of the Saviour! . . . I'm just sort of curious, friend, so don't you go imagining all sorts of things. You'd better go and find out, my friend, whether they aren't hatching something against me, and what *his* part in it is. That's what I want to know. You find it out for me, my good friend, and you'll see how grateful I'll be to you when you've done so."

"Very good, sir, and now, let me tell you that they have put Ivan Semyonych at your desk, sir, in your place."

"Ivan Semyonych? What? Is that so?"

"It was Andrei Filipovich who told him to sit there."

"Is that so? And what's the reason for that? Go and find out about it, my friend, find out for our Saviour's sake, find

out everything and I'll show my deep appreciation . . . But
don't go imagining . . ."

"Yes sir, very good, sir. I'll go at once. But aren't you
going in today, sir?"

"No . . . I just came to have a look today, my friend,
and later I'll thank you—you know what I mean, my friend."

"Yes sir. At your service." The copying clerk ran eagerly
upstairs, and Golyadkin remained alone.

"Looks bad," Golyadkin thought, "looks very, very bad!
Ah, it's really a bad business! But what did he actually mean?
What could that drunk have meant by his hints? Who's behind all this? Ah, I know! They probably found out about
me and made him sit in my chair. . . . But no, it was Andrei
Filipovich who put Ivan Semyonych there. But why should
he have done that? For what purpose? Well, they found out
and . . . That's Vakhrameyev's work. No, not him, he's as
stupid as a log; they're all working on it together, and that's
why they let that horrible creature into the department, and
set him on me and then that one-eyed German witch started
to complain. I suspected all along that all this intrigue wasn't
that simple and that there was something more behind all
this old wives' gossip. And that's exactly what I told Christian Ivanovich. I told him, they've sworn to cut my throat,
doctor, in the moral sense, that is, and so they are trying to
use Karolina Ivanovna. I can see that I have past masters of
intrigue to face here. It isn't Vakhrameyev. I recognize a
master's hand in it. As I said, Vakhrameyev is a fool. I know
who's working for them all; it's that creature, that fake! And
that's the only thing that gets him by here, and it partly
accounts for his success in high society too. Yes, I'd like very
much to know what his actual standing is today. But still,
why did they have to thrust Ivan Semyonych in? What the
devil do they need him for? Could they really not find anyone else? Although, whoever they put there, it would all
come to the same thing. As to Ivan Semyonych, I've been
watching him for quite a time. He's a nasty, unpleasant old
fogey—I've heard he lends money and charges Shylock interest. But I still say the bear is behind it all; it's always the bear!
That's how it all started. It was at the Izmailovsky Bridge . . ."

At this point, Golyadkin made a sour face as if he'd
bitten into a lemon, probably having thought of something
unpleasant. "Well, never mind," he thought, "I always keep
coming back to that . . . But why doesn't Ostafiev come

back? Has he got bogged down or did someone stop him there? A good thing I'm doing a bit of maneuvering on my own part, and trying to undermine them too. All I have to do is to give a coin to Ostafiev and he's on my side. Only, I wonder, is he really on my side? Perhaps they've got him on their side too and are using him for their own schemes. Why, the man looks like a real highway robber! 'No,' he says, 'nothing's going on. Thank you, sir, I appreciate it,' he says. Ah, the bandit!"

There was a noise. . . . Golyadkin shrank back and scuttled behind the stove. Someone came downstairs and went out into the street. "Who could it possibly be?" A minute later, there were steps again. . . . This time, Golyadkin was unable to restrain himself and stuck the tip of his nose out from behind the stove. He stuck it out and at once withdrew it, feeling as though it had been pricked with a pin. This time, of course, the person coming downstairs was none other than that depraved scandalmonger and schemer, and he was walking with his usual loathsome, mincing little steps, as though he were just about to kick someone. "The despicable creature!" our hero muttered under his breath, unable to help noticing that the creature had the huge green briefcase belonging to His Excellency under his arm. "He must be on a special errand again," Golyadkin thought, turning red and shrinking still further into himself out of sheer vexation.

Golyadkin Two passed without noticing him, and right away Golyadkin heard steps again. This time he felt sure it must be the copying clerk. And soon the sleek figure of a copying clerk came into sight. It wasn't Ostafiev though, but another clerk called Pisarenko. This surprised Golyadkin no end. "Why on earth does he have to drag others into our secrets? Ah, the barbarians! Nothing's sacred to them!" he thought and then turned toward Pisarenko: "Well, my friend, who sent you here?"

"It's about your business, sir. So far there's no news from anyone. We'll let you know, sir, if anything comes up."

"What's happened to Ostafiev?"

"He couldn't come himself, sir. His Excellency passed through his section twice. Indeed, sir, I can't stay either."

"Thank you, my friend, thank you, only tell me . . ."

"I assure you, sir, I haven't a minute. They keep asking for us every moment. . . . But if you'll stay here a bit longer, as soon as there's something new about your business, we'll let you know right away, sir."

"But first tell me . . ."

"I'm sorry, sir, I can't stay any longer," Pisarenko said, wriggling away from Golyadkin, who had seized him by his lapel. "I really can't, sir. But if you would stay here for a while longer, we'll certainly keep you posted."

"Just a second, my good friend, just one second! Now, my friend, see this letter here? I'll make it well worth your while, my friend."

"Yes, sir?"

"I want you to give it to Mr. Golyadkin."

"To Mr. Golyadkin, sir?"

"Yes, my friend, to Mr. Golyadkin."

"Very good, sir. As soon as I can manage to get away, I'll take it to him. And you'll wait here in the meantime, sir, won't you? No one will see you here, sir."

"No, my friend, you've got it all wrong. I'm not standing here so as not to be seen. . . . I won't stay here any longer, my friend. I'll go outside, into that sidestreet, you know, where there's a café. I'd rather wait there, and if anything happens you come over and let me know."

"Very good, sir, but please let me go now. I do understand, sir."

"And you can be sure that, for my part, I won't forget your services," Golyadkin shouted after Pisarenko, whom he had released.

"Seems to me the lout was a bit ruder toward the end," our hero thought, coming out diffidently from behind the stove. "I'm sure there's another snag somewhere. At first it was this and that . . . He was really in a great hurry. Well, perhaps there's a lot of work today. And His Excellency had been around twice. . . . But what's the cause of it all? Ah, there's probably nothing to it. Well, we'll find out soon enough . . ."

Golyadkin was about to open the door and slip out into the street, when suddenly His Excellency's carriage thundered up to the office building. And before Golyadkin had time to gather his wits, the carriage door opened and its occupant jumped out onto the sidewalk. That man was none other than Golyadkin Two who had been away on his errand for ten minutes or so. Golyadkin One remembered that the doctor's place was only a few yards away and thought, "So he has been there on a special errand."

In the meantime, Golyadkin Two took the green brief-case and some documents out of the carriage, said something to the driver, pushed open the door of the building, hitting Golyadkin One with it, deliberately pretended not to have noticed it to spite him, and rushed off upstairs.

"It's bad," Golyadkin One thought. "The business has taken a bad, bad turn! Ah, dear, dear me!"

He remained standing there motionless for half a minute or so, and then made up his mind. Without thinking any further, with his heart pounding violently and trembling all over, he followed the other upstairs into the office. And, as he discarded his overcoat and overshoes in the vestibule, he kept muttering under his breath: "Ah, whatever happens, happens! What is it to me really? I'm not involved in the whole business, remember!"

As Mr. Golyadkin stepped into his section, it was already growing dark. Neither Andrei Filipovich nor Anton Anton-ovich were in the room. They were both in the Director's office, presenting their reports. And apparently the Director himself was in a hurry to go over to make his own report to His Excellency. Because of this, and also because it was getting dark and closing time was drawing near, several clerks, especially the younger ones, were actively engaged in doing nothing at the moment when Golyadkin made his entrance; they had gathered in groups and were talking, arguing, and laughing. The very youngest even had a little game of pitch and toss going in a corner by a window.

Since he was a well mannered man and now felt a great need to conciliate and get along with people, Golyadkin im-mediately walked over to some of the clerks with whom he was on more friendly terms to wish them good day and so on. But it seemed to him that his colleagues reacted rather strangely to his presence. He was unpleasantly struck by a certain coolness, aloofness, perhaps even sternness in their reception of him. No one offered him his hand. Some simply said "hello" and then walked away; others just nodded. A few even pretended not to notice him, and looked the other way. But it was the youngest ones who were the most offen-sive, those young clerks who, Golyadkin used to say, knew only horseplay and how to take off and loaf at the first oppor-tunity. Now they gradually formed a ring around him, almost cutting off his retreat, and proceeded to stare at him with insulting curiosity.

This was a bad sign. Golyadkin felt that, and wisely decided not to pay any attention. Then an unforeseen event dealt what is called the *coup de grâce* to Mr. Golyadkin.

As he was living through his tensest moment of anguish, Golyadkin suddenly noticed Golyadkin Two among the young clerks surrounding him. Golyadkin Two was cheerful as usual, grinning as usual, bustling as usual, in brief, his usual playful, buoyant, chuckling, fawning, sharp-tongued, shifty self, the same as ever, the same as he had been yesterday, for instance, when he had popped up at another painful moment for Golyadkin One. Grinning, fidgeting, looking around with a smile that seemed to say "good evening" to everyone around him, he wormed his way into the group of clerks, shaking hands, slapping backs, patting shoulders, putting his arm around people, explaining what errand he had just done for His Excellency, where he had gone, whom he had seen, and what he had brought back with him; then, actually kissing some clerk, probably his dearest friend, right on the lips—in brief, he was acting exactly as he had acted in Golyadkin One's dream.

When he had skipped around to his heart's content and won everyone to his side whether he needed them or not, when he had exchanged enough amiabilities with all the clerks, Golyadkin Two suddenly stretched out his hand to his oldest friend, Golyadkin One, whom he apparently hadn't noticed before, although perhaps his gesture was just the result of a mistake. Probably also without thinking, Golyadkin One seized that hand, although he certainly had had time to notice his friend, and pressed it eagerly and warmly, squeezed it with a quite unexpected inner feeling, with a sort of tearful emotion. Whether our hero had been deceived by his vicious foe's first gesture, whether he had simply been caught unawares, or whether he had all of a sudden become aware of his utter helplessness—it is hard to say. The fact remains that Golyadkin One, in full possession of all his mental faculties, acting of his own free will and in the presence of numerous witnesses, solemnly shook hands with the man he had called his deadly enemy. But what was his amazement, indignation, and fury when the ignoble Golyadkin Two, noticing the mistake of the innocent man he had so callously and treacherously persecuted, rudely and without the slightest

compassion, pulled his hand out of Golyadkin Senior's grip.
Furthermore, Golyadkin Two then proceeded to brush his
own hand as though he had sullied it with something quite
unmentionable. And on top of that, he spat to one side,
making at the same time a most disobliging gesture; and
further still, he took a handkerchief from his pocket and
unabashedly wiped the fingers of his right hand one by one.
And all the time, Golyadkin Two kept looking around furtively, as was his loathsome habit, kept scrutinizing people's
faces, obviously anxious that everyone should see what he
was doing and thus gain as unfavorable an impression of Golyadkin One as possible. The repulsive behavior of Golyadkin
Two seemed to create indignation among the clerks, and
even the irresponsible young men displayed their displeasure. There was a roar of disapproval all around them. Golyadkin One couldn't have failed to grasp the wave of public
opinion in his favor, but suddenly a timely joke made by
Golyadkin Two took care of that, shattered Golyadkin One's
last hopes, and gave the advantage to his pernicious and
deadly foe once again.

"He is our Russian Faublas.* Allow me to introduce you
to this young Faublas," Golyadkin Two squealed with typical impudence, dancing about among the clerks and pointing
at the nonplussed, genuine Mr. Golyadkin. "Come, let's kiss,
my pet!" he went on with unbearable familiarity, coming
closer to the man he had so treacherously insulted a minute
before.

Golyadkin Two's joke seemed to have touched a responsive chord, for it alluded to a circumstance that was already
known to everyone. Our hero felt the heavy enemy hand
on his shoulder. But he had already made up his mind. His
eyes blazing, his face bloodless, and a faint little smile twisting his lips, he worked his way out of the circle of people
around him and in quick, uneven steps went in the direction
of His Excellency's office.

In the room just before that office he met Andrei Filipovich who was just leaving His Excellency. The room was
full of people who at that moment might have been considered complete outsiders as far as Golyadkin was concerned, but our hero just ignored that fact. He made a dash

---

* The main character of Louvet de Couvray's novel *Les amours
du chevalier de Faublas.*

straight for Andrei Filipovich and, surprised at his own boldness and praising himself for it, he stopped his superior, who
was considerably taken aback by such a direct attack.

"Ah! . . . What is it? What can I do for you?" the head
of the section said, without listening to Golyadkin who had
been spluttering something.

"Andrei Filipovich, sir, may I . . . I would like to have,
right away, Andrei Filipovich, to see His Excellency pri-
vately," Golyadkin said resolutely and distinctly, looking at
Andrei Filipovich with impressive determination.

"What? Most certainly not," Andrei Filipovich said,
measuring Golyadkin from head to foot with a look.

"I feel I have to, Andrei Filipovich, because, to my great
amazement, no one else here seems prepared to expose that
crook and imposter."

"Wha-ah-ah-t?"

"That low imposter, Andrei Filipovich."

"Too whom are you referring in those terms?"

"I have in mind a certain person, Andrei Filipovich. I
am within my rights, sir. I feel that our superiors should
encourage such impulses," Golyadkin added, apparently not
quite realizing what he was saying. "But, Andrei Filipovich,
I'm anxious that you should understand my praiseworthy
impulse and see that it indicates my total loyalty, because it
shows that I am entrusting myself completely to my superiors, as one entrusts oneself to one's father, sir, and it proves
that my chief is a father to me and that I accept his authority
blindly and trust him with my destiny. I'd like to tell him,
well, this is how it is, well and that's so and so." Golyadkin's
voice trembled, his face turned red, and two little tears
appeared on his eyelashes.

Andrei Filipovich was so surprised as he listened to
Golyadkin that he involuntarily reeled back a step or two
and threw an alarmed look around him. It is very difficult
to say how the whole business would have ended if the door
of His Excellency's office had not suddenly opened and His
Excellency himself, surrounded by some lesser officials,
emerged from it. Everyone in the room leaped up as if
pulled by strings. His Excellency called Andrei Filipovich
over to him, and started telling him something about pend-
ing business. Then they all set off, leaving the room behind
His Excellency, and Golyadkin suddenly became aware that
he was being left all alone. So he followed the procession

and took refuge under the wing of Anton Antonovich who was hobbling along behind the others with a worried air, or so it seemed to Golyadkin.

"Ah, I let my tongue run away with me again and made a new mess of things . . . but never mind . . ." he thought, and turning toward Anton Antonovich, he said:

"I have been turned down by everyone else and so I must turn to you, Anton Antonovich. To this moment, I am still at a loss as to the meaning of Andrei Filipovich's words. So please, won't you explain them to me if you can?"

"In time everything will be clear enough to you, sir," Anton Antonovich said sternly and solemnly, with an expression which intimated that he was not anxious to continue the conversation. "You'll find out soon enough. Indeed, you will be officially informed of it today."

"What do you mean by officially, Anton Antonovich? What's official about it?" our hero asked shyly.

"It's neither up to me nor up to you to decide, Yakov Petrovich. Our superiors will do just as they see fit."

"But why is it up to our superiors, Anton Antonovich?" Golyadkin said, growing more and more scared. "I see no reason why our superiors should be disturbed. Perhaps you have in mind something that happened yesterday?"

"No, no, it isn't what happened yesterday. There's something else that isn't right with you."

"But what isn't right with me, Anton Antonovich? There's nothing wrong with me, I'm sure."

"Well, who was it you were trying to drag into your intrigues then?" Anton Antonovich abruptly interrupted him. Golyadkin shuddered, went white, and looked completely annihilated.

"Of course, Anton Antonovich," he said in a hardly audible voice, "if the calumny spread by our enemies is heeded, while our answer to it is not, then, of course . . . then it is quite possible to suffer innocently, Anton Antonovich, to become an innocent victim."

"Yes, and so what about that unseemly act, your misbehavior, so damaging to the reputation of a respectable young lady belonging to a well known family to whom, moreover, you are so deeply indebted?"

"But what act exactly do you have in mind, Anton Antonovich?"

"You know very well what act. And now, what about

that other lady who, although poor, comes from an honorable foreign family? Are you also unaware of your praiseworthy behavior toward her?"

"Allow me, Anton Antonovich, please, just give me a chance to explain . . ."

"And what about your disloyalty toward and slandering of another person, indeed, your accusing another of your own little transgressions? How do you describe that sort of behavior, will you tell me?"

"But I never chased him away from my place, Anton Antonovich," our hero said, trembling in every limb, "and I had never instructed my servant Petrushka to say anything of the sort. . . . He was eating my bread, Anton Antonovich, taking advantage of my hospitality," Golyadkin added with such feeling that his chin began to jerk up and down, and the tears were about to gush from his eyes.

"It is you, Yakov Petrovich, who says that he ate your bread," Anton Antonovich said, with a certain slyness in his grin and in his voice which raked Golyadkin's heart.

"Allow me to ask you one thing, Anton Antonovich: Has His Excellency been informed of this whole affair?"

"Certainly he has! But, please leave me in peace now. I really have no time to go into it with you. . . . You'll know everything that there is to know today anyway."

"Please, Anton Antonovich, just one minute, just one more thing, please . . ."

"You'll say everything you have to say later."

"No, Anton Antonovich, I am . . . please believe me, sir, I am not one for freethinking. Indeed, I shun freethinking. I have even thought that for my part, I . . ."

"I know, I know, I've heard all that from you before."

"No, you haven't, Anton Antonovich, this is something different, something it will be pleasant for you to hear. As I was saying, Anton Antonovich, I have conceived the idea that since the Creator had a special design in creating two exactly identical men, and since the God-fearing authorities, having seen the hand of Providence in it, have provided a haven for these twins, it is all to the good, Anton Antonovich. You can see that it is all very good, and that I am very far from indulging in freethinking. To me, my wise and beneficent superiors are just like a father. Yes, that's what I say, Anton Antonovich, but I also say that a young man must have a job. . . . Please, Anton Antonovich, give me some support. . . . I just meant . . . In the name of God, please let me say one more thing, Anton Antonovich. . . ."

But Anton Antonovich was already far away. Our hero no longer knew where he was standing, what he was hearing, what he was doing, what was happening to him, what they were going to do to him. The shock had been too great.

With beseeching eyes he searched for Anton Antonovich among the crowd of clerks, so that he could justify himself further and tell him something that would convince him of his unconditional loyalty, and also slip in something flattering to Anton Antonovich personally. . . .

But gradually a new light began to dawn in Golyadkin's confused mind, a new, frightening light in which he saw in a flash a whole panorama of circumstances which he had never even suspected before. Then our hero felt a poke in his side. He saw Pisarenko.

"There's a letter for you, sir."

"Ah, so you went there, my friend?"

"No sir, it was delivered here at ten this morning, sir, by Mikheyev, the janitor of the house where Vakhrameyev lives."

"Very good, my friend, and I'll show you my appreciation."

Golyadkin slipped the letter into the inside pocket of his overcoat, buttoned it up, looked quickly around him and, to his tremendous surprise, realized that he was standing in the entrance hall of the department building, among a crowd of government employees, for this was office closing time. Up to that moment, Golyadkin was neither aware of this fact, nor did he remember putting on his overcoat and overshoes. Nor did he know how long he had been holding his hat in his hand. The government employees were all standing still, and appeared to be waiting respectfully for something. It so happened that His Excellency was standing by the door waiting for his carriage, which for some reason had failed to come for him in time, and while he was waiting, he had got engaged in a very interesting conversation with Andrei Filipovich and two councilors. At a few respectful steps from them stood Anton Antonovich and a few other officials, all of them smiling broadly because they realized that His Excellency was pleased to indulge in a joke. The clerks crowding on the stairs were also grinning amiably, waiting for His Excellency to laugh aloud again. The only person not smiling was Fedoseich, the fat-bellied doorman, who stood stiffly at attention with his hand on the door knob, preparing to perform his pleasurable daily duty: to open one half of the double door with one single sweep of his arm, and then, bending his whole body in an arch, let His Excellency pass out of the building.

But the happiest looking and the most obviously delighted person was Mr. Golyadkin's unworthy and ignoble enemy. He had even forgotten the other clerks for the moment, wasn't even busy buzzing and dancing about in their midst, trying to make up to one or the other of them. He had become all eyes and ears, the rest of his body having strangely shrunk, probably to make it easier for him to overhear what His Excellency was saying without taking his eyes off him. Only from time to time did his arms, legs, and head twist barely perceptibly, thus denoting the secret workings of his mind.

"Look at that face," our hero thought; "the nasty creature looks like His Excellency's pet already, no doubt about it. I'd give a lot to know how he manages to charm all of high society. He has neither brains nor character, nor education nor feelings. Ah, the lucky animal! He has really got around them all very quickly, and I'll swear he'll go much, much further yet with his luck! I would also give a lot to know what it is he keeps whispering in people's ears—what plots he's hatching and what secrets he's telling them. Ah, God, wouldn't it be nice if I could . . . Well, just ask him, as a favor . . . Well, make him see that it wasn't really my fault . . . Well, something to the effect that I won't do it again, that I'm sorry but that nowadays a young man must have a job, Your Excellency, and that I don't mind my menial position at all and that's the truth. I also won't protest any more and I'll take whatever comes to me with the utmost humility. Shall I do it then? But, after all, it's impossible to touch him. He won't listen to reason, the muddlehead. Well, never mind, let's have a go at it. I may just happen to catch him at the right moment. So, I think I'll try. . . ."

In his misery and anguish, feeling that he couldn't prolong his present situation, that the moment of decision had arrived, that he had to have the matter out with someone or other, our hero began moving slowly toward the spot where his unworthy and mysterious friend was standing. But at that very second His Excellency's long-overdue carriage rolled up thunderously to the curb. Fedoseich tore at the door handle, bent his body low, and let out His Excellency. All those who were waiting streamed toward the exit and, for a while, Golyadkin One found himself widely separated from Golyadkin Two.

"No, you won't get away!" our hero muttered, elbowing his way through the crowd, his eyes riveted on his objective. Finally the crowd dispersed. Our hero felt himself unfettered and rushed in pursuit of his enemy.

Chapter 11

G<small>OLYADKIN'S BREATH WAS</small> taken away; he was flying as if on wings after his fugitive foe. He felt tremendous energy bubbling up inside him. Yet, despite all that energy, Golyadkin was quite aware that a common mosquito, if such could have been found in Petersburg at that time of year, could easily have knocked him over with its wing. He knew that he himself was crestfallen and utterly weak, and that an outside force was propelling him, despite the fact that his legs were giving way under him and refusing to obey. But who knew, it might all turn out for the best. "Whether it is for the best or not," Golyadkin thought, almost suffocating from running so fast, "the game is lost and no doubt about it. I'm lost and that fact is signed and sealed."

Notwithstanding this view, our hero felt like one risen from the dead, like the victor of a strategic battle, when he caught hold of a corner of the skirt of his foe's overcoat, just as the latter had raised one foot to climb into a cab he had stopped.

"Sir! Sir!" he shouted to the ignoble Golyadkin Two, with whom he had finally caught up. "I hope, sir, that you . . ."

"Oh no, better have no hope at all," replied Golyadkin's unfeeling enemy, with one foot on the step of the carriage and the other still in the air, as he tried in vain to get into the cab. Golyadkin Two had both to keep his balance and to try to free his coat from Golyadkin One's grip into which the latter was putting his all.

"Yakov Petrovich, I must talk to you. It won't take ten minutes!"

"I'm sorry, I have no time at all."

"But please understand, Yakov Petrovich, please . . . Give me a chance to explain myself frankly, please, in the name of God, Yakov Petrovich, give me just one minute . . ."

"But don't you understand, my dear fellow, that I simply haven't the time," Golyadkin's ungenerous foe replied with offhand familiarity and sham heartiness. "I'd be glad to at any other time. I'd welcome the opportunity from the bottom of my heart, but just now—it's quite impossible."

Our hero thought: "The nasty creature!" and called out in anguish: "Yakov Petrovich, you must understand that I have never been your enemy. That is pure invention by ill-wishing people. . . . For my part, I'm willing . . . Listen, won't you come with me now, and I'll tell you everything, from the bottom of my heart, as you said so well a second ago. What about stepping into this café here? I'm sure everything can be explained in plain language . . . Yes, Yakov Petrovich, I'm certain that the whole misunderstanding will be cleared up."

"You want us to go into the café? All right, I don't object, but on one condition, my boy—I want you to give me a complete explanation of everything," Golyadkin Two said, stepping down from the cab and unabashedly patting our hero on the shoulder. "For an old friend like you, Yakov Petrovich, I'm even prepared to sneak in by the back alley as you once insisted. Ah, you rascal, there's no way of refusing you anything!" the false friend went on, bustling and buzzing around our hero.

The café where the two Golyadkins went was safely tucked away from the main thoroughfares and was completely deserted at this hour. A rather fat German woman appeared behind the counter as soon as she heard the bell ring. Golyadkin One and his unworthy companion passed into the second room where a puffy-faced boy with short-cropped hair was fiddling with the firewood in the stove, trying to revive a dying fire. Golyadkin Two ordered them some hot chocolate.

"Isn't she rather appetizing, that German woman? What do you say?" Golyadkin Two said with a sly wink at Golyadkin One, who turned red and said nothing. "Oh, I'm sorry, I forgot. I know your tastes," Golyadkin Two went on. "You go in for rather thin German women. Well, I admit they're not without charm either. Yes, you and I, Yakov Petrovich, we do have rather a weakness for those slender fräuleins who are so full of hidden charm. We rent rooms in their apartments, we corrupt their morals, we give them our hearts for their *bier suppen* and their *milch suppen* and give them all sorts of written promises—that's what we do—ah, you *Faublas*, you fickle lover!"

Thus Golyadkin Two made vicious but quite pointless allusions to a certain person of the female sex, all the while smiling at our hero with sham friendliness, pretending to be delighted with his company. But realizing that Golyadkin One was not stupid enough to be taken in that way, that he had much too much polish, manners, and upbringing not to see through him, that ignoble individual decided to change his tactics and to go over to an open attack. And so, having uttered that revolting remark, Golyadkin Two added insult to injury by patting our hero on the shoulder and then, not content even with that, started playing pranks which were quite inadmissible in good company. He repeated an earlier trick of his and pinched Golyadkin One's cheek; Golyadkin One flew into a rage at such an insult and . . . and took it silently. Of course, only for the time being.

"All that is only what my enemies say," he replied finally in a trembling voice, prudently restraining himself and glancing worriedly at the door. He realized that Golyadkin Two was in excellent spirits and likely to indulge in all sorts of little jokes which would be inadmissible in a public place and, generally speaking, unacceptable according to the code of high society.

"Well, in that case, just as you wish," Golyadkin Two replied to Golyadkin One's thought, putting down the cup he had emptied with such unseemly greed. "Anyway, I don't have much time to spare you. . . . So tell me, Yakov Petrovich, how's life been treating you lately?"

"I can assure you of only one thing, Yakov Petrovich," our hero said with cool composure. "I have never been an enemy of yours."

"Hm . . . But what about Petrushka? That's what he's called, isn't it? Yes, that's right. How is he—just the same as ever?"

"Yes, he's just the same as ever," Golyadkin One said, slightly surprised. "I don't know, Yakov Petrovich, but from my standpoint, from a frank, honorable standpoint . . . No, you're bound to agree yourself, Yakov Petrovich . . ."

"Yes, but as you know yourself, Yakov Petrovich," Golyadkin Two said in a soft and feeling voice, trying to sound like a sad man who is suffering from remorse and deserves compassion, "we are going through difficult times just now. I call on you as a witness, Yakov Petrovich—you're an intelligent man and I'm sure you'll judge correctly," Golyadkin Two added, trying vile flattery on Golyadkin One. "Life's no plaything, as you know yourself," he concluded ponderously, now impersonating a learned intellectual who is quite capable of discoursing on such an exalted topic.

"For my part, Yakov Petrovich," our hero answered with emotion, "scorning devious paths and speaking frankly and openly and being honorably aboveboard, let me firmly assure you that I am absolutely clean of any charges and that, as you know yourself, Yakov Petrovich, it was a mutual misunderstanding, and anything could happen—the verdict of society, the opinion of the slavish crowd. . . . I really mean it, when I say that anything can happen, Yakov Petrovich. What's more, if one were to pass a judgment, if one were to look at it from a noble, lofty viewpoint—I'll tell you boldly, without being coy, that it would even be pleasant for me to say that I was mistaken. I would be delighted to admit I was wrong. You know how it is yourself, being a man of intelligence and having a noble heart. Well, I am prepared to recognize everything without false shame," our hero concluded nobly.

"It's all a question of blind fate . . . But let's leave that," Golyadkin Two said with a sigh. "Let us rather spend the few minutes we have on more pleasant and useful talk, such as is fitting for colleagues. It's true that we haven't had an opportunity for a chat since that time. . . . And the blame for that cannot be laid at my door, Yakov Petrovich."

"Nor at mine!" our hero exclaimed heatedly. "My heart tells me, Yakov Petrovich, that all this is none of my fault. Well, so let's just blame fate then," Golyadkin One added in an altogether conciliatory tone. His voice had weakened and started to tremble.

"Well, how are things? And how is your health in general?" the abhorrent Golyadkin inquired in a syrupy voice.

"Just a little cough," our hero said even more sweetly.

"You'd better be careful. There are a lot of colds going around, and it's not so difficult to catch pneumonia. I must confess, I've already started wearing flannel underwear."

"You've said it, Yakov Petrovich, it's very easy to catch pneumonia," our hero said after a brief pause. "Yes, Yakov Petrovich, I realize now that I was in the wrong. And I still think with emotion of the happy moments we spent together in my poor, but I dare say, hospitable abode. . . ."

"Although that's not quite what you wrote in your letter," Golyadkin Two said with a reproach that for once was partly justified.

"But I admit I was wrong, Yakov Petrovich. It's quite obvious to me now, and I feel ashamed to look you in the eye. You can't imagine how ashamed I feel. Please, let me have that letter back and I'll tear it up here, right in front of you. Or if that's impossible, I beseech you to take it as meaning just the opposite of what it says. I was in error. Forgive me. I was completely wrong."

"What were you saying?" Golyadkin's false friend asked absentmindedly.

"I was saying that I've been completely wrong about you and I say it without any false shame . . ."

"Ah, enough about that. It's a very good thing you were mistaken," Golyadkin Two said rudely.

"I even had an idea, Yakov Petrovich," our open-hearted hero went on, without noticing the sneakiness of his false friend, "that two persons being created exactly alike . . ."

"Ah, so that was your idea!" And the notoriously good-for-nothing Golyadkin Two got up and picked up his hat. Still not realizing that he was being taken in, Golyadkin One got up too, smiling his open, friendly smile, trying thus, in his innocence, to cheer him up, to be nice to him, and so to resume their friendship.

"Well, good-by then, Excellency," Golyadkin Two suddenly cried out. Our hero shuddered, noticing something positively Bacchanalian in his enemy's expression, and, solely to get rid of him, he thrust two fingers into the unscrupulous fellow's outstretched hand. But the shameless thing that Golyadkin Two did then exceeded anything one could have expected. Having pressed Golyadkin One's two fingers, he decided to go once more through the shameless act he had performed before. The limit of human endurance was surpassed.

Golyadkin Two was already putting away in his pocket the handkerchief he had used to wipe his fingers when Golyadkin One burst into the next room, into which his enemy had darted, as he had a bad habit of doing. There he was, standing by the counter and eating pies as if nothing had happened. He looked like a very virtuous man and was paying compliments to the fräulein behind the counter. Beside himself, our hero rushed toward the counter, but he realized that "it would be quite impossible in front of a lady."

"Why, she's really not bad at all, this German woman. What do you say?" Golyadkin Two said, once again resuming his shoddy tricks and apparently reckoning that Golyadkin One's patience was quite inexhaustible. For her part, the fat German woman was staring at the two customers out of her blank, tiny eyes. Apparently she didn't understand Russian, for she even gave them a friendly smile. Our hero flared up at the shameless words of Golyadkin Two and, incapable of controlling himself any longer, he rushed at his enemy with the evident intention of tearing him to shreds and thus getting rid of him once and for all. But, with his usual disgusting shiftiness, Golyadkin Two was already safely out of reach. In fact, he had already reached the door. Of course, once he had overcome the first paralysis which was naturally caused by his surprise, Golyadkin One rushed madly after his offender, who was already getting into a cab whose driver was entirely in league with him. But at that moment, the fat German lady realized that her two customers had fled and began to ring her bell frantically. Our hero turned back and, almost in full flight, tossed her the money for himself and for the shameless man who had left without paying and, without waiting for the change, resumed his pursuit. Despite the delay, he managed to catch up with his friend again at the very last moment. Clutching onto the mudguard of the cab with all the strength at his disposal, our hero was dragged along the street for a while, making desperate efforts to clamber on board, while Golyadkin Two did his utmost to prevent him from doing so. The cabbie, meanwhile, urged on his broken-down nag with word, reins, and whip. The horse quite unexpectedly went into a gallop, biting at its bit and kicking at every third step, an old, bad habit it had. In the end, our hero succeeded in clambering on board. He faced his enemy, his back propped against the driver's back; their knees were locked and his right hand was on the fur collar of his depraved and merciless foe.

The enemies rolled about like that for a while in complete silence. Our hero could scarcely breathe. He was being badly jolted and was in peril of breaking his neck. What's more, his obdurate foe still refused to concede defeat and kept trying to push him out into the mud. To make things even worse, the weather was foul. Snow was falling heavily and was trying to slip under the collar of the genuine Golyadkin, whose overcoat had come unfastened. And with the snow and all, it was hard to see more than a few yards, so that our hero couldn't tell what direction they were going in or what streets they were passing along. Golyadkin One had the impression that something familiar was happening to him. He tried to recall whether he had had some premonition or whether he had dreamed something about it, perhaps just the night before . . . .

Finally his anguish turned into full-fledged agony. Leaning hard against his merciless foe, he tried to shout, but his cry died on his lips. . . . There was a second during which Golyadkin forgot what was going on and decided that it was all nothing really, that it didn't matter, that it was something that couldn't be explained, and that protesting would be a complete waste of time.

But at the very second when our hero had reached the conclusion that none of it mattered, an unexpected jolt completely changed the whole situation. Mr. Golyadkin fell from the carriage and rolled on the ground like a sack of flour, and while rolling thus, he quite justly admitted to himself that he had lost his temper a bit too hastily. When he got up, though, he realized that they had really reached their destination. The cab had stopped in the middle of a courtyard and our hero immediately realized that it was the yard of the house where Olsufy Ivanovich lived.

He saw at once that his friend was rushing into the house, probably on his way to Olsufy Ivanovich's apartment. In his indescribable anguish, Golyadkin was about to rush after him but, fortunately for himself, thought better of it. Not neglecting to pay the cabbie first, Golyadkin rushed out into the street and started to run without caring where he was going. The snow was coming down just as thickly as before, and it was still just as murky, dark, and damp. Our hero didn't run, he flew, knocking over men, women, and children who happened to be in his path, hearing all around and behind him frightened cries and squeals. But Golyadkin seemed quite unconscious and refused to pay attention to anything. He only came a little to his senses by the Semyonovsky Bridge, and then only because he had managed to knock over two women street merchants there, and this time had also fallen himself. "This still isn't the end of it," Golyadkin thought. "Everything may yet turn out all right," and he put his hand in his pocket, hoping that a silver ruble would make up for the scattered gingerbread, apples, peas, and all sorts of other junk.

While searching for the silver coin, Golyadkin's hand felt the letter that had been handed to him earlier that day by Pisarenko, and it was as though a new luminary had appeared over his head. Remembering that there was a tavern he knew close by, he hurried off there, and installed himself at a table on which a candle was burning. Ignoring everything around him, including the waiter who came to take his order, he broke the seal and proceeded to read the following message, which completely staggered him:

> To the magnanimous man who is suffering for me and who will always remain dear to my heart:
> I am suffering, I am perishing—save me! That schemer, that slanderer, that individual notorious for his pernicious tendencies has entangled me in his snares and I am lost. I have succumbed. But he disgusts me, whereas you! . . . They have separated us, they have intercepted my letter to you, and behind it all is that immoral creature who is taking advantage of his best feature—his resemblance to you. In any case, it is possible to be homely but to charm people with one's wit, one's strong feelings, and one's impeccable manners. . . .
> I am perishing! They are marrying me off forcibly, and the principal person involved in the maneuver is my father, my benefactor, State Councilor Olsufy Ivanovich, who apparently wishes me to get into high society this way. But I am resisting firmly, using all the means nature has put at my disposal.
> Wait for me with a carriage under the windows of our apartment tonight at nine o'clock sharp. We

are having a ball again. The handsome lieutenant is coming too. I'll come out and we shall flee.

Besides, you must realize that there are other government departments where it is possible to be of service to the country. In any case, you must remember, my dearest, that the main strength of innocence is innocence itself. Farewell. Wait for me with a carriage at the door of my house. I shall throw myself into the shelter of your embrace at exactly two o'clock in the morning.

Yours till the grave,
KLARA OLSUFIEVNA

Golyadkin was dumbfounded. White as his handkerchief, terribly agitated, and filled with anguish, he darted up and down the room several times, holding the letter in his hand. What made his situation even less pleasant was that, although he was quite unaware of it, he had become the center of the attention of everyone in the room. Probably the disorder of his dress, his walking, or rather running, to and fro, his gesticulations with both hands, and, possibly, some enigmatic words he may have dropped—all this must have helped to cause the poor impression Golyadkin left in the minds of those present. And the waiter also began to look at him suspiciously.

When he had recovered a little, Golyadkin found himself standing in the middle of the room, staring rather rudely at a respectable-looking old man who, having just finished his dinner and said his prayer of gratitude before an icon, had sat down again at his table and, in turn, was staring back at our hero.

Golyadkin looked around and realized that everyone in the room was looking at him in a most suspicious and unfriendly way.

Suddenly an army officer with a red collar on his tunic demanded the *Police Gazette* in a loud voice. Golyadkin shuddered, turned red, and instinctively lowered his eyes, and thus realized that his clothes were in a disorder that might have been considered intolerable even if he had been at home, let alone in such a public place. His trousers, his shoes, and his whole left side were splattered with mud, his right footstrap had snapped, and his frockcoat was torn in several places. With an agonized expression on his face, our hero returned to the table where he had sat while reading the letter, and saw the waiter coming toward him looking peculiarly rude and determined. Terribly embarrassed and utterly crestfallen, our hero stared down at the dirty plates left after someone else's dinner, at a soiled napkin, at the greasy knives and forks scattered on the table before him.

"Who ate that dinner?" he wondered. "Could it possibly have been me? Anything's possible. I ate my dinner without noticing. But how could I, really?"

Golyadkin looked up and caught sight of the waiter who was on the point of saying something.

"How much do I owe you, my friend?" Golyadkin asked in a trembling voice.

Loud laughter greeted these words; even the waiter grinned. Golyadkin realized that he had blundered again. He became terribly embarrassed, and put his hand in his pocket in search of his handkerchief, apparently just to be doing something. But, to the great delight of the others and to his own amazement, his hand emerged from his pocket holding, instead of the handkerchief, a phial containing a drug that Doctor Christian Ivanovich had prescribed for him four days or so before. "Get the medicine at the same chemist's," the doctor's voice echoed through Golyadkin's brain. He suddenly shuddered with horror. The dark, red-brown fluid passed in a flash before Golyadkin's eyes as the phial fell from his hand and broke. Golyadkin let out a yell and stepped back to avoid the spilled medicine. Every limb in his body was shaking, and cold sweat broke out on his temples and forehead.

"So my life *is* in danger!" he cried out.

This caused a general commotion in the room. Golyadkin was surrounded. Everyone was saying something about him and some, indeed, were praising him. But our hero was deaf, mute, and unmovable. He was indeed quite unaware of what was going on around him.

Then suddenly, as though something had suddenly set him off, he dashed out of the tavern, pushing those who tried to stop him out of his way. He managed to jump into the first cab he saw and was driven home in an almost unconscious state.

In the entry to his apartment, Golyadkin came across Mikheyev, the janitor from the department's office building.

The man held an envelope with an official government seal on it in his hand.

"I know, my friend, I know," our exhausted hero said in a weak, tired voice, "this is an official notification."

Indeed, the letter instructed Golyadkin to hand over the papers he was working on to Ivan Semyonych. Golyadkin gave a ten kopeck piece to the messenger and went back into the apartment. There he saw that Petrushka was collecting all his junk together, apparently with the intention of walking out on Mr. Golyadkin and going into the service of Karolina Ivanovna who had enticed him to come and take over Estafy's place.

Chapter 12

Petrushka swaggered into Golyadkin's room. There was a strangely casual air about his smug, flunkeyish face. Obviously he was about to do something he considered it his right to do. He was no longer part of this household and, although he was still a flunkey, he wanted it to be well understood that he certainly wasn't Golyadkin's flunkey.

"Well, my friend," our hero began, "what time is it, my friend?"

Without answering, Petrushka went behind the partition, came back and with a very independent air announced that it was already almost seven-thirty.

"Well, all right then, my friend, that's fine. Well, as you can see . . . It seems to me that this is the end between us, isn't it?"

Petrushka remained silent.

"So now, since everything is finished between us, I'd like you to tell me frankly, as a friend, where were you?"

"Where was I? I went to see kind people, sir."

"I know, my friend, I know. Well, I've always been pleased with your service and I'll write you a good recommendation. So you're going to work for them now?"

"Well, since you know it, sir, that shows that one never learns bad things from a good man."

"I know, I know, my friend, and since nowadays good people are rather rare, you'd better appreciate them when you find 'em. Well, and what about them?"

"Well, what about them, sir? But there's one thing I'm quite sure of and that's that I can't work for you any more."

"I know, my friend, and I respect you for it. I have always respected a good, honest man whether he was a servant or what have you."

"Why, to be sure, sir, the likes of me look out for what's best for them, and you know it, sir. That's just how it is, sir! And I understand that it'll be hard for you to get along without a good man."

"Right, brother, right. I feel it myself. . . . So let me pay you now and give you that recommendation. And let me give you a hug, my friend, as we say good-by. . . ." And when all this had been performed, Golyadkin addressed Petrushka in a solemn tone: "And now, my friend, I'll ask you for one last service. You see, my dear fellow, sorrow dwells even in gilded palaces, and there's no way of escaping it. As you know, my friend, I've always been nice to you." He paused; then, as Petrushka remained silent, he went on. "So, as I say, I've always been nice to you . . . Well, how much linen have I left now, my boy?"

"It's all there, sir. Six linen shirts, three pairs of socks, four shirtfronts, a flannel undershirt, two sets of underwear . . . You know very well, sir, that I haven't . . . To me, the things that belong to my master are sacred, sir. Perhaps, you and me, sir . . . well, you know yourself . . . But I've never been guilty of anything like that, sir . . ."

"I believe you, my friend, I believe you. That wasn't at all what I meant. You see, my boy . . ."

"I know, and you've said that already, sir. Why, when I was in the service of General Stolbnyakov . . . He let me go when he was moved to Saratov . . . He has an estate there, sir."

"No, my friend, I didn't mean that. Don't go imagining things. . . ."

"I know, sir, but as you know yourself, it's easy to sling mud at the likes of me, but, I dare say, sir, wherever I've served, everyone's always been pleased with me and I've worked, sir, for ministers, generals, senators, counts, in fact, I was even in the service of Prince Svinchatkin, of Colonel Pereborkin, of General Nedobarov, and I've been to their estates with them too, sir . . ."

"Yes, yes, my friend, all right, and like your other masters, I too am leaving town. . . . Well, every man must follow his own path and no one can tell which road he'll come out on. And so, my friend, help me to change my clothes now and then help me to pack my frockcoat, my sheets, blankets, and pillows . . ."

"Shall I tie it all in a bundle, sir?"

"That's right, my friend, do that, for who knows what may happen to us? And now, would you please go and get a carriage for me?"

"A carriage, sir?"

"Yes, a carriage, and a large one if possible, for I want to keep it for a certain time. But don't go imagining anything, my friend."

"And are you going far, sir, if you don't mind my asking?"

"I don't know yet myself. And the comforter, it could be put in the same bundle with the rest, don't you think? I rely on your judgment, my friend."

"Are you leaving right away then, sir?"

"That's right, my friend, right away. It turns out that I must go now."

"I understand, sir. I saw the same thing happen in our regiment, to a lieutenant, sir. He carried off a landowner's daughter . . ."

"Carried her off? How did that happen?"

"He just carried her off, sir, and they got married in the neighboring village. They'd planned it well in advance, sir. They chased them, but the late prince took them under his protection and so everything quieted down."

"So they got married, in the end—I see. But tell me, how come you know so much about that story, my friend?"

"Well, you know, sir, things get around, sir, and we end up knowing everything about everyone and no one can say that he's without a sin on his conscience. But let me tell you something, sir, let me give it to you straight, like a loyal servant, sir; you have an enemy, sir. You've a very big rival, very dangerous, sir. . . . And so now you know."

"I'm aware of that, my good friend, very much aware of it. And I'm relying on you to tell me what, in your opinion, I should do next."

"Well, if you really mean it, sir, if you want my advice and have really decided to go through with that plan of yours, sir, let me remind you that from now on you'll need sheets and blankets and such for a double bed and also a lady's cloak. Well sir, there's a woman lives downstairs in this house, sir, and she has a beautiful lady's cloak to sell, a real beauty, sir, with fox-fur trimmings and a satin lining. You ought to go down and have a look at it right away, sir."

"Very good, my friend, I agree. I rely upon you entirely, although perhaps that cloak . . . All right then, but let's be quick about it, for God's sake. Let's hurry! I'll buy that cloak, as long as it doesn't take long. It's almost eight now so, please, in the name of God, let's be quick!"

Petrushka left the bundle of sheets and blankets he had been putting together still untied and dashed out of the room.

Golyadkin picked up the letter but he couldn't read it. Seizing his triumphant face in both hands, he leaned against the wall, quite unable to keep his mind on anything or to do anything. Something strange was going on inside him. After he had waited what seemed to him a long time and neither Petrushka nor the lady's cloak had shown up, Golyadkin decided to go and see for himself what had happened to them. When he opened his apartment door, he heard a noise and voices coming from downstairs. Some women neighbors were arguing about something. He also heard Petrushka's voice and then steps approaching.

"Good God," Golyadkin moaned, wringing his hands in despair, "they're going to bring the whole town in here!" and he rushed back into his apartment.

When he was in his room again, he fell on his couch and buried his face in the pillow. He remained in that position for a minute and then, finding that Petrushka still didn't return, he leaped up again, put on his overshoes, his overcoat, and his hat, picked up his wallet, and tore downstairs.

"No, no, I don't need anything, my friend. I'll manage by myself, all by myself. I don't need you just now, but who knows, perhaps everything will come out all right in the end," Golyadkin muttered to Petrushka as he passed him on the staircase. Then he rushed out of the house into the yard and from there into the street. His heart felt faint. He hadn't decided yet how he was to act, what he was to do in this moment of extreme crisis.

"Oh God, what am I supposed to do now? Why did all this have to happen to me?" he cried aloud, hobbling hurriedly along the street, unaware of what direction he was going in. "Who needed it all? Why, if it hadn't happened, everything would've turned out all right in the end. Every-

thing would have been taken care of in one fell swoop. I'd
have let them cut off my finger, if it hadn't turned out well
in the end. In fact, I even know how everything would have
been arranged: I'd have said to him something like, 'Look
here, my good sir, that's not the way to act and we're not
used to that sort of behavior—imposture is of no use to our
country, sir, and since trying to pass as someone else is a
useless thing, then you're an utterly useless individual and
I want you to know it! . . .' Yes, that's quite right, but . . .
Well, no, that's not at all how it is really. It's not like that
at all . . . What am I chattering about, fool that I am? I'm
nothing but a suicidal idiot . . . Yes, but that's how it should
be done, you depraved creature! But where am I to go now?
What am I supposed to do with myself now? What am I good
for? Yes, what use can you be now, Golyadkin, you worthless, good-for-nothing failure? What now? She expects you
to get a carriage and bring it to her doorstep, because the
lady is afraid she'll get her feet wet if the carriage isn't there.
Who would've thought it? Ah, what a well bred young lady
she is! They've all praised you so much, and now you've
really distinguished yourself, ma'am! And I say all the trouble
comes from immoral upbringing! Yes, now I've seen and realized that the whole thing stems from looseness of principle.
Instead of giving her the rod when she was little, they stuffed
her with bonbons and other sweet things, and the old man
himself keeps doting on her and telling her that she's lovely
and beautiful and that he'll get her a count for a husband!
But now she's shown them her cards, as though saying, 'Here,
folks, have a look at the hand I have!' And instead of keeping her at home, they sent her to a finishing school run by
that French *émigrée*, Madame Falbalas, and now they can
go and admire the result of that upbringing! 'Wait for me
with a carriage,' she says, 'at such and such a time, in front
of my windows, and I want you to sing me a nice sentimental
Spanish serenade, because I am waiting for you and because
I know you love me; so come, we'll elope and we'll go and
live in a hut.' Well, it just can't be done, ma'am, and let me
tell you, it's even against the law to carry off honorable and
innocent girls from their parental homes. And anyway, what
need is there for it? Why can't you marry someone they
wish you to marry and put an end to all this business? I am
a government servant, ma'am, and this could cost me my

position and, possibly, it could even get me hailed into court, in case you didn't know.

"It's that German woman's work. All the trouble comes from her. She's the one who's lighted all these forest fires. It's all because a man has been slandered, because they invented that old wives' tale about him on the advice of Andrei Filipovich! Otherwise, why should Petrushka get mixed up in it? Where does he come in and what advantage can the lout derive from it? Oh no, ma'am, I'm very sorry but I can't oblige . . . It is you and not that German woman, ma'am, who are at the root of all the trouble. It's not the witch's fault, because the witch is a kind-hearted woman. It's all your fault, ma'am! There's a man perishing here, a man is losing himself and can do nothing about it. Who can talk of marriage under such conditions? And how is it all going to end? What wouldn't I give to know!"

Suddenly snapping out of these desperate thoughts, Golyadkin noticed that he was somewhere on Liteinaya Street. The weather was awful; it was snowing and raining at the same time, and a thaw had set in—exactly the same weather as on that terrible, unforgettable midnight when all Golyadkin's troubles had begun. "Who's talking about a little trip in a carriage in such weather?" Golyadkin thought. "It's death, simply death. . . . Ah, dear God, where on earth can I find a carriage around here? But what's that black thing around the corner? Let's go and investigate. . . . Ah, dear God!" He hobbled hesitantly toward the spot where he thought he'd seen a carriage.

"No . . . Well, here's what I'll do; I'll go back, go down on my knees, and humbly beg for forgiveness. I'll say something like, 'I place my life in your hands, Your Excellency. I implore you for your protection and I rely upon your magnanimity.' And then I'll tell him all about it, about all those unlawful goings on, and I'll tell him, 'I've come to you as to a father, Your Excellency, and so please do not allow my self-respect, my honor, and my name to be disgraced. Save me from a depraved, vicious man. . . . He is a different person, Your Excellency, and I'm a different person too, and let me assure you that I'm all on my own and strictly minding my own business. Believe me, Your Excellency. Therefore, it is quite impossible for me to be like him and so, I beseech you, sir, stop this godless and unauthorized impersonation, so that it won't create a precedent for others.' Our superiors certainly encourage us to come to them as to a father, and I say that there's even something heroic in my attitude in that respect. It's like coming to them and saying— you're like a father to me and I put my fate in your hands and will abide passively by your decisions!"

"Well, what about it, cabbie?"

"Need a cab, sir?"

"I need a cab for the whole evening."

"How far do you wish to go, sir?"

"I'll hire you for the evening and you'll have to drive wherever I tell you."

"Do you intend to go out of town, sir?"

"Possibly, my friend, possibly. I don't know yet myself. I can't tell you for sure. It just may be, my friend, that everything will turn out for the best in the end. . . ."

"Yes, sir, I wish that for everybody."

"Thank you, my friend, thank you. Well, so will you take me?"

"Do you want to hire me right away, sir?"

"Yes, right away . . . That is, you'll have to wait for me at the first place we go to. . . . But it won't take too long, I'm sure. . . ."

"Well, sir, if you're hiring me for the whole evening, I can't charge you less than six rubles. I couldn't do it, sir, in this weather. . . ."

"That's all right, my friend, thank you and don't worry. So I want you to take me now to that place."

"Please get in, sir, while I put things a bit straight here. Please, sit down, sir. Where do you wish me to drive you to now?"

"To the Izmailovsky Bridge, my friend."

The driver climbed up onto the box, and with tremendous difficulty jerked the pair of bony nags away from their trough of hay; then they drove off. But suddenly Golyadkin pulled the cord and, addressing the driver in a beseeching tone, asked him to turn the horses around and instead of going to the Izmailovsky Bridge to drive him to another street. The driver complied and, ten minutes later, the carriage stopped by the house where His Excellency resided.

Golyadkin alighted from the carriage, asked the driver to be certain to wait for him, entered the house and, his heart sinking, ran upstairs to the second floor and pulled the bell cord. The door opened and our hero found himself in the entry of His Excellency's apartment.

"Would you tell me, please, whether His Excellency is at home?" Golyadkin addressed thus the servant who opened the door.

"And what is it you wish?" the footman said, looking him up and down suspiciously.

"Well, you see, my friend, my name is Yakov Golyadkin. I am employed in His Excellency's department . . . I came in to . . . to explain, you see, to . . ."

"Wait, you can't go in just like that . . ."

"I can't wait, my friend. It's an urgent matter that mustn't be delayed. . . ."

"But on whose part are you here? Have you brought some papers or what?"

"No, my friend, I've come on my own account. Just announce me, my friend, say such and such has come with an explanation. You just announce me and I'll show you my appreciation. . . ."

"It's impossible, sir. His Excellency has company. You'll have to come again tomorrow morning at ten."

"Just go and announce me, my friend. I can't wait and I'll hold you responsible if . . ."

"What's the matter, are you afraid to wear out your shoe soles or what?" said another flunkey, who was sprawled on a stool in a corner and hadn't said a word until then. "Why, go in and announce him, man!"

"You know very well it ain't my shoe soles. He just won't receive visitors except in the morning."

"Still, go and announce him. Your tongue won't fall out."

"Sure, I can announce him and my tongue won't fall out, but you know we're not supposed to. All right, come inside."

Golyadkin went into the first room off the entry. There was a clock standing on the table there. Golyadkin looked at the time. It was eight-thirty. That gave him a sickly feeling. He was already thinking of giving up the whole thing when the long-legged footman placed himself in the doorway leading to the next room and announced Golyadkin's name in a stentorian voice. "What a throat that lout has!" Golyadkin thought in indescribable anxiety. "Why couldn't he have gone up to His Excellency and told him very quietly that I'd asked very humbly for him to give me a minute or so . . . But now, he's spoiled the whole thing and all my efforts have been in vain. Well, never mind. . . ."

But Golyadkin didn't have much time to think, for the footman came back, said, "Please follow me," and led Golyadkin into the study.

When Golyadkin entered that room he couldn't see a thing. It was just as though he had gone blind, although he had the impression that two or three figures had flashed in front of him. "Must be the guests," Golyadkin thought. At last, our hero clearly made out the shiny star on His Excellency's black dress coat, after which, his vision recovering by degrees, he discerned the dress coat itself, and finally he could see everything.

"Well, what is it?" Golyadkin heard the familiar voice next to him.

"I'm Yakov Golyadkin. I work in your department, Your Excellency."

"Well?"

"I've come here to explain . . ."

"Explain what? What do you mean?"

"Just to explain certain things, Your Excellency. . . ."

"But who are you?"

"I'm Yakov Golyadkin, Your Excellency, from your department."

"So, what do you want of me?"

"Well, I want to tell you, Your Excellency, that I consider you as a father and that I myself, I'll stand aside . . . I ask your protection from my enemies, Your Excellency."

"But what is this all about?"

"Well, as you know, Your Excellency . . ."

"Know what?"

Golyadkin remained silent. His chin was beginning to jerk.

"Well?"

"I thought it was . . . it was a praiseworthy thing, Your Excellency, for me to look up to my superior as to a father . . . And I thought I'd ask you to give me your protection, Your Excellency, I beseech you . . . with tears . . . and I . . . I be-believe that-that just imp-pulses m-must b-be encour-raged . . ."

His Excellency turned his back on Golyadkin who for several moments was unable to see anything through his tears. He felt a load on his chest, he had difficulty breathing.

He had no idea where he was and felt terribly ashamed and inexpressibly sad. God knows what followed. . . .

When he had recovered a bit, he realized that His Excellency was talking to his guests, and it sounded as though he were arguing rather forcefully with them about something or other. Then Golyadkin recognized one of the guests. It was Andrei Filipovich. He didn't recognize another, although there was something familiar about him too—a big, tall, elderly man with thick, graying whiskers around an expressive face with sharp, determined eyes. There was a decoration in his lapel and a cigar in his mouth which he kept puffing at without removing, as he nodded his head, glancing now and then at Golyadkin.

Golyadkin felt very embarrassed and looked away and, as he did so, noticed yet another rather peculiar guest. In a doorway that our hero had until then mistaken for a mirror, as had happened to him before, he saw HIM—you know who—a very, very close acquaintance of Golyadkin's. Golyadkin Two had been sitting in a small room all that time, busily writing something in a great hurry, but now he obviously had to get something and he came in carrying a file of documents under his arm. He walked up to His Excellency and, while waiting for His Excellency to give him his exclusive attention, managed quite adroitly to get into the conversation, placing himself slightly behind Andrei Filipovich, where he was partially hidden from Golyadkin by the cigar-smoking stranger.

Golyadkin Two appeared to be extremely interested in the conversation, listening to it with a most dignified expression on his face, nodding and at every moment peeking into His Excellency's eyes, grinning and looking imploringly at the others as if he, too, begged them to allow him to put a word in.

"Ah, the loathsome creature!" Golyadkin thought, instinctively taking a step forward. At that moment, His Excellency turned toward Golyadkin, walked over to him rather hesitantly and said:

"All right, go home now and I will look into your case. I'll have someone show you out," and at this point he glanced at the bewhiskered stranger, who nodded his head in assent.

Golyadkin felt very acutely that he had been misunderstood.

"One way or another," he thought, "I'll have to explain

myself. I'll say, you see, Your Exc . . ." As he lowered his eyes he suddenly saw to his immense surprise that there were white spots on His Excellency's shoes. "Could they really have burst at the seams?" he wondered, but then realized that His Excellency's shoes hadn't burst at all and that the white spots were actually the reflection of the light in them.

"That's what's known as a *highlight*," Golyadkin thought, "although that term is mainly used by artists, while otherwise such a reflection is called a *shine*."

At this point he raised his eyes and saw that it was high time for him to speak up, because otherwise the business might take a turn for the worse. . . . He took one step forward again.

"I'd like to state, Your Excellency," he said, "that it is impossible to get away with imposture in our time."

His Excellency did not answer. Instead he violently pulled a bell cord.

Our hero again took a step forward and went on: "He is a despicable and depraved man, Your Excellency," he said, dying of fright and pointing boldly at his twin who, at that moment, was busy buzzing around His Excellency. "That is just the way it is and, in saying this, I have one particular person in view."

Golyadkin's words caused a commotion. Andrei Filipovich and the bewhiskered stranger started nodding their heads; His Excellency pulled the bell cord impatiently to summon his servants; and then Golyadkin Two stepped forward.

"Your Excellency," he said, "I humbly ask your permission to speak." Golyadkin Two's voice and tone were strikingly self-assured; he obviously felt quite sure of his rights. "Now, sir, allow me to ask you," he said, turning toward Golyadkin One and thus anticipating His Excellency's permission to speak, "where do you think you are and what do you mean by talking like this in the presence of such people?"

Golyadkin Two was red with excitement and indignation; there were even tears in his eyes, so great was his agitation.

"Mr. and Mrs. Bassavrukov!" the footman roared fullthroatedly as he appeared in the doorway.

"A good, aristocratic name," Golyadkin thought. "They originate from the Ukraine," and at that moment he felt a friendly hand descend on his back, then another hand which also landed on his back. Golyadkin's despicable twin was bustling about in front of him, leading the way, and our hero clearly realized that he was being steered toward the door of His Excellency's study. "It's just like that time at Olsufy Ivanovich's," he thought when he was in the entrance hall, surrounded by two footmen and one twin.

"The overcoat! Get my dear friend's overcoat! The overcoat of my very best friend. Get it at once!" piped that depraved creature, snatching the garment out of the hands of a servant and throwing it over Golyadkin's head, just for the sake of a nasty, humiliating joke. Trying to free his face from his coat, Golyadkin distinctly heard the laughter of the servants. But he didn't stop to listen, and found himself already outside the apartment. The next thing he knew he was on the lighted stairs in Golyadkin Two's company.

"Good-by, Your Excellency," Golyadkin Two shouted to Golyadkin One.

"You low schemer!" our hero said, beside himself.

"All right, suppose I am?"

"And you're a depraved creature too."

"All right, so I'm depraved," replied Golyadkin's unworthy foe with characteristic impudence, looking unblinkingly down into Golyadkin's eyes from the landing where he stood, as though inviting him to continue.

Our hero spat in indignation and rushed out. He was so thoroughly crushed that he didn't even remember who helped him into the carriage, and only came back to his senses considerably later, at which point he realized that he was being driven along the Fontanka Embankment. "We must be on our way to the Izmailovsky Bridge," Golyadkin surmised and tried to remember something, but he couldn't, for something terrible that he couldn't explain was happening. . . . "Well, never mind," our hero thought as they drove on toward the Izmailovsky Bridge.

Chapter 13

The weather seemed to be trying to change for the better. The wet snow, that until then had been coming down in whole clouds, started to thin out and gradually stopped completely. The sky came into sight with little stars shining here and there. It was still damp, muddy, and close though, particularly for Golyadkin, who had great difficulty breathing as it was. His overcoat, drenched and grown heavy, sealed his whole body into a kind of unpleasantly damp envelope and weighed down his already weakened legs. A feverish tremor kept spreading over his limbs like an army of biting ants; sheer exhaustion caused a cold, sickly sweat to pour out of him, so that this time Golyadkin forgot to repeat his favorite phrase about everything—who knew?—turning out right in the end. Nevertheless, our steadfast hero still managed to assure himself that "after all, so far, it's not really all that bad," as he wiped the water from his face; it was streaming from all around the brim of his hat, which was so soaked it couldn't hold any more liquid. Having thus reassured himself, our hero tried to sit down on a rather big log lying near a pile of firewood in Olsufy Ivanovich's yard.

Spanish serenades and silk ladders were of course quite out of the question. What he was actually thinking about was a snug little corner that didn't even have to be perfectly warm as long as it was well out of sight and safe enough. He was thinking with considerable nostalgia of the corner in the back entry of Olsufy Ivanovich's apartment where he had spent two hours standing between a cupboard and some old screens among old household junk and discards. And it was no wonder he longed for it, for by this time Mr. Golyadkin had already been waiting in Olsufy Ivanovich's court-yard for over two hours. But that snug, discreet corner had certain drawbacks now that hadn't existed before. The first drawback was that, once having discovered the hiding place during the ball, they must certainly have taken the appro-priate measures to prevent his using it again. In the second place, he had to be here to see Klara's signal—for he felt sure she was bound to give some sort of a signal—"that's the way it's always done. It has been done before us and will be done after us."

Golyadkin remembered some novel he had read long ago in which the heroine, in an exactly similar situation, signaled to her Alfred by tying a pink ribbon to her window. But of course, with the damp Petersburg climate and, on top of that, its being night, a pink ribbon could not possibly be considered a suitable signal.

"No, silk ladders are definitely ruled out," our hero thought, "and I suppose I'd better wait here quietly and dis-creetly . . ." and he picked a spot just facing the windows by the pile of firewood.

It goes without saying that unknown people kept pass-ing through the yard, coachmen, postilions, and others, and besides, there was the rumble of wheels and the snorting of horses and so on. Nevertheless, it was a very convenient place to wait. He wasn't sure whether anyone had observed him up till now or not; but the spot he had picked, being so-to-speak in the shade, seemed safe enough: No one could see him, while he could watch everything. The windows of Olsufy Ivanovich's apartment were brightly lit. It looked as though they were having some sort of a reception that night too. But Golyadkin couldn't hear any music as yet. "So it's not a ball—just some other reception," our hero thought with a shudder. "Anyway, was it for tonight? Perhaps she made a mistake in the date? Anything could have happened. . . . That letter . . . perhaps it was written yesterday and I didn't get it in time because that oaf Petrushka got stuck some-where. . . . Unless it was written tomorrow . . . No, what I mean is, unless I had to go through with it—waiting with the carriage and all—tomorrow only . . ."

Golyadkin turned quite cold and plunged his hand into

his pocket for the letter to check the date. But, to his great surprise, he found no letter there.

"How can this be? Where could I have left it? Can I have lost it? Ah, that'd be the last straw!" he moaned. "And what if it falls into enemy hands? Perhaps it has already. Oh Lord, what will happen now? Ah, what a hell of a life! . . ."

It suddenly occurred to Golyadkin that when his hated twin had thrown the overcoat over him, he had done so in order to get hold of the letter of which he had somehow got wind from Golyadkin's enemies.

"Perhaps he has beaten me to it even now," our hero thought, "and the proof . . . Ah, who cares about proof!"

After the first shock, which had made him numb with terror, the blood rushed to Golyadkin's face. Groaning like a wounded beast, he took his burning head in his hands, sat down on the large log and, his teeth chattering, tried to think. But the thoughts wouldn't take shape in his head. Instead, he kept remembering faces and some separate events, now vaguely, now clearly, and all mixed up with the tunes of some stupid songs. . . . He was in a freakish state of anguish. "God, dear God!" our hero thought, during one of his brief lulls, stifling a sob in his breast, "grant me the strength, my God, to bear the inexhaustible depth of my torments! There is no doubt left now that I am lost, wiped out, and that it is in the order of things, for it cannot be any other way. In the first place, I've lost my position—I'm certain I've lost it . . . Ah, supposing things do get straightened out somehow. I suppose I have enough money to take care of me for a while, to get myself another apartment somewhere, to buy a few pieces of furniture. . . . Of course, I won't have Petrushka any more, but I'm sure I could manage without that lout. I could just be a lodger, for instance. Then I'd be able to come home and go out at any time that's convenient for me without Petrushka grumbling—that's why it's really better to be a lodger. . . . Ah, all right, even if all this is for the good, that's not what really bothers me now— I always keep switching to other things. . . ." And Golyadkin suddenly visualized his present position once more, and again seized his burning head in his hands.

"How much longer do you wish to wait, sir?" a voice resounded over Golyadkin's head. Golyadkin shuddered and saw his cabbie, who was also soaking wet and shivering. In addition, he was feeling terribly impatient at having nothing to do, so he had walked over to the wood pile where his fare was hiding.

"It won't be long, my friend, not long at all. Just wait a little more. . . ."

The cabbie walked off grumbling.

"What can he be grumbling about?" Golyadkin thought, feeling tears coming to his eyes. "Didn't I hire him for the entire evening? I am well within my rights, I'm sure. Now, since he's being paid for the whole evening, he can't say anything even if I elect to keep him standing here all the time. Everything depends on my wishes—if and when I wish to drive off, we'll drive off, and that's all there is to it. . . . As to my being here behind this stack of firewood, well, there's absolutely nothing unusual about that and he has nothing to say on the subject. If I wish to stand behind a stack of firewood, I'll stand there. I'm breaking no law in doing so! Yes, ma'am, that's exactly how it is, if you wish to know the truth! And let me tell you, ma'am, no one lives in a hut in our time. And, ma'am, I'd also like to remind you that you won't get far without virtue in this industrial age of ours, a truth which you yourself illustrate so disastrously . . . So you expect me to work as a court clerk and live in a hut on the seashore? Well, let me inform you, ma'am, that there are no court clerks on the seashore and, in the second place, they won't take me on even as a court clerk. Because just suppose for a minute that I put in a request to be taken on as a court clerk and to be protected from my enemy. Well, let me tell you, ma'am, that they have too many court clerks as it is, and you'd better remember that you're not at that finishing school run by that French émigrée woman, Falbalas, where you received your education, an education the effect of which you are so disastrously illustrating today. Virtue, ma'am, consists in sitting at home, respecting your father, and not thinking about marriageable young men until the proper time has come. Then, ma'am, marriageable young men will come of their own accord. That's how things are done. Of course, you must have some talents, such as playing a piece on the piano occasionally, speaking some French, having some idea of history, geography, the scriptures, and arithmetic. And that's all, except, of course, for cooking, because every self-respecting young lady must know her way around the kitchen too. And what do you actually have to offer? In the first place, my beauty, they won't let you go.

They'll catch you and lock you up in a convent right away. And then, ma'am, what do you expect me to do? Do you expect me to behave the way they do in some stupid novels, to climb up the nearest hill and dissolve into tears there while staring at the cold walls that separate you from me, and in the end die altogether as usually happens in bad German books and poems? Well, let me tell you in a friendly way that, to start with, that is not the way business is done. Then, you yourself need a good whipping and your parents too for allowing you to read French books, because no good ever comes of French books. They're pure poison, ma'am, deadly poison! Unless, perhaps, you imagine that we can elope and get away with it, go and live in that cabin by the sea and coo all sorts of loving feelings at each other, spend our lives like that in happiness and contentment, and then have an heir; and then you'll go to your papa and say to him something like, 'Here, papa, we have a little chick now and so won't you please take advantage of this great opportunity and remove your curse and give us your blessing?' No, ma'am! Again, let me assure you, that is not the way these things are done. In the first place, there won't be any cooing, so stop reckoning on it! Nowadays, my dear lady, a wife must please her husband in every single respect. As for tenderness, ma'am, we don't go for it very much in this industrial age of ours. Yes, ma'am, the times of Jean-Jacques Rousseau are past. Nowadays, for instance, a husband may come home from his office hungry and say, 'Isn't there a little snack ready, my love, a glass of vodka, say, and a piece of herring perhaps?' So you'd better have that vodka and herring ready, ma'am, I warn you. And while the husband is putting away that appetizer, he won't even glance at you, and maybe he'll tell you, 'Why don't you go to the kitchen, kitten, and see about the dinner.' Now, once a week or so, he may perhaps give you a kiss, but even if he does, he won't get too excited about it . . . Yes, that's how things are with us, my dear madam! Yes, and as I said, even if he kisses you, the chances are his mind will be elsewhere, and that's how it would be with us, if we did go through with it, and that's how you must look upon these things now . . . But actually, where do I come into it altogether? Why did you have to get me involved in your fanciful ideas? Ah, all that stuff about me being the man 'suffering for her, who will always remain dear to her heart,' and all that. Well, in the first place, let me tell you, ma'am, I am not a fitting suitor for you, because I am not adept at making compliments, and I'm not so good at conducting perfumed small talk with ladies about all sorts of rubbish either and, I must admit, I don't cut much of a figure. But then you won't find false shame or swagger in me, so that what I am saying to you now, I am saying in all sincerity. So that's how it is. All I have is a straightforward nature and lots of common sense. Also, I do not go in for intrigue and I'm proud of it. Yes, I'm proud to walk among good people without a mask, with my face well uncovered and, to tell you the whole story . . ."

All of a sudden, Golyadkin shuddered. The dripping red beard of his driver once again appeared behind the stack of firewood.

"Coming right away, my friend, I'm coming," Golyadkin said in a whimpery, trembling voice.

The cabbie scratched the back of his neck, patted his beard, then took a step forward and looked suspiciously at his fare.

"I'm coming. Just one minute, my friend. You see, I must . . . It will take me no more than one second . . . the thing is, my friend . . ."

"Looks like you ain't going to come at all," the cabbie said, resolutely coming up to Golyadkin.

"Yes, yes, my friend, I'm coming. I'm just waiting. . . ."

"I see, sir, but . . ."

"You see, my friend . . . Tell me, what village do you come from?"

"I come from a landowner's estate, sir."

"Are they nice people, the landowners?"

"They're all right, sir."

"Just stay here for a while, my friend. . . . Tell me, have you been in Petersburg long?"

"I've been driving a cab for a year, sir."

"And how do you like it?"

"I like it fine."

"To be sure, my friend, to be sure. I suggest you thank Providence. You should try to find yourself employment with a kind man. Kind people are rare nowadays and a kind man would give you clean clothes and food and drink, for that's the way a kind man is. And sometimes you'll find that tears fall even through gold, my friend, and you can see a sad example of it now, and that's how it is. . . ."

It looked as though the cabbie were sorry for Golyadkin. "All right, I'll wait some more," he decided, "but how long will you be?"

"No, my friend, I don't think I'll wait any longer. What do you think? I'm relying upon you, my friend. I won't wait here any longer."

"Then you're not coming at all?"

"No, my friend, and I'd like to show you my appreciation. How much do I owe you now?"

"Give me just what we agreed upon, sir. I've waited long enough and I'm sure you don't want to be unfair, sir."

"Here, brother, this is for you," Golyadkin said and paid the cabbie the full six rubles in silver. He decided definitely to leave quickly while the going was good, especially since everything was settled. He had let the cab go, and there was nothing more for him to do there. Golyadkin left the yard, went out into the street, turned left, and started to run without looking back.

"Who knows, perhaps it will all turn out for the best," he thought, "and in the meantime it looks as if I've avoided trouble." And indeed, a wonderful feeling of relief came over Golyadkin. "Ah, if only everything could be arranged!" he repeated but without much conviction. "I could perhaps try . . . Well no, I suppose I'd better handle it the other way . . . Unless, really, the best thing would be . . ."

Thus, hesitating, torn by doubt, debating with himself what would be the best way out of his dilemma, Golyadkin came to the Semyonovsky Bridge, by which time he had reached the reasonable and final decision to go back.

"That's the best thing," he thought. "I'd better handle it from another angle. I mean I'll act as an outsider, as a spectator, nothing more, and whatever happens there—it won't be any fault of mine. That's the way it's going to be now!"

And so, having decided to go back, our hero returned, considering himself now, thanks to that lucky thought, an outsider, not in the least involved in the whole affair.

"That's the very best way—you can watch everything and no one can hold you responsible for anything! That's smart!"

In other words, it was a sure thing—no risks involved. He had the answer. He was very calm when he reached the protective shelter of the stack of firewood and proceeded to watch the lighted windows with great intensity. But this time he didn't have to wait long.

Suddenly it became apparent that there was a strange commotion in the apartment. Faces appeared, curtains were pulled aside, whole clusters of people gathered at the windows, all of them staring out into the yard, searching for something or other there. Feeling secure behind his woodstack, Golyadkin, for his part, watched the general agitation with great curiosity, craning his neck with interest right and left as far as the short shadow of the stack allowed him without jeopardizing his safety. But then something happened that made him start and almost fall down in horror. It had dawned on him suddenly that they weren't just looking for something or someone, but for him, for Mr. Golyadkin. Yes, they were all looking in his direction. Running away was out of the question; they were certain to see him.

Feeling numb, Golyadkin pressed himself against the woodpile and at that very moment noticed that the treacherous shadow didn't cover him quite entirely. Our hero would have given anything to be able to slip like a mouse into a crack between two logs and sit there quietly and patiently, if only he had been given a chance. But it was quite impossible. In his agony, he started to stare boldly and openly up at the windows—that was all he could do now.

A stinging feeling of shame came over him. They had seen him. They had all noticed him at once, and now they were beckoning to him, nodding their heads, signaling to him to come up. He heard the click of some of the windows opening and several voices called out to him at the same time . . .

"I still don't understand why they don't whip young ladies of that type while they are still little girls," Golyadkin kept repeating under his breath, no longer knowing what he was saying.

Then, without his hat and coat, HE (it is obvious who) rushed out of the house, bustling, skipping, shuffling, perfidiously displaying his great delight at having found Mr. Golyadkin at last.

"Yakov Petrovich," piped that man notorious for his uselessness, "what are you doing here? You'll catch cold, you know! Won't you please come into the house?"

"No, thank you, Yakov Petrovich, I'm fine," our hero muttered in a subdued voice.

"No, Yakov Petrovich, you just can't stay here. They beg you to come in. They're waiting for us. 'Please,' they said to me, 'do us a favor and bring Yakov Petrovich inside.' So you see."

"No, Yakov Petrovich, I feel the best thing for me to do would be to go straight home. I'd really much rather do that," our hero said, simmering on a low flame and freezing with terror and shame all at the same time.

"No, no, no—that's quite out of the question!" chirped the repulsive man, "nothing doing. Let's go now!" And grabbing Golyadkin One by the arm, he dragged him across the yard toward the entrance door.

Golyadkin One had no intention of going along, but since it would have looked stupid if he had resisted and pulled in the opposite direction, he went. To say that he "went," however, may be misleading, for he had no precise idea of what was happening to him. Ah, what did it matter at this point anyway!

Before our hero had time to gather his wits or to straighten out his attire, he found himself in the drawing room. He was pale, disheveled, and harassed. He stared around him blankly and, to his horror, realized that the whole apartment was overflowing with guests. There were masses of people, including whole flowerbeds of ladies, and all of them were crowding around Golyadkin, pressing toward him, bearing him on their shoulders. And then he realized that he was being channelled in a particular direction.

"I'm sure I'm not being pushed out, toward the door," flashed through Golyadkin's head and, indeed, he was right. It was not toward the door that he was being directed but toward the armchair of Olsufy Ivanovich, near which stood Klara, looking pale, languid, and sad, although gorgeously attired. Golyadkin at once noted the pale little flowers in her black hair. They looked terribly effective. On the other side of the armchair stood Vladimir Semyonovich, wearing a black frockcoat with a new decoration in his lapel. Golyadkin, supported as we said before, was led straight to Olsufy Ivanovich's armchair. On one side he was flanked by Golyadkin Two, who, to Golyadkin One's great joy, looked benign and dignified now, and on the other side by Andrei Filipovich who wore the most solemn expression on his face.

"What can be going on?" Golyadkin wondered, but when he realized that he was being led to Olsufy Ivanovich, an idea struck him like a flash of lightning: what if they had intercepted that letter? And it was in great agony that our hero stopped before Olsufy Ivanovich. "What shall I do now?" he wondered. "Ah, I suppose the best thing would be boldness—I mean frankness, not without a touch of dignity. I'll just tell him, here is what happened, and so on."

But things seemed to be happening just the way our hero had feared they would. Olsufy Ivanovich received Golyadkin quite well, and although he didn't offer him his hand, he did glance at him and shake his gray, venerable head in solemn sadness but, at the same time, with a rather kindly air. At least such was Golyadkin's impression. Indeed, Golyadkin thought he saw a tear sparkling in Olsufy Ivanovich's lusterless eyes. When he raised his head, he thought he caught sight of a tear on Klara's eyelashes too, and indeed that something of the sort was happening to Vladimir Semyonovich also. As a matter of fact, Golyadkin felt that Andrei Filipovich's quiet, imperturbable dignity was worth all the tearful sympathy of the rest, such as, for instance, that young man who looked rather like an important state councilor and who, under the emotional impact of the moment, was sobbing bitterly.

Of course, it is possible that it all only seemed this way to Mr. Golyadkin because he himself had started to weep and could clearly feel the hot tears rolling down his cold cheeks.

Reconciled with men and life, loving at that moment not only Olsufy Ivanovich and all his guests, but even his pernicious twin who was now apparently no longer either pernicious or his twin, but a very pleasant person in no way connected with our hero, Golyadkin was about to lay his soul open before Olsufy Ivanovich. But, because of the overflow of his feelings, he was unable to express anything and, instead of speaking, simply placed his hand on his heart. . . .

Then Andrei Filipovich, wishing apparently to spare the sensitive feelings of the gray-haired old man, took Golyadkin a little to one side, leaving him there in what appeared to be a quite independent position. Smiling, muttering something under his breath, slightly bewildered but quite reconciled to men and life, our hero started working his way through the throng of guests. They all let him pass, looking at him with strange curiosity mixed with an unaccountable and mysterious sympathy. Golyadkin went into another room and met with the same considerate attention toward his person there. He vaguely heard many people following him step by step, heard them quietly commenting on every movement he made; he heard their whispers, glimpsed the way some of them shook their heads. Golyadkin was very curious to know what it was these people were whispering about and watching. He looked back and saw that Golyadkin Two happened to be near him. He felt an impulse to take the man by the hand, lead him to a corner of the room, and beg him not to abandon him at critical moments in the future. Golyadkin Two solemnly nodded his head, and firmly pressed Golyadkin One's hand. Our hero's heart leapt with a new overflow of feelings, although at the same time he was suffocating, feeling oppressed by all those eyes riveted on him. Then he noticed a councilor who wore a wig. The bewigged councilor was glaring at him and there was nothing of the general sympathy in that man's stern and penetrating gaze. Golyadkin decided to walk straight up to the councilor, to smile at him, and to explain to him . . . But somehow it didn't come off. At one point, Golyadkin almost fainted.

When he recovered, he noticed that he was turning within a wide circle formed by the guests. Suddenly someone called his name from the other room, and then the whole place resounded with shouts. There was a general commotion, an uproar, everyone rushed toward the door of the main drawing room. Our hero was carried out on people's arms, and he noticed that the hard-eyed, bewigged councilor was very close by his side. Then the councilor, taking Golyadkin by the arm, sat him down beside him, facing Olsufy Ivanovich's armchair, although at a quite respectable distance from it.

Everyone who happened to be in the room sat down, forming circles around Golyadkin and Olsufy Ivanovich. Everything grew quiet, all those people seemed to be observing a solemn silence with their eyes now fixed on Olsufy Ivanovich. Obviously, they were expecting something quite sensational to happen. Golyadkin noticed that Golyadkin Two and Andrei Filipovich took places next to the old man's chair, directly facing the bewigged councilor. The silence continued. Indeed, they were waiting for something.

"It's exactly like a family when one member is about to leave on a long journey. It's as though they were going to get up and say a prayer and then he'd go," our hero thought.

Suddenly there was a strange movement among the audience and Golyadkin's thoughts were interrupted. Something that he had been expecting all along happened.

"He's coming, he's coming!" cries resounded among the guests.

"Who's coming?" flashed through Golyadkin's mind, and he shuddered, experiencing a strange sensation. "It's time now," the councilor said with a significant look at Andrei Filipovich. Andrei Filipovich looked at Olsufy Ivanovich and Olsufy Ivanovich nodded solemnly.

"Let's get up," the councilor said, pulling Golyadkin to his feet. They all stood up. The councilor took Golyadkin One's hand while Andrei Filipovich took Golyadkin Two's, and they solemnly brought them together as the people around watched. Our hero looked around in bewilderment, but those around him immediately reminded him of what seemed to be his duty by pointing to Golyadkin Two. Golyadkin Two was offering him his hand.

"They want to reconcile us," Golyadkin One thought with emotion and rapturously offered his hand to Golyadkin Two. Then he offered him his cheek. The other Mr. Golyadkin did the same.

Suddenly Golyadkin One thought he saw a perfidious grin on the face of his treacherous friend. He seemed to be winking understandingly to the witnesses of the scene. Indeed, there was something quite sinister and threatening in the other Golyadkin's expression. Yes, it was the expression Judas had worn when he gave that kiss. Bells began to ring in Golyadkin One's ears, a veil fell before his eyes; he was under the impression that a whole file of exactly identical Golyadkins was breaking through every door of the drawing room. . . . But it was too late—the treacherous kiss resounded and . . .

Something completely unexpected took place. The main door leading into the drawing room slid open noisily and a man appeared in the doorway. The very sight of him sent icicles down Golyadkin's spine, although he had known all along that this would happen exactly the way it was happening now. Very solemnly, the stranger made his way toward Golyadkin. Golyadkin knew this figure very well indeed. He had often seen it before; indeed, he had seen it that day. The stranger was tall and thick-set; he wore a black frock-coat with a rather important decoration on it, and his face was framed in thick, graying whiskers. All he needed was a cigar in his mouth to make the resemblance really perfect. But it was his eyes, as we mentioned before, that froze Golyadkin with terror.

The terrifying man came up pompously and solemnly to the lamentable hero of our story, who stretched out his hand toward him. The stranger took hold of that hand and started to walk out of the room, drawing Golyadkin along behind him. . . .

Golyadkin turned around, looking bewildered and dejected.

"This is Yakov Petrovich Golyadkin, doctor," our hero heard a repulsive, piping voice right by his ear. "An acquaintance of yours of long standing, Christian Ivanovich."

Golyadkin turned his head and saw that ignoble man, his morally despicable twin. An indecent, vicious joy was radiating from his face. He was rubbing his hands in glee, shuffling his feet and buzzing around all and sundry. It looked as if he were about to go into a triumphant jig. Finally he leaped forward, snatched a lighted candle from the hands of a servant, and led the way for Christian Ivanovich and Golyadkin One. Our hero clearly heard how everyone present in the drawing room came rushing after them; people were struggling to get through the doorway, pushing one another; and then, he heard all of them, very clearly, repeating in a chorus after him, "All this is nothing," and reassuring him, "Don't worry, Yakov Petrovich, why, you're with an old friend of yours, Doctor Rutenspitz. You must surely remember him—Christian Ivanovich."

Finally they were out of the apartment on the brightly lighted staircase where a considerable crowd had also gathered. Then, downstairs, the door leading to the courtyard opened noisily, and Golyadkin found himself there alone with the doctor.

A closed carriage to which four horses, snorting impatiently, were harnessed was standing there. Smirking, Golyadkin Two tore downstairs in three leaps. It was he who opened the carriage door. The doctor firmly invited Golyadkin One to get in, although that firm gesture was not really needed, for, by now, there were enough volunteers to help our hero into the carriage. . . .

His heart sinking, Golyadkin looked back and saw that the whole brightly lighted staircase was teeming with people, that curious eyes were covering him from every angle, that even Olsufy Ivanovich was presiding in his armchair, which they had carried out onto the landing, and watching the proceedings closely and with great interest. Everyone was waiting. An impatient murmur ran through the crowd when Mr. Golyadkin turned his head toward them.

"I hope that there's nothing prejudicial in all this, nothing that could call down official disapproval upon my official position in the department?" our confused hero managed to say, and his words caused all those watching him to move their heads horizontally in denial—no, he had nothing to fear on that account.

Tears gushed from Mr. Golyadkin's eyes.

"In that case, I am ready—I entrust myself completely to . . . to Christian Ivanovich. . . ."

As soon as he had said that, a deafening, joyful roar came from those around him, and was echoed ominously by all the others who were farther away. Then Christian Ivanovich and Andrei Filipovich took Mr. Golyadkin under the arms and helped him into the carriage, while his double, in keeping with his usual perfidious ways, shoved him along from behind. The wretched Golyadkin glanced for one last time at everything and everybody and, feeling like a kitten at whom a bucket of icy water had just been thrown—if you will allow the comparison—climbed into the carriage. He was followed by Christian Ivanovich, who installed himself at his side. The carriage door slammed, the driver's whip whistled, the horses gave a tug and started off, and all the witnesses came running behind Golyadkin, the strident, shrill shouts of his enemies accompanying him as a farewell chorus. For a while, he could still see faces flashing behind the carriage window, but gradually they fell behind. Soon they were completely out of sight, except for Golyadkin's ill-wishing twin who, his hands thrust in the pockets of his green trousers, was trotting along with a smug expression, popping up now on one side of the carriage, now on the other, several times catching hold of the corner of the window, hoisting himself up by it, and throwing farewell kisses to Mr. Golyadkin. But then he too began to tire, popped up less and less often, and finally vanished from sight altogether, like all the others.

Golyadkin felt a dull ache in his heart. Blood rushed to his head, making it throb. He felt he was suffocating, and tried to unbutton his coat, to uncover his chest, to rub it with snow, to have icy water poured over it; finally he dozed off. . . .

When he awoke, he saw that he was being driven along some unfamiliar road which cut through a dark forest. The place was desolate and deserted. Suddenly he felt paralyzed with terror: Two burning spots, two eyes, were watching him in the darkness, and there was a sinister, satanic glee in those eyes. This was not Christian Ivanovich. Who was it? It was Christian Ivanovich but not the same one. It was another Christian Ivanovich, a horrible Christian Ivanovich!

"Doctor, Christian Ivanovich, it seems to me . . . I . . . I am all right," he began shyly, trembling and hoping to propitiate this horrible Christian Ivanovich by his meekness and submission.

"You will be given quarters at public expense with light, firewood, and service included, which is more than you deserve," Christian Ivanovich replied, and he sounded stern and terrifying like a judge handing down his verdict.

Our hero let out a yell and clutched his head. Alas, he had felt it coming for a long time.

THE ETERNAL HUSBAND

Chapter 1

Velchaninov

THE SUMMER CAME and, contrary to expectations, Velchaninov stayed in Petersburg. The trip to southern Russia was off and the end of the lawsuit was not in sight. That lawsuit over the land was getting out of hand. Only three months before, it had looked very simple, almost clear-cut, but then things had changed somehow, "and, in general, everything is changing for the worse," Velchaninov kept repeating to himself with perverse joy. He was using the services of a well-known, skillful, and expensive attorney and he didn't grudge the expense, but, impatient and suspicious as he was, he insisted on taking a hand in the matter himself, read documents, and drafted memoranda that his attorney kept discarding one after another, darted from one legal office to the next, made inquiries, and probably got in the way all the time. At least, so his attorney complained; he kept trying to pack him off to his country house.

But by then Velchaninov didn't dare leave town, even just to go to the country house. The dust, the stifling heat, and the oppressive white nights of Petersburg—that was what he enjoyed in town. The apartment in the vicinity of the Bolshoi Theater to which he had recently moved wasn't a great success either. "Everything's going wrong," he thought.

Every day he became more and more hypochondriac, but then he'd had a tendency toward hypochondria for a long time.

He was a man who had lived a lot and had had a varied life; he was no longer very young—thirty-eight, or even thirty-nine now—on whom, as he put it, "old age" had moved rather suddenly. He realized, though, that what had aged him wasn't so much the number of years as their quality, and that if senility was already setting in, it was internal rather than external. He was still quite a fine figure of a man—big, tall, with not a single silver thread in either his thick flaxen hair or his beard that reached halfway down his chest.

At first sight he might have struck one as a rather awkward man who was beginning to let himself go a bit; but upon closer examination one could see that he had himself well in hand and that he had been brought up as a gentleman. Even now, his manners were easy, self-assured, and even graceful, despite a certain crankiness and lumpishness he had acquired in his later years. He was still filled with the unshakable, arrogant self-assurance of a society man, the extent of which he didn't suspect himself, although he was not merely intelligent but could also display common sense on occasion, and he had an almost adequate education and a few indubitable talents. His open face had a ruddy complexion that, in the old days, had been as delicate as a girl's and had attracted the attention of the ladies, and even now, looking at him, many people thought "What a strapping, ruddy-faced fellow!" But it just so happened that the "strapping" fellow was suffering from hypochondria. His big blue eyes had had an all-conquering look in them ten years ago—they were so bright, so gay and carefree, that they charmed everyone he met. But now he was approaching forty and the brightness and kindness had all but vanished from his eyes, which were surrounded by a fine network of wrinkles; they had been replaced by the cynicism of a tired man who was perhaps a bit amoral, and also by a newly acquired suggestion of sadness and unreasoned but acute sorrow.

That sadness was most obvious when he was alone. And strangely enough, this gay, noisy, carefree man, who had been so good at telling funny stories just a couple of years before, now liked nothing more than to be alone. Despite the financial straits he was in, he deliberately broke off with many people with whom he could have kept up an acquaintance.

True, vanity had something to do with it, for a man with his suspiciousness and sensitivity could hardly have borne the company of his former acquaintances. But even his vanity underwent a gradual change when he was alone. It didn't diminish—just the opposite; but it started to degenerate into another, special form, and it began to suffer for reasons that would have been quite unthinkable in the past, for "higher considerations" than before, "if one can really say that considerations may be of a higher or lower order," as he put it himself.

Yes, he had come to that—he was worrying about loftier considerations to which he would never have given a thought in the past. In his own mind and conscience, he defined as loftier considerations those about which, in all conscience, and to his own surprise, he couldn't laugh when he was alone —that had never happened to him before. Of course, in the presence of other people it was quite another matter. He was very well aware, though, that if the situation changed, he would calmly discard all these "higher considerations" overnight, despite all his secret good resolutions, and would be the first to hold them up to ridicule, without, of course, admitting it to himself. And this was true despite a certain amount of independence of thought he had gained lately at the expense of the "baser considerations" that had dominated him until then. Ah, how many times, on getting up in the morning, had he felt ashamed of the thoughts and feelings he'd had during the hours of sleeplessness from which he had suffered lately!

He had noticed for some time now that he was growing oversuspicious about both important and unimportant matters, and he had resolved to trust his own judgment as little as possible. Still, there were facts whose reality could not be disputed. Lately, his thoughts and sensations had often been very different at night from what they were at other times, especially during the first half of the day. That surprised him so much that he told a prominent physician about it. It is true he knew him quite well and, it goes without saying, spoke about it in a jocular tone. He was told that the transformation and even splitting of thoughts and sensations during sleeplessness, and at night in general, is common among people who "think and feel intensely," that the convictions of a lifetime could change overnight under the effect of sleeplessness, when the most drastic decisions are taken without any apparent reason; but, of course, all this has its limits, and if the patient becomes very much aware of the splitting of his thoughts and feelings and it causes him suffering, it becomes an indisputable symptom of sickness, and it is urgent that something be done about it. The best thing would be a radical change of life and of diet, including going off on a trip. And, of course, a laxative could be of great help too.

Velchaninov didn't want to hear any more about it, but it had now been convincingly demonstrated to him that he was a sick man.

"And so all this stuff about loftier considerations is nothing but a sickness!" he often repeated sarcastically under his breath. He was longing to disagree with that.

But soon he began to experience in the mornings what had previously taken place during the exceptional hours of the night, but more biliously than at night, with rancor instead of remorse, and a sneer instead of heartfelt emotion. Actually, certain incidents from his past, even the very distant past, were emerging onto the surface of his memory "suddenly and God knows why," but presenting themselves in a peculiar way. For quite a long time, for instance, he had complained of a loss of memory—forgetting the faces of his acquaintances, who resented his cutting them when they met; and he would sometimes completely forget a book he'd read six months before. However, despite the obvious deterioration of his memory, which worried him, everything that touched upon the distant past, things he hadn't thought of for ten or fifteen years, was likely to crop up so clearly and with such an incredible wealth of detail that he felt as if he were reliving them all over again. He had so thoroughly forgotten some of those incidents that the very fact that he could remember them at all struck him as a miracle.

But that wasn't all, for, after all, people who have had varied experiences are bound to have some peculiar recollections. The extraordinary thing about it was that the incidents he remembered now came back as if they'd been arranged by someone else and were presented from a point of view that couldn't possibly have been Velchaninov's point of view at the time when they actually happened. Why was it that certain things he had done appeared to him now as outright crimes? And it wasn't just a matter of verdicts handed down by his brain, for he would hardly have trusted his gloomy, lonely, sick brain—it had reached a point where he cursed madly and even wept, even if only with inward tears. And to think that only a couple of years before, he'd never have believed it if he'd been told that the day would come when he would weep!

At first, however, the memories were of a nature to sting his pride rather than stir his heart—some social humiliations and failures, such as the slander of "some unscrupulous schemer" that had caused the doors of a house to be closed to him; or the relatively recent case when he had been publicly insulted but had not challenged the offender to a duel; or when he had been made the target of a very witty quip in the presence of several very pretty women but had failed to come up with a suitable retort. He also remembered a couple of unpaid debts, quite insignificant ones, it is true, but still, debts of honor he owed to people whom he had ceased to see and about whom he had started saying nasty things. He was tormented, too, at the thought (this only came at his worst moments, though) of the two substantial fortunes he had stupidly squandered. But soon memories came back that tormented his conscience for "loftier" reasons.

Suddenly, for instance, "for no special reason," he remembered the entirely forgotten figure of a kindly old civil servant, gray-haired and ridiculous, whom he had insulted once, very long ago, publicly and with impunity, just for the sake of showing off, just not to miss the opportunity of making a witty quip—and, indeed, it became famous and was often quoted. He had forgotten the incident so thoroughly that he couldn't even recall the old man's name, although all the circumstances surrounding the occasion came back to him with uncanny clarity. He remembered clearly that the old man had been trying to defend his spinsterish daughter who lived with him and about whom all sorts of rumors had been circulating. The old man had started to answer back and had lost his temper, then had suddenly burst into tears in front of everyone, which, it must be said, caused a certain sensation. It all ended in their filling him with champagne and having a great laugh at his expense. When Velchaninov thought now "for no special reason" of how the old man had put his hands over his face, sobbing like a child, it was as if he'd never forgotten it. And strangely enough, it had all seemed very funny to him at the time, while now he was particularly struck by certain details, such as the old man covering his face with his hands.

He also remembered how once, just for the sake of a joke, he had slandered a pretty woman who was married to a schoolteacher, and the slander had reached the husband. Soon after that, Velchaninov had left the small town without learning what the consequences of his slander were. But now he suddenly started imagining what those consequences might have been, and God only knows where his imagination would have led him had it not been for a much more recent recollection about the daughter of some shopkeepers, whom he had actually never really liked, of whom he had been ashamed, and with whom, for some unknown reason, he had had a child. He had then abandoned her as she was, with his child, without even saying good-by to her when he left for Petersburg, although it must be said in his favor that he had been in rather a hurry. Later, he had kept searching for her for a whole year, but had never been able to trace her.

Actually, such recollections cropped up almost by the hundreds, and in such a way that each of them seemed to drag scores of others behind it. Gradually, his vanity began to suffer too.

We have said that his vanity had taken on a certain peculiar, distorted form. That is correct. He had such moments of utter detachment—they were quite rare, though—that he would forget to be ashamed of not owning a carriage, of having to drag himself around on foot from one government office to another, of having become careless about his appearance. And if, at such moments, one of his old acquaintances had looked him up and down with a sarcastic air, or simply decided to cut him, his detachment would have been sufficiently great that he would not even have winced. Not simply pretended, but really not winced. Of course, such moments of detachment and exaltation were rare, but still his vanity was less and less involved in things around which it had previously been centered, and was becoming entirely invested instead in one matter that haunted him continually.

"It looks," he'd sometimes think sarcastically (and he almost always began by being sarcastic when thinking of himself), "as if there's someone up there worrying about setting my morals straight, who's trying to achieve it by sending me these nasty memories and 'repentant tears.' That's fine with me, but it's a terrible waste of time. It's like going hunting with blank cartridges. As if I didn't know for absolutely sure that, despite all this tearful remorse and self-condemnation, there hasn't been one single grain of inner strength in me in all the forty years of my stupid existence. Why, if tomorrow I were to be faced with the same temptation, if I found myself in a situation where it would be to my advantage to spread a rumor that that teacher's wife had accepted my presents—I am sure I wouldn't hesitate to spread it; and this time it would be even more disgusting on my part, since it would be the second time I'd been guilty of the slander. Or, suppose I were once again insulted by that same princeling—that widow's only son through whose leg I put that bullet—well, I'd challenge him again immediately and try to replace his remaining good leg with another wooden one. Well, isn't this remorse just like blank cartridges? So what's the point of it? And what's the point of reminding me that I don't know how to get rid of myself?"

And although he didn't slander the schoolteacher's wife again, or shoot anyone through the leg, the mere thought that it could happen, given the right circumstances, was driving him to despair . . . at least, at certain times. But who can be expected to suffer from remorse without let-up? Why, it is perfectly all right to have a rest now and then and to go out to the foyer for a drink during intermissions.

And that's exactly what Velchaninov did—he strolled around during the intermissions. Nevertheless, the further it went the less pleasant his life in Petersburg became. July was approaching. Sometimes he thought of dropping everything, even his lawsuit, and going somewhere, sort of casually—even, say, to the Crimea. But one hour later, he usually found the idea loathsome and laughed over it.

"These bad memories of mine won't stop in the South any more than anywhere else, and now that they've started pestering me, if there is a drop of self-respect left in me, I won't run away from them. And anyway, there's no need for me to flee. Why should I run away?" he went on, musing sorrowfully. "It's so dusty, so stifling here and the house is in such a mess; in the offices where I hang around among those busy people, there is so much mouse-like hustle and bustle, so much worrying; and all those people who have stayed in town, all those faces I see flashing by from morning to night, make such an open display of the boundless selfishness, simple-minded arrogance, and cowardice of their petty souls, that there is no better place for a hypochondriac to be. I am quite serious about it. Everything here is open and straightforward and nobody thinks of pretending, as they do in country houses in front of our ladies or at spas abroad. And so it is more deserving of respect, if only because of its frankness and simplicity. . . . No, I'm not going anywhere. I'll stay here, even if I burst!"

Chapter 2

The Gentleman with Crepe on His Hat

I**T WAS THE** third of July. An unbearably hot and stuffy day. A very busy one for Velchaninov. He'd spent the whole morning going from one place to another and, in the evening, he had to go to see a certain businessman who was also a state councilor, at his country house somewhere on the Black River, for he was to catch that gentleman at home by surprise. At around six, Velchaninov entered a rather second-rate French restaurant on the Nevsky Embankment near the Police Bridge, sat down at his usual table in a corner, and ordered his dinner.

His was a one-ruble dinner, not counting the wine—and he considered this austere fare a reasonable sacrifice necessitated by the precarious state of his affairs. While wondering how it was possible to swallow such garbage, he would nevertheless eat everything down to the last crumb and, each time, with such appetite that one would have thought he hadn't had anything to eat for three days. "There's something abnormal about it," he would comment under his breath when he happened to notice what an appetite he had.

But on that day he sat down to the table in the foulest

temper, angrily tossed his hat somewhere, put his elbows on the table, and plunged into thought. And if a neighbor had made too much noise, or the waiter hadn't understood him from the first word, he would have kicked up a big fuss and probably have made a loud scene, although he could be extremely polite or, if he chose, icily imperturbable.

They brought him his soup. He took the spoon and was about to dip it into the soup when instead he dropped it and jumped up from his chair. A thought had suddenly occurred to him—and God knows why precisely at that moment. He had just grasped the cause of his sadness, that peculiar and unique sadness of his which had been tormenting him for several days in a row now, pestering him, God knew how terribly and God knew why, and refusing to leave him alone. . . . But now he had grasped it all, understood everything, and it was as obvious to him as the palm of his open hand.

"It's all the fault of that hat," he muttered, in a flash of intuition, "that damned round hat with its disgusting mourning crepe around it—that's what's caused all the trouble!"

He started to think, and the more he thought the gloomier he became and the stranger the "whole incident" looked to him.

"But . . . but what sort of an 'incident' was it?" he protested, feeling distrustful of himself. "Is there anything in it that even remotely resembles an 'incident'?"

The whole business boiled down to this. About two weeks before—he wasn't really sure, but it seemed as if it was about two weeks before—on the corner of Meshchansky and Podyachesky streets, he had met a man wearing crepe on his hat. There was nothing very special about the man and he had passed by quickly, but as he passed he had looked at Velchaninov a bit too fixedly and, somehow, had immediately caught his attention. Velchaninov had the impression he had seen that face somewhere before. "But who knows how many thousands of faces I've seen in my lifetime?" he thought. "How can I be expected to remember them all!" And so, by the time he had walked on twenty yards or so, he had all but forgotten about the meeting, despite his strong first impression. But the effect of that impression lingered on for the rest of the day and it was quite an unexpected one—a sort of unprovoked anger.

Now, two weeks later, he remembered it all very clearly.

He remembered, too, that that day he hadn't understood why he felt so irritable and, to this moment, he still couldn't understand how he could have failed to make the connection between his bad mood in the evening and his morning encounter. But the gentleman in question had seen to it that he wouldn't be forgotten and, on the following day, they had met again on the Nevsky Embankment and again he had given Velchaninov the same fixed look. Velchaninov had spat but, having spat, was quite surprised at himself for doing so. True, though, there are faces that provoke a spontaneous, unaccountable revulsion.

"Yes, I'm sure I've seen him somewhere before," Velchaninov had muttered dreamily, about half an hour after the encounter. After that, he had been in a foul mood until nighttime. He had even had bad dreams. And still, it had never occurred to him that the sole cause of his special new dejection was that man with the crepe on his hat, although he had thought of him frequently during the evening. Indeed, he had even angrily remarked that he couldn't get "that kind of rubbish" out of his head. Even if it had been suggested to him that his anxiety might be due to the stranger, he would have dismissed the possibility as too humiliating to himself.

Then, a couple of days later, they had met again. This time it was on the crowded jetty where the Neva steamers stop. On this occasion, Velchaninov could have sworn that the man with the mourning band had recognized him and made a dash for him, but had been kept away by the crowd; he even thought that the stranger had "dared" to stretch out his hand toward him, maybe even called out his name, although Velchaninov hadn't been able to make out clearly what the man had said. . . .

"But who is the creature, after all, and why doesn't he come up and talk to me if that's really what he wants?" he wondered, irritatedly, getting into a cab and telling the cabbie to drive him to a place near Smolny Monastery.

Half an hour later, he was already arguing noisily with his lawyer and, later, during the evening and at night, he was again in a bad mood and so horribly depressed that he stood in front of a mirror wondering: "Perhaps I'm getting jaundice? . . ."

After that third encounter, he had met "no one" for five days and heard nothing about "that horrible man." Nevertheless, he kept thinking of the gentleman with the crepe band on his hat now and then. And Velchaninov was rather surprised to catch himself thinking about him: "Why, do I miss him by any chance? Hm . . . but it would seem he too has a lot of things to do here in Petersburg. . . . And who is it he's in mourning for? Probably we've met somewhere and he recognizes me but I don't recognize him. And why do some people wear those crepe bands? It somehow seems incongruous on them. I have a feeling now that if I got a closer look at him, I'd recognize him."

And something seemed to stir in his memory, like some known but somehow forgotten word that one tries hard to remember—you know it very well and you know that you know; you know exactly what it means, you keep coming close, but the word won't come to you, hard though you may try.

"It happened . . . it happened long ago . . . it happened somewhere . . . it happened here . . . here . . . Well, the hell with it! Who cares whether it happened or not, and why should I bother about that animal? It is really too humiliating."

He lost his temper altogether. But in the evening, when he remembered how he had lost his temper, he experienced a very unpleasant feeling—it was as though he had been caught red-handed by someone. He felt surprised and embarrassed.

"There must be something to it, if I lose my temper like that . . . for no apparent reason . . . just remembering . . ." He didn't complete this thought.

The next day he had an even worse fit of rage, but this time he had the impression that he had good reason for it and that he was perfectly right. It was "unheard-of insolence." They'd actually met for the fourth time. The man with the crepe had appeared as if he had sprung up from under the ground.

Velchaninov had just managed to catch that state councilor in the street whom he needed so badly and whom he had been going to surprise at his summer house again that day, because the official, whom he hardly knew, had obviously been trying to avoid him. Jubilant at having got hold of him, Velchaninov was walking at the official's side, hurrying, casting sidelong glances at his face, and trying hard to bring their conversation to a point where the sly old man would blurt out the needed piece of information. But the old official was quite a cool customer, and kept putting him off with laughter and silences and . . . Well—and just then, just at that moment which was so exceptionally important for him, Velchaninov had suddenly caught sight of the man with the crepe on his hat on the opposite sidewalk. He stood there looking fixedly at Velchaninov and the official. He followed them with his eyes, and may even have been sneering.

"Damn it, after all!" Velchaninov muttered furiously. He had given up pursuing the official and now ascribed his failure to the appearance of that "insolent creature." "Why is he following me around, that man, spying on me? Perhaps he's been hired by someone and . . . and I swear he's sneering at me! I swear I'll give him a taste of my stick! What a shame I don't carry a stick, though! . . . But I'll buy myself one. I won't let it go on like this. Who is he? I must find out who he is!"

Finally, three days after this last encounter, we find Velchaninov in his restaurant, as we have said, very much bewildered and agitated. By now, proud though he was, he had had to acknowledge it to himself. He finally bound to put two and two together—namely, that the reason for his two-week-long "special" depression and anxiety was none other than the man with the mourning band, "despicable creature though he may be."

"Even assuming that I am a hypochondriac," Velchaninov thought, "and that I am likely to make a mountain out of a molehill, it still doesn't make it any easier for me if all this *may be* nothing but my imagination. Why, if any such creature can so thoroughly upset a man . . . it is, then . . . it is . . ."

In fact, in today's encounter—the fifth—which had given Velchaninov such a shock, the mountain had presented itself to him in the guise of a molehill: this time the man had darted past Velchaninov and had not stared at him as he had the other times, nor shown a sign that he recognized him; quite the opposite—he had looked down and seemed to be very anxious not to be recognized himself. Velchaninov stopped, turned back, and yelled as loudly as he could:

"Hey, you with the crepe on your hat! Stop hiding! Who are you?"

The question, shouted at the top of his voice, was rather

incoherent, but Velchaninov only realized that after he had
uttered it. Hearing it, the man halted for a second, looked
surprised, smiled, was on the point of saying something, doing
something—he seemed to be torn by hesitation, and then
suddenly turned away and hurried off without looking back.
Velchaninov looked after him in amazement.

"And what," he thought, "if in reality it is not he who
is pestering me, but rather I who am pestering him? That
may be all it amounts to."

He finished his dinner and hurried to the state councilor's summer house. The official wasn't at home. He was
told that the councilor hadn't been back since morning and
probably wouldn't be back before two or three o'clock the
next morning, because he was attending a certain birthday
party in town. That was really too mortifying and, in a burst
of anger, Velchaninov decided to go to the birthday party
himself, and actually drove off in that direction; but, realizing on the way there that it would really be pushing things
a bit far, he got out of the cab, paid the cabbie, and set out
on foot for his apartment near the Bolshoi Theater. He felt
he could do with some exercise. He had to get a night's
sleep to calm his shattered nerves, and so he had to tire himself to avoid sleeplessness. It was already half-past ten when
he got home, for he had dismissed the cabbie quite a distance
from his place, and he certainly did feel tired.

The apartment, which he had taken in March and which
he had deprecated with such volubility, explaining that it
was just a temporary shelter, that he had "unexpectedly" got
stuck in town because of that "damned lawsuit," wasn't really
half as bad as he claimed. It's true, of course, that the
entrance was rather dark and grubby, but the second-floor
apartment consisted of two large, light, high-ceilinged rooms
separated by a dim entrance hall, one room giving on the
street, the other on the courtyard. This second room had a
small alcove adjoining it, obviously intended for use as a
bedroom, although Velchaninov used it to stow all sorts of
books and papers in, and slept instead on a sofa in the large
room that looked out on the street. The furniture was decent,
although second-hand, and he also had, left over from his
former prosperity, some valuable bronze and china knick-
knacks, some genuine Bokhara rugs, and even two rather nice
oil paintings. But it had all been in utter disorder, scattered
around and even covered with dust, ever since his maid

Pelageya had left for Novgorod to visit her family and had left him alone.

The fact that he, a single gentleman who was usually so particular about keeping up appearances, should keep a single female servant in his house was rather embarrassing to Velchaninov, although he was extremely pleased with Pelageya. The girl had worked for him ever since he had moved into the apartment in the spring—she'd been employed before by a family who'd moved abroad—and she had immediately put the place in good order. But once she had left, he hadn't dared to hire another maid. As to hiring a valet, he hadn't thought it worth while for such a short time and, anyway, he didn't like valets. And so it came about that it was left to Mavra, the janitor's sister-in-law, to do his rooms; he left her the key when he went out, but she didn't do a thing; she took her money, and probably stole from him as well. But by now he was quite beyond worrying about it and, indeed, was rather happy to be all alone in his apartment. Still, everything has its limits, and his nerves rebelled at times and refused to stand the "filth," and almost every time he came home he found he was unable to suppress a shudder of disgust.

This time, he hardly gave himself time to undress properly; then he threw himself on his bed, deciding irritatedly not to think of anything and to go to sleep within one minute. And, strangely enough, he did go to sleep as soon as his head touched the pillow—something that hadn't happened to him for almost a month.

He spent three hours in restless sleep, tormented by a dream such as a person with a temperature has. It was all about some crime he had committed and concealed from everyone, and now he was being accused of it by all sorts of people who poured into his room from heaven knows where. A huge crowd had already gathered around him, but more people kept crowding in, so that his door would no longer close and had to be left open. But the main interest was concentrated on a strange man who had once been close to him and who had been dead for some time, but who now suddenly came into Velchaninov's room.

The most painful part of it was that Velchaninov didn't know who the man was; he couldn't remember the man's name, although he knew that once upon a time he had been very fond of the stranger. Everyone else in the room seemed to be expecting the stranger to say The Word, to pronounce Velchaninov guilty or innocent, and they were quite impatient to hear it. But the man sat motionless at the table, refusing to speak. The din wouldn't stop, the agitation increased, and Velchaninov, suddenly losing his temper, went for the man, hitting him furiously for refusing to speak up, and deriving a strange pleasure from hitting him. His heart sank in horror, sorrow, and shame at having acted that way, but it was precisely this sinking of his heart that he found so pleasurable. Becoming completely frantic, Velchaninov hit the man a second and then a third blow, and went on hitting him, drunk with rage, fear, and infinite delight, no longer counting the blows he was landing on the man, but just hitting and hitting without stopping. He wanted to destroy *that*.

But then something happened; all the people around him started shouting and turned to face the door, as if waiting for something. The door bell rang three times, but with such violence that it sounded as though someone were trying to pull it out of its socket. Velchaninov woke up, immediately recovered his senses, and rushed to the door—he was absolutely convinced that the ringing of the bell had not been part of the dream, but that there really was someone ringing at his door. "It's much too unlikely," he decided, "that the bell should ring so clearly and realistically in a dream."

But to his great surprise, the ringing of the bell turned out to be just a part of the dream after all. He opened the door, stepped out onto the landing, looked around, but saw no one. The bell hung motionless. Puzzled but also rather relieved, he went back inside. As he was lighting a candle, he remembered that his door had been simply closed and that he hadn't bothered to lock it. In fact, he often neglected to lock the door at night, attaching no importance to the matter, and he had often been reproached for it by Pelageya. Now, he went back to the entry hall to lock the door. He opened it once more, again looked outside onto the landing, closed it, and fastened it with the inside hook, but again didn't bother to lock it with the key. The clock struck. It was two-thirty. So he had slept for three hours.

The dream had rather upset him and he was reluctant to go back to bed right away. Instead, he decided to pace the room "just for the time it takes to smoke a cigar." He put on some clothes, walked over to the window, pulled aside the heavy curtain, lifted the white blind behind it, and saw that the dawn was already breaking. Petersburg's light summer nights had always upset his nerves and, of late, had contributed to his insomnia, so that a couple of weeks ago he had ordered these special heavy curtains hung that allowed no light to filter through when they were fully drawn. Now, having let in the pale daylight and forgotten about the burning candle on the table, he was pacing the room, still weighed down by an oppressive, sickly feeling. He was still under the effect of the dream and was terribly distressed at having raised his hand to that man and then hit him again and again.

"But why should I feel so miserable about it when the man doesn't exist and never has existed!"

Then he started stubbornly repeating, "I'm getting really sick . . . I'm a very sick man now," as if trying to convince himself that that was the only explanation of his troubles.

As it was always painful for him to admit that he was aging and growing weaker, at his most wretched moments he exaggerated his deterioration, in an effort to exasperate himself.

"This is senility; I'm getting really old . . ." he muttered, pacing the room. "I'm beginning to forget things. I'm seeing ghosts, I have dreams with bells ringing in them. . . . Ah, damn it, I know from experience that such dreams indicate that I am feverish. . . . Well, that whole story with the mourning band may also be just a dream. . . . Yes, I'm sure I hit on the truth yesterday—it's me who is pursuing him, rather than him pursuing me. . . . I made up a whole epic about him and then climbed under the table in fear. And why do I refer to him as 'that creature'? In reality, he may be a very fine man. True, his face isn't too pleasant, although there's nothing ugly about it, and he's dressed like everyone else. . . . Only the queer way he looks . . . Ah, there I go again! I've got back onto the subject of that man! And what the hell do I care about the way he looks at me! Why, can I really not live without that candidate for the gallows! . . ."

Among other thoughts that occurred to Velchaninov, one really stung him: he suddenly felt convinced that the man with the crepe had known him quite intimately, and that if he smirked now when they met it was because he knew some important secret about him and consequently saw Velchaninov in a humiliating light. Without thinking what he was doing, Velchaninov walked over to the window to open it and let in the cool dawn air. Suddenly a violent shudder ran down his spine—this was something unheard of, something uncanny.

Before he'd got as far as opening the window, he slipped to one side, trying to get out of sight. Just across the street, in front of the window, the man with the crepe band on his hat was standing on the deserted sidewalk. He was facing the window but apparently hadn't noticed anything. He was simply examining the house with curiosity. It looked as if he were working something out, trying to decide what to do next. He lifted a hand and brought a finger to his forehead. Then he decided: he looked around and stealthily started to cross the street on tiptoe.

Now, here it was. He entered the door of Velchaninov's house that, in the summer, was often left unlocked until three in the morning. "He's coming here, after me," flashed through Velchaninov's head and he tiptoed hurriedly over to the door of his apartment and, breathing as inaudibly as he could, stood there behind the door, with his right hand resting gently on the hook he had fastened when he woke up, as he listened intently for footsteps on the stairs.

His heart was pounding so hard now that he was afraid it might prevent him from hearing the footsteps of the tiptoeing stranger. He didn't understand what was actually happening, but his senses were ten times more alert than usual. His recent dream seemed to have overflowed into reality. Velchaninov was naturally a brave man. At times he liked to show off his fearlessness in the face of danger, even when there was no one to admire him, just to admire himself. But this time there was something else as well. The moaning hypochondriac of a minute before was now a quite different man. Nervous, soundless laughter swelled in his chest. He guessed every movement of the stranger from behind the closed door.

"Ah, there, he's walking upstairs . . . he's on the landing now, looking around. He's holding his breath and listening. . . . He's creeping over here now. . . . He's touching the doorknob, turning it, trying it out. . . . He wasn't expecting to find my door locked. He knows, then, that I sometimes forget to lock it. . . . Ah, now he's trying the knob again. Does he imagine that the hook will come undone by itself? He doesn't feel like giving up, it seems. He hates having come for nothing. . . ."

And, indeed, it must have all happened very much as he

visualized it: there really was someone standing behind the door and quietly trying to turn the knob and, "of course he was pursuing a certain objective," having come all that way. But Velchaninov had already decided upon his further course of action and was waiting in a sort of rapture for the moment to act, getting ready, planning: he had an irresistible desire to unfasten the hook, to fling the door wide open, to face the "monster" and ask him: "Are you looking for something here, my dear sir?"

And so he did. He picked his moment, threw off the hook, pushed the door open, and came up against the man with the crepe band on his hat.

Chapter 3

Pavel Pavlovich Trusotsky

THE MAN WITH the crepe band seemed dumbfounded. They stood there in the doorway, staring into each other's faces. A few seconds passed. Suddenly Velchaninov recognized his visitor. A gleam in the visitor's eye indicated that he'd realized it. The next moment his face dissolved into the sweetest smile.

"I believe I have the pleasure of addressing Alexei Ivanovich Velchaninov?" he chanted almost tenderly, in a tone that was ridiculously incongruous under the circumstances.

"Could you possibly be Pavel Pavlovich Trusotsky?" Velchaninov managed to say at last, perplexedly.

"We used to see each other about nine years ago in T——, and if I may say so, we were rather close at the time."

"Yes . . . I suppose we were. . . . But it's three o'clock in the morning now, and for ten whole minutes you've been trying to find out whether my door was locked or not."

"It's three already?" the intruder exclaimed, taking out his watch and sounding very apologetic. "Indeed it is! Please forgive me, Alexei, I ought to have thought of the time when

I was coming here. How terribly embarrassing! If I may, I'll come by and explain and apologize one of these days. In the meantime . . ."

"Oh, no! If you have an explanation to offer, I'll have it right away!" Velchaninov said. "Step inside, please. Anyway, you came here in the first place with the intention of getting into my apartment, and not just for the sake of testing my locks in the middle of the night."

He felt both angry and at a loss, unable to make any sense of it all. He was even a bit ashamed of himself—there was nothing particularly dangerous or sinister about the situation, and out of what had looked to him like a nightmarish setting there had emerged nothing but the ridiculous figure of this Pavel Trusotsky. Actually, though, he couldn't really believe that it was all so simple, and an unpleasant presentiment lingered with him. He made the visitor sit in an armchair, and himself sat down on the bed one step away and bent forward, with his hands resting on his knees, waiting irritably for the man to speak, looking him up and down and trying hard to remember. But strangely enough, the other remained silent, apparently unaware that *he had to* speak up; indeed, he too seemed to be waiting for something and there was expectation in the look he fixed on his host. Possibly, though, he was feeling intimidated, like a mouse in a mousetrap. Finally Velchaninov lost his temper.

"Well, what are you waiting for?" he shouted. "Since you're not a ghost or a shadow in a dream, you'd better speak up! Or have you come here to impersonate a corpse! Come on, you owe me an explanation, sir!"

The visitor fidgeted, smiled, and said warily:

"I gather you're shocked at my coming at such an hour and . . . under rather peculiar circumstances. . . . Well, remembering our past relations and the way we parted, it seems strange to me too. . . . Actually, I had no intention of coming here, and if I did it was just by chance. . . ."

"Some chance! I watched you from my window, crossing the street on tiptoe."

"So you saw me, did you? Well, in that case you must know more about it than I do myself. But I see I am only irritating you. So let me tell you this—I came here about three weeks ago on business. . . . Why, I'm Pavel Trusotsky —you recognize me. . . . And my business consists of trying to get promoted and to be transferred to some other province.

But then all this is neither here nor there. . . . So, if you wish, the main point is that I've been here for three weeks already and I feel that I am deliberately dragging out the business that has brought me here—I mean that matter of my transfer to another government service. If I finally did obtain it, I might forget I'd got what I was after and, the way I feel now, not even budge from your Petersburg. I roam around the city as though I'd lost sight of my goal and, indeed, I believe I'm pleased that I have. In my present state of mind . . ."

"What sort of state of mind?" Velchaninov said, frowning.

The visitor looked him in the eye, picked up his hat, and pointed to the mourning band.

"*This* state of mind, see?"

Velchaninov looked blankly at the crepe, then into Trusotsky's face. Suddenly he turned red and became very agitated.

"Surely not Natalia!"

"Yes, it's her. Last March. Consumption—took only a couple of months. . . . And as you can see, here I am left . . ."

Trusotsky spread out his hands in a gesture of helplessness, holding his crepe-banded hat in his left hand and bowing his bald head very low and holding it in that position for at least ten seconds.

The sight of that gesture had a relaxing effect upon Velchaninov. A sarcastic, even aggressive smile twisted his lips. But it lasted only a second, for the news of the death of a lady whom he had known so long ago and whom he had also long since forgotten had had a surprisingly jolting effect upon him.

"Is it really possible!" he said, muttering the first words that came to him. "Why, then, didn't you tell me as soon as you came in?"

"Thanks for your sympathy. I do appreciate it, despite . . ."

"Despite what?"

"Despite all the years of separation, you've reacted to my bereavement and to me with a sympathy that cannot but fill me with deep gratitude. That's all I wanted to say. And it is not that I doubted my friends' loyalty—I could find true friends here even now—Stepan Mikhailovich Bagautov, for one. But the connection between us—we might really call it friendship, for I remember it with gratitude—was interrupted nine years ago. You never came back to T—— and we've never written to each other . . ."

Trusotsky chanted his words as if following a musical score. His head was still bent but, of course, he was watching very carefully what was going on.

By now, Velchaninov had somewhat regained his composure. The more he looked at Trusotsky and listened to what he was saying, the stranger he found him, and when the man stopped talking all sorts of queer incongruous thoughts flowed into Velchaninov's head.

"I wonder why I didn't recognize you before?" he cried, becoming quite animated. "Why, we ran into each other in the street about five times."

"Yes, I know! You kept running into me—it was twice, perhaps even three times . . ."

"You mean it was *you* who kept running into me, and not me into you!"

Velchaninov got up and quite unexpectedly burst into loud laughter. Trusotsky gave him an intent look and said:

"Well, you could very well have forgotten what I looked like, so there's nothing so extraordinary about your not recognizing me. And on top of that, I've had smallpox since I saw you last and that has left some traces."

"Smallpox?" That's right, he had had smallpox! "But how did you—"

"How the hell did I get into such a mess? One catches all sorts of things—that's how. One can never be sure."

"Still, I find it terribly funny. But go on, keep talking, my dear friend!"

"Well, and although I met you too . . ."

"Wait! Why did you say just now 'how the hell'? I was going to put it more politely than that. But please go on."

Somehow Velchaninov felt more and more like laughing. The first impression of shock and horror had been completely superseded by something else. He was now rapidly pacing the room.

Trusotsky went on: "I was saying that although I met you too, and although when I was on my way to Petersburg I had the firm intention of looking you up . . . But I repeat, I'm now in such a state of mind . . . I've been quite shattered since . . . since March."

"Yes, of course—you've been shattered since March. . . . By the way, do you smoke?"

"Well, as you know, in Natalia's presence . . ."

"I know that, but since March?"

"I wouldn't mind having a cigarette."

"Here. Light it and go on. Please go on, you're so . . ."

Velchaninov took a cigar, lit it, and sat down on his bed. Trusotsky looked at him.

"But you too seem to be in a very nervous state. You sure you're all right?"

"Don't you worry about my health, man," Velchaninov said with a sudden wave of anger. "Just go on talking."

His host's agitation seemed to please Trusotsky and his self-confidence increased.

"What more is there to say?" he asked. "Just try to imagine a man ruined by sorrow—not simply ruined, but destroyed radically, so to speak; a man whose life is completely changed after twenty years of marriage, a man who roams aimlessly through the dusty streets as if they were the open steppe, until he no longer knows who he is, and who finds a certain fascination in losing himself that way. And so it is quite natural if, after that, I came across someone I knew, even a close friend, that I'd purposely avoid him at such a moment. But at some other moment, I might remember and long to see some witness or participant of the recent yet irretrievable past, and the thought of him would set my heart pounding so that, in my desire to throw myself into the arms of that friend, I wouldn't care whether it was day or night, and would even risk waking him up at three in the morning. The only mistake I made was the matter of the hour, but about friendship, I was right, for now I feel amply compensated. As to the hour, I truly thought it was only just after eleven, and you must excuse me for it because of my state—I keep drinking my own sorrow and getting drunk on it, although it's not the sorrow that crushes me most, but the novelty of the situation . . ."

"I must say, you have a rather queer way of putting things," Velchaninov said, becoming very grave once again.

"Yes, I suppose I have a queer way of putting things."

"You sure you aren't joking?"

"Joking!" Trusotsky cried in pained surprise. "You say that, when I've announced—"

"Ah, for heaven's sake, don't talk about that!"

Velchaninov got up and started pacing the room again. He continued for five minutes. Trusotsky wanted to get up too, but Velchaninov shouted at him, "Sit still, sit still!" and he obediently sank back into the armchair.

"I must say, you have changed a lot!" Velchaninov said, suddenly stopping in front of Trusotsky as though just then struck by that idea. "It's fantastic how much you've changed! Incredible! You're a completely different man now!"

"There's nothing so surprising about that. Nine years, after all . . ."

"No, no, it isn't a matter of years. It's not even that you've changed so much physically. You've changed in another way . . ."

"That too can happen in nine years."

"Or perhaps since March!"

"He-he," Trusotsky sniggered slyly, "that's a rather playful idea. . . . But, may I inquire, in what way have I changed so much?"

"Why, it's quite obvious—the former Pavel Pavlovich Trusotsky was such a respectable, decent citizen, *un garçon bien sage*, while now, Trusotsky is just a *vaurien!*" Velchaninov said, having reached that state of irritation in which the most self-controlled people often begin to say things they'll regret later.

"I'm a *vaurien?* D'you really think so? No longer *un garçon sage?*" Trusotsky giggled delightedly.

"*Un garçon sage*, indeed! Hell, no, you're really *sage* now—wise to everything," Velchaninov said, and thought: "I am insolent with him, but the animal is even more insolent with me. . . . And anyway, what is he after?"

"Ah, my dear, dear Alexei!" Trusotsky suddenly exclaimed emotionally, stirring in his armchair. "Why should we care now? We're no longer in high society surrounded by the rich and the famous! We are two old and intimate friends who are having, we might say, a session of completely sincere recollections of our treasured past connection, in which the dear departed was the most precious link."

And he seemed so carried away by his feelings that he bowed his head low, as he had done earlier, and this time even covered his face with his hat. Velchaninov watched him with uneasiness and disgust, wondering: "And what if he is nothing but a buffoon? No, impossible, no! I don't believe he's been drinking . . . although he *could* be drunk—his face is rather red. But drunk or not, that wouldn't make any difference. What's he driving at? What is the animal after?"

"Do you remember, do you remember?" Trusotsky was shouting now, gradually removing his hat from his face and apparently more and more carried away by his memories. "Do you remember our drives to the country, our parties with dances, and those innocent games at the house of our most hospitable Semyon Semyonych? And do you remember the three of us spending the evening reading aloud? And the way the two of us first met—you came to see me one morning and asked me for some information concerning your lawsuit. . . . You even raised your voice . . . but then Natalia came into the room, and within ten minutes you became our closest friend, a friendship that lasted for exactly one year, just like in *The Provincial Lady*, that play by Mr. Turgenev. . . ."

Velchaninov was walking slowly up and down the room, looking at his feet and listening with impatient revulsion, but listening nevertheless.

"The thought of *The Provincial Lady* never even entered my head," he said, with a slight, angry tremor; "and why are you speaking in such a thin, squeaky voice and using words that obviously aren't your own? What's the point of it?"

"You're right. I mostly used to keep my mouth shut before," Trusotsky said hurriedly. "I preferred to listen while my late wife was talking. Do you remember how she spoke? What she said was always to the point! As to *The Provincial Lady*, and especially that Stupendiev character, the elderly husband, you're right there again. Why, we ourselves, my departed loved one and myself, when we spoke of you after you had left T——, used to compare our first meeting with you with the plot of the play. . . . The situation is really rather similar. As to Stupendiev—"

"What Stupendiev? Who the hell are you talking about?" Velchaninov shouted, even stamping his foot, so completely was he put out at the sound of that name.

"Stupendiev is the name of the husband in the play," Trusotsky squeaked in his most syrupy voice, "but that belongs to another period of our treasured memories, to the time following your departure from T——, when Mr. Bagautov bestowed his friendship upon us, just as you had done before, but in his case, a friendship that lasted a whole five years."

"Bagautov—who is he? Which Bagautov?"

Velchaninov suddenly stopped dead.

"Stepan Mikhailovich Bagautov, who befriended us exactly one year after you, and just like you, he—"

"Ah, I know, I know, of course!" Velchaninov said, suddenly remembering. "Why, of course, he stayed in T—— for quite some time."

"He certainly did. He worked in the Governor's office. He came from Petersburg, from the best society, and was such an elegant young man!" Trusotsky exclaimed in a really ecstatic tone.

"Yes, of course. How could I have forgotten? He too—"

"That's absolutely right—he too, he too!" Trusotsky repeated his host's careless words enthusiastically. "Yes, he too! And it was then that we staged *The Provincial Lady* in Semyon Semyonovich's private theater—Bagautov played the Count, I played the Husband, and my dear departed wife played the Provincial Lady, the title role. But later, on the insistence of my late wife, they took the part of the Husband away from me, ostensibly because I didn't fit into it. . . ."

"How the hell could you be Stupendiev? You're no Stupendiev, you're just Trusotsky," Velchaninov said rudely, no longer restraining his irritation. "But, since that Bagautov is also in Petersburg now—I saw him myself in the spring—why don't you go to see him too?"

"I've been dropping in at his place every single blessed day for three weeks, but it seems he's not receiving. He's not feeling well, it appears; won't have any visits! And I imagine he *is* dangerously ill—I found out from the most reliable sources. Terrible. He is a friend of six years! Oh, Alexei, I tell you, I am in such a state that I wish the earth would open up and swallow me. . . . On the other hand, though, there are moments when I long to throw myself into the arms of some of those former, let's say, witnesses and sharers of my past experience, just in order to burst into tears, yes, for nothing else—just to weep!"

"I see, but maybe you've had enough of that for today?" Velchaninov said cuttingly. "You ought to be satisfied, I suppose."

"Yes, indeed, I am satisfied, very much so!" Trusotsky cried, getting up at once. "It's four o'clock already and I have disturbed you so selfishly . . ."

"Listen, I'll come and see you myself, and then, I hope . . .

But tell me frankly and honestly—have you been drinking today?"

"Drinking? I haven't had a drop."

"Are you sure you didn't have anything before you came—or even earlier?"

"You know, Alexei, I'm sure you're feverish."

"I'll come and see you tomorrow before one—"

"I noticed some time ago that you seemed almost delirious," Trusotsky interrupted him, obviously enjoying this line. "I really feel terrible having caused you . . . through my awkwardness . . . Yes, yes, I'm going now! And you ought to lie down and get some sleep."

"But you haven't told me where you're staying!" Velchaninov said, suddenly remembering and calling after Trusotsky, who was walking toward the door.

"Didn't I tell you? I'm at the Pokrovsky Hotel."

"And where's the Pokrovsky Hotel?"

"Why, it's close to Pokrovsky Church, in a sidestreet . . . I can't remember the number or the name of the street, but it's just near the church."

"I'll find it."

"I'll be delighted to receive you," Trusotsky said, stepping out onto the landing.

"Wait!" Velchaninov shouted again. "You aren't going to take off, are you?"

"What do you mean by 'take off'?" Trusotsky asked. He had already gone a couple of steps down the stairs, but stopped and turned back. He stared at Velchaninov with his eyes almost popping out, and smiled.

Instead of answering, Velchaninov slammed his door, locked it carefully with the key, and put the hook on too. When he was back in his room, he spat in disgust, as if he had been in contact with something unclean. For five minutes, he stood motionless in the middle of the room, then flung himself on his bed without undressing, and a moment later was asleep. The candle, forgotten on the table, burned itself out.

Chapter 4

The Wife, the
Husband, and the Lover

HE SLEPT VERY DEEPLY, waking up at exactly nine-thirty. He sat up and started thinking about "that woman's" death. The shock he'd felt last night when he'd heard of it had left him feeling almost panicky, and also hurt. These feelings had been drowned out during Trusotsky's visit by a strange thought that had filled his mind. But now as he woke up, all that had happened nine years before came back to him in a blinding flash.

This woman, Natalia, the wife of "that Trusotsky"—he had fallen in love with her and had become her lover when he went to T—— on business (once again a lawsuit over a succession), remaining there for a whole year, although his presence wasn't really required all that time. The real reason for his staying there had been this affair. It and his love for her had taken such complete possession of him that he had become a real slave to Natalia, and would have done anything monstrous or senseless if she had ordered him to out of sheer whim. Neither before nor after had he ever experienced anything approaching it.

Toward the end of the year, when it seemed inevitable

that they must part, although only temporarily, Velchaninov had been in such despair as the fatal hour drew near that he had suggested to Natalia that she leave her husband and flee abroad with him, where they would settle down forever. But his plan was met with sarcasm and firm refusal from the lady (although she had encouraged those ideas of his at first, but that was probably out of sheer boredom, or to have a good laugh); and so, in the end, Velchaninov had had to give it up and leave all by himself.

And what happened? Well, in Petersburg, before even two months had passed, he was already asking himself the question that was to remain unanswered—did he really love that woman, or had it been nothing but an "infatuation"? And it was not at all a lack of emotional depth or a new passion that made him start wondering that way, for, during his first days in Petersburg, he moved through a sort of haze and it is very unlikely that he paid any attention to any woman, although he came across hundreds of them in society, which he had immediately re-entered. But, on the other hand, he knew very well that if he had found himself back in T—— he would have immediately fallen under that woman's oppressive spell again, despite all the questions he was asking himself.

Even five years later, he was still convinced of it, although by that time he was admitting it to himself angrily and remembering "that woman" with hatred. He was ashamed of that year in T—— and couldn't understand how he, Velchaninov, could have been so stupidly taken in. The entire memory of his passion had turned into a disgrace for him— thinking of it, he'd blush to the point of tears, and he was tormented by remorse. True, as a few more years went by, he managed to calm himself a bit; he tried hard to forget it all, and almost succeeded. But now, nine years later, the whole affair had been brought back to him so strangely by the announcement of Natalia's death.

Now, sitting on his bed, with a stream of murky thoughts pouring through his head, he was sure of one thing only: despite the "shock" he'd felt last night when he was told of Natalia's death, he was now feeling quite calm and composed about it. "Is it possible that I am not even sorry about her?" he wondered. He no longer hated her, and could judge her with greater detachment. In his present opinion, which had been formed quite some time before, after he had left T——, Natalia was just a lady belonging to "good" provincial society and he thought perhaps he had just "built up all that phantasy around her." However, he wasn't completely convinced that this opinion was correct, and he questioned it even now.

For one thing, the facts seemed to contradict it. That Bagautov, for instance, also seemed to have been completely under her spell. Bagautov really belonged to the best Petersburg society and was, at least according to Velchaninov, nothing but a "scatterbrain." Petersburg was the only place where he could possibly make a career. And yet, then, against his own obvious interests, he had stowed himself away in T—— for five years for the sake of that woman, thus sacrificing his future to her. If he had returned to Petersburg finally, it was only because he too had been "discarded like an old, worn-out shoe." So there must have been something about the woman—she must have possessed a gift for attracting, enslaving, and dominating men!

And yet, she didn't seem to be too well equipped to attract and dominate. She couldn't really be described as beautiful; one might even say, perhaps, that she was quite plain. She was already twenty-eight when Velchaninov had first met her. Her face, although it wasn't quite pretty, could look fairly animated at times, but her eyes were never pleasant to look at, for there was a certain excessive hardness in them. She was very thin; she was quite inadequately developed intellectually; her unmistakable intelligence was rather one-sided. She had the manners of a provincial society lady, although she had a good deal of tact; she had good taste, but it mostly consisted of an ability to dress.

Her character was strong, determined, and domineering, and there was no possibility of compromise with her—it was all or nothing. Under pressure, she displayed amazing strength and resourcefulness. She was generous and, at the same time, could be infinitely unjust and unfair. It was quite hopeless to argue with her—she was never impressed by the fact that two times two is four. She never thought she could be wrong, or guilty of anything. Her innumerable and constant love affairs and infidelities to her husband never seemed to weigh on her conscience. As Velchaninov put it, she was like a "Mother-of-God such as are appointed by the Khlysty sects, who has come to believe that that is what she really is," and Natalia also believed in the rightness of everything she did.

She was faithful to each one of her lovers as long as she hadn't tired of him. She liked to make her lovers suffer, but she also liked to reward them. She was of the passionate, cruel, sensuous type. She mercilessly condemned other people's deviations from accepted norms but was depraved herself, although nothing could make her admit her own ways were depraved. "Probably she *sincerely* doesn't know she is depraved," Velchaninov thought of her, while he was still in T—— and, let us note, while he was a party to her depraved ways himself. "She is," he thought, "one of those women who are destined to become unfaithful wives the day they are born. They never succumb while they are still unmarried; they must first be married—their husbands are their first lovers, but the wedding ceremony must come first. No woman finds a husband so cleverly and with greater ease. And it is always the husband who is to blame for the first lover. And everything, of course, is perfectly sincere and, to the last day, such women feel they have acted with perfect fairness and are, of course, beyond all blame."

Velchaninov was convinced that that type of woman really existed. But then, he was also convinced that there existed a corresponding type of man, husbands for such women, whose only real function was to correspond to the female type. In his opinion, such men were, in essence, made to be, above all, what might be called the *eternal husbands* of women of that type, or even better, *just* husbands and nothing else. "Such a man is born and grows up just to marry, and, having married, immediately becomes an appendage to his wife, even if he happens to have a personality all his own. The hallmark of such a husband is the well-known horns that he must wear as inevitably as the sun must shine, although he is never aware of it, nor can he be aware of it, by his very nature."

Velchaninov was deeply convinced that those two types of human being existed and that the Pavel Trusotsky he had known in T—— belonged to one of them. But, of course, last night's Pavel Trusotsky wasn't the same man he had been in T——. Velchaninov had found him incredibly changed, although he realized that he couldn't have failed to change and that that change was quite to be expected, since Trusotsky could only be what he was as long as his wife was alive; now he was only a part suddenly released from the whole, in other words, something strange and incongruous.

As to Trusotsky the way he'd been in T——, here's what Velchaninov remembered of him:

Certainly, back in T——, Pavel Trusotsky had been just a husband, nothing more. If he was, for instance, also in government service, it was only because, for him, his duties as an official had also become, in a way, one of his marital obligations: he served for his wife and for her social position in T——, although by nature he was quite a conscientious public servant. He was about thirty-five at the time, and he possessed a personal fortune that was really nothing to sneeze at. In the service, he had never displayed any outstanding ability, but neither had he ever shown himself to be inadequate. He was connected with the cream of provincial society, in which his standing was quite respectable. Natalia was highly respected in T——, and although she didn't seem particularly gratified by this, taking respect as a matter of course, she knew very well how to receive people and had trained Trusotsky so well that he displayed quite adequate manners even when they were entertaining the very highest personages of the province. Velchaninov even thought that Trusotsky might have brains, but he didn't have much chance to demonstrate them, because Natalia didn't like him to talk too much. Possibly he had many other characteristics, both good and bad. But his good points were kept sheathed, as it were, while his wicked propensities were almost completely inhibited.

Velchaninov had noted, for instance, that now and then Trusotsky betrayed an inclination to make fun of other human beings, but that that, among other things, was strictly forbidden to him. He was also fond of telling stories, but that weakness of his was also drastically curtailed: he was allowed to tell only colorless stories, and those only if they were short enough. Before, he had liked to spend an evening out with a group of friends occasionally and even to drink a bit with them, but that wayward tendency had been destroyed at the root. And with all that, an outsider couldn't tell from the first glance that this was a henpecked husband —Natalia appeared to be a loyal and patient wife, and perhaps she herself believed she was. It is possible that Trusotsky was madly in love with his wife, but no one would ever have suspected it, and that too was probably because of the domestic discipline imposed by Natalia.

During his year in T——, Velchaninov had often wondered whether Trusotsky suspected anything about his affair with Natalia. Several times, he had asked Natalia that, and had always received the rather irritated answer that her husband knew nothing, couldn't possibly know, and that anyway, "whatever there is, it's none of his business." Another notable trait of hers: she never laughed at her husband, never seemed to find him ridiculous or stupid, and was ready to defend him very forcefully if anyone else dared to show the slightest lack of respect. Having no children, she was naturally bound to become a society woman above all, but home life was also quite indispensable to her. Social life had never occupied her entirely, and she liked to run her own house and on occasion to sit down to some needlework too.

The night before, Trusotsky had mentioned their evening readings at T——. On those occasions, Velchaninov did most of the reading. Trusotsky also read and, surprisingly enough, did so very well. During these readings Natalia usually did some sewing, and always listened with calm and serenity. They read passages from Dickens' novels, some things from Russian magazines, and occasionally some "serious" stuff too. Natalia valued Velchaninov's culture highly, although she never mentioned the fact, apparently considering it an accepted and settled matter about which there was nothing more to say. Otherwise, she viewed books and learning with indifference, as something quite alien, although possibly useful to her, while her husband was at times positively enthusiastic about things of the intellect.

Velchaninov's affair with Natalia ended suddenly at a point where, for him, it had reached its peak and was becoming an obsession. He was simply dismissed, although when he was leaving town he had had no idea he was being "discarded like an old shoe."

About a month and a half before Velchaninov left town, a young artillery officer, fresh from military school, appeared in T—— and became a steady visitor at the Trusotsky house. And so, instead of three, there were now four of them. Natalia received the young man graciously, treated him just as a lady should treat a youth. Velchaninov suspected nothing, and, indeed, he had other things to worry about, for he had suddenly been informed that a temporary separation between him and Natalia was essential. One of the reasons for this was that Natalia suspected that she'd become pregnant and so, naturally, the best thing for him was to get out of the way quickly, for, say, two, three, perhaps four months, so that nine months from then her husband would be less likely to suspect anything, even if there was gossip. The argument was rather far-fetched, but still, after Velchaninov had made his passionate attempt to persuade her to elope to Paris or America with him, he had ended up by leaving for Petersburg alone, certain that he was leaving "just for a brief moment, that is, for three months at most," for otherwise he would never have agreed to go, whatever she had done.

Exactly two months later, he received a letter from Natalia with a request never to return, because she had fallen in love with someone else; as to her pregnancy, she informed him, she had made a mistake. She could very well have dispensed with informing him of that error—by then, it was all quite clear to him. He remembered very well about that young officer. So that was the end of the affair. And a few years later, he heard that Bagautov had gone to T—— and remained there for a whole five years. Velchaninov attributed the duration of that latest liaison to the fact that Natalia must have aged quite a bit, and aging had made her attachments longer-lasting.

He remained sitting up in his bed for almost an hour. Then he took hold of himself, rang for Mavra, ordered her to bring him his coffee, drank it in a hurry, dressed, and, as it was eleven o'clock, hurried off to Pokrovsky Church to look for the Pokrovsky Hotel. As he thought about the hotel, he found he felt quite differently about everything that morning. He felt rather ashamed of the way he had treated Trusotsky during the night, and now he wanted to make up for it.

He attributed last night's fantastic scene at the door to an accident, to Trusotsky's drunkenness, to all sorts of possibilities, although he still didn't actually know why he was going to take up again with the husband of his dead mistress, when everything between them had come to a natural end. There was something that attracted him; the man had left a certain impression upon him, and it was that impression that had prompted him to go.

Chapter 5

Liza

T<small>RUSOTSKY HAD NEVER</small> thought of "taking off," and God only knows why Velchaninov had suggested that he might the night before. It must have been because he was in a daze himself then. He entered the first grocery store near Pokrovsky Church and they pointed out the Pokrovsky Hotel to him, a few steps down a side street. At the hotel they told him that Mr. Trusotsky was now staying in an annex in their courtyard, where he rented a furnished room from Maria Sysoyevna.

Going up the narrow, damp, dirty stairs to the second floor of the annex where the rooms were, Velchaninov suddenly heard someone crying. It sounded like a seven- or eight-year-old child weeping bitterly. He heard half-smothered sobs amidst the stamping of feet and furious but subdued shouts in an adult voice. The adult was apparently trying to make the child be quiet and was very anxious that the crying should not be heard, although it was he who was making the most noise—his shouts came sharp and shrill, while the child seemed to be pleading haltingly for mercy.

Velchaninov reached a landing with two doors on each side of it, where he saw a very big, fat, disheveled working-class woman, whom he asked where Mr. Trusotsky lived.

She pointed to the door from which the crying was coming. The fat, purple face of the forty-year-old woman was indignant.

"Listen to him having himself a good time!" she said in an almost bass voice, and went downstairs.

Velchaninov was about to knock on the door but changed his mind, flung it open, and stepped inside. Trusotsky, in his shirtsleeves, stood in the middle of a smallish room, crudely but abundantly furnished, and, his face red and angry, was trying to silence a small, eight-year-old girl by shouts, threats, and—it seemed to Velchaninov—by some physical persuasion too. The child wore a short black woolen dress, rather shabby but respectable. She looked hysterical, and had stretched her hands out toward Trusotsky in a beseeching gesture.

At the sight of the intruder, the scene immediately changed: the girl darted off into the tiny adjoining room, and Trusotsky, looking at a loss at first, quickly recovered and dissolved into a smile, as he had done the night before when Velchaninov had suddenly opened his apartment door.

"Ah, it's you, Alexei!" he exclaimed, sounding very pleasantly surprised. "Why, I really didn't expect you. . . . But please, here, this way, please! Sit down, please! On the sofa . . . or rather, in that armchair, while I . . ." and he hurriedly put on his jacket, forgetting his waistcoat.

"Please don't go to any trouble. Stay as you are," Velchaninov said, sitting down on a chair.

"No, please allow me. I'd rather take the trouble. Well, now I look a bit more decent! But why are you sitting so far away in the corner? Here, take this armchair by the table. . . . Well, I really didn't expect . . ."

He sat down on the edge of a plain wooden chair like the one chosen by his "unexpected" visitor, turning it so that he was facing him.

"What, do you mean to say you weren't expecting me? I told you last night I would come and see you around this time, didn't I?"

"I never thought you would come, though. Especially when I thought over what had happened last night, I lost all hope of ever seeing you again."

Velchaninov looked around him. The room was in a mess—the bed hadn't been made, clothes were strewn all over the place, empty coffee cups, an open champagne bottle and a glass stood on the table among the bread crumbs.

He cast a sidelong glance toward the adjoining room—everything was quiet there. The little girl had become perfectly still.

"It's a strange time of day to be drinking that," Velchaninov remarked, pointing to the champagne.

"Just the leftovers . . ." Trusotsky said, embarrassed.

"Ah! it's incredible how much you've changed!"

"Yes, it's a bad habit, and I became afflicted with it sort of suddenly. I contracted it on that day, you know, and that's the honest truth. But don't worry, Alexei, I'm not drunk now, and you won't have to listen to a flood of nonsense like last night; but it's true—I've been in the habit ever since that day. And if someone had told me, even six months ago, that I'd let myself go like this and become what I am now, even if he'd showed me my own self the way I am today in a mirror, I would never have believed him."

"Does that imply that you were drunk last night?"

"Well, yes. . . ." Trusotsky admitted in a hardly audible voice, lowering his eyes. "Although I wasn't actually drunk then, but I had been a little earlier. I say that because I feel I ought to explain that I'm worse some time after I've been drinking—there's not much haziness left in my head, but some sort of unreasoned cruelty lingers in me, and also I feel my bereavement even worse then. In that state, I'm liable to do something silly and insult people for no reason at all. I must have behaved very strangely last night at your place, and you must think . . ."

"Why, don't you remember what happened there?"

"Of course I do. How could I help remembering?"

"Well, that was exactly what I thought and how I explained your behavior to myself," Velchaninov said in a conciliatory tone. "And I myself, I was rather irritable then and much too impatient—let me be the first to admit it. The thing is, I haven't been feeling too well lately, and your unexpected arrival in the middle of the night . . ."

"Yes, yes, the middle of the night!" Trusotsky said, shaking his head with an air of self-reproach. "I wonder what can ever have made me do it? But I'm certain I'd never have walked into your apartment if you hadn't opened your door yourself . . . I'd have gone away. You see, Alexei, I went to see you a week or so ago but you weren't at home, and it's possible that I would never have gone back. Although I'm in a terrible state these days, I do have some pride after all. And so, when we met before, in the street, I kept thinking to myself: 'He'll never recognize me. He's sure to turn away from me. Why, nine years—it's no joke after all.' And I never dared to come up to you and address you first. But last night, I'd been straying all over Petersburg and had lost all sense of time and . . . and that's the cause of everything!" He pointed to the bottle. "It's stupid, I know, very stupid! And if it had been another man in your place—because you did come to see me, disregarding my behavior for the sake of old times—I would've lost all hope of re-establishing relations with you."

Velchaninov listened to him attentively. The man seemed to be sincere, and there was even a certain dignity in the way he spoke. Nevertheless, he hadn't believed a word of what Trusotsky had said from the very first moment he had entered the room.

"Now let me ask you something, Pavel," he said. "I see you're not living alone here. . . . Who is the girl I saw here with you just now?"

Trusotsky somehow seemed surprised at the question. He raised his eyebrows as he looked at Velchaninov, but his look was pleasant and sincere.

"What do you mean—who is that girl? But that's Liza, of course," he said with a friendly smile.

"What Liza?" Velchaninov muttered, and a sudden shudder passed through his body.

The effect was all too sudden. When he had first caught sight of Liza, although he had been quite surprised, he had had no particular feeling or thought.

"Why, that's Liza, our daughter!" Trusotsky said smilingly.

"Your daughter? I never knew you and the late Natalia had any children," Velchaninov said diffidently and incredulously, in a very low voice.

"Why, of course we had. But I see now! How could you possibly have known! I don't know what I can have been thinking about—God sent her to us only after you'd left us!" Trusotsky jumped up from his chair, propelled by a certain agitation, although it appeared to be of a pleasant nature.

"I'd never heard about the child," Velchaninov said, turning pale.

"Of course, from whom could you possibly have heard

about her!" Trusotsky said in a warm, emotional voice.
"Why, the late Natalia and I, we'd lost all hope—why, I'm
sure you remember, yourself—and then, all of a sudden, God
granted us our wish! And the way I felt then, God alone
knows. It happened, I believe, exactly one year after you
left . . . no, wait, it wasn't quite a year. When exactly did
you leave T——? If my memory serves me right, it was in
October, or even November perhaps. . . . Am I right?"

"I left T—— at the beginning of September, on the
twelfth to be exact. I'm sure of it. . . ."

"In September? Is that so? Well, I must be quite a bit
off," Trusotsky said, sounding very surprised. "But if that's
so, you left on September twelfth and Liza was born on May
eighth, which makes it, September, October, November, De-
cember, January, February, March, April—well, only eight
months and something. And if only you knew how my late
wife . . ."

"Well, show her to me then . . . call her in . . ." Velchaninov said in a faltering voice.

"Certainly, certainly!" Trusotsky said, becoming very
agitated. He'd been about to say something, but whatever it
was, he must have decided that it was no longer necessary.
"I'll introduce you to each other right away!" and he hurried into the adjoining room.

Three or even four minutes passed. Hurried whispers
came from the room. Then the child's voice reached Velchaninov. She must be begging him not to force her to come
out, he decided. At last they emerged from the little room.

"She's very bashful," Trusotsky said. "She's so shy and
proud . . . she takes after her late Mama a great deal."

Liza was no longer crying. She kept her eyes fixed on
the floor as her father led her in by the hand. The child was
rather tall for her age, very thin, and extremely pretty. She
quickly raised her light blue eyes to the visitor, gave him a
curious but sullen look, and lowered them again. There was
in her gaze that seriousness and mistrust with which many
children when left alone with a strange person will examine
him from their corner; but, there was something else in that
look, something not at all childlike—or at least that was how
it struck Velchaninov. Trusotsky brought the girl up to him.

"This gentleman used to know Mama and was our good
friend . . . Come on, don't be so shy. Give him your hand!"

The girl bent slightly forward and gave Velchaninov her hand.

"Natalia never wanted to teach her to curtsy. She wanted her just to give her hand and bend slightly forward—the English way, you know," Trusotsky explained, watching Velchaninov closely.

Velchaninov knew that he was being closely observed, but he no longer tried to conceal his agitation. He sat motionless in his chair, holding Liza's hand in his and looking at her intently. But something seemed to be worrying Liza. She seemed to have forgotten her hand in the strange man's and, without taking her eyes from her father's face, was listening fearfully to what he was saying. Velchaninov immediately recognized the child's blue eyes and was even more struck by the extraordinary fairness of her complexion and the color of her hair—those characteristics were all too significant for him. On the other hand, the oval shape of her face and the line of her lips reminded him vividly of Natalia. In the meantime, Trusotsky was telling him something with great emotion. Velchaninov, whose thoughts had been elsewhere, caught only the last sentences:

". . . and so, you can't even imagine our joy, Alexei, when God presented us with this gift! To me, at least, Liza's arrival meant everything! If it was God's will that my quiet happiness should be destroyed, I'd still have the child, I said to myself, and that at least was something I could be certain of!"

"And Natalia?" Velchaninov asked.

"Natalia?" Trusotsky repeated, screwing up his face. "Well, you remember how she was—she never said much about how she felt. But then, when she said good-by to the child on her deathbed . . . Well, it all came to light then! Now, I just said 'on her deathbed,' but actually, suddenly, the day before her death, she was angry and worried and said that they were giving her too many drugs of all sorts, that all she had was a very ordinary fever and that our two doctors understood nothing; that as soon as Koch came back —that old army doctor, remember?—he would get her back on her feet within two weeks. . . . And even later, only five hours before the end, she remembered that in three weeks it would be the birthday of an aunt of hers and that we had to go and visit her at her estate, for she was Liza's godmother. . . ."

Suddenly Velchaninov stood up. He still held Liza's hand in his. He thought he had detected a reproach in the ardent gaze the child had fixed on her father.

"Is she all right?" he asked, in a queer, hurried tone.

"Well . . . she seems to be quite well, although . . . although the way things turned out . . ." Trusotsky said, a bitter note slipping into his solicitous tone. "She's a strange child, very nervous by nature, and then, after her mother's death, she was ill for two weeks, sort of hysterical. Why, I suppose you must've heard her crying when you came in . . . D'you hear that, Liza, do you? And what was it all about? It was because when I go out and leave her here, she thinks I don't love her the way I loved her when her Mama was alive. Well, that's what she reproaches me for. What a thought to occur to a child who's at an age when she should still be playing with toys! And since we've been here, she hasn't even had anyone to play with."

"What do you mean? You're all alone with her here?"

"Yes, we are all alone, except for a cleaning woman who comes in once a day."

"And she stays here all alone while you go out?"

"Why, of course! When I went out last night, for instance, I even locked her in that little room of hers, and that's why we were having all those tears today, as a matter of fact. But what choice did I have? Judge for yourself: two days ago she went down without me and a boy in the courtyard threw a stone at her and hit her in the head. Or else she runs downstairs in tears, asking everyone around where I've gone. That's not right, is it? But I am not much better either— sometimes I go out for an hour and then stay away until the next morning—like last night, for instance. Even so, luckily the landlady unlocked the door for her while I was away, because she was calling out for a locksmith to break the lock. Yes, I'm quite ashamed about it all, and perhaps I look like a heartless monster or something to people. . . . Yes, it must all be due to my blankness of mind, to my present state. . . ."

"Papa," the girl said shyly and hesitantly.

"There you go again! Remember what I just told you!"

"No, no, Papa, I won't, I won't . . ." the girl said, clasping her hands. She looked terrified.

"This can't go on," Velchaninov said, speaking suddenly in a changed voice and sounding imperious and impatient now. "Why, you are a well-off man, so how can you? . . . In the first place, why are you in this sordid house? Why must you live in these surroundings?"

"In this house? What's the difference? We probably won't stay here more than a week anyway and, as it is, we've spent quite a lot of money—which counts up whether one is well-off or not—"

"All right, all right, that'll do!" Velchaninov interrupted him with growing impatience, his tone implying that whatever the other might say, he, Velchaninov, saw through him and knew why he was saying it. "Listen, man, I want to propose something to you: you just said you intended to stay here for another week, maybe two. Well, I know of a home here, a family I've known for over twenty years—the Pogoreltsevs. He, Alexander Pogoreltsev, is a privy councilor, and I suppose he might even be useful to you in connection with your business. They are away in their summer villa now. They have a truly luxurious summer place. Mrs. Pogoreltsev is like a sister . . . like a mother to me. They have eight children. If you'll let me, I'll take Liza and drive her over there right away. They'll be delighted to have her and will be very nice to her and treat her like their own daughter."

Velchaninov didn't make the slightest effort to conceal his extreme impatience.

"Well, I just don't think it can be done," Trusotsky said with a wriggle, looking up with a sly air into Velchaninov's eyes.

"And why can't it be done?"

"How can I let the child go just like that? Of course, with a sincere friend like you, I don't say . . . But after all, you suggest she go and stay with completely unknown people, who, moreover, belong to such high society that I am not at all sure they'll want to associate with us."

"Come on, I just told you that I am like a member of the family in that house," Velchaninov said, almost shouting in his annoyance. "Klavdia—that's Mrs. Pogoreltsev—will be delighted to have Liza if I ask her. She'll treat her as if she were my own daughter. . . . Ah, damn it, you understand very well. You're just talking for the sake of talking. What you say makes no sense!" And Velchaninov even stamped his foot.

"I just meant that it might look rather strange, mightn't

it? You see, I'll have to come and see her too sometimes, for, after all, she can't be all the time without her father and, he-he-he, it would be awkward to go to the home of such important people."

"They are very nice, simple people, nothing 'important' about them!" Velchaninov shouted. "I'm trying to explain to you that they have a lot of children. She'll come back to life there and that's why I want to take her there. And you, I'll introduce you to them tomorrow if you wish. Yes, I even feel that you ought to go out there, sort of to thank them. Yes, we'll go there every day if you want."

"You make it sound really so . . ."

"Nonsense! And what's more, you know it yourself. Listen, come over to my place early in the evening. You can both spend the night there, then we'll all drive out to the Pogoreltsevs' early in the morning, so as to be there before noon."

"Ah, you're really very, very kind! Even inviting us to spend the night at your apartment," Trusotsky said with feeling, deciding all of a sudden, apparently, to accept. "And where, by the way, is this summer house of theirs?"

"In Lesnoye."

"All right, but what about her dress? For you see, if she's going to stay with such a distinguished family and, what's more, at their summer residence . . . Well, you understand, I'm sure, how a father feels . . ."

"Well, what about her dress? She's in mourning, isn't she? How could she wear anything else? Her dress is very adequate really, although, of course, her linen could be a bit cleaner, I suppose . . . and her kerchief . . ."

"She must go and change immediately," Trusotsky said, becoming very busy, "and we'll collect the rest of her linen —it's at the landlady's. She took it to wash—"

"Then you should send for a carriage," Velchaninov interrupted him, "and the sooner the better."

But then an obstacle arose—Liza categorically refused to go. She had been listening in terror and, had Velchaninov paid any attention to her while he was trying to convince Trusotsky, he would have seen the utter distress in her eyes.

"I am not coming," the child said firmly in a low voice.

"You see, just like her mother all over again!"

"No, no, I'm not like Mother!" Liza cried out, wringing her little hands, as though defending herself from an accusation. "Papa, Papa, if you leave me . . ." All of a sudden she rushed at the bewildered Velchaninov. "If ever you try to take me away, I—"

But before she had time to finish, Trusotsky caught her by the shoulder, almost by the scruff of the neck, and, without even bothering to disguise his anger now, dragged her to the small adjoining room. Whispering and subdued weeping could be heard from there again. Velchaninov was about to follow them in there himself, but Trusotsky hurriedly reappeared and, with a twisted smile, informed him that "she'll be ready in just one second." Velchaninov couldn't stand the sight of the man and kept looking past him.

Maria Sysoyevna, the landlady, was summoned. This was the same woman whom Velchaninov had met on the landing. She started to pack Liza's linen into a small, pretty-looking suitcase.

"Is it you, sir, who's taking the child?" she asked Velchaninov. "She'll stay with your family—is that it? You're doing a good thing, sir. She's a nice, quiet child and you'll be saving her from Sodom."

"Come, come, Maria, what are you talking about?" Trusotsky mumbled.

"Come, come, indeed, man! Or are you trying to say that you haven't made a Sodom here? Is it right to let a child who can understand see all the disgusting things that go on here? The carriage is here, sir. Where is it you're going—to Lesnoye?"

"Yes, yes . . ."

"All right, good luck to you."

Liza came out of the other room. She was pale, and looked at the floor as she picked up her suitcase. She never once looked in Velchaninov's direction. She restrained herself and, at parting, didn't throw herself into her father's arms as she had done earlier; apparently she was avoiding looking at him too. He gave her a proper paternal kiss and patted her on the head. As he did so, her lips twitched and her chin began to tremble. But she still didn't raise her eyes to her father. Trusotsky was pale too, and his hands were trembling. Velchaninov noticed that especially, despite the fact that he was trying very hard not to look at him. Velchaninov was in a terrible hurry to leave now. "After all, it's none of my fault," he was thinking. "It just had to be this way."

When they got downstairs, the landlady kissed Liza good-by effusively and it was only when they were already installed in the carriage that Liza raised her eyes to her father. She screamed, stretched out her arms toward him, and, the next second, would have jumped out and flung herself at him. . . . But the carriage drove off.

Chapter 6

An Idle Man's
New Fancy

"ARE YOU FEELING SICK?" Velchaninov said in alarm. "Shall I tell the driver to stop and get you some water?"

She raised her eyes to him in bitter reproach.

"Where are you taking me?" she asked in a sharp, resentful voice.

"They're wonderful people, Liza, and they're staying in a very nice summer house right now. . . . They have a lot of nice children and they'll like you very much, I'm sure. Please don't be angry with me, Liza. You must understand I'm doing all this because I'm sure it's the best thing for you. . . ."

Anyone who knew Velchaninov would have been surprised to see him at that moment, very surprised indeed.

"You . . . you . . . you're bad, you're very, very bad!" Liza said, gasping and trying to control the tears that were right on the verge, her beautiful eyes sparkling with resentment.

"But Liza, I—"

"You're bad, bad, bad!"

She wrung her hands. Velchaninov was completely at a loss.

"Liza, dear, if you only knew what you're doing to me."

"Is it true he'll come to see me tomorrow?" she asked peremptorily.

"Yes, of course it's true. I'll bring him myself."

"He doesn't do what he promises," Liza whispered, looking down.

"Why, doesn't he love you, Liza?"

"No, he doesn't."

"Was he nasty to you? Did he treat you badly?"

She looked at him sullenly without answering. Then she turned away again and sat with her eyes on the floor.

He began to speak, trying to reassure her. He spoke heatedly, feeling feverish. She was listening to him with hostility, but listening nevertheless. The fact that she was paying some sort of attention to him encouraged him greatly, and he even went into a lengthy explanation of what drinking could do to a man. Then he told her how fond he was of her and that from then on he was going to keep an eye on her father for her. At last she lifted her eyes and gave him a long, intent look. He told her that he had known her Mama before, and realized that he had caught her interest. Then, little by little, she started answering his questions, too, but very reluctantly and only in monosyllables. The most important questions she left completely unanswered—she wouldn't say a word about anything touching her relations with her father.

While they were talking, Velchaninov again took her little hand in his and held it, and again she didn't pull it away. In the end, her resistance broke down a bit further and she yielded some of her secrets. From her vague answers, he gathered that she had once loved her father more than her mother, because he had loved her more than her mother had. But when her Mama was dying she had kissed her a great deal and cried, and then everyone had left the room and the two of them had stayed all alone. . . . And so now, she loved her Mama more than anyone in the world, and every night she loved her more than anyone . . .

Liza was really a very proud girl though, for when she realized she had given away some of her secrets, she fell silent again and gave Velchaninov a look loaded with hatred. Toward the end of the drive her hysterical state subsided, but she sank into a brooding mood and looked at him with the sullen, gloomy distrust of a trapped little wild animal. On the other hand, she didn't seem to be too much worried about being taken to stay with people she had never seen before. Velchaninov realized that she was tormented by something else—that she felt embarrassed before *him*, that she was ashamed because it had needed so little effort to convince her father to let her be taken away, because, indeed, it looked as if he was glad to get rid of her.

"She's ill," Velchaninov thought, "perhaps very ill; she's suffered so much. . . . Ah, the nasty, drunken creature! Now I understand everything!"

He urged the driver to hurry. He hoped the country air, the garden, the children, the change of surroundings would do her good, and that, later . . .

He had no doubts about what was going to happen "later." He had clear, well-defined hopes for the future. About one thing, above all, he was quite sure: he had never yet felt the way he was feeling now, and he knew that he would go on feeling that way as long as he lived. "It's a goal in life, it's life!" he thought rapturously.

Many thoughts flashed through his head, but he avoided stopping and examining any of them in detail and, without such an examination, everything seemed clear and certain. His main plan of action took shape by itself.

"It should be possible to influence that horrible creature by combined efforts," he mused, "to make him leave Liza in Petersburg with the Pogoreltsevs, at least temporarily, and go back by himself; for otherwise, why should he torment her like that?"

At last they arrived. The Pogoreltsevs' summer place was really very lovely. A noisy group of children rushed out to the gate to meet them. Velchaninov hadn't been there for a rather long time, and the children, who liked him a great deal, noisily expressed their delight at seeing him. One of the bigger ones called out to him as soon as he saw him, "How's your lawsuit going?" That question was at once caught up by the little ones, who repeated it again and again amid squeals and laughter—here they were, teasing him about that endless lawsuit of his. But as soon as they saw Liza they crowded around her and examined her with the silent, intent curiosity of children.

Then Klavdia Pogoreltsev appeared on the veranda, followed by her husband, and they too greeted him with a laughing query about the lawsuit.

Klavdia was thirty-seven years old, a big, handsome, dark-haired woman with a fresh, ruddy complexion. Her fifty-five-year-old husband was an intelligent, quick-witted, and, above all, a gentle and kindly man. And just as Velchaninov had said, their house was a second home for him.

But there was something special about their relations. About twenty years or so before, Velchaninov, who was then a student and hardly more than a boy, had almost married Klavdia. It was their first love—an ardent, ridiculous, and beautiful love. In the end, however, Klavdia had married Pogoreltsev; and when they met again five years later, they had drifted into a serene friendship. But their relations had always kept a warmth and a peculiar glow, and Velchaninov's memories of that friendship were pure and without reproach, perhaps the only memories of that sort he possessed. Here, in this family, he was simple, straightforward, unaffected; he was kind to the children and spoiled them, put on no airs, admitted all his failings. He often swore to the Pogoreltsevs that he would soon give up society and come and live with them for good, never to leave them again. And he meant it seriously, for he toyed with the idea even in his private thoughts.

He told them everything he thought he should tell them about Liza, although he needn't have bothered with explanations—a simple request that they allow her to stay with them would have been quite sufficient. Klavdia kissed "the poor orphan" warmly and promised him to do everything possible to make the child feel at home. The children took charge of Liza, and they ran off into the garden to play.

After a lively half-hour's conversation, Velchaninov rose and started to take his leave. He was in a great hurry; they noticed this, and remarked that he hadn't been to see them for three weeks and now wouldn't stay more than half an hour. He laughed and swore that he would come back the following day. He was told then that he seemed much too agitated for his own good. Suddenly he took Klavdia by the hand and led her to another room, explaining that he had forgotten to tell her something very important.

"Do you remember what I told to you alone—something that even your husband doesn't know—about that year I spent in T——?"

"I remember it only too well. You've spoken of it often enough."

"Spoken of it! I was confessing, confessing to you alone! I never told you the name of that woman—it was Trusotsky, the wife of that man I told you about. . . . Well, she's dead, and this little girl, Liza, is her daughter . . . my daughter."

"Are you sure? Couldn't you be making a mistake?" Klavdia asked, somewhat breathlessly.

"Yes, yes, I am absolutely certain!" Velchaninov said ecstatically, and he proceeded to sum up the whole story for her as best he could. He talked very fast and sounded terribly agitated. Klavdia had heard it all before, except for the name of the lady; for the mere thought that anyone who knew him, even Klavdia, might some day meet Mrs. Trusotsky and find out that this was the woman that he had loved so much terrified him. And so he had never revealed "that woman's" name to anyone.

"And the husband doesn't know either, does he?" Klavdia asked.

"He . . . he m-must know. . . . The thing is—I am still in the dark," Velchaninov said nervously. "But he knows it—I felt sure of it both last night and today. But I must find out exactly how much he knows, and that's why I'm in such a hurry now. He is coming to my place tonight. I still don't understand—how could he have found out about it?—I mean, found out *everything?* About Bagautov, he knows everything; no doubt about that. But what about me? You know how good wives are at hiding things from their husbands in these cases. Even if an angel descends from heaven and tells him, the husband would still rather believe his wife. Don't shake your head and don't condemn me. I blamed and condemned myself for everything long ago. . . . You see, I was so certain he knew all about me when I went to see him this morning that I allowed myself to become further compromised in his eyes. Would you believe it, I felt guilty for having treated him so rudely during the night. I'll tell you more about that some other time. The whole point of that nocturnal visit of his was his uncontrollable desire to let me know that he knows he has been wronged, and who was the guilty party. Yes, that was the reason for his stupid visit, drunk as he was. But it's quite natural, coming from him—he simply came to make me feel my guilt. In general, I was altogether too impetuous last night and this morning—I gave myself away. Why did he have to turn up just at a moment when I was feeling so low? . . .

"And let me tell you, he's even been cruel to Liza. He was making the child unhappy, and I suppose that too was just to vent his bitterness on someone, even a child! Yes, he is embittered! Insignificant and colorless though he may be—he is a badly embittered man. Otherwise, he is nothing but a buffoon; although, before, he did manage to look like a respectable man. Still, it is quite natural that, under the circumstances, he should have started behaving so waywardly. We must view that with Christian charity! And you know, my dear, I want to treat him very differently now—I want to make it up to him, be nice to him—that would even be a 'good deed' on my part. Why, after all, I have done him a wrong, haven't I? And listen, let me tell you something else now: when I was in T——, it so happened that once I had to have four thousand rubles urgently and he gave them to me just like that, without any IOU or anything. Indeed, he was only too happy he could be of some help. And, mind you, I took that money from him. I took it as though he were my friend . . . my friend! . . ."

"Be careful now," Klavdia said in alarm. "You're in such an excited state that it makes me quite worried for you! Of course, from this minute on, Liza will be just like a daughter to me, but there is still a lot here that hasn't been cleared up. But the main thing—be cautious. You must be circumspect! You know, when you are happy or in a state of elation, as you are now, you tend to be a bit too generous," she added with a smile.

They all came out to see Velchaninov off. The children and Liza, who had been playing in the garden, came along too. They seemed to regard her with even greater astonishment than they had at first. Liza was utterly confused when Velchaninov kissed her in front of everyone and again assured her fervently that he would bring her father along with him when he came back the next day. Up to the last moment, she just looked at him in silence; but as he was about to leave, she suddenly seized him by the sleeve and pulled him aside, looking at him beseechingly and obviously wanting to say something to him. He immediately took her into the house.

"What is it, Liza?" he said gently and encouragingly. But she continued to look around apprehensively and then dragged him a little further away, apparently wanting to be quite out of sight of the others. "Well, Liza, what is it? Tell me."

She remained silent, hesitating, her blue eyes staring at him, and every feature of her fine little face expressing a wild terror.

"He . . ." she whispered as if raving in a nightmare, "he will hang himself . . ."

"Who will hang himself?"

"He will . . . he! He wanted to hang himself during the night . . . In a noose . . ." the little girl said hurriedly, gasping for breath. "I saw him! He wanted to hang himself in a noose, and he told me so, he did! Yes, and he wanted to do it before, he always wanted . . . I saw him at night . . ."

"That's impossible!" Velchaninov whispered, completely at a loss.

All of a sudden, Liza kissed his hand. She began to cry, hardly able to catch her breath between sobs, and begging him for something that he couldn't make out from her hysterical babble. He was never to forget, to the end of his days, the tormented face of that frightened and exhausted little girl, looking at him as if he were her last hope.

"How can she love him so much?" he wondered with sickly impatience as he drove back to town. "But she told me herself that she loves her mother more than him now. . . . Unless she really hates rather than loves him. . . . And what is this about hanging himself? The fool hang himself? . . . I must find out, I must! The whole thing must be settled once and for all, as quickly as possible."

< no>Chapter 7

Husband and
Lover Kiss

HE WAS IN a great hurry to "find out." "I was so flabbergasted at first I couldn't think straight," he kept repeating to himself, reliving the moment when he had first seen Liza. "But now, I must find out." He was in such a hurry to "know" that he was on the point of ordering the driver to take him straight to Trusotsky's place, but he immediately changed his mind. "No, let him come to me himself instead, and in the meantime I'll try and get some of that damned legal business out of the way."

He got down to his business very earnestly, but he soon began to feel that he couldn't concentrate and decided that the best thing to do was to give up for the day. After five, when he was on his way to eat, a funny idea occurred to him for the first time: perhaps it was true after all that he was only hindering his case by interfering in the lawsuit, by fussing around various government offices and constantly pestering his lawyer, who had begun hiding from him now. This idea made him burst into cheerful laughter. "If that idea had occurred to me only yesterday, I'd have been awfully mortified," he thought, becoming even more cheerful. Despite his cheerful mood, however, he was becoming more and more absent-minded and restless. Then he grew thoughtful, and though he tried to pin his restless thoughts to one thing after another, he found he couldn't. "I must see that man!" he decided finally. "I must first puzzle him out; only when I have done so will I be able to decide what to do. It's a duel!"

When he returned home at about seven, he found that Trusotsky wasn't waiting for him, which at first surprised him; then, in turn, it made him angry, despondent, and finally frightened. "God only knows how this will end!" he said to himself, now walking up and down the room, now stretching himself out on his sofa, and every minute glancing at the clock.

It was already almost nine when Trusotsky appeared. "If that man had been cunningly trying to upset me for his own ends," Velchaninov thought, "he couldn't have succeeded better—I feel quite unhinged now." And somehow this thought cheered him up and he suddenly became very gay.

He asked in a cheerful tone why Trusotsky hadn't come in all that time. The man grinned crookedly and sat down in an off-hand manner. He casually tossed his hat with the crepe band onto another chair. His attitude had changed greatly. Velchaninov took good note of that.

Calmly, without wasting words, with none of the excitement he had shown in the morning, he told Trusotsky, as if making a report, how he had taken Liza to the country house, how warmly she had been received by his friends, how good it would be for her health. And then, gradually, as though forgetting about Liza, Velchaninov started talking only about the Pogoreltsevs—what nice people they were, how long he had known them, what a good and influential man Pogoreltsev was, and so on. Trusotsky wasn't listening very attentively, and from time to time he stole a sly, sidelong glance at the narrator.

"You're quite an impulsive man, I see," he mumbled with a particularly unpleasant grin.

"You seem to be in a rather nasty mood tonight," Velchaninov said, annoyed.

"And why shouldn't I be nasty, just like everyone else!" Trusotsky snapped, like a beast leaping out of its corner. It even looked as if he had been waiting for an opportunity to leap out of it.

"Suit yourself," Velchaninov said with a laugh, "but I was merely worried that something might have happened to you."

"Well, something has happened!" Trusotsky announced, as if he were very proud of the fact.

"What exactly?"

Trusotsky let some seconds pass before answering.

"Stepan Bagautov, you know, that elegant young Petersburg dandy . . . well, he played a dirty trick on me, you know. . . ."

"Why, did he refuse to see you again, or what?"

"N-no . . . just the opposite, in fact—I was received at last and I even had the privilege of contemplating his features. Only he happened to be dead."

"What! Bagautov dead?" Velchaninov cried in tremendous surprise, although there was really nothing so incredible about this piece of news.

"Yes, he is dead. My unforgettable friend of five years! He died yesterday at about noon, and I didn't even know! Perhaps he even died just at the moment when I was over at his place inquiring about his health. They are burying him tomorrow, and he is already in his coffin. It is lined with crimson velvet trimmed with gold. . . . He died of brain fever. So they let me in and I could at last look at his face. I told them I was a true, close friend of his, and that's why they let me in. And what has that sincere friend done to me now, I ask you? Why, he was perhaps my main reason for coming to Petersburg!"

"But you sound angry with him," Velchaninov said laughingly. "I'm sure he didn't die on purpose, just to spite you."

"I'm just trying to tell you how much his death hurts me; he was a dear friend of mine and this is what he meant to me."

Quite unexpectedly Trusotsky placed two outstretched fingers above his bald head like horns and let out a quiet, low, protracted chuckle. He sat like that, chuckling, with his horns on his head, for at least half a minute, looking into Velchaninov's eyes with a sort of arrogant, malicious exultation.

At first Velchaninov froze, as if he had seen a ghost,

but he immediately snapped out of it and a sarcastic and insultingly calm smile slowly appeared on his lips.

"And what do you mean by that?" he asked carelessly, drawing out his words.

"This represents horns," Trusotsky said cuttingly, at last removing his fingers.

"You mean your horns?"

"Yes, my own; my own, personal, rightfully acquired horns," Trusotsky said with a horrible grimace.

They remained silent for a while.

"I must say you're a brave man!" Velchaninov said at last.

"Why, because I showed you the horns? But you know what, Alexei, I think you'd better offer me something. Why, I used to entertain you every blessed day in T——. My throat feels quite parched—you ought to send out for a bottle of something."

"Certainly. You should have mentioned it earlier. What would you like?"

"Why what would *I* like? It's what *we* would like, because, of course, we'll drink together, won't we?" Trusotsky said challengingly, but also with a strange anxiety, looking worriedly into his host's eyes.

"Would champagne do?"

"Of course. We haven't come to vodka yet."

Velchaninov got up unhurriedly, rang for Mavra, who came up from downstairs, and ordered the champagne.

"To our joyful reunion after a nine-year separation," Trusotsky chuckled rather awkwardly and quite unnecessarily. "For now you are the one and only true friend I have left. Stepan Bagautov is no longer with us! It's just like the poet who said:

> 'Great Patroclus gone forever
> Vile Thersites still alive.'"

At the word "alive," Trusotsky poked himself in the chest.

Velchaninov thought: "Why don't you come out with it, you pig? I hate innuendos." He was seething with fury, and found it hard to restrain himself.

"Tell me this," he said with an audible note of annoyance. "Since you quite openly accuse Stepan"—he no longer referred to the man as just Bagautov—"it would seem you should be pleased that he is dead. So why are you so angry about it?"

"Why pleased? What should I be pleased about?"

"I suppose that's how a man in your position would feel."

"He-he-he! You're quite wrong then about the way I feel . . . A sage once said that while a dead enemy is a good thing, a live one is even better, he-he-he!"

"But you had plenty of time, I believe—five years or so—to enjoy him alive," Velchaninov said with impatient insolence.

"But do you imagine I knew then?" Trusotsky snapped again, like a cornered animal glad to pass to the attack, apparently welcoming the cue Velchaninov had offered him. "I wonder what you take me for?" he growled, and a new, unexpected expression gleamed in his eye and completely transformed his slyly twisting leer into a fierce scowl.

"Is it really possible that you never suspected anything in all that time?" Velchaninov said, suddenly sounding dumbfounded.

"So you really think I knew! Is that it? Ah, these Jupiters among us! A man is just a dog in your eyes, and you judge all others by your miserable selves. . . . There, swallow that!" Trusotsky brought his fist down on the table furiously. But immediately afterward he got frightened of what he had done and looked up at Velchaninov with apprehension.

Velchaninov drew himself up.

"Listen, Pavel, you can very well understand that it makes little difference to me whether you knew about those goings-on or not. If you didn't—it's all to your credit, I'd say. . . . But what puzzles me is, what made you pick on me as your confidant?"

"I wasn't angry with you. . . . Forgive me. It had nothing to do with you," Trusotsky muttered, looking at the floor.

Mavra came in with the champagne.

"So here it is!" Trusotsky shouted, welcoming the diversion. "Give us a couple of glasses, my good woman, quick! Wonderful! We won't ask you for anything more, my dear. . . . Ah, I see it has already been uncorked! Honor and glory to you, gentle creature! So all right now, be on your way!"

And regaining his courage, he again gave Velchaninov an insolent look.

"Admit though," he suddenly said with a chuckle, "that

you're very curious about whether I knew or not—and it isn't true that you don't care, as you claim. I am even quite sure that you would be terribly disappointed if I just got up and left without any further explanation."

"I don't think I would mind if you did leave."

Trusotsky's smile said: "Ah, you liar!"

"Well, let's get down to business." He poured champagne into the glasses. "Let's drink to something," he said, raising his glass. "Here, to the health of our departed friend Stepan Mikhailovich Bagautov!" and he drank.

"I'm not drinking to that," Velchaninov said, putting down his glass.

"Why not? Isn't it a pleasant thing to drink to?"

"Tell me, were you drunk when you came in just now?"

"I have had a few drinks. . . . But why?"

"Nothing special. I simply thought that last night and this morning you sincerely missed the late Natalia. . . ."

"And what makes you believe now that I don't sincerely miss her?" Trusotsky snapped at him again, as if worked by a spring.

"That's not really what I wanted to say. But admit it, it is quite possible that you're wrong about the late Stepan Bagautov. It is a very grave accusation you are making."

Trusotsky smiled and winked slyly.

"I bet you'd love to know how I found out about it, wouldn't you?"

Velchaninov flushed. "Let me tell you once more—I don't care," he said, thinking: "Shouldn't I throw him downstairs, along with the bottle?" and his face became even redder.

"Never mind," Trusotsky said, pouring himself another glass. "I'll explain to you in a minute how I found out about *everything*, and thus gratify your ardent curiosity. . . . Yes, ardent, because you're a very inflammable man, Alexei, very inflammable indeed! Just give me a cigarette, because ever since last March . . ."

"Here, help yourself."

"Because since last March, Alexei, I've become quite depraved, and here is how it happened. As you know, old man," he said, becoming more and more familiar, "consumption is a very curious disease. Consumptives die all over the place, when they never even suspected they were ill and about to die. I'm telling you, only five hours before she died,

Natalia was preparing to go to visit her aunt at her estate about thirty miles away. And then you, perhaps, are aware of the habit, or shall we call it weakness, of certain ladies, and perhaps even of certain gentlemen, for preserving all sorts of old rubbish, such as love letters. It would seem, though, that the safest thing would be to throw them into the stove—wouldn't you think so? But no, these people scrupulously keep every scrap of paper in their drawers and suitcases, and they even arrange them in years and by dates and categories. I don't know whether that makes them feel better or what, but I suppose it might be conducive to happy memories.

"So as she was planning to drive out to visit her aunt, only five hours before her death, Natalia naturally never suspected that her end was so near, and she was just waiting for that Doctor Koch to come. And it just so happened that she passed away leaving the little ebony box with mother-of-pearl inlay and silver trimmings standing on her bureau. Ah, it was such a pretty little family casket with a nice little silver key to it, that she had inherited from her grandmama. Well, and it was that box that revealed everything that had happened during the whole twenty years, all arranged according to the years and days, all of it, without anything left out. And since Stepan Bagautov had a definite weakness for literature and had once even sent a very passionate short story to a magazine, I found perhaps a hundred of his creations in that ebony box—oh, of course, they were spread over five years. There were other contributions too, with Natalia's annotations on them. . . . Well, what do you think, isn't that a pleasant thing for a husband to discover?"

Velchaninov quickly thought that he had never sent a single note to Natalia, and that even after he'd left for Petersburg the only two letters he had written to T—— had been addressed jointly to Mr. and Mrs. Trusotsky, as had been agreed beforehand. And when, later, Natalia had informed him of his dismissal, he hadn't even answered.

When he had completed his story, Trusotsky remained silent for a full minute, looking at Velchaninov with an insistent, questioning smile.

"Well, why didn't you answer my little question?" he asked at last, with an obviously painful effort.

"What little question?"

"Why, whether you think it is very pleasant for a husband to make such a discovery on opening his wife's little ebony box?"

"What business is that of mine!" Velchaninov said, shrugging angrily.

He got up and started pacing the room.

"I bet you're thinking now, what a pig that creature is to point to his own horns himself. Am I right? He-he-he! You're a very fastidious man, you know!"

"I wasn't thinking about that at all. I simply believe that the death of a man who had offended you has been a considerable shock to you and, on top of that, you've had too much to drink. I don't see anything so unusual in all this story. I understand very well that you'd have preferred it if Bagautov were alive, and I am prepared to sympathize with your disappointment, although—"

"But what need, in your opinion, do I have for Bagautov?"

"That's your private business."

"I bet you had a duel in mind, didn't you?"

"Damn it all!" Velchaninov shouted, abandoning himself more and more to his anger. "Well, I thought that a self-respecting man wouldn't lower himself, in such a case, to ridiculous babbling and playing stupid pranks and making disgusting hints and pitiful complaints that degrade him even further. I thought that a self-respecting man would act more openly. . . ."

"He-he-he! And what if I don't happen to be a self-respecting man?"

"Well, that again is your private business. But then, if that's so, what the hell do you need Bagautov for?"

"Perhaps just to have a good look at that dear friend of mine; we could, for instance, have drunk a bottle together."

"He wouldn't have even agreed to drink with you."

"Why do you say that? *Noblesse oblige*, you know! Take yourself, for instance. You're drinking with me, all right, so why shouldn't he? In what respect is he better than you?"

"Well, I didn't drink with you either."

"Why have you become so proud all of a sudden?"

Velchaninov suddenly laughed loudly and nervously.

"God damn it," he said, "you're really a predatory type, while I thought you were nothing but an 'eternal husband'!"

"What do you mean by 'eternal husband'? What sort of

animal is that?" Trusotsky asked, all attention and pricking up his ears.

"Well, it is a special type of husband, but it would take me too long to explain to you. And by the way, you'd better get the hell out of here—it's time you went. I'm really quite sick and tired of your company."

"But what did you say about my being 'predatory'? You said something about my being 'predatory'—what was it?"

"I said that you were a predatory type. I meant it sarcastically, if you want to know."

"What sort of type is a 'predatory' type, Alexei? Please tell me, tell me for God's sake, or for Christ's sake."

"Enough, enough!" Velchaninov shouted, losing his temper again. "It's time you went. Out with you now!"

"No, my good man, it's not enough, even if you're sick of me, it's still not enough!" Trusotsky said, also jumping up. "And it's not enough, because before I leave here we must have a drink together, to each other. Let's do that and then I'll go, but now it's still not 'enough' yet!"

"Tell me, Pavel, are you going to get the hell out of here or aren't you?"

"I'll get the hell out of here all right, but we must have a drink first. You said you didn't want to drink with *me* personally, while I want you to have that drink precisely with *me*."

He was no longer grimacing, no longer chuckling. Everything in him had changed again and he had become quite a different man from what he had been a second before. Velchaninov was quite puzzled by this new transformation.

"So let's have that drink, Alexei—better not say no!" Trusotsky said, taking hold of Velchaninov's arm, squeezing it hard and looking into his face with a strange expression.

Obviously it was not just a question of whether they were going to have a drink together or not.

"Well, all right," Velchaninov muttered, "where's the stuff?"

"There's just enough of the 'stuff' left for two glasses. It's good clean stuff, you know, so let's clink glasses and drink it up. Here's your glass, sir; now be so kind as to take it."

They clinked glasses and drank.

"Well, if it's like this, if it's like this . . . well, then!" Trusotsky suddenly clutched at his forehead and froze in that position for a number of seconds. Velchaninov was under the impression that at any moment the man was going to utter his *ultimate* word. But Trusotsky didn't utter anything. He just looked up at Velchaninov, winked, and smiled with his former sly smile.

"What do you want of me in the end, you drunkard, you!" Velchaninov screamed frantically, stamping his foot hard on the floor. "Are you trying to make a fool of me, or what?"

"Stop shouting. Stop it! Why do you have to shout?" Trusotsky said hurriedly, waving his hands at him. "I'm not trying to make a fool of you, not in the least! Do you have any idea what you've become for me now?" And unexpectedly seizing Velchaninov's hand, Trusotsky brought it quickly to his lips before Velchaninov realized what was happening.

"That's what you have become for me, sir! And now, I'm prepared to get the hell out of here."

"Wait, wait," Velchaninov called after him when Trusotsky was already by the door. "I forgot to tell you . . ." Trusotsky turned toward him, and Velchaninov, turning very red and looking away, muttered as quickly as he could: "I think you ought to go to the Pogoreltsevs' tomorrow . . . you ought to make their acquaintance and thank them. I really think you—"

"Of course, of course, I understand," Trusotsky said, acquiescing with great readiness and waving his hand to signify that Velchaninov didn't really have to remind him of it.

"And then, Liza is very anxious for you to come. I promised her—"

"Liza?" Trusotsky came back from the door. "Liza? Do you have any idea what Liza has meant and still means to me? Yes, she still does!" he screamed, almost in a fit. "But then . . . Ha! We will come back to that later, but now . . . Well, it was not enough for me our having a drink here, Alexei—I must have something else to be satisfied." Trusotsky put his hat on the chair and stared at Velchaninov, gasping for air, as he had done before. Then all of a sudden he blurted out:

"Kiss me, Alexei!"

"You're drunk!" Velchaninov shouted, reeling back.

"So I am. But still you must kiss me. Go on, Alexei, do it! Why, didn't I just kiss your hand myself?"

Velchaninov remained silent for a few moments, feeling

as though he had been hit on the head with a club. But suddenly he bent down—for he towered a whole head over Trusotsky—and kissed him on his lips, which reeked of liquor. Actually, he wasn't absolutely certain whether he had kissed the fellow or not.

"Well, if that's the way it is, if that's the way it is . . ." Trusotsky shouted again, in drunken enthusiasm, his red eyes sparkling. "Now, it's like this—I was thinking to myself: 'Is it possible that this one too? Well, if he too,' I said to myself, 'then who on earth could I trust after that?'" and Trusotsky burst into tears. "So you understand now, you are the only friend I have left!" And he rushed out of the room, holding his hat in his hand.

Velchaninov remained standing motionless for some moments, just as he had after Trusotsky's first visit.

"Ah, the drunken buffoon!" Velchaninov said, and shrugged. "That's all he is," he repeated firmly when he had undressed and got into his bed; "definitely—that and nothing more!"

Chapter 8

Liza III

Next morning, while waiting for Trusotsky, who had promised to be prompt, in order to go to the Pogoreltsevs' with him, Velchaninov was taking sips from his cup of coffee, smoking, and thinking that he was like a man who has waked up in the morning and remembers every other second that he has been slapped the night before.

"Ah," he thought, "the fellow understands the situation only too well, and he'll use Liza to avenge himself on me." That thought filled him with great fear.

The sweet image of the poor child flashed before his mind's eye. His heart pounded in his chest at the thought that he was going to see *his own* Liza very soon, perhaps within a mere two hours. "No doubt about it," he said to himself heatedly, "she has now become my only goal in life. What do I care now about all those slaps and all those memories! And I can't even understand how I've lived until now. . . . That disorder, that sadness . . . But nothing's the same now, everything's new and different!"

But despite his rapture he grew more and more pensive.

"He'll drive me mad with Liza, that's obvious! And he will torment her too. Yes, that's how he can get at me and make me pay for *everything*. Hm, of course, I can't tolerate his behaving again the way he did last night." Velchaninov suddenly went all red in the face. "And why doesn't he come now? It's already after eleven!"

He waited a long time. His anguish grew. At half-past twelve, Trusotsky still hadn't shown up. The thought that he might deliberately stay away for the sake of tormenting him, just as he had the night before, which had been smoldering in him for some time already, finally reduced him to a state of complete exasperation. "He knows how much I depend on him," Velchaninov thought. "How will I face Liza without him? What will happen to her?"

At one o'clock he couldn't stand it any longer, and drove over to the Pokrovsky Hotel. In the annex there he was told that Trusotsky hadn't returned home until nine in the morning, that he had then stayed for fifteen minutes or so and had gone out again. While the maid was telling him this, Velchaninov was standing by Trusotsky's closed door, absent-mindedly fiddling with the door handle. Then he pulled himself together, snorted with disgust, and asked the maid to take him to Maria Sysoyevna. But the landlady had heard he was there and came out herself.

She was a kindly woman, "a working-class woman with nobility in her heart," as Velchaninov described her later to Klavdia Pogoreltsev. She first inquired how "the little girl" was, and then told him a few things about Trusotsky. If it hadn't been for the child, she said, she would have got rid of him long ago. They had moved him from the hotel to the annex because of his scandalous ways. Wasn't it shocking, for instance, to bring a whore to his room when there was a child there old enough to understand? Indeed, she had heard him shouting at Liza: "She'll be your mother if I so decide!" Yes, believe it or not, a whore! But even she couldn't stand it and spat in his face. And after that he went for the child again: "You're no daughter of mine," he shouted, "you're just a little bastard!"

"Oh, really . . ." Velchaninov muttered, horrified.

"I'm telling you, I heard it with my own ears. And I say that even if a man's blind drunk, it's not right for him to carry on like that in front of the little 'un—for even a little 'un can figure out in the end what's what. And so the child kept crying and she was miserable all the time.

"And then, on top of everything, a bad thing happened in the hotel—a clerk, I believe, took a room there, and during the night he hanged himself; they say he'd spent some money that wasn't his, or something. A lot of people gathered around and what do I see but the kid walking around, for Mr. Trusotsky was out, just the way he was most of the time. I see her down the corridor peeping from between the people's backs at the dangling body, and she had a queer look in her eyes, too. I quickly took her and brought her here and, I'm telling you, she was trembling like a little leaf, the poor little thing, and her face went all gray, and as soon as I got her in here she fell down and twisted and kicked, and she only just pulled through. Must've been some kind of a fit or something, for after that she was often sick.

"Well, when he came back and found out what had happened, he started pinching her all over—for he went for pinching the child more than beating her, Mr. Trusotsky did. Then he got himself good and drunk and started threatening her: 'I,' he says, 'I'll hang myself too, and when I do that it'll be all your fault. Here, do you see that curtain cord over there? Well, that's what I'll use to hang myself with,' and he made a noose right there in front of her. And the little girl put her poor little arms round him and cried out, real miserable like: 'I won't, I won't, I won't do it ever again!' Ah, it breaks my heart to think of her. It's a real shame!"

Although Velchaninov had expected to hear rather strange things, he was so shocked by what the woman had told him that he couldn't quite believe it. But the landlady told him much more. Once, she told him, if it hadn't been for her, Liza would probably have jumped out of the window.

Velchaninov left the annex feeling like a drunk man. The words, "I'll kill the mangy dog by cracking his head open with my stick," kept going through his brain again and again.

He hired a cabbie and drove off to the Pogoreltsevs'. Before they had left the town, the carriage was brought to a stop at the crossroads by the canal—a funeral procession was crossing over the bridge. On either side of the bridge, carriages and people were waiting. It was a rich funeral and the string of vehicles following it was very long. Suddenly, in the window of one of the carriages, Velchaninov caught sight of Trusotsky's face. He would have thought he'd made a mistake if Trusotsky himself hadn't leaned out of the window and, grinning widely, nodded to him. He seemed terribly pleased to see Velchaninov, and even started waving to him from the window. Velchaninov jumped out of the cab and, despite the crowd, the police, and the fact that Trusotsky's carriage was already driving onto the bridge, rushed right up to the window. Trusotsky was alone in the carriage.

"What's come over you!" Velchaninov shouted. "Why didn't you come? What are you doing here?"

"I'm paying off a debt," Trusotsky chuckled roguishly, screwing up his face. "Come, come, don't shout. I am seeing off the mortal remains of my true friend Stepan Bagautov."

"That's absurd! You're a drunk and a madman!" Velchaninov shouted even louder, although for one second he'd been rather taken aback. "Get out of that carriage! You're coming with me!"

"I can't. I must pay my debt, yes, my debt . . ."

"I'll drag you out if you don't come by yourself!" Velchaninov screamed.

"But if you do, I'll call for help. You can be sure I will!" Trusotsky said, still with the same chuckle, as if they were having a little game, although he did move away from the window to the opposite corner of the carriage.

"Look out, look out! You'll be run over!" a police officer shouted.

From the other side of the bridge, a carriage had somehow succeeded in getting through and was causing quite a commotion. Velchaninov was forced to leap back out of its way and at once he found himself hopelessly separated from Trusotsky's carriage. He gave a snort of disgust and made his way back to his cab.

"Anyway, I couldn't take him there in that state," he said, still full of surprise and alarm.

He repeated to Klavdia what Maria Sysoyevna had told him, and also reported the strange scene at the funeral procession to her. Klavdia became very thoughtful.

"I'm very worried about you," she said. "You must break off all relations with him, and the sooner the better."

"He's just a buffoon, nothing else!" Velchaninov cried challengingly. "You don't imagine, by any chance, that I'm afraid of him, do you! And how could I possibly break off with him when Liza is involved? We must think of Liza first!"

And Liza was in bed, ill. The night before she had become feverish and they were expecting a well-known doctor to come from town. They had sent for him at daybreak.

This all helped to upset Velchaninov still more. Klavdia took him to see the sick girl.

"I was watching her yesterday," she said, stopping by the door of Liza's room. "She is a very proud and serious little thing. She feels quite hurt and ashamed because her father has abandoned her and left her with us. I believe that's all there is to her illness."

"Abandoned? What makes you think he had abandoned her?"

"Why, the very fact that he allowed her to be brought here, to a family he knows nothing about, and even the fact that he sent her with a man whom she also hardly knows and whose relations with her father are, to say the least—"

"But it was I who took her, almost by force, and I don't find . . ."

"Oh, good gracious! And Liza, who is only a child, sees it all! Well, in my opinion he'll simply never come."

When Liza saw Velchaninov, she didn't seem surprised. She only smiled sorrowfully and turned away her hot, feverish head. She said nothing to his timid reassurances and to his firm promises that tomorrow, for sure, he would bring her father. As he left the room, he suddenly burst into tears.

The doctor did not come till the evening. He examined the child and gave everyone a bad scare by asking why they hadn't called him earlier. When told that she had only become ill the night before, he wouldn't believe it at first. "Everything will depend on how things go tonight," he said; then he gave all sorts of instructions and left, promising to return first thing in the morning.

Velchaninov wanted to stay there overnight, but Klavdia insisted that he should go to town and try once more to bring back "that monster."

"I'll tie him up if I must and carry him here!" Velchaninov said in a frenzy, and the thought of tying the man up and bringing him back with him took hold of Velchaninov so firmly that he felt very impatient to carry it out.

"I don't feel in the least guilty before him any more," he told Klavdia as he was leaving. "I take back all the slobbery, despicable things I said yesterday," he added with revulsion.

Liza lay with her eyes closed. She seemed asleep. She appeared to be feeling a bit better. Velchaninov bent over her carefully, longing to kiss even a corner of the bedclothes as he was leaving. But Liza suddenly opened her eyes and, as if she had only been waiting for this opportunity, whispered:

"Take me away."

It was a quiet, sad request. There was no trace of yesterday's irritation in her voice, although she sounded as if she knew very well that her request could not possibly be granted. And as soon as the dejected Velchaninov started assuring her that it couldn't be done, she closed her eyes, and she didn't say another word, as though she hadn't heard or seen him at all.

He told the driver to take him directly to the Pokrovsky Hotel. It was already ten o'clock, but Trusotsky wasn't at home. Velchaninov, burning with impatience, paced up and down the corridor for a whole half-hour. Finally, Maria the landlady assured him that Trusotsky certainly wouldn't be back before daybreak.

"Well then, I'll be back here at daybreak too," Velchaninov decided, and he left for home in a state of fury.

But, to his amazement, when he entered his house Mavra told him that last night's visitor had been waiting for him ever since nine o'clock.

"The gentleman even had his tea here and then sent me out for a bottle, like the one you had last night. He gave me a five-ruble bill to get it."

Chapter 9

An Apparition

P<small>AVEL</small> T<small>RUSOTSKY</small> had made himself very comfortable. He sat in the chair where he'd sat on his previous visit, smoking a cigarette and sipping his fourth glass, which he'd just poured himself out of the bottle. The teapot and an unfinished cup of tea also stood on the table near him. His face was flushed and he was beaming with contentment. He had discarded his coat and sat in his waistcoat.

"Please forgive me, my dear friend," he cried, leaping up and reaching for his coat as soon as he saw Velchaninov. "I just took it off to enjoy the moment even more."

Velchaninov took a threatening step toward him.

"I hope you aren't quite drunk yet, and that it's still possible to talk to you?"

Trusotsky seemed somewhat nonplussed.

"Well, not quite. Of course, I've had a few for the departed, but . . . I'm not quite done yet."

"Can you understand me?"

"I am here precisely to understand you."

"If you can, I'll start by telling you that you're a vicious and repulsive creature!" Velchaninov shouted, his voice cracking.

"If you start by that, perhaps you'll finish by that too,"

Trusotsky protested feebly, obviously rather scared by his host's violent outburst. But Velchaninov kept shouting, ignoring what the man said.

"Your daughter is ill. She's dying. . . . Have you decided to abandon her, or what?"

"Is she really dying?"

"She's ill, very critically ill."

"Perhaps she's just having one of those fits."

"Stop talking rot! She is dangerously ill—understand?—and you ought to have gone to see her, if only—"

"To thank those people for their hospitality. I understand, I understand perfectly, my dear, nice Alexei. You're so perfect . . ." Trusotsky suddenly caught Velchaninov's hand in both of his and, in a fit of drunken sentimentality, started begging him for forgiveness, appearing to be on the verge of tears. "Please, please, Alexei, don't shout at me like this. As things stand now, it won't matter in the least whether I drop dead here and now, or fall into the Neva and drown there in my drunken state. But we can always get there in time to pay that visit to Mr. Pogoreltsev."

Velchaninov collected himself and managed to get his anger somewhat under control.

"You're drunk, and so I don't quite understand what you actually mean when you say all that," he said sternly. "Of course, I'd be glad any time to have things out with you. In fact, on my way here, I . . . But I must warn you—this time I'll take my precautions, and so I want you to spend the night here, in my place, and tomorrow morning we will drive over to the Pogoreltsevs'. Yes!" Velchaninov suddenly started to scream again. "I won't let you out of here; and if I have to, I'll tie you up, hand and foot, carry you down, and throw you into the carriage myself! . . . Do you think you'll be comfortable on that sofa?" he asked, pointing breathlessly at a wide, soft sofa that stood on the opposite side of the room from the sofa on which he himself slept.

"Oh, any place will do . . ."

"Not any place—you'll sleep on this sofa. Here, take these sheets, blanket, and pillow and make your bed at once."

Velchaninov had taken all the things out of the closet and was tossing them into Trusotsky's obediently outstretched arms. For a while, Trusotsky stood in the middle of the room loaded with the bedclothes, with a broad grin on his drunken face. But when Velchaninov threateningly repeated his order, he got down to work. He pushed away the table, and huffing, puffing, and panting, started to unfold the sheets and spread them on the sofa. Velchaninov went over to give him a hand. He felt quite pleased with his guest's submissiveness and fear.

"Drink up what there is in your glass and lie down," Velchaninov said, again in a tone of command which he was unable to get away from. "Was it you who sent the woman for the wine?"

"Yes, I did so on my own initiative. I knew you wouldn't send for liquor any more."

"It's a good thing you know that, but there are a few more things I want you to know. I warn you once more: I've taken all the necessary precautions and I won't stand your drunken goings-on any more, your kisses and all that sort of thing!"

"I understand very well myself, Alexei, that something like that would only be possible once," Trusotsky sniggered.

When he heard that answer, Velchaninov, who had been pacing up and down the room, stopped almost solemnly in front of Trusotsky.

"Listen, Pavel, you are a clever man. I give that to you. But I assure you you are on the wrong track. Speak openly, be straightforward, and I give you my word I'll answer anything you care to ask me."

Trusotsky again produced his broad grin, which by itself was enough to drive Velchaninov into a frenzy.

"Stop that!" Velchaninov shouted again. "Stop play-acting. I see through you! I repeat: you have my word of honor that I am prepared to tell you *everything*, and that you'll receive any sort of satisfaction you care to demand, whether it is possible or impossible. Ah, I wish to heaven you could understand me!"

"If you're really so obliging," Trusotsky said, cautiously moving a bit nearer to him, "I would be very interested in what you meant yesterday when you mentioned something about the 'predatory type'."

Velchaninov gave a sound of disgust and started pacing the room again, even more rapidly than before.

"No, Alexei, don't snort like that, because I am highly interested and, in fact, I have come here especially to check . . . Please forgive me, my tongue won't obey me too well. Why, I read over there in a magazine something about the 'predatory' and the 'meek' types . . . in the literary section, and I suddenly remembered about it this morning. But I've forgotten what it said, and, to tell you the truth, I never understood it too well. What I'm actually trying to find out now is whether the late Bagautov belonged to the 'meek' or the 'predatory' type. You could tell me perhaps, Alexei?"

Velchaninov was still pacing in silence.

"A predatory type," he said, stopping dead, in a sudden outburst of fury, "is a man who'd sooner have slipped some poison into Bagautov's glass when drinking champagne with him to celebrate a pleasant reunion—as the two of us did last night—than have followed his coffin to the cemetery as you did, out of God knows which of your hidden, underhand, disgusting aspirations, and for the sake of stupid play-acting that degrades you yourself above all!"

"You certainly are right that he wouldn't have gone to the funeral. . . . But you really have it in for me tonight . . ."

"The predatory type is not the man," Velchaninov went on in a rage, ignoring him, "who imagines all sorts of cock-eyed things, calculates what is fair and what is legal, and finally goes over the insults he has suffered, like a lesson, and starts moaning and making a show of himself, hanging himself on people's necks—and, in fact, spending all his time on it and . . . Tell me, is it true that you wanted to hang yourself? Is it the truth?"

"I may have said something like that when I was drunk, but I really can't remember. And then you see, Alexei, it doesn't fit us too well somehow to go around slipping poison into champagne glasses. Besides, I am making quite a good career in the government service, and I also have a nice little bit of capital, so that I could perhaps re-marry if I felt like it. . . ."

"And then, you'd risk being sentenced to hard labor too."

"Yes, to be sure, that's also an unpleasant prospect, although nowadays they'd find some mitigating circumstances, I dare say. But let me tell you an awfully funny little story, Alexei, that I remembered driving over here in the cab and wanted very much to tell you. You said something a few seconds ago about 'hanging oneself on people's necks.' Do you remember Semyon Livtsov, by any chance? He stayed with us sometimes in T——. Well, then, his younger brother, also a young gentleman from Petersburg, was on the Governor's staff and had all sorts of very brilliant qualities. Once he got into an argument with Colonel Golubenko and he considered himself insulted. It happened in the presence of ladies, including even the lady of his heart. Nevertheless, he decided to swallow the insult. Well, soon after that, Golubenko stole the heart of Livtsov's lady, offered her his hand in marriage. Well, what do you think happened? That Livtsov had become a sincere friend of Golubenko's—they'd completely made up their quarrel—and he even insisted on being his best man at the wedding. And when they came home from the ceremony, he congratulated Golubenko and kissed him in front of all the local high society, including the Governor; and then, in his tailcoat and with his hair all curled, he went and stuck a knife into Golubenko's belly, and you should've seen that bridegroom topple over. Yes, and just think of it— the best man at his wedding! Isn't that shameful?

"But that's nothing yet—the worst was that once he'd stuck the knife into his belly, he turned away and started rushing around and shouting: 'Ah, my God, my God! What have I done!' And the tears were streaming down his cheeks and he flung his arms around people and hung himself on their necks, even the ladies' necks. 'Ah, what have I done? What,' he shouted, 'did I do just now?' Ha-ha-ha, he really tickled me to death, the fellow! Of course, one felt a bit sorry for Golubenko perhaps; but after all, he pulled through in the end too."

"I really don't see why you had to tell me that story," Velchaninov said with a threatening frown.

"Well, because the fellow did stick his knife into that belly, didn't he?" Trusotsky said with a chuckle; "although, obviously, he wasn't of the type you mentioned; in fact, I'd say he was more like a drop of snot than a man, since, out of sheer fear, he forgot his manners entirely and, in the presence of the Governor, started hanging himself on various ladies' necks. Yet he did stick that knife where he wanted to, and so got his point across. That's the only reason why I brought it up."

"Get the hell out of here, out!" Velchaninov howled in a voice that was not his own. "Get out with your gutter filth. That's what you are yourself—gutter filth! Do you think you can scare me, just because you bully a child! You miserable, cowardly creature, you low, low, low hypocrite!" he shouted, unaware of anything, and gasping with every word.

Trusotsky's face twitched. His drunkenness seemed to have vanished, and his lips trembled.

"Is it you, Alexei, who is calling *me* a low hypocrite? *You* calling *me* that?"

But Velchaninov managed to get hold of himself.

"I am prepared to apologize," he said, after a brief pause of gloomy hesitation, "but on condition that you yourself start acting openly this very minute."

"If I were in your place, Alexei, I would apologize unconditionally."

"All right then, so that's how it will be," Velchaninov said after another brief pause. "I ask you to forgive me. But please understand, Pavel, that as things stand now, I don't feel I owe you anything any more, and I'm referring to the *whole business*, and not just the present incident."

"That's all right. What's the point of keeping score?" Trusotsky sniggered, but he was looking at the ground.

"If that's the way you feel, so much the better! So drink up your wine and go to bed, because I still don't intend to let you go."

"Ah, the wine . . ." Trusotsky said a bit disconcertedly, but he walked over to the table and drank the glass that had been poured out quite a while before. Perhaps he had had a good deal to drink before, for his hand was shaking badly and he spilled some wine on the floor, on his shirt, and on his waistcoat. But he drained the glass to the last drop, as if it were unthinkable to leave anything in it; then he carefully replaced the empty glass on the table, went back to his bed, and started to undress, as he had been told.

"Wouldn't it be better, though, if I didn't spend the night here?" he asked unexpectedly, holding in his hand the shoe he had already taken off.

"No, it wouldn't be better," Velchaninov snarled without looking at him; he was still pacing the room.

Trusotsky undressed and slipped under the bedclothes. A quarter of an hour later, Velchaninov blew out the candle and also went to bed.

He was falling asleep amidst a crowd of tormented thoughts. Something new had appeared out of the blue to complicate the "business" even further, and, at the same time, he was ashamed of his fears.

Just as he was dozing off, a slight rustling woke him up. The room was quite dark, for the curtains were drawn, but

Velchaninov, who was looking intently toward Trusotsky's sofa, thought he could see that the man was no longer lying down, but was sitting up.

"What's going on?" Velchaninov shouted.

"A ghost . . ." Trusotsky answered after a while, in a hardly audible voice.

"What ghost?"

"Over there, in the other room—I think I saw a ghost."

"Whose ghost?" Velchaninov asked after a pause.

"Natalia's."

Velchaninov got up and looked across the entrance hall into the other room, the doors of which were always left open. There were no curtains over the windows in that room, and so it was relatively light now.

"There's no one in that room. You're drunk, that's all. Come on, lie down!"

Velchaninov went back to bed and pulled the blanket over him. Trusotsky stretched himself out, too, without saying a word.

Ten minutes or so later Velchaninov suddenly asked, "Have you ever seen a ghost before?"

"Yes . . . I have once," Trusotsky said in a weak voice, after a long pause.

After that there was silence. Velchaninov couldn't have said for sure whether he had fallen asleep or not during the following hour; then all of a sudden he turned over. Perhaps it was a light noise that had wakened him, but he thought that there was something white in the middle of the dark room. It was moving toward his sofa and had now reached the center of the room. He sat up in his bed and looked intently into the darkness.

"Is that you, Pavel?" he asked, and his own weak voice in the darkness sounded very strange to him.

There was no answer, but there could no longer be any doubt that someone was standing there.

"Is that you, Pavel?" he repeated, so loudly that even if Trusotsky had been in his bed and asleep he would certainly have answered.

But again there was no reply. Instead, he thought he saw the white shape move a bit closer to him. Then something strange happened inside him: something seemed to have been released in him and, as he had earlier in the evening, he started to scream in a mad voice, panting at every word:

"If you fancy you can scare me, you drunken buffoon, I'll turn to the wall and put my head under the sheet, and I won't turn again till morning. That'll prove to you, you stupid clown, how much you impress me. . . . And you can stay standing there all night if you wish . . . I spit into your eye, understand!"

And he spat furiously toward the spot where he assumed Trusotsky was at that moment; then he turned to the wall, put the sheet over his head, as he had said, and remained motionless in that position. A dead silence followed. Whether the ghost kept moving toward him or remained still, he didn't know, but his heart was pounding violently. At least five minutes had passed when suddenly, two steps away from him, he heard Trusotsky's weak voice:

"I just got up to look for . . ." He named an indispensable household item. "I couldn't find it over there, on my side. I wanted to see whether there was one here, near you."

"So why didn't you answer when I shouted?" Velchaninov asked in a breaking voice after half a minute.

"I got scared. You screamed so loudly, I got frightened."

"Over there, to the left, in the little cupboard by the door. Light the candle."

"Oh, I'm sure I can manage without the candle," Trusotsky said humbly, walking toward the corner. "Please forgive me, Alexei, for bothering you like this. . . . I felt so drunk all of a sudden, then . . ."

Velchaninov didn't answer. He lay with his face turned to the wall, and he remained like that, without turning or stirring, for the rest of the night. Was he so anxious to keep his word and prove to himself how much he despised the man? He didn't know himself what was going on inside him. He was in a state of nervous strain bordering on delirium. He couldn't go to sleep for a long time. And when he awoke at around nine in the morning, he sat up hurriedly as if someone had shaken him. But Trusotsky was not in the room. There was only the empty, unmade bed there. The man himself had escaped.

"I knew it!" Velchaninov growled, slapping himself on the forehead.

Chapter 10

The Cemetery

THE DOCTOR'S FEARS were justified—Liza's illness took a turn for the worse and she was now far more ill than Velchaninov or Klavdia would have imagined possible. When Velchaninov arrived before noon, he found the child unconscious. She was burning hot. Later he claimed that she smiled at him and even stretched out her hot little hand toward him. Whether this was true or he had just imagined it to make himself feel a bit better, he had no chance to check. Liza had become unconscious during the night and remained unconscious during her whole illness. On the tenth day after she had come to the Pogoreltsevs' country house, she died.

It was a terrible time for Velchaninov, and the Pogoreltsevs were very alarmed about him. He spent the greater part of those painful days with them. Toward the end, he'd stay for hours sitting all alone in some corner, his mind apparently completely blank. When Klavdia tried to talk to him he hardly answered her, and was obviously anxious to be left alone. Klavdia said that even she had never expected it would give him such a shock. He could bear only the presence of the children; with them he even laughed occasionally, but then, too, he'd suddenly get up and go on tiptoe to Liza's room to have a look at her. Sometimes he thought she recognized him. Like the others, he had no hope that she'd recover, but he refused to go very far away from the room in which she was dying, and usually sat in the room next to it.

Twice during that time, however, he displayed tremendous energy. He suddenly got up, rushed off to Petersburg to get the most famous doctors, organized whole medical consultations. The second and last consultation was held on the day before the girl died. Three days earlier, Klavdia spoke to Velchaninov about the necessity of finding "that Mr. Trusotsky, because, in case the worst happens, we can't bury her without him." Velchaninov mumbled something to the effect that he would write to him. Then Mr. Pogoreltsev declared that he himself would have him traced by the police. Finally Velchaninov wrote a two-line note and left it at the Pokrovsky Hotel. As he'd expected, Trusotsky was out again, and he left the note with Maria Sysoyevna.

At last, when Liza died on a beautiful summer evening as the sun was setting, Velchaninov seemed, as it were, to awaken. When they laid out the dead girl on a table in the drawing room, dressed in a pretty white dress that belonged to one of Klavdia's daughters, and with flowers in her folded hands, Velchaninov walked over to Klavdia and, his eyes flashing wildly, declared that he was going to get the "murderer" and would bring him back right away. Disregarding the suggestion that he wait till the following day, he drove off to the city.

He knew where he could find Trusotsky, for it was not just in search of famous doctors that he had been to Petersburg while Liza was ill. There had been moments when he imagined that if he were to bring Trusotsky to the dying child, she might recover, and then he had rushed all over the place like a madman, trying to find the man. Trusotsky was still staying in the hotel annex, but it seemed quite futile to look for him there.

"He may stay away for three days on end," the landlady informed him, "and even if he comes in by chance, he's usually drunk; he hardly ever stays more than an hour and then off he goes again. He's gone to pieces completely now."

A waiter at the Pokrovsky told Velchaninov that for quite some time now Trusotsky had been in the habit of visiting some women on the Ascension Embankment. Velchaninov immediately located the ladies in question. They had no trouble remembering the man who'd loaded them with presents and champagne, and they were able to identify him by the crepe on his hat. At the same time, they showered abuse on him because he had stopped coming to see them. One of the girls, named Katia, said that she could find the man at any time.

"He never leaves that Mashka Stupidov and he has more money than he knows what to do with; and that Mashka, by the way, should be called Bitchidov, not Stupidov; she's been in the hospital, you know. If I wanted to turn her in, they'd pack her right off to Siberia."

Katia, however, was unable to locate Trusotsky that time, although she did promise to tell Velchaninov the next time exactly where to find his man. And it was on her help that Velchaninov was relying most.

He got to town that evening at about ten, and immediately went over to Katia's establishment, asked for her, paid the proper person compensation for her absence, and went with her to look for Mashka and Trusotsky. Velchaninov wasn't quite sure yet what he'd do with Trusotsky if he found him—kill him, or simply inform him of his daughter's death and explain that his cooperation was needed to have her buried.

At first they met with failure—it transpired that Mashka and Trusotsky had had a fight, and that some cashier had whacked Trusotsky on the head with a stool. For a long time they were unable to find him. At last, at two in the morning, Velchaninov bumped into him as he himself was going out of one of the establishments in which they'd suggested he should look for him.

Trusotsky, quite drunk, was being led to the establishment by two ladies, one of whom was supporting him by the arm. They were followed by a big man who apparently thought he had a claim on something or other, and was shouting full-throatedly and threatening Trusotsky with all sorts of horrors. Among other things, the man was shouting that Trusotsky had "exploited" him and "poisoned his life." Apparently some money was involved. The ladies seemed rather frightened and were in a great hurry to get inside. When Trusotsky caught sight of Velchaninov, he rushed toward him with wide-open arms, as if he were being murdered.

"Please, dear Alexei, help me!"

Just one look at Velchaninov's athletic figure made the claimant retreat in a hurry, while Trusotsky triumphantly brandished his fist in the direction of his withdrawing foe, letting out a victorious squeak. Then, without knowing why, Velchaninov caught him by the shoulders and shook him so hard that the drunk man's teeth began to rattle. Trusotsky immediately grew quiet, staring at his tormentor with frightened, drunken eyes. At a loss what to do with him next, Velchaninov pushed him down, forcing him to sit on the edge of the sidewalk.

"Liza is dead," he informed Trusotsky.

Trusotsky's eyes were still fixed on him as he sat on the edge of the sidewalk, supported by one of the ladies. Finally, he understood, and his face twisted.

"Dead . . ." he whispered in a peculiar way, and Velchaninov wasn't certain whether it was one of his unpleasant grins or some sort of a twitch that had distorted his face, but a moment later Trusotsky raised his right hand painfully and tried to make a sign of the cross. The cross didn't come off too well, though, and his trembling hand fell back to his side. After another little while he slowly got to his feet, clutching onto his lady and, using her as a support, he went on his way, seeming quite unaware of everything, including Velchaninov. But Velchaninov again caught him by the shoulder.

"Can't you understand, you drunken slob—we can't bury her without you!" Velchaninov cried, beginning to pant again.

Trusotsky turned his head toward him.

"D'you remember . . . that lieutenant . . . artillery lieutenant?" he mumbled with a thick tongue that wouldn't move in his mouth.

"Wha-a-at!" Velchaninov shouted, as a painful shudder ran down his spine.

"He . . . he is . . . he's her father. . . . It's him you need . . . find him to bury her. . . ."

"You're lying!" Velchaninov screamed, like someone who suddenly realizes he is a lost man. "You're just saying that out of spite. I knew you'd have prepared something like this for me!"

And, beside himself with fury, he raised a terrifying fist over Trusotsky's head. In another second, he might have killed the man with a single blow. The ladies shrieked and darted out of the way, but Trusotsky didn't even blink an eye. His face was distorted by a paroxysm of animal hatred.

"I'm sure you know where you can go according to that good old Russian expression?" he said in an almost sober voice, uttering the quite unprintable phrase of abuse. "Well, you'd better take yourself off there, you bastard!"

He twisted his body violently to get out of Velchaninov's clutches, pulled back, and almost fell; his lady friends took hold of him then and ran off, squealing, almost dragging Trusotsky along behind them. Velchaninov didn't pursue them.

The next day at one o'clock, a middle-aged, uniformed official presented himself at the Pogoreltsevs' country house and politely handed Klavdia a package addressed to her by Pavel Trusotsky. The package included a letter with three hundred rubles enclosed in it, and the legal documents necessary for Liza's burial. Trusotsky's letter was brief, polite, and very decent. He thanked Mrs. Pogoreltsev for her kindness toward the little girl, for which only God could repay her. He wrote that he wouldn't be able to attend his beloved, unhappy daughter's funeral, vaguely mentioning his own poor state of health; he would have to leave all the arrangements in the hands of Mrs. Pogoreltsev, who had already demonstrated her angelic kindness. The enclosed three hundred rubles were to cover the burial expenses and also those incurred during the child's illness. And if, by any chance, there was anything left over from that sum, he humbly requested that it should be spent on a requiem mass for the soul of the departed Liza.

The official who had brought the letter was unable to offer any additional explanation; it even appeared that Trusotsky had had to use some persuasion to make the man do the errand for him and put the package personally into the lady's own hands. Pogoreltsev was almost offended by the mention of "the expenses incurred during the illness," and decided that while fifty rubles could be kept for the burial— a father couldn't, after all, be prevented from burying his child—the remaining two hundred and fifty had to be returned forthwith to Mr. Trusotsky. But Klavdia, who had the final say, decided that instead of the two hundred and fifty rubles, Trusotsky should get a receipt from the cemetery chapel saying that the money had been paid for requiem services for Liza's soul. That receipt was later handed to

Velchaninov for him to send to Trusotsky, which he did by the next mail, addressing it to the annex of the Pokrovsky Hotel.

The funeral over, Velchaninov disappeared from the Pogoreltsevs' country house. For two weeks he roamed alone all over the town, colliding with people in his absent-mindedness. At other times, he spent days on end stretched out on his sofa, oblivious to the most ordinary things. Several times the Pogoreltsevs invited him to come and stay with them. He thanked them, said he would come, and immediately afterward forgot all about it. Once Klavdia came to fetch him herself, but she didn't find him at home. The same thing happened to his lawyer, who at last had an important piece of news for him: he had very adroitly settled the lawsuit and his opponents had agreed to an amicable arrangement by which they were to compensate him quite generously for the disputed portion of the inheritance they were claiming. All the lawyer needed now was Velchaninov's consent. When he at last found him at home, the lawyer was very surprised at the apathy and indifference with which his formerly over-anxious client received the good news.

The very hottest days of July came, but Velchaninov was unaware of the season. His grief had grown in his heart like a ripening abscess and he was constantly aware of it in his painfully lucid thoughts. His main sorrow was that Liza had died before she had learned how agonizingly he loved her. His whole goal in life had flashed by him in such a happy glow, and suddenly dissolved in eternal darkness. That goal had consisted mainly, he thought now, of making Liza aware every day, every hour of her life, of his love for her. "And there can't be any higher goal for a human being, there can't be!" he mused sometimes in gloomy exaltation. "And even if other goals are possible, none of them is more sacred than that!" At other times he felt: "Loving Liza would have cleansed and redeemed all my earlier debauched and useless existence; and instead of being preoccupied with myself, an idle, depraved, and washed-out man, I would have cherished and prepared for life a pure and beautiful creature and, for her sake, everything would have been forgiven me and I would have forgiven myself everything."

All these conscious thoughts always brought with them the heart-breaking image of the dead child. He reconstructed her pale little face, with every expression he knew; he remembered her in her coffin, amidst the flowers, and in the coma, with her open, immobile eyes. He remembered that when she had been laid out, he had noticed, God knows why, that one of her fingers had turned dark during her illness. This had struck him so, and he had become so sorry for that poor little finger, that it occurred to him then and there to find Trusotsky and kill him. Before that, he had been "sort of unfeeling."

Was it wounded pride that had tormented her young heart and driven her to death, or was it the three months of suffering at the hands of her father, who had switched from love to hatred, who had abused her with foul words, had made fun of her terrors, and had finally abandoned her to strangers? He thought about it constantly, imagining all sorts of possibilities and variations.

"Have you any idea what Liza was to me?" he'd suddenly remember Trusotsky exclaiming when he was drunk, and he felt now that there was more than a pose in it, that there was a true love there too. Then how could the monster have been so cruel to the child whom he loved—was it really possible? But each time he quickly dismissed that question, brushing it aside, for there was something terrifying in it, something unbearable for him, something that had remained unanswered.

One day, without knowing how he got there, he found himself in the cemetery where they had buried Liza and, once there, found her grave. He hadn't been to the cemetery since the funeral, for he had thought it would cause him unbearable suffering, and so he did not dare to go. But strangely enough, when he bent down and kissed the gravestone, he suddenly felt much easier. It was a clear evening; the sun was setting; lush, bright green grass grew around the graves; nearby, a bee was humming in a rosebush; the wreaths and flowers left on Liza's grave by Klavdia and the children were lying there, half their petals and leaves scattered about. For the first time in many days, something resembling hope filled his heart. "It feels so peaceful!" he thought, sensing the stillness of the cemetery and looking at the clear sky. His soul was filled with a flood of pure, quiet faith.

"Liza has sent this to me. It's she who is talking to me," he thought.

It was getting quite dark when he left the cemetery and went home. Not far from the cemetery gate there was an inn, or some sort of an eating place, and through the open windows he saw the customers sitting at the tables. He saw a man sitting right by the window, and suddenly he thought he recognized Trusotsky and that the man had also seen him and was examining him with curiosity. Velchaninov went on and soon heard someone hurrying to catch up with him. Trusotsky was running after him. Probably a conciliatory expression on Velchaninov's face had determined him. When he caught up with him, Trusotsky smiled with his usual, drunken smile, although he wasn't really very drunk.

"Hello," he said.

"Hello," said Velchaninov.

Chapter 11

Trusotsky Thinks
of Marriage

VELCHANINOV WAS SURPRISED to hear himself answer
"hello." It struck him as strange that he felt no anger whatever toward the man and that there was something quite
different in his feelings, a sort of new impulse.

"What a nice evening," Trusotsky said, looking up
searchingly into his eyes.

"So you haven't left yet," Velchaninov said, not as a
question, but just thinking aloud as he walked on.

"It took longer than I expected, but in the end I did get
that promotion. I suppose I'll be going the day after tomorrow."

"You got the post you wanted, then?" Velchaninov was
really asking now.

"Why shouldn't I have?" Trusotsky said, his face twisting suddenly.

"Oh, I was just asking," Velchaninov said appeasingly,
but he frowned and cast a sidelong glance at Trusotsky. Then
he noticed with surprise that the man's hat and suit looked
infinitely better than what he had been wearing a couple of

weeks before. "What was he doing sitting by the window in that eating place?" Velchaninov wondered.

"I wanted to tell you yet another happy piece of news, Alexei," Trusotsky said, speaking again.

"Happy news?"

"I'm going to get married."

"You're *what?*"

"Well, after sorrow comes happiness—that's how it always goes in life. I would've liked very much, Alexei . . . But I don't really know whether I ought to . . . You seem to be in such a hurry . . ."

"Yes, I am in rather a hurry, as a matter of fact . . . and I don't feel too well either." Velchaninov suddenly felt an intense urge to be rid of the man, and his new warm impulse toward him vanished.

"What a shame! I'd have liked—"

Trusotsky stopped short without spelling out what it was he would have liked. Velchaninov said nothing.

"In that case, we'll talk about it some other time, if we meet . . ."

"Yes, that's it—later," Velchaninov said very quickly, without looking at him and without stopping. For a minute or so they walked on in silence, Trusotsky still trotting at Velchaninov's side.

"In that case, good-by," Trusotsky said at last.

"Good-by, and I wish you . . ."

Velchaninov arrived back home, once again completely upset. He couldn't stand any contact with "that man." As he was getting into bed, he thought again: "Why was he hanging about near the cemetery?"

Next morning, he finally decided to go and see the Pogoreltsevs. He felt rather reluctant—sympathy from anyone, even such close friends, was painful to him. But they seemed to be really worrying about him and he had to go. He somehow felt very ashamed to face them now.

As he was finishing his breakfast he was still deliberating with himself about whether to go or not, when, to his great surprise, Trusotsky came to see him.

After their meeting of the day before, Velchaninov had not thought the man would come to see him again, and he was so perplexed that he didn't know what to say. But Trusotsky took charge of everything, said good morning, and sat down in the same chair he'd sat in three weeks before, during his nighttime visit. A peculiarly vivid recollection of that visit suddenly came back to Velchaninov and he looked at his visitor with a mixture of alarm and distaste.

"Surprised to see me, aren't you?" Trusotsky said, guessing how Velchaninov felt.

He seemed altogether much more off-hand than he had the day before, although at the same time it was evident that he was also more afraid. His appearance this morning was very curious: he was not simply well-dressed—there was even some pretension to elegance in his light-weight summer jacket, his light-colored, tight-fitting trousers, his bright waist-coat, his gloves, and the gold lorgnette that he'd suddenly started to wear. His linen was immaculate, and he gave off a delicate scent of perfume. The whole figure of the man was grotesque and it also suggested something strange and unpleasant.

"I realize very well, Alexei, that my coming here must have greatly surprised you," he said, wriggling in his chair, "but then, between people, there always remains—and I maintain should remain—some loftier link. By that I mean that it is above all the vicissitudes and unpleasantnesses that may take place. . . . Well, don't you agree?"

"Please, Pavel, come to the point quickly," Velchaninov said, frowning.

"All right, then. I'll tell you in two words," Trusotsky rattled off in a hurry. "I am going to get married and I am leaving now to join my fiancée. I'm leaving right away. Her family is staying in a villa out of town. Now, I would like you to do me the honor of allowing me to introduce you to my fiancée's family. Yes, I've come here to ask you for a very great favor." Trusotsky humbly lowered his head. "Namely, to accompany me there."

"Accompany you where?" Velchaninov gaped at him, his eyes bulging with astonishment.

"To the villa of my fiancée's family. Please forgive me, I'm so excited that it may sound to you as if I'm raving, but I'm so afraid you may refuse . . ." and he looked tearfully at Velchaninov.

"So you're asking me to come with you, right now, to see your fiancée?" Velchaninov asked, looking him quickly up and down as if unable to believe his ears.

"Well . . . yes . . ." Trusotsky said, terribly abashed now, "but please don't be angry. I don't mean to be presumptuous. I'm just asking you very, very humbly, as a great favor. Perhaps I was too hopeful in imagining that, under the circumstances, you wouldn't refuse."

"In the first place, it's quite impossible for me," Velchaninov said, writhing in his chair.

"It's just that it's something I wanted so very, very much," Trusotsky went on, imploring him; "although, I must admit, I also have a special reason for wanting you to come with me. But I wanted to explain that reason to you later, and now I'm just begging you humbly. . . ." And he got up to mark his great deference and respect.

"But it's quite impossible. You must understand that yourself," Velchaninov said, rising too.

"It's perfectly possible, Alexei. In the first place, I intended to take you along as a friend, and, in the second, you are already acquainted with these people. It's to the summer house of the Zakhlebins that I want you to come. You know Zakhlebin, the state councilor, don't you?"

"What, Zakhlebin?"

This was the state councilor whom Velchaninov had been trying unsuccessfully to catch a month before and who, as it turned out, had been using his influence on behalf of Velchaninov's opponents in the lawsuit.

"Yes, sure, him," Trusotsky said, smiling, encouraged by Velchaninov's astonishment. "The very fellow with whom you were walking once, trying to talk to him, while I watched you from the opposite sidewalk, waiting for you to leave him so that I could talk to him myself. He and I worked in the same department about twenty years ago, but when I thought I'd go and talk to him after he was through with you, I still didn't have the idea . . . It only came to me all of a sudden a week or so ago."

"But listen, they're a very highly respected family," Velchaninov said with rather naïve surprise.

"And what if they are?" Trusotsky asked with a grimace.

"Oh, I didn't mean, of course . . . But as far as I could observe when I was there—"

"Yes, yes, they remember your visit," Trusotsky caught him up cheerfully, "and although you missed the rest of the family that time, the state councilor himself remembers you very well and holds you in great esteem. And I mentioned you to him with the greatest respect, of course."

"But you only lost your wife three months ago!"

"But you don't imagine, do you, that the wedding will take place right away? No, we'll wait for another nine or ten months, until the year of mourning is over. Believe me, it's all right and proper. To begin with, Mr. Zakhlebin has known me since I was a boy, and he also knew my late wife. He knows my service record and, finally, he knows that I have money and also that I have obtained a promotion now—and all that has weight."

"So she's his daughter, I suppose?"

"I'll tell you everything in order," Trusotsky said with a shiver of pleasure. "Do you mind if I light a cigarette? But anyway, you'll see for yourself today. To start with, business-like men like Mr. Zakhlebin are sometimes very highly valued in Petersburg, once they have managed to catch the eye of their superiors. But still, except for his salary, bonuses, expense accounts, and such, he has nothing substantial, nothing that could be described as real capital. And so, although they live well, they can't put anything aside with a family like theirs.

"Judge for yourself. Mr. Zakhlebin has eight daughters and only one boy, and he's still very young at that. So if he were to die tomorrow, all that would be left after him is a meager pension and eight young damsels; now just think of the cost of buying each of them a pair of shoes—a whole fortune in itself. Five of these eight young ladies are already of marriageable age; the oldest is twenty-four—a lovely girl, you'll see for yourself—and the sixth in age is fifteen and still going to school. So, obviously, husbands must be provided for the five older ones in good time and, for that purpose, the father must start by taking the girls out—which, however, is rather expensive. And at this point I suddenly turn up. I am the first prospective husband in their house and they know for certain that I have substantial capital. Well, that's just about it," Trusotsky concluded his enthusiastic explanation.

"And so you've proposed to the eldest, I take it?"

"N-no, not quite . . . I'm actually asking for the sixth daughter I mentioned—the one who's still studying in high school."

"What? Really?" Velchaninov couldn't help laughing. "But I thought you said she was only fifteen?"

"She's fifteen now, but in nine months she'll be sixteen and three months, so what's wrong with that? But since it would be improper for me to marry right away, we're not as yet officially engaged. It's just an understanding between the parents and me. Believe me, everything's perfectly proper."

"So it's not definite yet, is it?"

"Yes, it is definite, quite definite; and believe me, everything's perfect."

"And does she know?"

"Well, they pretend, for convention's sake, that she hasn't been told yet, but how could she fail to know?" Trusotsky said with a pleased grin. "So, what do you say, Alexei—will you do me that great favor?" he concluded very bashfully.

"But what need is there for me to come there with you? But," he added quickly, "since I'm not coming with you in any case, there's no need for you to give me any reasons why I should go."

"But Alexei, please . . ."

"You don't really imagine that I'll just get into a carriage with you and drive out there, do you?"

His feeling of revulsion and dislike for the man, which had abated for a few minutes during Trusotsky's story about his engagement, had returned. Another minute and he would perhaps have thrown him out altogether. He even felt angry with himself too.

"Come, Alexei, get into the carriage with me. You won't regret it!" Trusotsky implored in an emotional voice. "No, no, no!" he cried, waving his hands, when he saw Velchaninov make a determined and impatient gesture. "Wait, Alexei, don't reject it outright. Perhaps you've got me wrong—believe me, I know only too well that we aren't a couple of comrades, bosom friends. Why, I'm not crazy enough not to see that. And then, I want you to understand that if you do me the favor of coming with me now, it won't place any obligation on you in the future. Anyway, since I myself am leaving for good the day after tomorrow, it will be as if you'd never even come with me, as far as you're concerned. Let this day be an exception. As I was coming here, I was basing my hopes on the fact that there are certain things that arouse generosity in your heart, which, in fact, have aroused it very recently. . . . I believe I've expressed myself plainly enough, have I not?"

Trusotsky's excitement had reached a high mark. Velchaninov watched him with a strange expression on his face.

"You're asking some favor of me," he said, sounding as

if he were trying to work something out. "You're so insistent that it sounds suspicious to me. I want to know more about it."

"The only favor I'm asking of you is to come with me. And when we come back from there, I'll tell you everything, just like at confession. Please, Alexei, you can trust me!"

But Velchaninov continued to refuse, especially because he was conscious of an oppressive and spiteful feeling stirring in him. The notion had first crept into his mind when Trusotsky appeared and mentioned his fiancée. From that point on, out of sheer curiosity or some obscure fascination, he had felt tempted to go along with Trusotsky. And the more the temptation grew, the more strongly he resisted. He sat with his face resting on his hand, hesitating. Trusotsky kept buzzing on, trying to convince him.

"All right, I'll go," Velchaninov suddenly consented, getting up agitatedly with a look almost of alarm on his face.

Trusotsky was delighted.

"Please, Alexei, get dressed now," he said, bustling happily around Velchaninov. "Please dress as elegantly as you know how."

Velchaninov thought to himself: "Why on earth is he going there himself—the strange fellow . . ."

"This is not the only favor I'm expecting from you, Alexei. Since you've agreed to come, I would like you to give me some advice too."

"To advise you about what, for instance?"

"Well, to start with, about the crepe. What do you think is better—to keep it on or take it off?"

"Please yourself."

"No, I'd like to know what you would have done if you'd worn crepe? In my personal view, I'd say if I kept it, it would suggest the constancy of my feelings and therefore would present me in a flattering light."

"Obviously, take it off."

"So it's 'obviously' now?" Trusotsky became thoughtful. "No, I suppose I'd better keep it on."

"Just as you please," Velchaninov said, and thought, "He doesn't trust me. I like it better that way."

They went out. Trusotsky looked approvingly at the elegantly dressed Velchaninov, and he himself somehow looked more respectable and dignified. Velchaninov was quite puzzled by Trusotsky, and also by himself. A fine carriage was waiting for them at the gate.

"I see you even had the carriage ready. Were you really so sure I'd come with you?"

"I rented the carriage for my personal use but, as a matter of fact, I was almost certain that you'd agree to come," Trusotsky said, looking like a perfectly satisfied man.

"I say, Pavel," Velchaninov said with an irritated little laugh when they were installed in the carriage, "aren't you taking me a bit too much for granted?"

"But you, Alexei, you can hardly call me a fool for that, can you?" Trusotsky said with emotional finality.

The thought, "And what about Liza?" flashed through Velchaninov's mind, but he immediately pushed it away, afraid of committing a blasphemy. And suddenly he felt that he was horribly despicable at that minute and that the idea that had led him to accept Trusotsky's invitation was a wretched, dirty idea; he felt like leaving everything and getting out of the carriage, even if he had to beat Trusotsky unconscious to do it. But when Trusotsky spoke, temptation took hold of him again.

"Tell me, Alexei, do you know anything about jewelry?"

"What sort of jewelry?"

"Diamonds."

"I do."

"I thought of making her a little present. Advise me—should I, or shouldn't I?"

"I don't think you should."

"But I'd like to so much," Trusotsky said, fidgeting in his seat. "But I can't decide what I should buy. Should I get her a whole set, that is a brooch, earrings, and a bracelet, or just one single item?"

"How much do you intend to pay?"

"I'd say four or five hundred rubles."

"Whew!"

"Do you mean that's too much?" Trusotsky asked in alarm.

"Buy her a bracelet for a hundred rubles."

Trusotsky was quite disappointed. He was eager to spend as much as possible on the present and to buy the "whole set." He insisted. They stopped at the jeweler's. In the end, however, they bought only a bracelet, and not even the one Trusotsky wanted but another one chosen by Velchaninov.

Trusotsky would have liked to get both. When the jeweler, who had at first asked a hundred and seventy rubles for the bracelet, came down to a hundred and fifty, he was rather displeased—he would have been delighted to pay all of two hundred for it, if the man had insisted on that price.

"It doesn't really matter if I'm in a bit of a hurry with presents," he said, holding forth rapturously, when they set out again. "They're not high society people; they're just simple folk. Anyway, innocence loves little gifts," he said, grinning slyly. "You laughed when I told you she was fifteen, Alexei, but that's just what caught my fancy, my dear friend, the very fact that she still goes to school carrying her schoolbag with all those exercise books and pens inside it! Yes, it was the idea of the schoolbag that really got me. It's innocence rather than beauty that attracts and fascinates me, Alexei. I imagine her giggling with some little girl friends of hers in a corner. Ah, the way they laugh, oh dear, dear me! And what makes them laugh like that? Well, perhaps because the kitten has jumped down from the chest of drawers onto the bed and rolled itself into a ball. . . . Ah, they have the scent of fresh apples, those . . . I say, shall I take off that crepe?"

"Whatever you say."

"Off it comes!"

He removed his hat, tore off the crepe, and tossed it out onto the road. Velchaninov saw that his face was beaming with bright hope when he replaced the hat on his bald head.

"Is he really like this, then?" Velchaninov thought, a wave of real loathing sweeping over him again. "He must have something tricky on his mind in bringing me here. I can't imagine he really reckons on my magnanimity," he went on, pondering and almost becoming offended at this last thought. "What is he—a buffoon and a fool, or 'the eternal husband'? Ah, it's quite impossible, after all!"

Chapter 12

At the Zakhlebins'

As VELCHANINOV HAD REMARKED, the Zakhlebins were an eminently respectable family, and Zakhlebin himself a rather prominent government official. But what Trusotsky had said about them was also true: they lived very well, but if the father were to die there would be nothing left behind.

Zakhlebin welcomed Velchaninov warmly and from a former "foe" became a friend.

"Congratulations! It's much better this way," he told Velchaninov with a pleased, important air as soon as he set eyes on him. "It was I who was all for settling it out of court, and that lawyer of yours, Peter Karlovich, is worth his weight in gold when it comes to such matters. Well then, I'd say you'll get sixteen thousand or so now, and without trouble, delays, or unpleasantness. Otherwise it could've gone on for another three years."

Velchaninov was immediately introduced to Mrs. Zakhlebin, a rather overflowing, middle-aged lady with a plain, tired face. Then the daughters sailed in, singly and in pairs, but somehow there seemed to be too many of them, maybe ten or twelve—Velchaninov lost count because they kept coming in and going out. There must, obviously, have been some summer friends from the neighboring villas among them.

Zakhlebin's summer home was a large wooden structure in nondescript style, with additions dating from different periods. Surrounding it was a big garden, which, however, the Zakhlebins had to share with three other families, an arrangement that obviously promoted closer relations with the girls of the three households.

From the first words, Velchaninov gathered that he was expected, and that he had been almost solemnly heralded as a friend of Mr. Trusotsky's who was anxious to meet the family. Being very perspicacious and experienced in these things, he soon detected something peculiar in the way he was received: the parents were a bit overcordial, and the girls looked at him in a rather peculiar manner and had obviously paid particular attention to their dress (although, it must be said that it was a holiday anyway). He became suspicious, wondering whether Trusotsky hadn't tricked him and, without spelling it out in so many words, had suggested that he was some sort of a bored bachelor, a man of good society and rather well off who might be on the point of "settling down," especially since he had just come into an inheritance. It would seem that such was very much the impression of the eldest Miss Zakhlebin, the twenty-four-year-old Katia, whom Trusotsky had described as a young person of great charm. Her costume and the way her luxuriant hair was arranged made her stand out from among her sisters. Her sisters and the unrelated maidens looked as though they knew for certain that Velchaninov had come to make the family's acquaintance just in order to "look Katia over." The looks they exchanged, and even certain snatches of their conversation that reached him in the course of the day, confirmed him in this surmise. Katia was a tall, gorgeously curvaceous blonde with a very sweet face and a quiet, passive, even sleepy, disposition.

"Strange that a girl like her should still be available," Velchaninov thought, watching her with considerable pleasure, "even when there's no dowry to go with her. Of course, soon there'll really be too much of her, but there are so many men who'd go for her as she is today."

The other sisters weren't at all bad either, Velchaninov decided, and even among their girl friends he found a few amusing and even pretty faces. He began finding the whole adventure great fun, apart from the fact that he had come there with a special idea in the first place.

Nadia, sister number six, the high-school student and Trusotsky's prospective bride, kept everyone waiting. Velchaninov was so impatient to see her that he surprised himself, finding it quite ridiculous. Finally she made an effective appearance, accompanied by a sharp, lively brunette with a funny face, called Maria, of whom Trusotsky was obviously very much afraid. This Maria was a young woman of twenty-three, sharp-tongued and smart. She was a governess in a family who were close friends of the Zakhlebins'. For a long time she had been received in their house like one of their own and she was thought a great deal of by the Zakhlebin daughters. Obviously Nadia felt in great need of her just now.

From the first glance, Velchaninov saw that all the girls, even those from the neighboring households, were against Trusotsky; and two minutes after Nadia had made her appearance, he knew that she too loathed him. Velchaninov also noticed that Trusotsky was quite unaware of it or, at least, was determined to ignore anything of the sort. Without any possible doubt, Nadia was the best-looking of the sisters —a dark little girl with a wild, untamed look and the boldness of a nihilist; a roguish imp with blazing eyes, with a flashing although often cruel smile, with amazing lips and teeth; with a slender, graceful figure and an intense little face revealing incipient thought but still full of childlike charm. One could tell she was fifteen by the way she walked, by every one of the words she used. Later, it turned out that Trusotsky had really seen her for the first time carrying an oilcloth schoolbag, which she'd discarded soon afterward.

The presentation of the bracelet was a flop, and left quite an unpleasant impression. As soon as his "fiancée" entered the room, Trusotsky went over to her with a smirk. He offered her the bracelet to "thank her for the great pleasure he had experienced" when Nadia, during his last visit, had sung a romantic song, accompanying herself on the piano. He got all entangled, failed to finish what he was trying to say, and stood there helplessly pushing the case with the bracelet into Nadia's hand, while she refused to accept it.

Flushed with anger and embarrassment, she drew back her hands. Then she turned rudely toward her mother, whose face betrayed confusion, and said in a loud voice: "I don't want it, *Maman*."

"Take it and say thank you!" her father said in a calm, stern tone, but obviously he too was rather displeased with

Trusotsky's gesture. "Quite, quite unnecessary . . ." he muttered disapprovingly to Trusotsky.

Nadia had no choice but to take the case containing the bracelet. She lowered her eyes and curtsied as very small girls do—suddenly bobbing down and then just as suddenly popping up again, as if worked by a spring. One of her sisters wanted to look at the present and Nadia handed her the case as it was, still unopened, indicating thus that she herself didn't even want to see it.

The bracelet was taken out and circulated from hand to hand, but everyone looked at it in silence, some even with sarcastic smiles. Only the mother mumbled something about the bracelet's being "really charming." Trusotsky looked as if he would have liked to sink into the ground.

Velchaninov came to his rescue.

He suddenly began to talk about the first thing that came into his head and, within five minutes, he had monopolized the attention of all those present in the drawing room. He was extremely good at society small talk—he knew how to sound quite sincere and how to look as if he believed that those listening to him were just as sincere as he himself was. When there was need for it, he could look convincingly like the happiest and gayest of men. He was also very good at inserting a sharp, witty remark, an insinuation, or an amusing pun into a sentence, quite casually, as if he considered it hardly worth any attention, whereas, in fact, his witty insertion—and, indeed, perhaps the whole monologue—may have been carefully planned and rehearsed, and have been used before.

But on this occasion, his skill was assisted by his feelings; he was in the right mood, something inspired him. He was quite certain of his triumph and knew that within a few moments all eyes would be turned toward him, that all those people would be listening to him alone, would respond only to him and laugh only at what he said. And sure enough, laughter was soon to be heard and others gradually got into the conversation—he was perfect at drawing people into a conversation—and three or four voices started talking at the same time.

Mrs. Zakhlebin's dull, tired face was almost radiating joy now, and the same was true of Katia, who looked at Velchaninov and listened to him quite spellbound. Nadia watched him furtively and distrustfully—apparently what she had heard had prejudiced her against him. That only spurred Velchaninov on. But the sharp-tongued Maria managed to get in a sharp thrust at him: she asserted—quite gratuitiously, by the way—that Trusotsky had spoken of him as a childhood friend, which would have made him at least seven years older than he was. But even the wicked governess liked him. Trusotsky was really perplexed. He had, of course, some idea of his friend's social charms and, at the beginning, was delighted with his success; he kept chuckling and trying to take part in the conversation. But somehow he gradually grew pensive, and later even dejected, and his dejection became quite obvious in his troubled face.

"Ah, you're one of those guests who doesn't need to be entertained!" Zakhlebin decided cheerfully, getting up and preparing to go upstairs, where, despite the holiday, he had to go through a few documents. "And to think that I thought you were the worst hypochondriac among the younger men. The mistakes one makes sometimes!"

There was a piano in the drawing room. Velchaninov asked who it was who went in for music, and then suddenly turned toward Nadia.

"I understand you sing?"

"Who told you that?" Nadia said shortly.

"Mr. Trusotsky."

"It's not true. I only sing to amuse myself. I don't even have a real voice."

"Well, I have no voice either, but I still sing."

"All right, so why don't you sing something? If you do, I'll sing something for you too," Nadia said, her eyes sparkling. "But not now—perhaps after dinner. I hate music," she added, "and I am really sick and tired of that piano; why, the singing and the piano never stop from morning to night in this house! Take just Katia alone—ah, what a racket she makes!"

Velchaninov at once took this as a cue, and it turned out that, of them all, Katia was the only one who played the piano seriously. He began to urge her to play. Everyone was very pleased that he had turned his attention to her, and the *Maman* even went quite red in the face in her joy.

Katia got up very cheerfully and walked over to the piano. Then, quite unexpectedly, even to herself, she too turned crimson, and she felt very ashamed that she, who was already twenty-four and was so big and tall, was blushing like a little girl—it was written all over her face as she sat down to play. She played something by Haydn, performing it neatly, although without very much feeling, but perhaps this was because she was feeling rather shy. When she had finished, Velchaninov showered praise, not on her, but on Haydn, and especially on the little piece she had just played. She was obviously so pleased and looked at him with such tremendous gratitude as she listened to him extolling Haydn rather than herself, that Velchaninov couldn't help looking at her with more warmth and interest, his eyes saying: "Why, but you're a nice one!" Everyone in the room understood that look, and so did Katia.

"Your garden looks lovely!" he said, addressing everyone in the room and pointing to the glass doors of the balcony. "What about all of us going out into the garden?"

"Yes, let's go, let's go!" happy squeals answered him, and it looked as if he had guessed everyone's wish.

They stayed in the garden until dinnertime. Mrs. Zakhlebin, who had really been longing for a nap all that time, couldn't resist the general impulse and followed the others; then, however, she thought better of it and remained on the veranda, where she sat down comfortably, soon dozing off. In the garden, relations between Velchaninov and the girls became even warmer. Two very young men from the neighboring villas joined the group—one a university student, and the other still attending high school. Each of these two immediately latched on to *his* girl, and it was obvious that they had come for that purpose. A third young man, a disheveled twenty-year-old boy in huge blue spectacles, came over and, frowning gravely, started a very tense whispered conversation with Maria and Nadia. He looked Velchaninov sternly up and down and apparently considered it necessary to display immense contempt for him.

Some of the girls suggested that they should play games; Velchaninov inquired what sort of games and was told that they liked them all, including tag. Later in the evening, he was told, they'd play "proverbs," a game in which all except one sit down, and that one goes out; while he is away, the rest chose a proverb, say, "More haste, less speed." Then he is called in and everyone in turn tells him a sentence prepared in advance, so that the first speaker's sentence includes the word "more," the second's "haste," and so on. The guesser has to pick out the key words and reconstruct the proverb from them.

"That must be great fun," Velchaninov remarked.

"No, it's an awful bore," two or three voices answered at the same time.

"Or else we could play 'theater,'" Nadia said suddenly, turning toward him. "Do you see that thick tree over there with a seat around it? Well, behind that tree are the wings of the stage where the actors wait to come on—the King, the Queen, the Princess, the Young Man, whatever one decides to be. And then each actor comes onto the stage whenever he feels like it and says anything that comes into his head. Well, sometimes something comes of it."

"Sounds very nice," said Velchaninov, again approving.

"No, that's an awful bore too, really. At first it's quite fun, but toward the end no one knows how to finish it and it simply makes no sense. But perhaps with you in it, it would turn out to be interesting; because at first we thought you were Mr. Trusotsky's friend, but apparently he was just bragging. . . . I am awfully pleased you came . . . for a special reason," Nadia said, giving Velchaninov a serious and meaningful look, after which she immediately turned toward Maria.

One of the little girls from a neighboring villa, whom he had hardly noticed before, whispered in Velchaninov's ear: "If they play 'proverbs' in the evening, they'll all be pulling Mr. Trusotsky's leg, so you'd better pull it too!"

"What a good thing you came here—it's so dull otherwise," another girl, whom he actually hadn't noticed at all, remarked to him in a very friendly tone. God knew where she'd appeared from, with her red hair and freckles and her funny face flushed from walking and the heat.

Trusotsky's uneasy feeling grew. In the garden Velchaninov and Nadia became very friendly and she no longer looked at him distrustfully, as she had done earlier; she seemed to have removed the chip from her shoulder now, and laughed, jumped about, and squealed without restraint; twice she even seized Velchaninov's hand. She seemed to be enjoying herself greatly and paid little attention to Trusotsky; in fact, she almost ignored him.

Velchaninov became certain that there was actually a plot against Trusotsky. Nadia and some of her friends dragged Velchaninov to one side, while some of the other girls

maneuvered Trusotsky in the other direction under all sorts
of pretexts. But Trusotsky kept escaping and came darting
back to Nadia and Velchaninov, now and then sticking his
bald head between the two of them. As time went by, he lost
all restraint and then the absurdity of his gestures and movements was really quite unbelievable. Velchaninov couldn't
help noticing also that Katia understood very well by now
that he hadn't come there to look her over—the interest he
was showing in Nadia by itself eliminated that. But her face
remained just as sweet and friendly as before and it seemed
that she was quite happy just to be there and listen to what
the new visitor had to say. Anyway, the poor thing wasn't
too good at taking part in a conversation.

"What a nice person your sister Katia is!" Velchaninov
whispered to Nadia.

"Katia? I don't know anyone nicer and kinder than her!
She's our angel here, and I am in love with her!" Nadia said
enthusiastically.

Finally, at five, it came time to have dinner, and it was
quite evident that it wasn't just another meal, but a dinner
organized especially for the new guest. There were two special dishes added to the ordinary dinner fare, and one of them
was so extraordinary that no one could name it. And besides
the usual wines, there was a bottle of Tokay to impress the
guest; toward the end of the meal, for some reason, they even
served champagne.

Old man Zakhlebin had one glass too many to drink, and
that put him in such a cheerful mood that he was prepared
to laugh at everything Velchaninov said.

In the end it was more than Trusotsky could stand and,
spurred on by the spirit of competition, he too decided to
produce a witticism. He had a go at it and immediately a
delighted burst of girlish laughter came from the end of the
table where he sat next to Mrs. Zakhlebin.

"Papa, Papa, Mr. Trusotsky has also made a pun!" two
of the middle Zakhlebin girls shouted at the same time. "He
says we are 'damsels who dazzle . . .'"

"So you go in for puns too?" Zakhlebin said to Trusotsky in a patronizing tone. "I didn't catch it. What did he
say?" He was smiling in advance.

"He said we're damsels who dazzle . . ."

"Yes? Well, where's the pun?" the old man said, still
not understanding and smiling with even greater good humor.

"Oh, Papa, you're really terrible! Why, 'damsels,' and then 'dazzle,' and that's it."

"Aha, I see!" the old man said, rather perplexed. "Hm . . . Well, I'm sure he'll manage a bit better next time," and he burst into gay laughter.

"It's all right, Mr. Trusotsky, no one can excel in everything," the sharp-tongued governess Maria said rather loudly, teasing him. "Oh, good Lord, Mr. Trusotsky's got a bone stuck in his throat!" she exclaimed, leaping up from her chair.

This produced a certain commotion, which was just what Maria wanted. Actually, Trusotsky had only swallowed some wine the wrong way when he had taken a drink to hide his embarrassment over the unsuccessful pun, but Maria assured everyone that she herself had noticed he'd swallowed a fish bone and that it was very dangerous and that she had known people who'd died from such an accident.

"Slap him on the back!" someone advised.

"Yes, that's the best thing in such cases," Zakhlebin said, approving loudly, and in less than a second there were volunteers to render him that service—Maria, Nastia, the funny-faced red-headed girl who'd also been invited to dinner, and, finally, the mistress of the house herself—all of them anxious to slap Trusotsky on the back. Trusotsky, who had jumped up from his chair, was trying to avoid the lady volunteers and assuring everyone that it was simply a little wine that had interfered with his breathing, that in one second he'd stop coughing and be all right. At last everyone realized that it was all a prank played by Maria.

"You're really quite impossible, Maria," Mrs. Zakhlebin said to her in as stern a tone as she could, but she couldn't keep it up and burst out laughing herself. As she hardly ever laughed, this in itself also produced a certain effect.

After dinner they all went out onto the terrace to have their coffee.

"What lovely days we're having!" Mr. Zakhlebin said, condescendingly expressing his approval of the weather as he looked out over the garden. "If only we were to have a little rain now . . . Well, I think I'll go upstairs and have a little after-dinner rest while you people have a good time!"

As he was leaving, he patted Trusotsky on the shoulder.

When they went out into the garden again, Trusotsky suddenly came up to Velchaninov and pulled at his sleeve.

"May I have a word with you? . . . It won't take a minute," he whispered.

They walked off onto an isolated side path in the garden.

"Not again, not here . . . I'm sorry, I just won't stand for it this time . . ." he hissed, breathless with fury, and clutching Velchaninov by the sleeve.

"What are you talking about?" Velchaninov said, looking at him round-eyed.

Trusotsky's lips were moving, and he was grinning fiercely and glaring at him.

Impatient girlish voices reached them. "Where are you? Where have you disappeared to? Everything's ready!" Velchaninov shrugged, and went to join the girls. Trusotsky followed him.

"I'm willing to bet he asked you to lend him your hanky!" Maria said. "He didn't have one last time either."

"He always forgets something," a Zakhlebin sister put in.

"Mr. Trusotsky has forgotten his handkerchief, *Maman!* You know, Mr. Trusotsky has forgotten his hanky again! Mr. Trusotsky has another cold, *Maman!*" several voices shouted.

"Why didn't you tell me, Mr. Trusotsky? You're really so terribly formal!" Mrs. Zakhlebin said in a singsong voice. "You mustn't neglect a head cold . . . I'll send you a hanky right away. . . . Anyway, how is it that you keep getting colds?" she added, walking off, pleased to have a pretext to go inside.

"I happen to have two handkerchiefs and no cold, ma'am," Trusotsky shouted after her. But she obviously hadn't heard him, and a few moments later, as Trusotsky was trotting along behind the rest of the group, trying to keep as close as possible to Velchaninov and Nadia, a panting maidservant caught up with him and handed him a handkerchief.

"Let's play. Let's play 'proverbs'!" The shouts came from all sides, as if they were expecting all sorts of things from that game.

They picked a place and installed themselves on benches. It was Maria who had to guess, and they demanded that she go rather a long way off and not try to overhear. While she was gone, they picked a proverb and distributed the words everyone had to slip into his sentence. She came back and guessed immediately.

The proverb was: "If a dream gives you a fright—there's God's mercy and His might."

After Maria, it was the turn of the disheveled fellow in blue spectacles. They insisted that he stand by the arbor with his face turned toward the fence—they wanted to make quite sure that this one at least wouldn't overhear. The gloomy young man did as he was told, with a scornful expression on his face, as if it were all quite beneath him. When they called him back, he couldn't guess a thing; he went around twice, listened to every sentence offered him twice over, pondered at length with a grim expression, but couldn't make out anything. They teased him.

The proverb was: "A prayer to God, a service to the Tsar, never get lost whoever you are."

"That's a revolting proverb!" the gloomy young man muttered indignantly, retreating to his seat.

"Ah, this is a terribly boring game! A real bore!" voices cried.

It was Velchaninov's turn to guess. They sent him even further away than the others; he complied, and also failed to guess.

"This is really no fun!" more voices exclaimed. "A dreadful bore, this game."

"I suppose I'll go next," Nadia said.

"No, no, it's Mr. Trusotsky's turn!" several girls shouted, and the company regained some of its animation.

They led him off all the way to the fence, put him in a corner facing away from them, and, to prevent him from peeking, placed the funny-faced redhead to guard him. Trusotsky, who had regained his self-confidence and was almost cheerful again, wanted to do dutifully what he was asked, and stood as stiff as a tree trunk, looking at the fence and not daring to turn his head. The redhead guarding him stood twenty steps away toward the company, near the arbor, and kept exchanging frantic signs with the girls in the group. Evidently they were all expecting something, and were very excited; something was afoot. Then the redhead waved her hands and immediately all the girls jumped up and dashed madly off somewhere.

"You must run too!" ten whispers instructed Velchaninov, sounding almost horrified because he hadn't taken to his heels.

"What's the matter? What's going on?" he asked, following the girls.

"Be quiet, don't make so much noise! Let him stand there and admire the fence while we all take off. And here comes Nastia too."

Nastia, the redhead, was running as if she were on fire, waving her arms. Finally, they all reached the other side of the pond at the far end of the garden. When Velchaninov arrived there too, he heard Katia arguing with all the other girls, especially Nadia and Maria.

"Katia, darling, don't be angry!" Nadia was saying, kissing her.

"All right, then, I won't tell Mother, but I won't stay here myself, because what you're doing isn't nice. It'll hurt the poor man's feelings—standing there alone by that fence."

She left because she felt sorry for Trusotsky, but the others remained implacable, as merciless as ever. When Velchaninov joined them again, they demanded that he too ignore Trusotsky and pretend nothing had happened.

"And now, let's have a game of tag!" the red-headed Nastia called out in rapture.

It took Trusotsky at least a quarter of an hour to find the rest of the group. He must have spent two thirds of that time standing by the fence. Playing tag turned out to be great fun—the girls laughed and screamed with delight. Livid with rage, Trusotsky again went over to Velchaninov and again seized him by the sleeve.

"Just one minute, please."

"Ah, there he goes again with his secrets!" a girl shouted.

"He's going to ask you for a hanky again!" some voices called after them.

"Now this time, it's you. . . . You're the cause. It's certainly you—" Trusotsky said through gritted teeth.

Velchaninov interrupted him to give him some friendly advice—he should cheer up, for otherwise they'd never stop teasing him.

"They're playing tricks on you just because you're so ill-humored all the time, while others are enjoying themselves."

To Velchaninov's surprise, his words had a tremendous effect upon Trusotsky, who quieted down to such an extent that when he rejoined the company there was a very guilty look about him, and he obediently agreed to take part in whatever games were suggested.

They didn't bother him for some time after that, and for half an hour or so he was treated just like anyone else, so that before the half-hour was over, he had regained most of his spirits. In all the games, whenever he had to pick himself a partner, he took either the red-headed Nastia who had betrayed him, or one of the Zakhlebin sisters. Velchaninov was surprised to notice that Trusotsky never dared to address Nadia herself, although he hung around her all the time, thus accepting as a matter of fact his position as a spurned and ignored suitor. But despite all this, they played another trick on him in the end.

They were playing hide-and-seek. The one who hid was allowed to move around anywhere within the confines of the territory asigned to him. Trusotsky, who had succeeded in concealing himself behind a thick shrub, suddenly decided to leave his hiding place and make a bolt for the house. They saw him, and cries resounded. He ran upstairs to the mezzanine, thinking of a room there where he could hide behind a chest of drawers. But the redhead tore upstairs after him, stole up to the door on tiptoe, and turned the key on him. As soon as this was done, the game was suspended and the whole crowd once again rushed off to the other end of the garden, beyond the pond. After ten minutes or so, Trusotsky peeked out of the window. There was no one around. He didn't dare shout for fear of waking up the parents. The cook and the maid had received strict instructions not to answer if he called. Katia would have opened the door for him, of course, had she not dozed off in her room where she had sat down to think quietly for a bit after leaving the party. And so Trusotsky remained locked up for almost an hour. At last, as if by chance, the girls started walking past the window in twos and threes.

"Well, Mr. Trusotsky, why don't you come and join us? We're having such a wonderful time over there! We're playing 'theater' and Mr. Velchaninov is impersonating the Young Man. . . ."

"What are you waiting for, Mr. Trusotsky? You're really dazzling!" other girls cried out as they passed by.

"What's dazzling?" came Mrs. Zakhlebin's voice. She had just awakened and had decided, while waiting for tea, to watch how the "children's games" were going in the garden.

"Why, Mr. Trusotsky is dazzling, of course," they answered, pointing to the window where Trusotsky's face, pale with rage, could be seen smiling wryly.

"Why should a man sit all alone while everyone is having such a good time!" the mother of the family said, shaking her head disapprovingly.

In the meantime, Nadia condescended to explain to Velchaninov what she had meant earlier when she had said that she was pleased that he had come "for a special reason." The explanation took place on a deserted garden path. Maria had called to Velchaninov, who was playing in some game or other and getting quite bored with it, led him to the path, and left him alone there with Nadia.

"I am quite convinced by now," Nadia began boldly, in a quick patter, "that you aren't at all such a friend of Mr. Trusotsky's as he wanted us to believe. I believe that you alone could render me one tremendous service: here is that nasty bracelet he gave me." She took the case out of her pocket. "Would you please give it back to him right away, because I myself will never address him again as long as I live. And also, would you please tell him from me never to try to force his presents on me again. For the rest, I'll manage to make him understand what's what through other channels. Now, will you be so good as to do what I am asking?"

"Please, I would appreciate it very much if you left me out of it!" Velchaninov almost shouted, making a defensive gesture with his hands.

"What? Leave you out of it?" Nadia said, gaping at him, immeasurably surprised by his refusal. The tone which she had planned so carefully broke down and she found herself on the verge of tears. Velchaninov laughed.

"You see, it's not that . . . But—how shall I put it?—I have my own accounts with him—"

"I knew you were no friend of his, and that he was lying!" Nadia interrupted him heatedly. "I'll never consent to marry him, let me tell you! Never! I don't even understand how he could dare . . . Only you must give him back his disgusting bracelet, for how can *I* do it? I want him absolutely to get it back this very day and to understand what's what. And if he goes and complains to Papa, he'll be in real trouble, I promise you!"

At that moment, the disheveled head of the bespectacled young man popped up from behind a bush.

"You must give him back that bracelet!" he said furiously, rushing up to Velchaninov. "You must do it, if only in the name of women's rights! That is, if you yourself are capable of fully grasping that social problem . . ."

He didn't have time to finish, for Nadia tugged violently at his sleeve, pulling him away from Velchaninov.

"My God, how stupid you are, Predposylov!" she shouted at him. "Go away and don't you ever try to eavesdrop again! I told you to keep much farther away, didn't I?" She stamped her foot, and even when the young man had disappeared behind the bushes she still kept walking angrily up and down a stretch of the path, her eyes flashing and her joined hands extended before her, the palms together.

"It's incredible how stupid they are!" she said, planting herself in front of Velchaninov. "I see you're laughing, but think how hard it is for me!"

"It's not because of *him*, is it? *He* can't be the cause of your reaction, can he?" Velchaninov said, laughing.

"Of course not! How could such a thought even occur to you?" Nadia said, turning red and beginning to smile. "That fellow is only a friend of *his*. But I can't understand how *he* picks his friends. They all refer to this one as a future leader, but I don't understand what they mean by it. . . . So listen, Mr. Velchaninov, I have no one to turn to but you, and you must tell me once and for all—will you give the bracelet back to him, yes or no?"

"All right, give it to me."

"Ah, you're so nice, so kind!" Nadia said, becoming radiant and handing him the case containing the bracelet. "And to repay you, I'll sing all evening for you, because I'm terribly good at singing, and that was a lie I told you when I said I hated music. Ah, I wish you'd come here just once more, because then I would tell you every, everything about this and many other things besides, since you're so nice and so kind, just as kind as . . . as Katia."

And, indeed, when they returned to the house for tea, she sang two romantic songs for him in a voice that was not quite set and still unformed, but that was rather pleasant and strong. When they came in from the garden, Trusotsky was already sedately sitting with the parents at the tea table on which the large family samovar was boiling, standing amid the family teaset of Sèvres china. He must have had urgent matters to discuss with the parents, since he was leaving in two days for a whole nine months. He hardly paid any attention to those coming in from the garden, and completely ignored Velchaninov. It was also obvious that he hadn't "squealed" on Nadia to her Papa, and that, for the time being at least, everything was peaceful and quiet.

But when Nadia started to sing in the drawing room, he immediately went in there. He asked her something and Nadia ignored him, but he didn't seem to be perturbed or discouraged by it. He placed himself behind her, assuming an attitude that suggested that that was his rightful place and that he wasn't going to yield it to anyone.

"Now it's Mr. Velchaninov's turn to sing! Sing us something, Mr. Velchaninov!" several girls shouted at once, crowding around the piano. Velchaninov sat down confidently; he was to play his own accompaniment. The parents came into the drawing room too, and Katia, who had been pouring the tea, followed them in.

Velchaninov picked a song by Glinka that is almost forgotten now.

"Oh, hour of bliss when your lips speak of love!
    Your cooing is tender as that of a dove . . ."

He sang it, addressing only Nadia, who stood at his elbow, closer to him than any of the others. What was left of his voice indicated that once upon a time he'd had a fine one. Velchaninov had heard that song performed by Glinka himself about twenty years before at a stag party given by a composer friend, when he himself was still a student. Glinka had been in the right mood and had performed all his favorite songs, including this particular one. At that time, Glinka too had not had much voice left, but Velchaninov remembered the extraordinary effect produced by the song and felt that no drawing-room singer, however skillful, could have achieved a comparable effect. In that song, the tension of passion rises with every word, and precisely because of that extraordinary tension, the least insincerity, the smallest exaggeration or affectation, such as would so easily pass unnoticed in an opera, would distort and destroy the whole idea behind it. In order to sing that slight but unusual piece, what was needed above all was truth—a true, complete inspiration, genuine passion, or at least a complete poetic understanding of that passion. Otherwise, the song was bound to sound quite insipid, or even ugly and indecent.

It is quite impossible to express the whole tension of passion without evoking revulsion, unless there is the saving grace of truth and *sincerity*. Velchaninov remembered that he himself used to sing the song quite successfully. He had almost assimilated Glinka's way. But now, from the first verse, indeed from the very first sound, true inspiration seized him and quivered in his voice. With every word of the song, his emotion burst forth more boldly and a true outcry of passion came through the closing verse when, his blazing eyes on Nadia, he sang the last words:

"And now, grown bolder, in your eye I gaze,
 My lips I bring closer to your lips ablaze,
 And all I can think of is kiss, kiss and kiss,
 To kiss your sweet lips in an orgy of bliss! . . ."

Nadia shuddered as though frightened and made a hardly perceptible movement backward; then the blood rushed to her cheeks and, for a split second, Velchaninov thought he saw a response in her embarrassed, almost frightened face. The expression of the other girls presented a mixture of rapture and bewilderment—one would have guessed that they all felt that it wasn't permissible, that it was indecent to sing like that, and yet, all their girlish faces were flushed, their eyes asparkle, as if they were still waiting for something. And among all the other faces, Velchaninov saw Katia's in a flash and it struck him as almost beautiful at that moment.

"That's quite a romantic song!" Zakhlebin muttered, somewhat taken aback. "I wonder, however, whether it's not a bit . . . well, a bit strong? It's very pretty, but yes, a bit strong I'd say . . ."

"Yes, it is rather—" Mrs. Zakhlebin began, but Trusotsky didn't give her a chance to complete her sentence. He leaped up, rushed forward like one beserk, seized Nadia by the arm, and pulled her away from Velchaninov; then he rushed back to him and stood there staring at him wildly, soundlessly moving his quivering lips.

"Come . . . just for one minute . . ." he brought out at last.

Velchaninov realized that in another moment the man

might do something even more senseless. So he quickly took Trusotsky by the arm and, ignoring the general commotion, walked out with him onto the veranda and from there a few steps into the garden, where it had grown almost completely dark.

"You must understand that we must leave right away, this very minute!" Trusotsky said.

"No, I really don't understand that—"

"Do you remember," Trusotsky said in a frenzied whisper, "when you demanded that I tell you *everything*, down to the very last word. . . . So the time has come for me to tell you everything down to the last word. Let's go, then!"

Velchaninov thought for a second, looked at Trusotsky again, and agreed to go.

The announcement of the guests' sudden departure made the parents wonder, and caused great indignation among the girls.

"At least have another cup of tea," Mrs. Zakhlebin insisted weakly.

"Why did you get so excited all of a sudden, old man?" Zakhlebin asked Trusotsky in an irritated voice, but Trusotsky only stood there in silence with a faint smirk on his face.

"Mr. Trusotsky, why are you taking Mr. Velchaninov away from us?" the girls cooed plaintively, at the same time casting angry glances at him. And Nadia gave him such a fierce look that he seemed to shrink under it. But he didn't give way.

"Mr. Trusotsky is right, though. He has reminded me of some very important business I might miss," Velchaninov said laughingly, taking Zakhlebin's hand and bowing to Mrs. Zakhlebin and the daughters, showing special warmth when he came to Katia, something that everyone noticed.

"Thank you for coming to see us, and we'll always be delighted to see you here," Zakhlebin said in conclusion.

"We were so pleased to have you . . ." the mistress of the house enthusiastically seconded her husband's statement.

"Come back, Mr. Velchaninov, do come back!" some of the girls called out from the veranda when he had climbed into the carriage and installed himself next to Trusotsky. And it seemed to him that there was one voice that had murmured lower than the others: "Please come back, dear Mr. Velchaninov! . . ."

"It must be the little redhead," Velchaninov thought.

Chapter 13

On Which Side
Is There More?

HE COULD STILL THINK about the redhead, but already annoyance and regret were pressing on his heart. Indeed, during that whole day, when it would have seemed he had had such a good time, anguish had never once left him. Even before he had sung the romantic song, he had not known how to rid himself of it and that was why, perhaps, he had sung so emotionally. "How on earth could I let myself go like that, tear myself away from everything?" he thought reproachfully, but he soon felt that whining like that only degraded him more, and the best thing under the circumstances would be to get angry.

"Idiot!" he whispered, giving Trusotsky a sidelong glance as he sat quietly next to him.

Trusotsky maintained a dogged silence, concentrating on something, preparing himself for some action, from time to time removing his hat and wiping his forehead with a handkerchief.

"Look at him sweating," Velchaninov thought with loathing.

Trusotsky only opened his mouth to ask the driver: "Is there going to be a thunderstorm?"

"Yes, sir, and what a one! It's been coming on all day."

And true enough—the sky had turned dark, and flashes of lightning could be seen far off.

It was already half-past ten when they reached town and, as they approached Velchaninov's house, Trusotsky suddenly asked him in a very considerate tone:

"I'll come up to your place with you, all right?"

"I see, but I must warn you that I'm not feeling at all well . . ."

"Oh, I promise I won't stay long."

As they were entering the house, Trusotsky stepped into the janitor's lodge for a moment to say something to Mavra.

"What did you want in there?" Velchaninov asked him as Trusotsky caught up with him on his landing.

"Nothing really . . . the driver . . ."

"I won't allow you to drink in here."

There was no answer. Velchaninov lit a candle and Trusotsky immediately sprawled out in an armchair. Velchaninov stood in front of him, frowning.

"I also promised to tell you my own final word," he began, trying to control his irritation, "and here it is: I consider that by now all business between us has been settled and that we have nothing more to talk about—yes, nothing, do you hear! And so I wonder whether it would be best if you left right away and I locked my door behind you."

"Let's settle our accounts, please, Alexei," Trusotsky said very meekly, looking into his eyes.

"Settle our accounts!" Velchaninov said in great surprise. "What a strange thing to say! What sort of accounts do you wish to settle? Would it be, by any chance, that final word of yours, that ultimate secret that you promised to reveal to me?"

"That's just it."

"We have nothing more to settle—everything has been settled between us," Velchaninov said proudly.

"Do you really think so?" Trusotsky asked in a strange, penetrating voice, holding his hands against his chest with the fingers interlaced.

Instead of answering, Velchaninov started pacing the room, muttering sorrowfully, "Liza, Liza," his heart pounding.

"After all, just what is it you wanted to settle?" he asked after a rather prolonged silence. Trusotsky, who had been following him with his eyes all the time as he paced about the room, still held his interlaced hands against his chest.

"Don't go there any more," Trusotsky said beseechingly, almost in a whisper, as he got up from his seat.

"What? Is it only that?" Velchaninov laughed spitefully. "I must say you've kept constantly surprising me today," he began sarcastically, but suddenly his face changed. "Listen to me now," he said sadly and with great sincerity. "I don't think I've ever degraded myself as I did today; in the first place by agreeing to go with you, then by what happened there. . . . It was so petty, so pitiful that I feel I dirtied myself by allowing myself to become involved. . . . Ah, but what's the use!" he cried suddenly, as if remembering something. "Listen, you've just happened to find me in a sick, irritated state. . . . Well, no need for me to find excuses! I won't go there any more and, believe me, I have no special interests there whatever," he concluded firmly.

"Do you really mean it? Do you?" Trusotsky said, without hiding his joy.

Velchaninov looked at him scornfully and went back to pacing the room.

"It sounds to me as if you'd decided to make yourself happy, whatever happens," he couldn't abstain from remarking.

"Yes, that's right," Trusotsky confirmed naïvely in a hardly audible voice.

Velchaninov thought: "The fact that he is a clown and is only wicked out of sheer stupidity still doesn't enable me not to hate him, and knowing that he's not even worth hating doesn't really help either."

"I am an eternal husband!" Trusotsky said with a humble, self-deprecating, ironic smile. "I picked up that phrase from you long ago, Alexei, at the time when we were still together in T——. As a matter of fact, I learned many phrases from you that year. And so when you used the phrase 'eternal husband' the last time I was here, I understood."

Mavra came in bringing a bottle of champagne and two glasses.

"You'll have to forgive me, Alexei. You know very well

that I can't do without this. . . . Please don't take it as insolence on my part. Consider me as an inferior, not worth your
anger."

"All right," Velchaninov said with distaste; "but I assure
you, I don't feel well."

"I'll be very quick. It won't take a minute. I must have
just one glass, because my throat is . . ."

He greedily emptied a glass, looking at Velchaninov almost tenderly. Mavra went out.

"Disgusting!" Velchaninov said in a whisper.

"Just the little girl friends," Trusotsky said cheerfully,
suddenly becoming quite animated.

"What? What are you talking about? Ah, you're back
on that subject . . ."

"Just the little girl friends! And then she's still so young,
still pouts and puts on graceful airs and all that—delightful!
And later, you know very well, I'll become her slave. She'll
enter society, be treated with respect, and become completely
different . . ."

Velchaninov, feeling the case in his pocket, suddenly decided that the time had come to return the bracelet, but Trusotsky was still holding forth.

"You, for instance, just mentioned that I am determined
to be happy; well, for that I must get married, Alexei,"
Trusotsky said in a confidential, almost touching tone. "For
otherwise, what'll become of me? You can see for yourself."
He pointed to the bottle. "And this is only one hundredth of
my vices. I could never manage without being married, without a new faith. . . . I assure you, I'll come back to life if
I do."

"But why are you telling me all this?" Velchaninov asked,
almost bursting out laughing, although the whole thing
sounded incredible enough to him. "Now tell me one thing—
why did you have to drag me there in the first place? What
did you need me for?"

"Just to test—" Trusotsky said, becoming somehow embarrassed.

"Test what?"

"The effect. You see, Alexei, I've only been looking
around over there for a week," he said, growing more and
more embarrassed; "and when I saw you yesterday, I said to
myself: 'I haven't seen her yet in the presence of strangers,

that is, in the company of men other than myself' . . . Now I realize that it was a rather stupid idea, quite unnecessary . . . I was just overanxious. It's just my horrible nature, I suppose. . . ." He suddenly raised his head and blushed.

Velchaninov was wondering if that was the whole truth. He was amazed.

"And?" he asked.

Trusotsky smiled sweetly. But there was a hint of slyness in his smile.

"Ah, nothing but delightful childhood! Ah, those little girl friends! But I do wish you could forgive the stupid way I behaved toward you, Alexei. It'll never, never occur again, never."

"Yes, if only because I'll never go there again myself."

"Well, that's partly what I had in mind."

Velchaninov felt a bit jarred.

"But, after all, I am not the only man in the world," he said, irritated.

Trusotsky flushed again.

"It makes me sad to hear you say that, Alexei. After all, I have great respect for Nadia Zakhlebin . . ."

"Excuse me, excuse me, I didn't mean anything. . . . I only felt a bit surprised that you should so highly estimate my capacities and . . . and that you should have relied on me so trustingly . . ."

"I relied on you precisely because it followed all the rest . . . after what happened before . . ."

"If that's so, does it follow that you still consider me an honorable man?" Velchaninov said, and came to a sudden stop. At some other time, he would have been quite shocked himself at the innocence of his own question.

"I always did, and still do," Trusotsky said, lowering his eyes.

"Yes, of course, but that wasn't what I meant. . . . I only wanted to say that despite all the prejudices . . ."

"Yes, despite all the prejudices."

"And what about when you were on your way to Petersburg?" Velchaninov said, unable to abstain from asking, although he fully realized the monstrousness of his curiosity.

"And when I was on my way to Petersburg too—I considered you a highly honorable man then. I've always had the greatest respect for you, Alexei," Trusotsky said, raising his eyes and looking openly now, without a trace of embarrassment, into the eyes of the man opposite him.

Velchaninov suddenly became frightened. He didn't want anything to happen. He didn't want a certain line to be overstepped through his own fault.

"I like you, Alexei," Trusotsky said, as if having made up his mind now, "and I was very fond of you all that year you spent in T——. You didn't notice it," he said, to Velchaninov's horror, in a slightly quivering voice, "because I was too insignificant compared to you to let you know how much you meant to me. And perhaps I was right to keep it to myself. And during the nine years after you left, I always remembered you because I'd never known in all my life a year such as that one." Trusotsky's eyes began to glisten in a peculiar way. "I also remembered many of your opinions and words. I always thought of you as a man who reacts warmly to every human feeling, as an intelligent and highly educated man with ideas of his own. 'Great ideas come rather from great feeling than from great intelligence,' as you yourself put it. Although you may have forgotten it, I remember it very well. And so, I always relied upon you, as on a man with great feeling, and so I trusted . . . yes, believed, despite everything . . ."

His chin suddenly began to twitch. Velchaninov felt panicky. The unexpected turn their talk had taken had to be cut off quickly.

"That'll do, Pavel, please!" he said, blushing in impatient irritation. "And what on earth makes you say all these things!" he suddenly shouted. "Why do you have to latch onto a sick, tired, irritated, almost delirious man and try to drag him down into your dark hole? Why, it's all nothing but a figment of your imagination, a mirage, a lie, a shame, unnatural and, what's worse, quite out of all proportion! Yes, that's the most shameful thing about it! And it's all a lot of nonsense—we're both slimy, disgusting people. And I can prove to you, not only that you don't like me, but that you loathe me as much as you're capable of loathing anyone, and that you've been lying, although you weren't aware of it yourself. You took me there with you not at all for the ridiculous purpose you told me about—not at all to test your fiancée, which is quite an idea, really—but simply because you were angry with me yesterday and decided to take me there and show her to me, as if to say, 'See that one? She's lovely, isn't she? Well, just try something with her. See whether it works this time!' You challenged me. Perhaps you didn't know it yourself, but it was so just the same, because you felt it all deep down inside you. But, you understand, it is impossible to issue such a challenge without hatred, and therefore you certainly hated me!"

He was tearing back and forth across the room, shouting out his words and feeling more and more annoyed and degraded by the thought that he himself was descending to Trusotsky's level.

"I wanted to make up with you, Alexei!" Trusotsky suddenly said in a hurried whisper, and his chin began to twitch again. A furious rage swept over Velchaninov. He felt he had never been so insulted before.

"I repeat again!" he screamed. "You've latched onto a sick, nerve-racked man. . . . You're hanging round his neck in the hope of tearing from him some impossible promise while he is delirious! Try to understand then that we belong to two different worlds, and that . . . that there's a grave between us now!" he added in a frantic whisper, then regained his self-control.

"But how can you know what that little grave means to me?" Trusotsky said, his face becoming distorted and going completely white. He took a step toward Velchaninov and, with a ridiculous but terrifying gesture, struck his chest with his fist. "We both know that grave and we stand on either side of it, although there's much more on my side than on yours! Yes," he went on, whispering and madly pounding his chest, "there's more, there's more, much more . . ."

A loud, powerful ring at the doorbell brought them both to their senses. The bell rang so violently that it seemed the person who had pulled it was deliberately trying to tear it out of its socket.

"No one's ever rung my bell like that," Velchaninov said, perplexed.

"It's certainly not for me . . ." Trusotsky whispered shyly, having at once become his usual self again.

Frowning, Velchaninov went to open the door.

"Mr. Velchaninov, I presume?" a young, resounding, and strikingly self-assured voice came from the entrance hall.

"What can I do for you?"

"I have good reason to believe that one Trusotsky happens to be here with you at this moment. I must see him right away."

Velchaninov was on the point of kicking the arrogant young man downstairs, but he thought better of it and stepped out of the way, gesturing the stranger in.

"Mr. Trusotsky is in here. Please come in."

Chapter 14

The Pledged Ones

THE YOUNG MAN who walked into the room was twenty or perhaps less, to judge by his handsome, self-assured, snub-nosed face. He was of above average height and quite well-dressed, or rather everything he wore seemed to fit him very nicely. Thick black locks fell on his forehead, and his bold, dashing dark eyes had a striking quality about them. Only the fact that his nose was rather thick and turned up prevented him from being really perfect. He walked in with an air of great importance.

"I believe I have the opportunity of addressing Mr. Trusotsky," he said in a measured tone, with special emphasis on the word "opportunity," by which he made it clear that he didn't consider it either an honor or a pleasure.

Velchaninov began to understand, and apparently Trusotsky also had an inkling of what it was all about, for he looked worried, although he stood his ground.

"I don't believe I have the honor of knowing you," he said with dignity, "and therefore I don't see what business I can have with you."

"You'll first hear what I have to say, and only then express your opinion," the young man said, in an arrogant, lecturing tone and, taking out a tortoise-shell lorgnette that hung on a cord, examined the bottle of champagne that stood on the table. When he was through with his scrutiny of the bottle, he folded up the lorgnette and turned to Trusotsky.

"My name is Alexander Lobov."

"What has that to do with me?"

"Why, haven't you heard of me?"

"I can't say I have."

"Actually, how could you have? But I've come here on important business that concerns you directly. May I sit down, though? I'm rather tired."

"Sit down," Velchaninov invited him, but the young man had already done so. Despite a growing pain in his chest, Velchaninov was quite interested in this insolent youth, for in his pretty, rosy young face, he thought he recognized some remote resemblance to Nadia.

"You sit down too, then," the young man suggested to Trusotsky, casually indicating with his head the chair opposite him.

"I prefer to stand."

"You may get tired. And you, Mr. Velchaninov, I suppose you may stay."

"I have nowhere to go. I happen to be in my own house."

"Just as you like. Actually I'd prefer you to be present while I have things out with this gentleman, for Nadia Zakhlebin has spoken very well of you to me."

"Is that so? Whenever did she get around to that?"

"Immediately after you'd left, for, like you, I've just come from there. So here's what it is, Mr. Trusotsky," he said, again turning toward Trusotsky, who was still standing. "We, that is, Nadia Zakhlebin and myself"—he clipped out his words through his teeth, sprawling nonchalantly in the armchair—"we have been in love with each other for a long time and we happen to be pledged to each other. Now, you happen to be an obstacle in our way and I've come here to suggest that you clear out of it. Do you intend, yes or no, to follow my suggestion?"

Trusotsky literally reeled under the impact of this request, but the next moment a sarcastic grin appeared on his lips.

"No, I have no intention whatever of following it," he said sharply.

"Is that so!" The young man turned in his armchair and crossed his legs.

"I don't know who you are and it doesn't seem to me that there's any point in our going on with this conversation," Trusotsky said and, having said that, decided to sit down.

"I warned you you'd get tired," the young man said in an off-hand tone. "Now, as to who I am, I have already had the occasion to inform you that my name is Lobov, and that Miss Nadia Zakhlebin and I are pledged to each other, so it's impossible for you to say you don't know who I am. Nor can you believe that we have nothing to talk about. Not even to speak of myself, Nadia, whom you are pestering with your rather insulting attentions, is very much involved in the matter, and that in itself is sufficient reason for us to have things out."

All this was thrown at Trusotsky almost through clenched teeth, and the young man hardly bothered to shape his words. While he was speaking, he unfolded his lorgnette and, at one point, looked at Trusotsky through it.

"Just a minute, young man, just a minute—" Trusotsky cried in shrill irritation, but the other immediately came back at him.

"At any other time, I would certainly have forbidden you to call me 'young man,' but in this particular instance you must realize yourself that my being a young man constitutes my main advantage over you, and I'm sure you'd give an awful lot to be even a little younger."

"Ah, you milksop!" Velchaninov whispered.

"However that may be, sir," Trusotsky said, pulling himself up with an air of great dignity, "I still don't consider the reasons advanced by you—very doubtful and questionable reasons at that—sufficient to continue this discussion. I realize that this whole thing is nothing but a meaningless, childish affair. Tomorrow I'll ask Mr. Zakhlebin what it is all about, and now I must request that you leave."

"See the sort of man he is!" Lobov shouted, addressing Velchaninov and unable to sustain his previous tone. "It's not enough for him that they all but chased him away, sticking their tongues out at him—now he wants to go and squeal on us to the old man! Isn't that proof, you stubborn man, that you're trying to take the girl by force, that you're buying her from her senile father, who, by virtue of an outdated and barbarous custom, still has control over her? Hasn't she shown you sufficiently how much she despises you? Why, otherwise, do you think your ill-mannered gift, that bracelet, was returned to you? What else do you need to make you understand?"

"No one has given any bracelet back to me, and what you're saying is quite impossible," Trusotsky said with a shudder.

"What's impossible? Hasn't Mr. Velchaninov returned the bracelet to you?"

"Ah, you be damned!" Velchaninov muttered under his breath, and said aloud: "As a matter of fact, Miss Nadia Zakhlebin did ask me to return this case to you." He frowned. "I tried to get out of it, but she insisted. . . . Here it is . . . I'm sorry. . . ."

He took the case from his pocket and, in great embarrassment, put it down in front of the dumbfounded Trusotsky.

"Why did you wait until now to return it to him?" Lobov asked him sternly.

"Evidently because I hadn't got around to it," Velchaninov said, scowling.

"I find that very strange."

"What did you say!"

"It *is* strange, to say the least. You must agree, yourself. I am willing to believe, however, that there has been some sort of a misunderstanding somewhere."

Velchaninov had an impulse to get up and pull the pert youth's ears for him, but instead he suddenly snorted and burst into a loud laugh, straight in his face. The boy began to laugh too then. But Trusotsky felt quite differently about the whole thing. If Velchaninov had seen the horrible look Trusotsky gave him when he was laughing at Lobov, he would have understood that at that moment the man had passed the fatal line. . . . But Velchaninov, although he hadn't seen the look, realized he had to support Trusotsky.

"Look here, Mr. Lobov," he began in a friendly tone, "without going into other reasons, I wish to call your attention to the fact that, in asking for Miss Zakhlebin's hand, Mr. Trusotsky presents certain advantages: in the first place, everything about him is well known to her worthy parents; in the second place, he is very well off and holds an excellent and respected position. And so it stands very much to reason that he should be surprised to see a rival like you—that is, a man who, although he may have considerable qualities, is still so very young. He cannot seriously consider your challenge, and so is quite justified in asking you to end this conversation."

"What does that mean—'so very young'? I was nineteen a month ago, and legally I have been old enough to marry for a long time. So that takes care of that."

"But I cannot imagine a father who'd be willing to allow his daughter to marry you at this time, even if you were a future multimillionaire or some great benefactor of mankind. A nineteen-year-old person cannot even be responsible for himself, while you are trying to take upon your conscience the future of someone else who is just as much of a child as you are. Well, that doesn't strike me as very honorable either, I must say. I have allowed myself to express my opinion on this point because you yourself asked me to act as intermediary between you and Pavel Pavlovich Trusotsky."

"Ah, then his name really *is* Pavel Pavlovich," Lobov said. "I really don't know why, but I was under the impression that it was Vassily Petrovich Trusotsky. And now let me tell you," he said, looking squarely at Velchaninov, "you don't surprise me in the least—I knew you were all the same! In fact, I was quite surprised when I was told you were a man with a fairly modern outlook. But, of course, that is neither here nor there. What matters is that there is nothing that is not honorable about my position, and I'll try to explain to you why, on the contrary, it is extremely honorable. I've promised her in the presence of two witnesses that if she ever fell in love with another man, or simply came to regret having married me, I would immediately hand her a signed confession of adultery and thus support her petition for a divorce. Moreover, as a further guarantee, in case I later tried to back out of that agreement, on the very day of our wedding I would sign her an IOU for one hundred rubles which would enable her to make her claim and have me imprisoned. Thus, as you can see, everything has been taken care of, and I am not jeopardizing anyone's future."

"I bet it was the other fellow—what's his name?—the one with the blue glasses who thought that one up for you!" Velchaninov cried mirthfully.

Trusotsky chuckled.

"What's this gentleman chuckling about? Yes, you're right, it was that man's idea, and you must agree that it's quite clever—it completely gets around the stupid marriage laws. Of course, I expect to remain in love with her always and she finds the whole arrangement infinitely funny; but still, isn't it cleverly arranged? In any case, it is so honorable that not every man would dare to go into such an arrangement."

"In my opinion it's not honorable at all; if anything, it's rather disgusting."

"Again, I'm not in the least surprised to hear you say that," Lobov said with a shrug, after a brief silence. "It's long since that sort of thing has ceased to astonish me. My friend Predposylov—the one with the blue glasses—could explain to you that your failure to understand the most natural things is due to your distortion of the simplest feelings and concepts, caused, in the first place, by your long, senseless life, and in the second place, by your idleness. However, I still hope that we have simply failed to understand each other so far, in view of the favorable things I've heard said about you. How old are you? Fifty?"

"Let's get to the point, please."

"Please forgive my indiscreet question. I didn't mean to offend you. So I will get back to business. I am not at all a future mulitimillionaire, as you put it—what a thought!—I am what I am, although I have complete confidence in my future. I have no wish to become a hero or anyone's benefactor, but I am fairly certain to be able to provide for myself and my wife. Of course, as of now, I don't own a thing and, as a matter of fact, I have been brought up in the Zakhlebin family since I was a small boy—"

"How's that?"

"I just happen to be the son of a distant relative of Mrs. Zakhlebin, and when my parents died, when I was only eight, old Zakhlebin took me into his house and later sent me to school. He's rather a kind man, if you want to know."

"I already know it."

"Yes, but he is also too much of a blockhead. But now I have become quite independent of him; I want to earn my own living and not owe anything to anyone."

"When, actually, did you become independent of him?" Velchaninov inquired.

"I'd say about four months ago."

"Now I understand everything quite clearly—you are a

couple of childhood friends. Well, have you found yourself
a job?"

"Yes, in the office of a notary. I get twenty-five rubles
a month. Of course, it's only temporary, but when I proposed
to her I didn't even have that. At that time I was working for
the railway for ten rubles a month . . ."

"Why, have you really made an official proposal of marriage, then?"

"I have—three weeks ago."

"And what was the result?"

"At first the old man laughed very hard, then he became
angry. They locked her in a room. But Nadia held her
ground very courageously. As a matter of fact, though, the
old man had had it in for me from the time I threw up my
job in a government department where he had placed me, to
go to work for the railroad. I repeat, at home he is a nice,
simple man, but when he's in his office he thinks he's Jupiter
or something! So, of course, I let him understand that I no
longer appreciated his ways too much. But, actually, the main
trouble started with the head of my department—that fellow
took it into his head to complain that I had been rude to
him, when all I had said was that he wasn't adequately developed. So I dropped them all and am now working for my
notary."

"And what were you getting in the government service?"

"Phew, I wasn't even on the regular staff! But then, the
old man paid me a living allowance, for he is really a decent
fellow, as I told you. But still, we won't give in. I realize, of
course, that twenty-five rubles isn't enough to support a wife
comfortably, but I expect to be taking part soon in the running of Count Zaviletsky's neglected estates, in which case
I'll get three thousand a year for a start. Otherwise, I'll try
to qualify as a lawyer. There's a general demand for educated people nowadays. . . . Ha! Did you hear that thunder?
We're about to have a big thunderstorm and I am very lucky
to have got here without getting caught in it, for, you know,
I came all the way here on foot."

"But wait a minute—if that's so, how could you have had
time to talk everything over with Nadia? Especially when
they don't receive you there."

"And what about the fence? Didn't you notice a red-
headed girl called Nastia?" Lobov said, laughing. "Well, she,

for one, was very helpful. And then there was Maria. . . . Why are you screwing up your face? Are you afraid of the thunderstorm, by any chance?"

"No, it's not that. . . . But I'm not feeling well at all. . . ."

Velchaninov really had an acute pain in his chest. He got up and started pacing the room.

"Oh, I see. I'm so sorry to have disturbed you!" And the young man jumped up from his seat.

"You're not disturbing me, really," Velchaninov said, trying to be polite.

"What do you mean, I'm not disturbing you? 'When Kobylnikov's belly aches' . . . as Shchedrin said. . . . Do you like Shchedrin, by the way?"

"Yes, I do."

"Me too. Well, Mr. Trusotsky, let's settle this business of ours," Lobov said, almost laughingly. "I'll rephrase my question to make it easier for you to understand: Do you agree to officially renounce your claim to Nadia and to notify her parents of that fact in my presence?"

"I have not the slightest intention of doing so," Trusotsky said, rising from his seat with a fierce, exasperated expression. "Moreover, I must ask you to spare me your company, because you have been talking nothing but stupid, childish stuff."

"Watch out," the young man said with a supercilious smile, shaking his finger at him, "you'd better be sure you're not underestimating me, for an underestimate like that could leave you God knows where. Let me warn you that in ten months, after you'll have spent a lot of money and worn yourself out a great deal, you'll renounce Nadia yourself. And if you don't, it will be even worse for you! You're like a dog in the manger now, if you will excuse the comparison —you can get nothing out of it yourself so you're just preventing others. Out of sheer humanitarianism, I appeal to you —use your reason! Force yourself to reason, just for once in your life."

"I would appreciate it if you'd spare me any further lecturing," Trusotsky said furiously, "and as to your dirty hints, I shall take all the necessary precautions tomorrow, the most strenuous precautions, indeed."

"Dirty hints? What are you talking about? The dirt is in your head if you think that way. Still, I'm willing to wait until tomorrow. But then, if . . . Ah, that thunder again! Good-by then—very pleased to have met you." He nodded to Velchaninov and ran off in a hurry, in the hope, apparently, of getting back before the storm, so that he would not be soaked in the rain.

Chapter 15

Getting Even

"Did you see? Did you?" Trusotsky said, rushing over to Velchaninov as soon as Lobov had left.

"Yes, decidedly, you have no luck," Velchaninov said casually. He wouldn't have said that if he hadn't been irritated and depressed by the growing pain in his chest. Trusotsky jerked back, as if he had been burned.

"So it was because you were sorry for me that you couldn't bring yourself to give me back that bracelet, wasn't it?"

"I simply didn't get around to it."

"You were sorry for me from the bottom of your heart, like a loyal friend."

"All right, if you insist—I was sorry for you," Velchaninov said with annoyance.

Nevertheless, he told Trusotsky briefly how Nadia had insisted on giving him the bracelet, almost forcing it on him.

"You must realize that nothing else would have induced me to take it; I have enough trouble without that."

"But you were swept off your feet and you took it!" Trusotsky chuckled.

"That sounds rather stupid, coming from you. However, you have some excuse, considering the state you are in. . . .

But, don't you see yourself now that I had no part in the business, that there are others . . ."

"Nevertheless, as I said, you were swept off your feet," Trusotsky repeated, sitting down and pouring himself a glass. "Perhaps you imagine now that I'll yield to that nasty brat? Oh no, I'll sweep the floor with him. I'll go there tomorrow and I'll make mush out of him. Yes, I'll see to it that the pestilence is smoked out of the nursery. . . ."

He gulped down the drink and poured himself another one. In general, he was behaving most off-handedly.

"Ah, the dear kiddies—little Nadia and little Alex Lobov! How sweet! . . ."

He was beyond himself with spite. There was another powerful thunderclap, followed by a blinding flash of lightning, and rain started to pour down, as if out of a bucket. Trusotsky got up and closed the window that had been open.

"Did you hear him ask you whether you weren't scared of the thunderstorm? He-he-he! Just imagine—Velchaninov afraid of a thunderstorm! And then that remark about the bellyache—like that Kobylnikov in Shchedrin. And asking you whether you were fifty? Don't you remember?" Trusotsky kept sniggering.

"I suppose you've . . . made yourself at home here . . ." Velchaninov said, hardly able to pronounce the words in his pain. "I'll lie down . . . you do as you please."

"I suppose you wouldn't even kick a dog out on a night like this!" Trusotsky cried in an offended tone, obviously looking for a reason to get offended.

"All right, sit, drink . . . even spend the night here if you must," Velchaninov said, stretching himself out on a sofa and letting out a slight moan.

"Me spend the night here? Are you sure you wouldn't be too scared?"

"What do you want?" Velchaninov said, suddenly lifting his head.

"Nothing special. I just said whatever came into my head. But what about the last time I spent the night with you? Didn't you get a bad fright that time, or did I just dream it up?"

"You're so stupid!" Velchaninov said with annoyance, and turned to the wall.

"Never mind that," Trusotsky said.

Velchaninov was quite sick, but somehow he fell asleep

within a minute after he had lain down. The great nervous strain he had had to go through that day in his already poor state of health had suddenly caused his resistance to snap, and he felt as weak as a small child. But the pain won out in the end. After an hour, it broke through his sleep and exhaustion and he got up.

The thunderstorm had quieted down; the room was filled with tobacco smoke; the bottle on the table was empty; Trusotsky was asleep on the other sofa. He lay prostrate, his head on the sofa cushion; he was dressed and even wearing his shoes. His lorgnette had slipped out of his pocket and dangled at the end of its cord, almost reaching the floor. His hat lay on the carpet by the sofa. Velchaninov looked at him dejectedly and started pacing the room, doubled up with pain, for he could no longer stay still. As he moved around, he moaned and thought of his pain.

He was afraid of the pain in his chest, and he had good reason to be. He'd started having attacks of this sort long before, but they had come at long intervals—every year or two. He knew that they came from the liver. It started with a dull, vague, irritating pressure which built up at some point, perhaps in the pit of the stomach, or higher up, in his chest. Then the pressure kept increasing, during a period of as long as ten hours sometimes, and it reached such a level and the pain became so unbearable that he felt it was the end. During a previous attack, the pain had kept increasing for ten hours; and when it had finally subsided, Velchaninov had been left so weak that, lying in his bed, he had hardly had the strength to move his hand, and was allowed by the doctor only a few teaspoonfuls of weak tea and a small piece of bread soaked in broth, such as one would give to an infant.

These attacks were brought on by different things, but always when his nerves were already badly shattered. It was quite strange, too, how such an attack passed. Sometimes he managed to catch it at the very start—during the first half-hour or so—and treat it with simple compresses. Then it would pass off; but at other times, as during his last attack, nothing helped, and only toward the end did the pain subside a bit, after he had taken several doses of emetics. Later, his doctor admitted to him that he had been sure it was actually a case of poisoning.

Now there was a long time to go until morning, but he was reluctant to send for a doctor in the middle of the night. He didn't think much of doctors anyway. But as the pain became even worse, he was unable to control himself and started moaning so loudly that Trusotsky woke up and sat up on his sofa, staring in bewilderment at his host, who was now pacing madly about through the two rooms. The bottle of wine Trusotsky had drunk had somehow affected him more than usual, and it took him a long time to make out what was going on. At last he understood and rushed toward Velchaninov, who muttered something unintelligible to him.

"I know what it is—it comes from the liver!" Trusotsky cried, becoming suddenly very animated. "I knew a fellow called Peter Posolnukhin . . . he had the same sort of thing—it's the liver. You ought to put a compress on it, as Peter always did. . . . Why, a thing like this could kill you otherwise. Shall I run down and call Mavra? All right?"

"No, no, don't . . . I don't need anything. . . ." Velchaninov tried irritatedly to brush him off.

But Trusotsky seemed beside himself for some reason, as if it were a matter of life and death concerning his own son. He wouldn't be put off and kept insisting on the compress, and also wanted Velchaninov to swallow two or three cups of weak tea—not just hot but really boiling tea, and to be of any use, it had to be really gulped down!

Without asking for Velchaninov's consent again, he ran downstairs, brought Mavra up, and the two of them lit the samovar in the kitchen, which hadn't been used for a long time. Then Trusotsky put the sick man to bed, after undressing him, and tucked him in with a blanket, and in twenty minutes or so the tea and the first compress were ready.

"This is a hot plate—white-hot practically!" he said in an almost rapturous tone, placing a heated plate wrapped in a towel on Velchaninov's sore chest. "There's nothing else around that we could use as a compress, but plates are fine. I swear on my honor, they're good for you. I know it from that Peter I mentioned. . . . Otherwise, one could easily die from a thing like this. Now gulp down the tea . . . Don't worry about scalding your mouth. . . . Why, life is more important, don't you think? . . . Ah, what a fuss . . ."

He drove the poor, sleepy Mavra quite crazy; he wanted the plates changed every three or four minutes. After the third plate and the second cup of boiling tea he had been forced to gulp down, Velchaninov felt a certain relief.

"Good! Now we've weakened the pain a bit, and that's a good sign. Thank God!" Trusotsky shouted joyfully, and he rushed to get a fresh plate and another cup of boiling tea.

"If only we could break that pain—yes, if only we could turn it off . . ." he kept muttering all the time.

Half an hour later the pain was almost gone, but the patient was so exhausted that, despite Trusotsky's ardent pleas to accept one more "little warm plate," Velchaninov wouldn't hear of it. His eyes were closing from weakness.

"Sleep . . . sleep . . ." he beseeched feebly.

"Well, all right," Trusotsky said, finally resigning himself.

"You, please stay for the night. . . . What time is it?"

"Almost two. . . . A quarter of. . . ."

"So stay here. . . ."

"All right, all right, I will."

One minute later the patient called Trusotsky again.

"You . . . you . . ." he muttered, when Trusotsky ran over to him and bent down toward his head, "you are a better man than me . . . I understand every, everything now. . . . Thank you. . . ."

"Go to sleep, just go to sleep," Trusotsky whispered, and trotted back to his sofa on tiptoe.

As he was falling asleep, Velchaninov could still hear Trusotsky, making his bed, quietly undressing, blowing out the candle, and lying down on his sofa, all the time hardly allowing himself to breathe so as not to disturb him.

There is no doubt that Velchaninov fell asleep very soon after the candles had been blown out—that, he was quite sure of afterward. But during all the time he was asleep, up to the very moment when he woke up again, he dreamed that he wasn't asleep, that he couldn't go to sleep, try as he might, despite his terrible weakness. Then he dreamed that he was beginning to have hallucinations while still awake, and that it was beyond his power to get rid of the apparitions crowding around him, although he was perfectly well aware that they were the products of delirium, and not reality.

The visions were quite familiar to him: his room was filled with people and the door leading toward the entrance hall was open; people were coming in from the street and lining up on the staircase and on his landing. At his table, which stood in the middle of the room, sat a man, just as in

the dream he'd had about a month before. Just as in that
dream, the man was sitting with his elbows on the table and
refused to talk, although this time he wore a round hat with
a crepe band on it. "So it was Trusotsky that time too?"
Velchaninov thought, but when he looked into the man's
face he realized that the silent man was someone else altogether. "But why is he wearing that crepe, then?" Velchaninov asked himself in bewilderment. The shouts and the din
made by the people crowding around the table were quite
unbearable, and it sounded as though they were even angrier
with Velchaninov than they had been in the other dream;
they kept threatening him with their fists and shouting something to him that he couldn't make out. "But I know very
well that I am just delirious," he thought. "I know I couldn't
go to sleep, and I've just got up because lying still became too
depressing." The shouts, the people and their gestures, however, were so real, so convincing, that at times he had doubts
about it. "Can it really be just a hallucination? What do these
people want of me? But if it weren't a hallucination, wouldn't
their shouting wake Trusotsky sleeping there on the other
sofa?"

Then something happened, and this time, as in the other
dream, they all suddenly rushed out onto the stairs and there
was a terrible scrimmage by the door, because another crowd
was trying to get into the apartment from outside. This new
crowd was carrying something large and heavy, for he could
hear the loud sound of the porters' feet on the steps and
their gasping voices calling out: "We're bringing it, we're
bringing it!" Everyone's flashing eyes were turned on Velchaninov now, and they were pointing threateningly and
triumphantly at the staircase. No longer doubting that this
was no delirium but reality, Velchaninov stood on tiptoe,
trying to look over the heads of the others to see what they
were carrying. His heart pounded wildly, and suddenly, just
as in the other dream, he heard three powerful rings at the
bell; and once again, the sound was so clear, so real, that it
seemed quite obvious that such ringing couldn't be just part
of a dream. He let out a scream and awoke.

But unlike that other time, he didn't rush toward the
door. What thought directed his first movement, or whether
he had any thought at all at that moment remains unclear,
but it was as though someone had whispered to him what to
do: he leaped up in his bed and threw himself forward, with

his arms outstretched, as if warding off an attack from the direction of Trusotsky's sofa. His hands came into immediate contact with other hands that were already stretched out over him. He caught hold of them in midair, held on firmly to them. . . . Someone had really been standing by his bed, bending over him.

The heavy curtains were drawn, but it wasn't completely dark, because a dim light filtered in from the other room where there were no such curtains. Suddenly a sharp, smarting pain stung the palm and fingers of his left hand and he understood in a flash—he had caught the blade of a knife or a razor and was clutching it desperately in his hand. . . . At that moment something fell on the floor with a dull thud.

Velchaninov was perhaps three times stronger than Trusotsky, and yet they struggled for a long time—for three full minutes. Finally Velchaninov got him down onto the floor and twisted his hands behind his back. But then, for some reason, he felt an irresistible urge to tie those twisted hands together. Holding the would-be murderer with his wounded left hand, Velchaninov fumbled with his right for the curtain cord. It took him a long time to find it, but finally he caught the dangling end and tore it from the window. He himself was surprised that he had the great strength needed. During those three minutes, neither of the two uttered a word, and all that could be heard was their heavy breathing and the muffled sounds of their struggle. At last Velchaninov succeeded in tying Trusotsky's hands behind his back; he threw him onto the floor, got up, pulled the curtain aside, and lifted the blind.

The deserted street was already quite light. Velchaninov opened the window and stood there for a few seconds breathing deeply in the fresh air. It was a little after four. He closed the window, walked unhurriedly over to his chest of drawers, took a clean towel and wound it tightly around his wounded left hand to stop the blood that was flowing from it. Crossing the room, he had stepped on the open razor that lay on the carpet. He picked it up, closed it, and put it back in his shaving case that he had left that morning on the small table next to the sofa on which Trusotsky had slept. Then he put the shaving case into the drawer of his desk and locked it with a key. It was only when he had done all that that he went over to have a look at Trusotsky.

In the meantime, Trusotsky had managed to get up from

the floor and install himself in an armchair. He had only
his underwear on, and his feet were bare. The sleeves and
back of his shirt were stained with blood, but it was Velchaninov's blood, not his. It was obviously Trusotsky; but,
at first glance, someone stumbling across him by chance
might have failed to recognize him, so different was he from
his usual self. He sat in an awkward upright position enforced
by his hands being tied behind his back, his face suffering,
distorted, and greenish, his whole body shaken by shudders.
He turned his lusterless and seemingly blank stare on Velchaninov and kept it fixed on him. Then, unexpectedly, a
vacuous smile twisted his lips and, gesturing with his head
at a jug standing on the table, he said in a rasping half-
whisper:

"I'd like some water . . ."

Velchaninov filled a glass and held it up to the man's
lips. Trusotsky drank greedily, taking three big gulps, then
lifted his eyes and looked intently into Velchaninov's face,
and went back to drinking without a word. When he had
finished, he took a deep breath. Velchaninov took a pillow
and his clothes and went into the other room, locking Trusotsky in the first room.

The pain in his chest had gone completely but the weakness had returned after his violent effort, for which he had
had an infinite supply of strength that came from God knows
where. He tried to figure out what had happened, but he
couldn't organize his thoughts—the shock had been too
great. His eyes would close for minutes on end, perhaps for
as much as ten minutes, but then he would jump up with a
start, remember what had happened, raise his sore hand
wrapped in the blood-soaked towel and think with feverish
intentness. He came to one firm conclusion, namely, that
Trusotsky had really wanted to cut his throat, but that possibly he had had no idea of it fifteen minutes before he had
tried. Possibly his eye had taken in the shaving kit unthinkingly in the evening, and the impression had simply remained
stored somewhere in his memory. Anyway, as a rule, Velchaninov always kept his razors locked in a desk drawer,
and it was only that morning that he had taken them out to
trim some odd hairs that stuck out around his mustache and
his sideburns, as he did now and then.

"If he'd planned to kill me beforehand, he'd have had a
knife or a pistol with him and not relied on my razors, which

he'd never seen until last night," was one of the points Velchaninov made to himself.

At last it struck six. Velchaninov got up, dressed, and went into the other room to see Trusotsky. As he was unlocking the door, it struck him as strange that he had locked Trusotsky in instead of letting him go altogether. To his surprise, his prisoner was completely dressed, having managed to untie his hands. He was sitting in the armchair, but stood up immediately when Velchaninov came in. His hat was already in his hand and his worried look seemed to say: "Don't try to talk. We've nothing to say to each other, no need to speak . . ."

"Go away," Velchaninov said, "and take that case with you," he added as Trusotsky started to go. Trusotsky had already reached the door, and now he came back, took the case with the bracelet in it from the table, put it in his pocket, and walked out of the room. Velchaninov followed him to the entrance hall, to lock the door behind him. For the last time their eyes met. Trusotsky stopped and for five seconds or so they gazed into each other's eyes as though they were both hesitating over something. Finally, Velchaninov waved his hands weakly.

"So go on, then," he said in a low voice, and locked the door.

Chapter 16

Analysis

AN IMMENSE, EXTRAORDINARY joy descended upon him; something was over, done with; he felt that a horrible anguish had lifted and dissipated. It had lasted for five weeks. He raised his left hand, staring at the blood-soaked towel, and muttered under his breath: "No, this time it's really all over. . . ." And that morning, for the first time in three weeks, he hardly thought of Liza, if at all, as if the blood from the gash in his hand had made him quits with that misery too.

He realized very well that he had escaped a deadly danger. "These people," he mused, "who a minute beforehand don't know themselves whether they're about to cut a man's throat or not—when they once have a knife in their trembling hands and get the first feel of hot blood on their fingers, they'll not only kill you, but cut your head off afterward 'just to make sure,' as convicts say. . . ."

He couldn't bear to stay indoors, and went out into the street, convinced that he absolutely must do something right away, or something terrible would happen to him. He roamed through the streets, waiting for something. He was longing to meet someone, talk to someone, even to a stranger; and that was the only reason why it occurred to him that he ought to go to a doctor and have his hand properly bandaged.

The doctor, whom he knew, examined the wound with a great deal of curiosity, wondering how it could have happened. Velchaninov put him off, joking, burst out laughing, and was on the point of telling him everything, but restrained himself. The doctor felt his pulse and, when informed about last night's pain in the chest, persuaded him to take a sedative he happened to have on hand. He also reassured Velchaninov about the cut.

"It can't possibly have any very grave consequences," the doctor said.

Velchaninov laughed again and assured him that the only consequences he knew of were excellent.

An all but irresistible desire to tell *everything* even to complete strangers seized him a couple more times that day. One time it was with a man he had never set eyes on before, and with whom he started a conversation in a teashop. Up till then, he had always loathed addressing strangers in public places.

He entered a stationer's, bought a newspaper, went to his tailor's and ordered himself a new suit. The thought of going to the Pogoreltsevs was still unpleasant to him, and he avoided thinking of them. Anyway, he couldn't possibly go out of the city—it was as if he were expecting something there. He greatly enjoyed his dinner, spoke to the waiter and to a customer sitting at the next table, drank half a bottle of wine. The thought that last night's attack might recur never even entered his head. Indeed, he was convinced that his affliction had been over the very moment he'd fallen asleep in a state of utter weakness, to wake up an hour and a half later and cope with the would-be murderer with such amazing vigor, and hurl him so easily to the floor.

In the evening, however, he became dizzy, and something resembling last night's nightmare would overcome him now and then for a second or so. When he got home it was already quite dark, and he was somewhat taken aback by the sight of his room. His apartment gave him an uneasy, sinister feeling. He walked from one end of it to the other a few times, even inspecting the kitchen, in which he had hardly ever set foot before. "They heated the plates here last night," it occurred to him. He carefully locked his entrance door and lighted the candles earlier than usual. As he was locking the door he remembered that, about half an hour

earlier, as he was passing by the janitor's lodge, he had called
Mavra out and asked her whether Mr. Trusotsky hadn't come
to see him during his absence, as though Trusotsky could
really have been asking for him.

Once he had locked the door, Velchaninov unlocked his
desk drawer and unfolded "last night's razor" to have a good
look at it. There were still some tiny specks of dried blood
visible on the white bone handle. He replaced the razor in
his shaving case and again locked it in the desk drawer. He
felt sleepy and knew he must lie down right away, for otherwise "tomorrow I won't be any good for anything." That
"tomorrow" loomed before him, for some reason, as a fateful
"ultimate" day. But the thoughts that had never left him
during the day, even while he was walking in the streets, kept
buzzing and rattling in his aching head without let-up, and
he kept thinking and thinking and couldn't go to sleep for a
long time.

"If it is a fact that he came for me with a knife *acci-
dentally*," Velchaninov kept repeating to himself, "had the
idea really never occurred to him before, even if only in the
form of a daydream in a moment of spite? . . ."

And finally he came up with a rather peculiar answer:
Trusotsky had wanted to kill him, but it had never once
occurred to the future would-be murderer that he did. In
other words—Trusotsky didn't know he wanted to kill Velchaninov. It made no sense, but that was the way it was.
"He didn't come here either to get himself transferred to a
new post or to find Bagautov," Velchaninov decided, "although he did something about his job, and became so furious when Bagautov died. . . . He utterly despised the fellow.
No, he came here because of me, and that was why he
brought Liza along with him. . . . But did I myself expect
him to try to cut my throat?" Velchaninov decided that he
had, from the moment when he'd seen Trusotsky in the
carriage following the procession to Bagautov's grave. "It's
as though I'd been expecting something ever since. . . . Although, of course, not that, not that he'd try to cut my
throat. . . . And were they really true," he exclaimed, suddenly raising his head from the pillow and opening his eyes,
"all those things that madman told me about his love for me,
when his chin was trembling and he was pounding his chest
with his fist?"

"It was the absolute truth!" he decided, tirelessly examining and analyzing everything he knew about the business. "That Quasimodo from T—— was stupid and generous enough to come to love the lover of his wife, in whose behavior he had found *nothing* suspicious during twenty years of marriage! He respected me for nine years, cherishing my memory and treasuring my words and opinions. And I had no inkling of it! He couldn't possibly have been lying to me yesterday. But did he really love me yesterday when he was telling me about that love, and also when he mentioned that he would 'settle our accounts'? Yes, he loved me *out of spite*, and that sort of love is the strongest. . . .

"But it may have happened, and probably did, that I produced a tremendous impression upon him when I went to T——, for that's just the sort of thing that might happen to such a Schiller in the shape of Quasimodo! He saw me a hundred times larger than life because my coming was such a shock to him in his philosophical isolation. . . . I'd like very much to know what exactly it was about me that struck him so. Perhaps, though, it was just because I always had a fresh pair of gloves and knew how to wear them. Quasimodos love esthetics. They certainly do! Gloves can have a sufficient effect upon some of the noblest souls, especially the 'eternal husbands' of this world. They'll fill in the rest themselves a thousand times over, and will fight for you if you want them to. Ah, how much he thinks of my powers of seduction! Well, perhaps it was those powers of seduction that made the greatest impression upon him. And the way he cried out that time: 'If this one too—in whom can I believe now!' After such a cry one might as well turn into a wild beast. . . .

"Hm, he came here with the intention of 'embracing me and weeping on my shoulder,' as he rather nauseatingly put it himself; actually, he came to murder me, while thinking he was coming to embrace me and weep on my shoulder. And he brought Liza along with him, too. But what would have happened if I'd really wept with him? He might well have forgiven me then, because he was longing to forgive me. . . . But then, at the first clash, it all turned into drunken antics, a real farce, and finally into disgusting, old-womanish whining about having been wronged—those horns, those horns he made on his forehead! Yes, he deliberately got drunk before he came here, to be able to let himself go and say all those things, and even to do that clowning, for in a sober state he couldn't possibly have made himself talk like that. . . . But he enjoyed the clowning—he surely did! And wasn't he pleased with himself when he managed to force that kissing stuff on me. Only, he still didn't know then how it would end—in embracing me, or in trying to cut my throat. Of course, it actually turned out in the best possible manner for him: he got both things—the most natural solution! Yes, Nature abhors freaks and destroys them with such 'natural solutions.' The most freakish freak is a freak with noble feelings, and I know it from my own experience, Pavel Trusotsky! To a freak, Nature is no loving mama, but a cruel stepmother. Nature gives birth to a freak, and instead of taking pity on him she tortures him, and serve him right, too. Tears and embraces are unforgivable even for decent people in our time, not to mention freaks like you and me, Pavel!

"Yes, and he was foolish enough to take me to see his 'fiancée.' Oh, good Lord—'his fiancée! Only such a Quasi-modo could think up a thing like being 'reborn into a new life' through the medium of Miss Zakhlebin's innocence! But it was really none of your fault, Pavel Trusotsky, because you're a freak, and so everything about you is bound to be freakish, including your hopes and dreams. But freak though you were, you had your doubts about the dream, and that was why you had to have the high approval of Velchaninov, whom you so revered. Yes, you needed Velchaninov to con-firm to you that it was not just a daydream, but the real thing. And so he took me there because of the faith he had in me, because he trusted in the nobility of my feelings, per-haps imagining that we would fall into each other's arms and burst into tears at the sight of her innocence. But, of course, that 'eternal husband' was bound to punish himself some time or other, and it was to punish himself that he took the razor —true, by sheer accident, but still, he did take it. . . . 'The fellow did stick his knife into that belly . . . and in the presence of the Governor. . . .' And by the way, did he have anything of the sort in mind when he told me that story about the best man? And what was really going on in his mind the night when he got up out of bed and stood in the middle of the room? Hm, I doubt that he was just playing a *joke* on me that time. He got up for natural reasons, but when he realized that I was scared, he kept me for ten min-utes without answering me because he got a big kick out of my being so scared of him. . . . Yes, and possibly that was the first time something of that sort dawned on him, as he stood there in the darkness.

"And yet, if I hadn't forgotten my shaving kit on that little table by his bed, probably nothing would have happened. Is that true? Is it? Sure—hadn't he been avoiding me before? He didn't come to see me for two whole weeks, and he kept hiding from me in order to spare me! Yes, and he picked Bagautov first, and not me. And didn't he jump up in the middle of the night to heat those plates, trying to take his mind off the razor and turn his feelings to tenderness. . . . Yes, he was trying to save both himself and me with those hot plates! . . ."

And the sick head of the former society man kept on hammering out thoughts in this way for a long time, turning them inside out and outside in, again and again, until finally peace descended upon him. The next morning when he woke up, he still had the same old headache. But along with it there was a quite *new* and unexpected horror.

That horror stemmed from a positive conviction that had suddenly come to him: that he, Velchaninov, the man of the world, would, of his own volition, go that day to see Pavel Trusotsky. Why? What for? He didn't understand a thing about it himself. All he knew was that, for some unknown purpose, he was going to drag himself over there.

However, this madness—he couldn't call it anything else —developed to such a degree that it made an apparently rational pretext for itself: even yesterday he had visualized Trusotsky going back to his room, locking the door and hanging himself, just like that clerk about whom Maria Sysoyevna had told him. That vision turned gradually into an irrational but inescapable certitude. "But why should the idiot hang himself?" he kept repeating, breaking in on his own thoughts every minute. Then he remembered Liza's words, and thought: "Although I'm not so sure at all that in his place I wouldn't hang myself too."

In the end, instead of going to have his dinner, he went over to Trusotsky's. "I'll just inquire from Maria Sysoyevna," Velchaninov decided. But before he had even stepped out of his house, he halted in front of his door and thought, turning red with shame: "Can it really be that I'm dragging myself over there to 'fall into his arms and weep'? Am I really after that nauseating bit of nonsense which would make my ignominy complete?"

But the providence that watches over all decent and respectable people saved him from the "nauseating bit of nonsense."

He had been in the street hardly more than a few seconds when he practically collided with Alexander Lobov. The young man was breathless with excitement.

"I was just running over to your place. . . . Well, what do you think of your friend Mr. Trusotsky now?"

"So he did hang himself! . . ." Velchaninov muttered wildly.

"Who's hanged himself? Why?" Lobov said, gaping at him.

"Ah, never mind, I just said it like that. What is it you want?"

"I must say, though, that you have a rather peculiar turn of mind! He hasn't hanged himself at all. Why should he? On the contrary—he's left. I took him to the station, put him on the train, and sent him off. I've just come from there. But the man sure drinks! You can take my word for it: between the three of us—Predposylov came too—we emptied three bottles, but you should have seen the way Mr. Trusotsky went at it. When he was already in the train, he kept singing songs and remembering you, blew kisses, sent you his regards. But he is a nasty, despicable character, isn't he?"

Lobov was obviously drunk—his red face and shining eyes and the tongue that wouldn't quite obey him attested to that.

Velchaninov laughed full-throatedly. "So you two ended up drinking to friendship. Ha-ha-ha! You fell into each other's arms and wept! Ah, you couple of Schillers! You poets, you!"

"Stop calling me names, please. I want you to know that he's given up everything *there*. He went there yesterday and again today. He sneaked shamelessly. They locked Nadia up. There was shouting, there were tears, but we won't give up! . . . But I must say, the way he drinks is really something! And he's so *mauvais ton* . . . No, I didn't really mean *mauvais ton*, but what's the word? . . . And he kept talking about you, but how can he compare himself to you! You're a self-respecting man, after all, and at one time you really used to belong in the best society and it's only now that you're forced to stay away—I suppose because you're hard up. . . . But I'll be damned if I could make *him* out."

"Was it he who spoke of me in those words?"

"Yes, those were his words, so don't get offended. To be a decent citizen is more important than belonging in high society. . . . I say that because in our present-day Russia, it is quite impossible to figure out whom one ought to respect. You must agree that it is a symptom of a bad disease of the century when one doesn't know whom to respect. Do you agree?"

"I do, I do; but tell me about him. How was he?"

"He? Who? Ah, yes! Why did he keep repeating: 'That fifty-year-old *but* ruined Velchaninov'? Why did he say *but* instead of *and?* He laughed and repeated it maybe a thousand times. Then he climbed into his carriage, sang a song, and began to weep. Really disgusting! I even felt sorry for him, with all I'd had to drink too. Ah, I hate fools! He left without a kopek. He kept throwing money to the beggars to pray for the peace of soul of Elizaveta. Who was she—his wife, I suppose?"

"His daughter."

"What's the matter with your hand?"

"I cut it."

"Never mind, it will heal soon enough. . . . You know what? The hell with him after all, and it's a damn good thing he's gone. But I'm willing to bet you that, wherever he settles, he'll get married again right away, won't he?"

"But you too want to marry, don't you?"

"Me? Ah, that isn't the same thing at all. Ah, you're really a strange man! If you're fifty, he must be at least sixty already. Let's try to be a bit logical, sir. And do you know what? I used to be a pure Slavophile once upon a time, but today we're looking for the sun to rise in the West. . . . Well, good-by now, I'm glad I met you downstairs and so didn't have to walk all the way up. . . . No, don't ask me to come in now. I have absolutely no time. . . ." And he started to run.

"Ah, I'm really crazy," Lobov said, turning back. "Of course, I came here with a letter for you. . . . He sent it. Here it is. Why didn't you come to see him off?"

Inside the envelope there was not one single line written by Trusotsky. It contained a letter written by someone else. Velchaninov recognized the handwriting. It was an old letter —the paper had turned yellow and the ink had faded. It had been written about ten years before, and was addressed to

Velchaninov in Petersburg two months after he'd left T——. But the letter had never reached him. Instead, he had received a different one—that was obvious from the contents of the yellowed letter. In this one, Natalia said good-by to him forever, just as in the missive he had received, and also admitted to him that she was now in love with another man. However, she didn't hide her pregnancy from him. On the contrary, she promised him that she would some day find a way to turn over the yet unborn child to him. She wrote that she felt both of them had other obligations from now on, that their friendship had thus been sealed forever. In brief, it wasn't any too logical, but she had always the same objective in view—that he should spare her his love. She would even allow him to come to T—— in about a year to have a look at the baby. God only knew why she'd changed her mind and sent him the other letter instead of this one.

Velchaninov was very pale as he read it, but he kept imagining Trusotsky when he had discovered this letter and read it for the first time, standing before the little ebony box inlaid with mother-of-pearl that had come down to Natalia from her family.

"He too must have turned pale as a corpse," he thought as he chanced to catch sight of his own face in a mirror. "He must have read it, closing his eyes and re-opening them again in the hope that the letter would have changed into blank white paper. . . . He must have repeated the experiment at least three times."

Chapter 17

The Eternal Husband

ALMOST EXACTLY TWO years had passed since the foregoing story. One fine summer's day, we meet Mr. Velchaninov in a carriage of our beautiful, recently opened railroad. He was going to Odessa to stay with a friend of his, for a change of scene and also for another, rather pleasant reason—through his friend he hoped to meet a very fascinating woman whose closer acquaintance he was very eager to make. Without going into detail, we may say that he had changed, or rather improved, very much in the past two years. Hardly any trace of his former hypochondria remained. Of the various "reminiscences" and anxieties resulting from his illness that had started plaguing him two years before in Petersburg, at the time when his lawsuit was going rather badly, nothing was left except for some secret shame over his past fears. But even that was partly compensated for by the certainty that it would never happen again, and that no one would ever find out about it. Of course, the fact that he had stopped appearing in society at that time, had become slovenly in his dress, and had kept hiding from everyone was inevitably noticed. But he so readily acknowledged those failings of his, doing so in his old, eminently self-assured tone, which he had regained, that everyone who mattered immediately forgave him his temporary defection. And even those whom he had ceased to acknowledge came to him themselves, their hands outstretched and, without asking him any annoying questions, treated him as though he'd just come back from a long trip taken to arrange some private affairs of his that were none of their concern. The reason for all these favorable changes was, beyond doubt, the successful conclusion of the lawsuit. Velchaninov got only sixty thousand rubles, which is not such a big sum; nevertheless it was quite important to him. In the first place, he felt he was back on firm ground and thus rid of his mental insecurity; now he felt sure that he wouldn't squander this money as he had squandered the two previous fortunes, and that it would last him as long as he lived.

"No matter how shaky the social edifice may become, and what slogans they may be shouting from the rooftops," he pondered now and then, watching and listening to the extraordinary things going on in Russia, "whatever transformations people and ideas may go through, I'll always be able to afford a delightful, tasty dinner like the one I am about to have now, and so I am prepared for every eventuality."

This delicate, almost voluptuous concept took complete possession of him and transformed him not only in his moral outlook but also in his physical appearance: he looked a different man, no longer the sluggish fellow he'd been two years earlier who had kept getting involved in unseemly incidents. He looked cheerful, serene, and dignified now—the ominous wrinkles around his eyes and on his forehead had become almost smoothed out, and even his complexion had changed. He had a fresher, rosier color in his face.

At the present moment he was comfortably installed in a first-class railway carriage and was toying with a pleasant idea. There was a new line that branched off to the right after the next stop. He thought of deviating momentarily from his direct route, taking that new branch line, getting off at the third stop, and going to pay a visit to a lady he knew who had just returned from abroad and was spending some time in an isolation that was so dull for her but that might just now be so welcome to him. And so he had an opportunity to spend his time just as pleasantly as he would in Odessa, and the lady in Odessa would come later anyway. Nevertheless he still hesitated, waiting for something to make up his mind for him.

In the meantime they were drawing near a station; and the "something" wasn't long in coming either.

The train stopped at that station for forty minutes, so that the passengers were able to have their dinner there. At the entrance to the dining room for first- and second-class passengers there was the usual impatient and hurried throng and, as often happens, a disturbance took place. A lady, who was very pretty although somewhat overdressed for travel, emerged from a second-class carriage dragging after her with both hands a very young, nice-looking Uhlan officer who was trying to get loose from her. The young officer was very drunk and the lady, evidently some senior relative of his, wouldn't let go of him. Probably she was afraid that he would make a beeline for the bar. Meanwhile, in the crowd, the officer was jostled by a young merchant who was also quite disgustingly inebriated. This young merchant had been stuck at this stop for two days, drinking and throwing money around, surrounded by a bunch of newly acquired friends, and never managing to catch the train in time and pursue his journey.

An argument ensued. The officer shouted. The merchant showered him with abuse. The pretty, dressy lady was in despair as she tried to pull the young Uhlan from the scene of the quarrel, repeating "Mitya, Mitya . . ."

For some reason, that struck the merchant as being really a bit too much. True, everyone around was laughing, but the young merchant became even more incensed, feeling it outraged his sense of decency.

"Listen to her 'Mitya, Mitya,'" he said, in a scandalized tone, imitating the lady's high-pitched voice. "They're shameless, even in public now!"

And, making his way unsurely toward the chair into which the lady had sunk, pulling the Uhlan down next to her, he looked her up and down with infinite scorn and said:

"Ah, you poor whore, dragging that tail of yours behind you!"

The lady let out a plaintive little shriek and looked around for help. She was both embarrassed and frightened and, to make things even worse, the officer suddenly twisted himself out of her grip and, with a yell, tried to get hold of the merchant. But before he reached him, he slipped and fell back onto his chair. People laughed even louder, and no help seemed to be forthcoming until Velchaninov went up, grabbed the merchant by the collar and pushed him at least five steps away from the frightened woman.

That was the end of the incident, for the merchant, considerably sobered by the shove as well as by Velchaninov's impressive figure, was immediately whisked away from the scene by his companions. The dignified countenance of the well-dressed gentleman also had a considerable effect on those who had been laughing—they fell silent. The lady blushed deeply and, on the verge of tears, assured him of her great appreciation. The Uhlan, muttering "Thank you, thanks," was about to offer Velchaninov his hand, but at the last moment decided instead to stretch himself out on the chair.

"Oh, Mitya!" the lady moaned reproachfully, helplessly clasping her hands.

Velchaninov liked both the adventure and the whole set-up. The lady was quite attractive—apparently a rather well-off provincial woman, richly but tastelessly dressed and with rather peculiar manners—in brief, she had everything that made the success of an elegant gentleman from the capital most likely if he happened to have such designs. They started to talk. The lady seemed very indignant with her husband, who had suddenly vanished from the compartment and thus caused all this trouble—he apparently always managed to vanish when he was needed.

"He always has to go to the lavatory then . . ." the officer mumbled.

"Ah, Mitya!" the lady cried in despair again.

That husband of hers must be in for some trouble, Velchaninov thought, and said:

"What's your husband's name? I'll try to find him for you."

"Pavel Pavlovich . . ." the Uhlan mumbled.

"So your husband's name is Pavel Pavlovich?" Velchaninov asked with curiosity, and suddenly the familiar bald head thrust itself between him and the lady. In a flash, he saw the garden of the Zakhlebins' house, the innocent games, and the tiresome bald head thrust between him and the young Nadia.

"So here you are at last!" the lady cried, with a hysterical edge to her voice.

It was Pavel Pavlovich Trusotsky in person, and he stared at Velchaninov with a stunned, horrified expression, as one might stare at a ghost. The shock was so great that for some time he obviously couldn't make out a thing in the furious, reproachful stream of words being poured on him by his wife.

At last, with a shudder, Trusotsky understood the horrible situation: his own responsibility for the incident, Mitya's state, that the "*Monsieur*," as the lady for some reason referred to Velchaninov, had acted as their "savior and guardian angel, while you, you're never around when you're needed!"

Velchaninov began to guffaw.

"Why, but we are sort of boyhood friends!" he exclaimed, addressing the surprised lady and casually putting his right arm around the shoulders of the wanly smiling Trusotsky. "Hasn't he ever mentioned Velchaninov to you?"

"No, he never has," the lady said, a bit taken aback.

"Well, you'd better introduce me to your wife, my fickle friend!"

"This is Mr. Velchaninov, Lympa dear . . ." Trusotsky said, and shamefully fell silent in the middle of his sentence. His wife blushed and her eyes sparkled wildly, probably because he had addressed her as "Lympa dear."

"And imagine, he never even informed me of his marriage and, of course, never invited me to his wedding. . . . But you, Olympiada—"

"Olympiada Semyonovna," Trusotsky prompted.

"Semyonovna . . ." the Uhlan, who was about to fall asleep, echoed.

"But you must forgive him now, for the sake of this reunion of friends, for my sake. . . . He's such a considerate husband—I know!" And Velchaninov gave Trusotsky a friendly pat on the back.

"I just stayed behind . . . for one second only, my dear," Trusotsky said, trying to justify himself.

"And you left your wife to be insulted!" Lympa cried, immediately going for him. "When you're not needed, you're there; but when you're needed, you aren't."

"When not needed, you're there; when needed, you aren't . . ." the Uhlan repeated.

Lympa was so agitated that she was almost breathless. She knew very well that she shouldn't keep on like that in front of Velchaninov. She blushed with embarrassment, but was unable to restrain herself.

"You're really so impossibly cautious when there's no need for it!" she blurted out.

"Under the bed . . . he keeps searching for her lovers under the bed—when there's no need . . . when there's need . . ." Mitya stammered, becoming suddenly very excited too; there was no stopping him any more.

But in the end everything worked out nicely enough. They got on quite friendly terms. Trusotsky was sent to get some coffee. Lympa told Velchaninov that they were on their way from O——, where her husband worked, to their country estate, where they intended to spend a couple of months; that it was not at all far from that station—only twenty-five miles or so; that they had a beautiful house and garden there; that they were expecting guests to come and stay with them; that, besides, they had nice neighbors; that if Mr. Velchaninov thought he would like to come and stay with them in their "seclusion," she would receive him as her guardian angel, because she couldn't think without shuddering of what might have happened had it not been for him . . . and so on and so forth. In brief, if he came she would receive him as her guardian angel.

"And savior, savior . . ." the Uhlan muttered enthusiastically.

Velchaninov thanked her politely and said that he would be delighted at any time, that he was a man of leisure and could dispose of his time as he pleased, and that Mrs. Trusotsky was really too amiable. And he immediately engaged her in a light conversation into which he managed to introduce two or three well-turned compliments.

Lympa blushed with sheer delight, and when Trusotsky returned with the coffee she informed him that Velchaninov had graciously accepted her invitation, that he would stay with them for a whole month, and that he would join them in a week. Trusotsky smiled sheepishly and said nothing. Mrs. Trusotsky indicated him with her head, her shoulders, shrugged and raised her eyes to heaven. At last they parted—with more thanks to the "guardian angel." Trusotsky led off his wife and the Uhlan to help them into the railway carriage.

Velchaninov lighted a cigar and paced up and down the platform, knowing that Trusotsky would come running over to have a little talk with him until the last bell rang, warning that the train was about to leave. And that's exactly what happened. Trusotsky came with an alarmed expression in his eyes and on his whole face. Velchaninov laughed, took him affectionately by the elbow, walked to the nearest seat with him, sat down, pulled Trusotsky down next to him, and waited for him to speak first.

"So I hear you're coming to see us . . ." Trusotsky mumbled.

"I saw it coming!" Velchaninov laughed loudly. "You haven't changed in the least! You didn't seriously think, did you, that I was really coming to stay with you, especially for a whole month! Ha-ha-ha!"

Trusotsky shuddered with relief.

"So you aren't really coming!" he cried, without trying to conceal his joy.

"Of course I'm not!" Velchaninov said with a conceited laugh, although he couldn't quite understand why it should strike him as so funny as all that. And yet he felt more and more like laughing.

"You're serious about what you said, are you?" Trusotsky even jumped up from the seat, trembling in suspense.

"Why, I've already told you I'm not coming! Ah, you're really funny!"

"But how shall I explain it to my wife when you don't turn up in a week, when she's expecting you?"

"That's nothing. Tell her I broke a leg, or something."

"She won't believe that," Trusotsky said in a plaintive little voice.

"And you'll catch it then, won't you!" Velchaninov was still laughing. "But tell me, my dear friend, I am right in surmising that you hold your beautiful wife in awe, am I not?"

Trusotsky tried to smile, but it didn't come off. Velchaninov's refusal to come was all to the good, but he didn't at all like the off-hand way in which he had spoken of his wife. He winced. Velchaninov noticed it. Meantime, the second bell rang and a shrill voice came from the carriage window, calling Trusotsky. Trusotsky became very agitated, but didn't rush off; apparently he was waiting for Velchaninov to assure him once more that he wouldn't come.

"What's your wife's maiden name?" Velchaninov inquired, as though he were unaware of Trusotsky's painful expectation.

"Her father was our priest," Trusotsky said, anxiously glancing at the train and listening for the final bell.

"I understand. You married her for her beauty."

Trusotsky winced again.

"And who is that Mitya fellow?"

"He? He's just a distant relative of ours—he's the son of a first cousin of mine who died. He was disrated for misconduct but has been reinstated in his rank again now. We have equipped him and all that. He's just a rather unfortunate young man. . . ."

Well, everything seemed in order, Velchaninov thought; the old set-up again.

"Pavel!"

There was even greater irritation in the female voice coming from the carriage window.

"Pavel Pavlovich!" a hoarse male voice called out too.

Trusotsky's agitation increased and he was about to dart off, but Velchaninov caught him by the elbow.

"Wouldn't you like me to go up to your wife now and tell her how you tried to cut my throat? Wouldn't you like it just!"

"Please, please, what are you saying!" Trusotsky exclaimed, horrified. "God forbid you should do anything of the sort!"

"Pavel!" "Pavel Pavlovich!" the voices clamored for him again.

"All right, off you go!" Velchaninov said, releasing him and continuing to laugh good-humoredly.

"So you definitely aren't coming?" Trusotsky murmured despairingly, even folding his hands prayerfully with the palms inward.

"I swear I won't come! But you'd better run along or you'll be in trouble!" And Velchaninov graciously offered him his hand with a flourish. . . .

But then a shudder passed through him—Trusotsky had pulled his own hand back.

The third and last warning bell rang.

Within one second, something strange happened to both of them. Both seemed transformed. Something snapped, as it were, inside Velchaninov, who up to that point had been laughing. Furiously, he caught Trusotsky by the shoulder.

"Since I held this hand out to you," he hissed, showing him the palm of his left hand on which a scar could clearly be seen, "I'm sure you'd better accept it!" Velchaninov was whispering, his lips completely white, and twitching.

Trusotsky had also turned pale and his lips, too, were

twitching. And, on top of that, his whole face twisted convulsively.

"And what about Liza?" he whispered breathlessly and, right away, his lips, cheeks, and chin began to quiver, and tears poured from his eyes.

"Pavel, Pavel!" the rasping shout came from the window of the carriage, sounding as if someone were screaming for help. And then the bell rang.

Trusotsky snapped out of it, threw up his hands in despair, and dashed toward the train that had already started. Somehow he managed to get aboard and make his way to his carriage.

Velchaninov remained at the station, boarding the train only in the evening. He resumed his journey as he had planned it originally. He didn't feel like visiting the lady who was staying in the nearby district—he was in no mood for that just then.

But he was later to regret it!

The painting on the cover
of this Bantam Classic
is by Michael Leonard.

BANTAM CLASSICS

are chosen from the whole span
of living literature. They
comprise a balanced selection
of the best novels, poems, plays
and stories by writers whose works
and thoughts have made an indelible
impact on Western culture.

Bantam Modern Classics

BANTAM CLASSICS

COLLECTIONS

(Edited by Milton Crane)

Wait 'til you see what *else* we've got in store for you!

Send for your FREE catalog of Bantam Bestsellers today!

This money-saving catalog lists hundreds of best-sellers originally priced from $3.75 to $15.00—yours now in Bantam paperback editions for just 50¢ to $1.95! Here is a great opportunity to read the good books you've missed and add to your private library at huge savings! The catalog is FREE! So don't delay—send for yours today!